HEMLOCK
BAY

MARTIN EDWARDS: WINNER OF THE CWA DIAMOND DAGGER 2020

Gallows Court and _Blackstone Fell_ Longlisted for the CWA Historical Dagger

'Martin knows more about crime fiction than anyone else working in the field today. He's always been a fan of the genre and his passion shines through in his work: the fiction, the non-fiction and the short stories. In his editing, he's brought new writers and forgotten favourites to discerning readers. I'm delighted his work is being recognised in this way.'
Ann Cleeves

'Martin's fiction alone makes him a truly worthy winner of the Diamond Dagger. His editorial excellence, his erudition, his enthusiasm for and contributions to the genre, his support of other writers, and his warm-hearted friendship are the icing on the cake.'
Lee Child

'Martin Edwards is a thoroughly deserved winner of this prized award. He has contributed so much to the genre, not only through the impressive canon of his own wonderfully written novels, but through his tireless work for crime writing in the UK.'
Peter James

'Martin is not only one of the finest crime writers of his generation. He is the heir to Julian Symons and H.R.F. Keating as the leading authority on our genre, fostering and promoting it with unflagging enthusiasm, to the benefit of us all. I'm delighted that our community can show its gratitude by honouring him in this way.'
Peter Lovesey

'Martin Edwards is a wonderful choice to receive the Diamond Dagger. He's a very fine writer but has also devoted huge energy to both the CWA and Detection Club – all done quietly and companionably, which is a rare thing. I love a man who takes care of archives. I am delighted for him, but as we always say: it's for lifetime achievement – but please don't stop what you do so well!'
Lindsey Davis

'Martin Edwards is not only a fine writer but he is also ridiculously knowledgeable about the field of crime and suspense fiction. He wears his learning lightly and is always the most congenial company. He is also a great champion of crime writing and crime writers. His novels feature an acute sense of place as well as deep psychological insights. As a solicitor, he knows the legal world more intimately than most of his fellow novelists. He is a fitting winner of the Diamond Dagger.'
Ian Rankin

ALSO BY MARTIN EDWARDS

The Lake District Mysteries
The Coffin Trail
The Cipher Garden
The Arsenic Labyrinth
The Serpent Pool
The Hanging Wood
The Frozen Shroud
The Dungeon House
The Crooked Shore

The Rachel Savernake Series
Gallows Court
Mortmain Hall
Blackstone Fell
Sepulchre Street

Fiction
Take My Breath Away
Dancing for the Hangman

The Harry Devlin Series
All the Lonely People
Suspicious Minds
I Remember You
Yesterday's Papers
Eve of Destruction
The Devil in Disguise
First Cut is the Deepest
Waterloo Sunset

Non-Fiction
Catching Killers
The Golden Age of Murder
*The Story of Classic Crime in
100 Books*
The Life of Crime

HEMLOCK BAY

MARTIN EDWARDS

HEAD
ZEUS

An Aries Book

First published in the UK in 2024 by Head of Zeus,
part of Bloomsbury Publishing Plc

9 7 5 3 1 2 4 6 8

A catalogue record for this book is available from the British Library.

ISBN (HB): 9781035909803
ISBN (E): 9781035909797

Cover design: Meg Shepherd

Printed and bound in Great Britain by
CPI Group (UK) Ltd, Croydon CR0 4YY

MIX
Paper from
responsible sources
FSC
www.fsc.org   FSC® C171272

Head of Zeus
First Floor East
5–8 Hardwick Street
London EC1R 4RG

WWW.HEADOFZEUS.COM

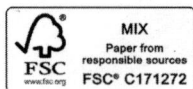

Dedicated to Ann Geraghty, Lea Doran, and Jo Wright, with grateful thanks for your friendship, hard work, and support, keeping me going in the 'day job' for more years than any of us would have imagined.

MARTHA TRUEMAN'S SKETCH MAP OF HEMLOCK BAY (NOT TO SCALE)

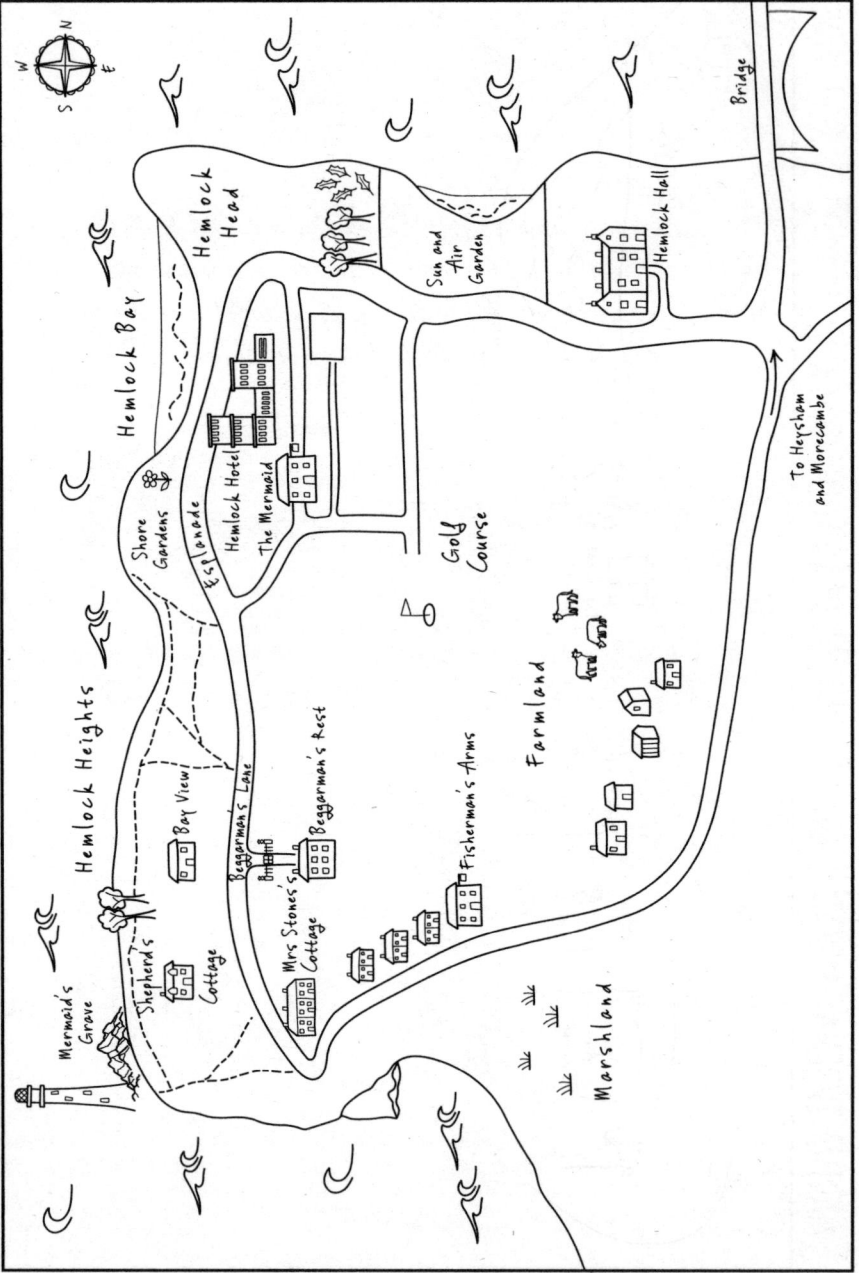

N
W E
S

Bridge

Hemlock Head

Hemlock Bay

Hemlock Hall

Sun and Air Garden

Shore Gardens

Esplanade

Hemlock Hotel

The Mermaid

Golf Course

To Heysham and Morecombe

Hemlock Heights

Bay View

Beggarman's Lane

Beggarman's Rest

Fisherman's Arms

Farmland

Mermaid's Grove

Shepherd's Cottage

Mrs Stone's Cottage

Marshland

MARTHA TRUEMAN'S SKETCH MAP OF HEMLOCK HEAD (NOT TO SCALE)

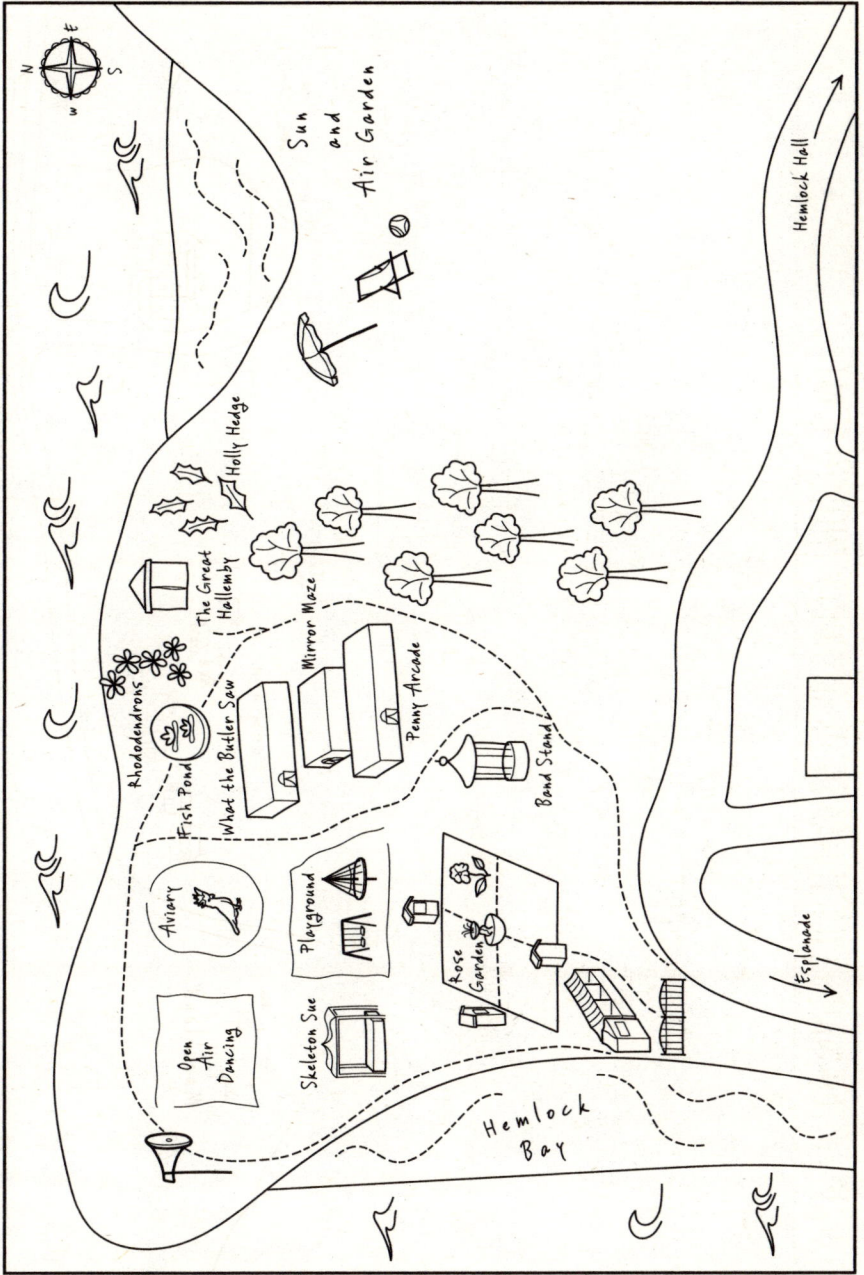

Prologue

'I'm frightened,' she said.

He moved to join her at the window. They had to look up through the grille to see passers-by on the other side of the iron railings. People going about their business in the Temple, unaware of the pair in the basement room, let alone that they were discussing death.

'Don't be, my dear,' he murmured. 'Haven't we discussed this endlessly? We reached an agreement.'

A hollow laugh. 'Always the lawyer, darling! Any minute now you'll threaten to sue for breach of contract.'

'Please don't make a joke of it, not at a moment like this.' He clasped her arm. 'Didn't we explore every avenue? It's hopeless, we both see that. There simply is no alternative.'

She expelled a long sigh. 'I suppose you're right.'

Outside, hooves clattered on the cobbles. A man with a braying voice hailed an acquaintance. The sun had slipped out from behind the clouds and in the outside world, life was going on as usual. Although not for everyone. A newspaper vendor repeated his hoarse cry.

'Death of Sir Arthur Conan Doyle!'

He took her in his arms and kissed her. He felt her body trembling, but gradually she became still. When finally he moved away, she dabbed a tear from the corner of her eye and stared through the window at the stone steps leading up to the street.

Facing him on the shelf was a bulky tome. *Archbold's Pleading, Evidence & Practice in Criminal Cases.* And now he was about to commit the ultimate crime. He shook his head, scarcely able to believe what he was about to do.

Opening the drawer in his desk, he took out the revolver. A Webley Mk IV, once the property of his father, who had fought in the Boer War. He'd loaded the bullets before her arrival. The bird's head grip of moulded vulcanite felt comfortable in his hand. The gun was designed for emergency use, at close range.

Well, this was certainly an emergency.

'You're not having second thoughts?' she asked in a small voice.

Fear had paralysed her. She couldn't move even if she wanted to.

'No,' he said. 'No second thoughts.'

He lifted the revolver and squeezed the trigger.

I

Basil Palmer's Journal

1 January 1931

My New Year's resolution is to murder a man I've never met. This is no sudden decision. For almost six months it's brewed in my mind. Ever since I lost my beloved Alicia.

Since I was a boy of ten, I have celebrated each new year by making a resolution. Reticent by nature, and fearful of failure, I've never mentioned this to a soul, but I've pursued each aim with a zeal that would startle those around me. Other people see me as meek, mild-mannered, and middle-aged, the very model of a modern chartered accountant. My reputation for reliability and attention to detail has enabled me to make a success of my practice, but nobody would think of me as remorseless. Respectable, yes. To my core.

My previous resolutions have, I must admit, lacked daring. To commit oneself to abstaining from alcohol or losing half a stone in weight is a very different kettle of fish from deciding to murder a fellow human being.

I cannot confide in a living soul. That goes without saying. Yet my private thoughts demand an outlet. I don't underestimate the obstacles that lie ahead. If not recorded in black and white, my plans might remain pipe dreams. Writing about them somehow brings them alive.

'You're a creature of habit,' Alicia liked to say, tossing her lovely fair curls.

She knew me so well. Whenever I encounter a difficulty, I find it helps to order my thoughts by writing them down. This method suits my temperament and has helped me to unravel knotty problems, typically concerning my clients' difficulties with the Inland Revenue. My new goal is by far the most ambitious and extraordinary I have ever attempted. Hence the need for this journal. I shall destroy it as soon as the deed is done. In the meantime, the chances of anybody laying their hands on it are nil.

The first challenge is this. The man I wish to kill is called Louis Carson. I do not, however, know where he lives or what he looks like. In truth, I know nothing about him.

Except that he deserves to die.

7 January

I'm a God-fearing man.

By instinct, I am law-abiding. My only experience of criminality is another old habit, of driving at speeds in excess of the pitiful maximum prescribed by the Motor Car Act of 1903. How ironic that the first of this month, which marked my momentous New Year's resolution, also saw the repeal of that absurd and widely flouted statute. From now on, I am no longer guilty of breaking the law when I drive at more than twenty miles per hour. Before the year is out, however, I shall have committed a premeditated murder.

Is it strange that my conscience scarcely troubles me? I

don't think so. I am filled with a sense of purpose, reinforced by rereading what I wrote on New Year's Day. I have no doubt that I am doing the right thing. Ridding the world of wickedness.

All I need to do is find Carson and then devise a plan for his elimination that does not expose me to the risk of arrest. A tall order? Perhaps, but there is no stopping me. Losing Alicia numbed me. My life lost any sense of purpose. Now, I detect a glimmer of light at the end of a long, dark tunnel. If I can remove Louis Carson, I may be able to move forward. I have no wish to be treated as a common criminal or to finish up on the gallows. True justice doesn't require my death. It requires the elimination of Louis Carson.

8 January

How to murder a man in such a way that I never become a suspect? I've consulted several volumes of *Notable British Trials* in the British Museum so as to gain an understanding of mistakes commonly made in cases of premeditated homicide. I find it depressing to study the blunders of even the most intelligent of killers. Crippen's panic, for instance, at a moment when he had come within an ace of persuading the police that his wife was still alive!

I console myself with the reflection that the annals of crime concern cases where the perpetrator was identified and apprehended. I have no known link with Louis Carson and this is a huge advantage which I shall exploit to the full.

Even as I write these words, the blurred outlines of an answer to my question begin to form through the mist in my mind. I must create a false identity. Someone who comes into being solely for the purpose of killing Louis Carson and then disappears without a trace.

I must become someone else.

12 *March*

My initial preparations are complete. It has taken little more than two months for me to embark upon a double life.

To my surprise, I've found the whole business exhilarating. Professional life in Guildford offers little scope for the imagination to roam. I cannot deny there have been occasions when, in a fit of exasperation, even my dear Alicia described me as dull or boring. These characteristics merely reflect the nature of my work. Books need to balance and the demands of double-entry accounting discourage a spirit of adventure. I'm neither as humourless nor as uncultured as Alicia, during our infrequent but dispiriting arguments, was wont to suggest.

In my youth I dabbled in amateur theatricals, receiving considerable encouragement from a kindly teacher. An unfortunate incident involving one of my fellow pupils led to the master's sudden departure from the school, and thereafter I had few opportunities to develop my thespian talents. My New Year's resolution allows me to rediscover the pleasures of playing a part.

I have always found the Irish accent mellifluous and easy to imitate. My second Christian name happens to be Seamus, thanks to a flight of fancy on the part of dear Mamma, who once visited the Emerald Isle. I chose the surname Doyle because I've always enjoyed the late Sir Arthur's stories; not so much the detective stories as the novels of long ago, chivalrous times such as *The White Company*.

The most convincing lies are seasoned with truth. To pose as garage hand or a retired county cricketer, for instance, would be an act of folly. Much as I love cars and the summer game, I would struggle to maintain the charade for any extended period of time. I am a professional man and it makes no sense to pretend otherwise. Given that my history of ill-health has caused me to study innumerable medical dictionaries, pretending to be a doctor, recently retired and back from foreign climes, should present few problems.

So Mr Basil Palmer has become Dr Seamus Doyle, late of South Africa and fifty-five years old. Adding to my age was easier than subtracting a few years; even dear Alicia occasionally accused me of becoming old before my time. Dr Doyle has a mild stoop and is never seen without large tortoiseshell spectacles with round tinted glass and a nose-piece lined with cork for comfort. In a radical departure from a three-piece suit and bowler hat, Dr Doyle dresses nattily – the colonial influence – and has a taste for garish bow ties. His headwear alternates between a tweed trilby and, on sunny days, a panama. He smokes an occasional Havana, even though it makes him cough.

As far as the rest of the world is concerned, Dr Doyle is comfortably off, without being so rich as to attract unwanted attention. He has deposited healthy amounts of cash in his recently opened account with the National Provincial Bank and has taken rooms in Gower Street.

Dr Doyle is, despite his bow ties, inconspicuous and often absent from London. Nobody has taken any notice of him at all while he prepares the ground for committing a perfect murder.

15 March

To find Carson, I need help. Reluctant as I am to involve others in my scheme, I have no choice. The man could be anywhere, doing anything.

The solution is to engage the services of an enquiry agent. In the normal course of events I would give a wide berth to such individuals, who are so often mixed up in the seamy business of procuring evidence for the divorce courts. Luckily, I know just the man.

I came across his name eighteen months ago. One of my clients is a prosperous merchant of timber and building supplies, and in conducting the annual audit of the business, I discovered discrepancies between the figures for incoming and outgoing stock. The scale of losses was putting the future of the business in jeopardy. The managing director, a hard-bitten fellow rather ironically named Cheetham, called in a private investigator from London. The man soon concluded that the thefts were an 'inside job' of some sophistication. I never met the detective, but I saw his reports, which were concise yet meticulous in matters of detail.

'Fellow used to be a copper,' Cheetham told me when I expressed my approval of the thoroughness of the investigation. 'Not sure why he left Scotland Yard – some funny business, I heard – but he was recommended to me as the best man for the job.'

McAtee, the man in question, proposed that he should apply for a job with the firm as a store hand. Cheetham duly recruited him and within a fortnight, he had pinpointed the long-serving yard foreman and the company secretary as co-conspirators. His comprehensive dossiers enabled Cheetham to press charges and the business was saved. His fee was hefty, but he more than earned it.

Tracing Louis Carson is unlikely to prove straightforward. In any event, I need to be careful. If people remember me making enquiries about him, it might have serious repercussions. Far better to use an intermediary to discover his present whereabouts. I never met Joseph McAtee, but all the evidence suggests that he is persistent, well organised, and discreet. In other words, the right man for the job.

18 March

Today saw the first setback in my quest for justice.

I called McAtee this morning, from a public telephone booth. He answered cheerily and confirmed that he was available to accept new instructions, but as I began to explain what I wanted, he cut me short.

'Yes, yes, Dr Doyle, that's all well and good. But I don't take on new clients by phone. You need to come in to see me.'

'Is that really necessary?'

'Absolutely essential. Can we arrange an appointment so you can tell me all about this little job of yours? Does next Monday morning suit?'

'It isn't very convenient. Surely if I give you...'

'A personal briefing is vital, I'm afraid.' Beneath the jollity, there was evidently an unbending will. 'Much easier to discuss these things face to face. I'm sure you see the sense of that, Doctor. Better to examine the patient than listen to an account of symptoms on the blower, eh?'

The analogy failed to impress me. 'I thought that if I

explained everything fully and sent a payment on account of costs to be incurred...'

'Sorry, Doctor, no can do. You see, you'll want to be satisfied of my bona fides...'

'Oh, I have no concerns on that score. You come highly recommended.'

'Very kind of somebody. May I ask who pointed you in my direction?'

'If you don't mind, I'd rather not say. It was a sensitive affair and your name was given to me in strict confidence. Indeed my friend was impressed with your own discretion.'

'Delighted to hear it. Now, as I was saying, when a client engages someone in my line, what's sauce for the goose is sauce for the gander, if you follow my meaning.'

'Actually, I'm not...'

'These things cut both ways,' he said briskly. 'You're placing your faith in me. By the same token, I need to be satisfied that everything is open and above board.'

'Please. I can assure you...'

'No offence intended, Doctor, don't get the wrong end of the stick.' A slight pause. 'But I need to see the cut of a client's jib, if you'll pardon the expression. You've gathered that I have a reputation, and I place a high value on it.'

Given my understanding that McAtee had left the police under a cloud, I thought this was rich, but plainly he was in no mood to relent.

'Very well.' I drew in a breath. 'If you will... allow me a little time to think about it.'

'Excellent, Doctor. I shall wait to hear from you.'

Without more ado, he put down the phone.

So I am left in a quandary. I am nervous about revealing myself to an experienced detective. Will his keen eyes see through my subterfuge? I have some confidence in my ability to carry off my impersonation of an Irish medical man, but there is another reason for concern. The fewer people who can connect Dr Seamus Doyle with Louis Carson, the better.

But, as Cheetham said, this man McAtee is at the head of his peculiar profession. Can I afford not to hire his services?

20 March

I have made up my mind. Life is never free of risk and it is self-deception to believe otherwise. Even if McAtee never met me, he would be aware that I'd engaged him to hunt Carson down.

The more I think about it, the more my confidence grows. If I can persuade an experienced detective to believe in the existence of Dr Seamus Doyle, I will have passed my first serious test with flying colours. It is one thing to fool a bank clerk or a landlady, quite another to deceive a man such as Joseph McAtee.

I shall telephone him later today to arrange a meeting.

27 March

Tonight I am tired but relishing the heady delights of having played a part to – if not perfection, then to the very limits of my ability.

I travelled to London last night, assuming the guise of Dr Doyle for an evening meal in Bloomsbury before spending the night in Gower Street in readiness for my appointment at ten o'clock the next morning.

McAtee's office is on the first floor of a scruffy building tucked away in a side street near King's Cross. He has no secretary, the battered Underwood on his desk indicating that he types his reports himself.

In person, he dwarfs me. Broad-shouldered and balding, he has a ready smile and pumped my hand with such vigour that I feared he would break a bone. He is a man of fifty and quite unlike the sleuth-hound of my imagining. The resemblance to a genial grocer is so marked that I half expected him to urge me to buy some cauliflowers.

'Good of you to make the time to come over, Doctor,' he said, as if I'd done him a special favour rather than acceding to a condition he'd imposed. 'I'm sure you're a busy man. Patients to see and drugs to dispense?'

The wooden chair he'd ushered me into was as unsteady as it was uncomfortable. I felt at a disadvantage, as if at any moment it might give way beneath me.

'I'm retired,' I said briefly. 'I returned to Britain recently after a long time in South Africa.'

'Marvellous country!' He gave me a searching look. 'The Cape, was it?'

My heart sank. 'You're familiar with that part of the world?'

He beamed. 'Sad to say, Doctor, I don't have much time for travelling. Maybe one of these days, eh? By comparison you are quite a globetrotter. Which part of Ireland are you from, may I ask?'

'I was born in Wexford. But let me get right to the point. I need you to trace someone for me. Is that the kind of work you undertake?'

'Certainly, certainly.' He rubbed his hands, his expression gleeful. 'This isn't a divorce matter, then?'

I shook my head.

'Splendid, a change is as good as a rest! I get a lot of business in connection with unhappy marriages and, between you and me, it can become a trifle… samey. Makes me glad I never tied the knot myself. May I ask a question before we proceed? What if the individual you seek does not wish to be found?'

For all the bland amiability of his words, I detected a sharpness in his pale blue eyes as he studied my reaction.

I let out a sigh. 'I'm a bachelor and not in the best of health. After so many years out of the country, I've lost touch with the people I knew. I have no close family left and given my uncertain health, it's only sensible to consider making a will. There are a number of people I'd like to consider as heirs. One of them is the man I'd like you to find. The son of a friend of mine who once did me a great kindness.'

McAtee beamed. 'I'm sure you're good for many years to come, Doctor!'

I tried to look wistful. 'If only I shared your confidence. But that is immaterial. The question is whether you are able to trace Louis Carson.'

'What can you tell me about him?'

'Very little, I'm afraid. I didn't know his father well, which made me all the more grateful for his generosity. He and his wife died when Louis was still quite young. I never met the boy and can't even give you a description. I heard a vague rumour once that he'd had a difficult time after losing his parents. Got into bad company, more than likely. So he may be down on his luck and in desperate need of financial help. On the other hand, he may be highly respectable and making a success of his life. All I can really tell you is that about nine months ago, he was in Brighton.'

'And how do you know that?'

'He sent a postcard to a mutual friend, who hadn't heard of him for many a year. It arrived out of the blue last June. My understanding is that Louis wasn't enjoying a holiday at the seaside, he was actually living in the town. More than that, I'm afraid, I cannot say.'

McAtee rubbed his chin. 'Not much to go on, Doctor.'

I ventured a smile. 'Now you understand why I need to engage your services.'

'Well, what about this mutual friend? He might be able to shed more light...'

'Impossible,' I interrupted. 'He died recently, while travelling abroad.'

'Pity.' McAtee rubbed his nose.

'I doubt he could have helped. By the way, I should emphasise that I don't want Louis Carson to become aware of the enquiries I'm making.'

'No?'

'Definitely not.' I paused. 'If, for instance, I find that he is disreputable, I should not wish to mention him in my will.'

'Very well, that's understood. What sort of age is he?'

This was one of the questions I'd dreaded, because I simply had no idea. I gave a heavy sigh.

'I'm afraid I'm far from sure.'

'Rough idea?'

'Perhaps late thirties,' I said, hoping that my guesswork wasn't absurdly inaccurate, 'but quite possibly older than that. Forty-plus. I'm sorry to be so vague.'

McAtee raised his eyebrows. 'Not easy to make bricks without straw, Doctor.'

The time had come for me to take a risk. 'Of course, if you feel that the task is beyond you, I'll understand.'

McAtee leaned across his desk. 'So you want me to find

one Louis Carson, last heard of in Brighton nine months ago? You don't know the man's age or what he looks like?'

'When you put it like that,' I said, risking a rueful smile, 'it does sound as if I'm asking the impossible.'

'One thing you learn in this business, Doctor, is that nothing is impossible.' He relaxed back in his chair and folded his arms. 'Very well, then. Shall we discuss terms?'

And that was that. He asked no more awkward questions and was no doubt happy to accept a sum on account of his fee and expenses that was as much as, in these depressed times, many working men can earn in half a year.

'When can I expect to hear from you?' I asked as I was leaving. 'I am away from home a good deal at present, but you have my address for correspondence.'

'I'll report once a fortnight,' he said. 'Sooner, if I turn anything up.'

With that, I made good my escape.

4 *May*

McAtee has repaid my faith – and my sizeable investment – in him. This afternoon I arrived at Gower Street and found a letter waiting for me. He said he believed he had located the man I sought and would be glad to supply further information if I called into his office at my convenience.

I preferred to telephone. Our first meeting had gone as well as I could have hoped, but I did not want to risk subjecting myself to his scrutiny once again. What if I made the mistake of revealing my true feelings about Louis Carson?

Fortunately, McAtee did not insist on my making another appointment to see him in person.

'You're in luck, Doctor,' he said breezily. 'You gave me a haystack the size of St Paul's Cathedral, but I finally managed to hunt down your lost needle.'

'Congratulations.'

'Thanks. You were right, by the by.'

'About what?' I tried to keep the surprise out of my voice.

'Carson's age. He's forty.'

'What can you tell me about him?'

'The details will be in my report, but you may like to know that he's married.'

'Really?' Somehow I'd imagined Carson as a single man.

'There are no children, if that's a complication that bothers you.' I shook my head. 'His wife's name is Pearl. She's worked in shops and as a nurse, but mostly she's been in service.'

I could only feel pity for the woman. 'You will let me have a full description of him? I'd prefer to get a clear picture of the fellow in my mind before I approach him.'

'I can do better than that. You can have a snapshot I took when I tracked him down. Don't worry, he didn't see me.' He paused. 'If you're still considering the possibility of making him your heir, you may want to know that he doesn't have a criminal record. Neither does his wife.'

I gripped the receiver so hard that it hurt. 'Is that so?'

'And he's not short of a few bob. To say the very least.'

I made a non-committal noise and waited. I had the impression that McAtee was keen to assess my reaction to what he said, and I was determined to give nothing away.

'Yes, he's acquired some business interests in the north of England. Buyer's market these days, of course, and he's taking full advantage.'

Of course he has, I thought grimly. Carson specialises in taking advantage of people.

'So he is no longer in Brighton?'

'Correct. That didn't half complicate the business of tracing him, believe me. But this is your man, as sure as eggs is eggs.'

'How confident are you?'

'I'd stake my life on it.' He sounded affronted, as if I'd cast doubt on his professional integrity. 'I've checked exhaustively; that's why my investigation took a good while. Nobody else by the name of Louis Carson has lived in Brighton for the past three years.'

'Where is he now?'

We were coming to the crunch. I had a vague fear that Carson might be living the high life in the south of France or on Capri.

'Still living by the seaside. His adopted home has become a fashionable watering hole.'

'He's moved there permanently?'

'Yes, he's gone into partnership with the fellow who built the resort and has taken charge of the main hotel in town. I took his picture from a shelter as he walked by. He was strolling along the cliffs as if he owned them. Maybe he soon will.'

'So where exactly is this place?'

'Lancashire.' McAtee made it sound as remote as the North Pole. 'Name of Hemlock Bay.'

2

'**M**arvellous, don't you think?'

Rachel Savernake stood back to admire the painting Cliff Trueman had hung above the art deco sideboard. The latest addition to her collection occupied pride of place in the elegant drawing room of Gaunt House.

In the whole of London, there were few finer residences in private hands. An outsider would expect the domestic staff to number upwards of a dozen, especially given that Rachel had money to burn. Yet between them, Trueman, his wife Hetty, and sister Martha did everything necessary. No blood tie connected Rachel with the Truemans, but the four of them were as tight-knit as the closest family. There was no question of anyone else working at Gaunt House.

Trueman, shirtsleeved, folded his beefy arms and scowled at the hotchpotch of bright colours and irregular lines. A dozen examples of surrealist art jostled for attention in the drawing room, but this was the most inscrutable of all.

'Put me out of my misery. What is it?'

She raised her eyebrows. 'Do I gather you're unmoved by the artist's vision?'

His grunt was eloquent. 'You want my honest opinion?'

'Always.' She smiled. 'Though I suspect I'll live to regret it.'

'I can't fathom what you see in this stuff. It makes no sense to me. Looks like something out of a kindergarten.'

She pretended to flinch. 'I asked for honesty, not brutality.'

'Look at it, a jumble of meaningless shapes. I can't make head nor tail of it. What's the point? It's not as if you need to cover up a damp patch. I daren't think how much you forked out for it.'

'Don't try to guess,' she said gaily. 'I'd be heartbroken if you dropped down dead in front of me. I paid a fair price, let's leave it at that.'

'You were robbed, whatever you spent.'

'Believe me, I beat the dealer down until he was almost sobbing with pain. My final offer was a fraction of his original asking price. His first sale in a month, so it was easy to drive a hard bargain. The Slump has devastated the demand for fine art.'

'Fine art?' The big man's face creased with incredulity.

'Fine art, yes.' A touch of steel entered her voice. 'The strangeness of surrealism enchants me.'

He shook his head. 'Takes all sorts. You always were one of a kind. Determined to go your own way.'

'Believe me, the best avant-garde artists of today will be admired long after you and I have shuffled off this mortal coil. Quite apart from its intrinsic merit, this painting will prove an excellent investment. Not that I have any plans to sell.'

'Pity.'

She laughed. 'You're such a curmudgeon. A true Philistine.'

As she spoke, Martha Trueman bustled in. Like Rachel, she was in her mid-twenties. As far as the outside world was concerned, she worked as a housemaid. Within these four walls, she and Rachel were as close as twins.

'He enjoys being grumpy,' Martha said. 'Anyone would think he's in his dotage. If I didn't know better, I'd never believe he's not quite forty.'

Her brother glared. 'Age doesn't come into it. Don't tell me you can make any sense of a series of random splodges?'

Martha considered the artwork. 'I like the vivid shades of orange and brown, yellow and blue. The way he's mingled them together is… intriguing.'

'Highly diplomatic.' Rachel pointed to a squiggle in the bottom right hand corner. 'But your detective skills are getting rusty. The artist is female.'

Moving closer to the painting, Martha screwed up her eyes and peered at the tiny signature.

'Virginia… Penrhos?'

Trueman made a scornful noise. 'Looks like she finds it hard enough to write her own name, let alone paint.'

'Don't underestimate her,' Rachel said. 'I'm the first to admit that her work is uneven, but I admire her ambition. Her willingness to take chances. She's one of the women taking surrealist art in fresh directions.'

'You said the same about Damaris Gethin,' Trueman said in a low voice. 'Didn't do her any good.'

'No.'

Rachel's expression darkened. A few weeks earlier, the shocking death of Damaris Gethin had led the pair of them to a fatal rendezvous in a house in a quiet cul-de-sac in Rye. They would never forget Sepulchre Street.

Martha wasted no time in changing the subject. 'Virginia Penrhos... mmm... the name rings a bell.'

'You must have heard of her. When we arrived in London eighteen months ago, she was still quite obscure, but since she turned to surrealism, her reputation has come on in leaps and bounds. She has an eye for publicity and a taste for sensation.'

'Wasn't she in the news some time ago? Something rather scandalous?'

'Last summer, a gallery in Camden Town held an exhibition of her work. Surrealist versions of the naked female form. Virginia Penrhos announced her intention to appear in the nude at the private viewing. The aim, she insisted, was to display her artistic integrity.'

'Among other things,' Trueman muttered.

'She claimed to be making an emotional connection with her models. Standing together with them, making the point that the anonymous figures are as important to art as the artists who paint them.'

'It's coming back to me now,' Martha said. 'She stirred up quite a fuss.'

'Guardians of public decency were duly outraged.'

'When are they not?'

'Questions were asked in the House of Commons about declining moral standards.'

Martha gave a playful smile. 'Thank goodness for our Members of Parliament. We can always rely on them to behave with the utmost integrity.'

'Rather like the newspaper barons. Leader articles ranted and the forces of law and order were urged to do the right thing. Public protests were threatened. Virginia Penrhos was warned she faced prosecution if she went ahead with her plan.'

'And did courage fail her?'

'Courage never came into it. She issued a defiant statement saying that under duress she'd told the gallery owner to cancel the private viewing. The statement even included a catchy line for the headline writers. Because she didn't wish to expose him to the risk of prison, she'd chosen not to expose herself.'

Martha laughed. Her brother sighed.

'Virginia didn't stop there,' Rachel said. 'Her forced surrender was a Pyrrhic victory for tyrannical and outdated conventions, buttressed by a debased and archaic legal and social system. As for the art critics and the rest of the cultural establishment, they only cared about Old Masters and their Young Mistresses. They'd spat in the faces of women with independent minds who longed to break free of cultural enslavement.'

'At least she got all that off her chest,' Martha said.

'Whatever you think of her work, Virginia Penrhos is as smart as her own paint. She gained all the publicity she could dream of without so much as peeling off a garter.'

Trueman jerked a thumb at the wall. 'What's so fascinating about this particular masterpiece?'

'Look closely,' Rachel said. 'Notice anything unusual?'

'Easier to spot something that *isn't* unusual,' he retorted.

Martha inspected the painting. 'Is it… a seaside scene?'

'Bravo! Yes, once your mind is attuned to her style, you see the sun and the sea and the sand. As well as that shadow cast over the rocks by cliffs. And a lighthouse.'

'Yes! It's almost like an optical illusion.'

Rachel turned to Trueman. 'Now does anything strike you?'

Grudgingly, and for the first time, he gave the picture

more than a cursory glance. After fully half a minute, he straightened.

'Is that a person, obscured by the shadow? Sunbathing on the rocks? Face down?'

'I doubt Virginia Penrhos was portraying a sun worshipper. Any other ideas?'

'Give me a hint.'

'There's such a stillness about the figure.'

Trueman and his sister stared at the painting.

'I see what you mean,' Martha said softly. 'It's ambiguous, but...'

'Art's almost always ambiguous.'

'And alliterative?'

Rachel laughed. 'So what do you think?'

'A dead body? Is that why the limbs are stretched out in such an unnatural pose?'

'Yes,' Rachel said. 'Once the penny drops, you see that it must be a corpse.'

'Someone who jumped from the cliffs? Or the lighthouse?'

'Or was pushed.'

Hetty sighed. 'You're incorrigible.'

'What is the painting called?' Martha asked. 'The title might give us a clue.'

'Quite right. Virginia Penrhos named it after a watering hole in Lancashire. Not a product of her imagination, but a resort on the north-west coast.' Rachel smiled. '*Hemlock Bay.*'

'Hemlock Bay?' Hetty Trueman poured from the sterling silver teapot with infinite care. 'The name rings a bell, but I've no idea why.'

The residents of Gaunt House were taking afternoon tea

out on the roof garden, high above the leafy square. There was a conservatory and a swimming pool and far-reaching views across London. The fragrance of blue agapanthus lilies scented the air. The garden was an oasis of calm in the heart of the capital.

Martha was racking her brains. 'Is it… notorious?'

Hetty raised her eyebrows. 'Notorious?'

'In some circles, yes,' Rachel said. 'I've become intrigued by the place.'

'We all know what that means.' Hetty sighed. 'You won't rest until you've found out everything you can about the place. Go on, I can see you're bursting to tell us.'

Rachel laughed. 'I've devoured *The Illustrated Guide to Hemlock Bay*. Before the war, hardly anyone knew it existed. There was just a small bay with a splendid beach, flanked by a stretch of sheer cliffs on one side and a tiny, secluded cove on the other side of a steep strip of headland. Fishermen and farmhands lived in scattered cottages and there was an old, decaying manor house. The main landmark, close to the cliffs and a treacherous outcrop of rock, was an old lighthouse.'

'Sounds pleasant,' Hetty said. 'Not overwhelmed by crowds.'

'To the north, a narrow channel of water cut the area off from Heysham and Morecambe. Because there was no bridge, you could only reach Hemlock Bay by going miles out of your way. If you made the journey, there was nothing to do but admire the scenery. As the crow flies, it wasn't so far from Blackpool. In every other respect it was a world away.'

'I can't be doing with Blackpool,' Hetty said. 'Too brash and noisy.'

'The tower is marvellous,' Martha said dreamily. 'On a clear day you can see north Wales.'

Hetty made a face. 'You'd never catch me going up there. I've no head for heights.'

'I love the Illuminations and riding along the front on the tram. And there are three piers. No wonder they call it the Wonderland of the World.'

'Three piers in one resort?' Hetty retorted. 'If that isn't overegging the pudding, I don't know what is. Give me Morecambe any day.'

'We went to Morecambe on our honeymoon,' Trueman said. 'Stayed at a guest house on the front. Rained every day we were there.'

'I still have happy memories,' his wife said.

Rachel tasted her drink and gave a nod of approval. 'Ah, Darjeeling. The champagne of teas. Actually, you weren't many miles from Hemlock Bay. Not that you'd have wanted to interrupt your marital bliss with such a tedious journey.'

Hetty blushed. 'Rain or no rain, we had a lovely time, and I'll say no more than that.'

'Turner was one of the few visitors to venture as far as Hemlock Bay. He travelled there on a sketching trip and said it was as pretty as Paradise. A glowing endorsement, but nothing much changed in the next hundred years. No candyfloss, no saucy postcards. Only a legend about a mermaid displaying her charms on the rocks.'

'The rocks in your painting?' Martha asked.

Rachel nodded. 'In bad weather, those coastal waters are extremely dangerous. In olden times, ships were often wrecked on the rocks and sandbanks beneath the cliffs. Some were deliberately lured to their doom. The fishermen and farmers of Hemlock Bay supplemented their income by smuggling contraband through a maze of underground passages. Rather less romantic than the folk tale about a beautiful mermaid who lazed on the rocks, combing her luxuriant tresses and distracting sailors from their attempts to navigate a safe passage. Lancashire's very own Lorelei.'

'The smugglers were explaining away their own crimes?'

'Yes, it's always convenient to blame someone else for one's own misdemeanours. In the story, the mermaid's shameless bosom-flaunting was responsible for one disaster after another until finally the widow of a drowned sailor took a terrible revenge.'

'What did she do?'

'She swam up behind the mermaid, slit her throat, and left her on the rocks to bleed to death. The outcrop became known as Mermaid's Grave.'

'So your painting shows Mermaid's Grave?'

'Virginia Penrhos's version of it, yes.' Rachel paused. 'But in modern times, Hemlock Bay has changed out of all recognition.'

'What happened?'

'Before war broke out, a bridge was built over the stream, shaving a good half-hour off the journey by road. Motorists who made detours to the coast liked what they saw. Of course, natural beauty wasn't enough for trippers. They needed somewhere to stay and expected to be entertained when they got there.'

'That kind of place draws speculators like moths to a candle.' Hetty shook her head. 'Such a pity. Does Hemlock Bay now have three piers of its own?'

'Not so much as a single jetty, you'll be delighted to hear. A rich man called Jackson got in ahead of everyone else. He bought a lot of land cheap and set about developing a small and select seaside resort, complete with esplanade, fashionable hotel, and eighteen-hole golf course. No expense spared, no opportunity missed. The lighthouse had been decommissioned and he turned it into a residence for visitors to rent. Pleasure grounds were built on Hemlock Head, which divides the main bay from the small cove. There's dancing, an aviary, all sorts of amusements.'

Hetty sniffed. 'Fun for all the family?'

'Turner's phrase was adopted by the advertising men. The amusement park is modestly known as Paradise.'

'Paradise? Sounds more like purgatory.'

'Jackson is supposed to be a civilised fellow. Cambridge-educated and married to a glamorous American.'

'Ha!' It wasn't clear whether Hetty's scorn was targeted at the wife's nationality or Jackson's alma mater. Or both.

'They met and married shortly after war broke out. He was fighting in France and there was every chance he'd be killed as soon as he went back to the front.'

'But he survived?'

'Thankfully, yes. Meanwhile, her great-uncle died. He'd become her guardian while she was still a babe in arms, after her parents were killed in a car crash in San Diego. She came into the fortune the old man made during the California Gold Rush.'

'Lucky her,' Hetty said.

'Sounds romantic to me,' Martha said.

'A bit of both, I gather. Her money allied with his vision for the future. Jackson was never a typical hard-bitten speculator, not simply in it to soak the trippers and make a quick profit before finding fresh fields to conquer. He and his wife fell in love with Hemlock Bay. They settled there permanently.'

'A modern-day lord and lady of the manor?' Martha said.

'Exactly. With two boys to carry on the line in due course. Jackson rebuilt the crumbling old manor house and turned it into a luxurious family home. His achievements were recognised eighteen months ago. He was given a knighthood, the ultimate seal of respectability.'

'Or badge of corruption, depending on your point of view.'

Rachel finished her drink. 'Jackson and his wife seem to have won over the locals. He's limited the amount of new building and that sort of exclusivity always appeals to people who are already there. He even squashed proposals to build another bridge that would carry a branch line of the railway into his new resort.'

'To keep out the common herd?'

'Whatever his faults, he doesn't sound like a snob.'

'But so many people don't own a car.'

'They can travel by coach. He didn't want his resort to be overrun, or to destroy the natural beauty that attracted people in the first place. Such a small resort could never compete with bigger towns like Morecambe, let alone Blackpool. His dream was to make Hemlock Bay somewhere special. A haven for the discerning visitor, if you believe the advertisements.'

Martha wasn't impressed. 'You mean genteel and boring?'

'Hardly. The Slump has affected everyone. Sir Harold Jackson is presumably no exception, but he's nothing if not enterprising. Last summer, he opened a new venture with much fanfare.' Rachel allowed herself a smile. 'The Hemlock Sun and Air Garden. Proudly advertised as an Eden of Education and Enlightenment.'

Hetty's eyes narrowed. 'You don't by any chance mean…?'

'Yes, a club for nudists, with its own beach in the cove on the far side of Hemlock Head. The Garden boasts complete privacy and the grounds are patrolled by a watchman with a big dog to deter intruders. Tall hedges and spreading oaks protect the members from prying eyes as they prance around in the open air, playing volleyball and listening to lectures about the benefits of frolicking *in puris naturalibus*.'

'Latin!' Hetty said darkly.

'An excellent language for asserting moral superiority. In return for a handsome fee, you can cast off your clothes and your inhibitions. Hence Hemlock Bay's recent notoriety. Several newspapers have kicked up a fuss about the nudist craze. They're furious that Britain has become engulfed by a wave of depravity disguised as healthy outdoor living.'

'Jacob Flint's rag is in the vanguard, then?' Trueman said. 'Frothing with outrage, as usual?'

'The *Clarion*? They aren't the worst offenders, but of course they'll seize any opportunity to trumpet moral indignation on behalf of their long-suffering readers.'

'You've done a lot of homework,' Martha said. 'As usual. What I don't understand is why you're so interested in Hemlock Bay?'

'The Virginia Penrhos connection was the starting point. You know I like to research paintings before I buy. She comes from the Welsh gentry, but she moved to Hove to pursue her passion for painting. She wasn't an overnight success, but she always refused to compromise her artistic integrity.'

Trueman made a scornful noise. Rachel smiled at him.

'I admire her single-mindedness. Of course it helped that she had plenty of money. She kept working on her technique and in the past year or two she has finally begun to make a name for herself. This spring, she moved to Hemlock Bay.'

'Permanently?'

'The dealer who sold me the picture told me she's taken a six-month tenancy of the lighthouse.'

'The lighthouse in the painting?'

'Exactly. Her decision to move astonished the dealer. Mind

you, he regards anywhere north of Watford as barbarian territory.'

Martha laughed. 'I bet she wants to recruit a fresh supply of models from the Sun and Air Garden.'

'I'm curious. Virginia Penrhos already lived by the sea. So what prompted her to move from one end of the country to the other?'

'Obviously the place took her fancy. If Hemlock Bay was good enough for Turner…'

'There's something else.' Rachel's face clouded. 'While I was looking up Hemlock Bay in the newspapers, one paragraph caught my eye.'

'Why was that?' Martha asked.

'There was a report of an inquest into the death of a young man from Liverpool. He'd jumped off the cliff at Hemlock Bay.'

A brief silence was broken only by a distant rumble of traffic from the streets below.

'Very sad, but if he was out of work and depressed…'

'On the contrary, Edward Hillman worked in the offices at the Mersey Docks and was engaged to be married. What's more, he'd recently won a jackpot on the football pools.'

'Gamblers,' Hetty said, as if that explained everything. 'They are unhappy people.'

'Not when they are winning. He seemed like someone with everything to live for. Hence the story made the national news.'

'You know what they say.' Hetty was never afraid to give them the benefit of her homespun wisdom. 'There's nowt so queer as folk.'

Rachel exhaled. 'I find it hard to understand.'

'You're not suggesting he was murdered?'

'No. An elderly couple who were visiting on holiday, and a local dog-walker both saw Hillman approach the cliff edge. He was on his own. Unless they were lying, nobody else was around, certainly not close enough to give him a shove. Before the witnesses knew what was happening, he'd jumped.'

'How dreadful.'

'What puzzles me is this. There was no indication that Hillman had any links to Hemlock Bay, other than the fact he'd taken his elderly mother there for a short holiday. Yet he made a special journey there to end his life. Why?'

'There aren't many other cliffs in Lancashire.'

'Unfortunately there are a hundred other options for someone who wants to kill himself.' Rachel shook her head. 'It strikes me as a peculiar choice. Yet it must have some significance.'

'A lot of things are peculiar in this day and age,' Hetty said. 'You can't worry your head about all of them.'

'I can't help feeling curious, given that the same small resort also exerts a powerful attraction on an artist whose work I admire. So much so that she's painted a picture of the place, featuring a corpse and a lighthouse. And then gone to live in the lighthouse.'

The older woman sniffed. They all knew what she was thinking. *Curiosity killed the cat. And one day it will kill you.*

'Do you think there's a connection between the body in the painting and the young man from Liverpool?' Martha asked.

Rachel shook her head. 'From what the dealer told me, there's no doubt that Virginia Penrhos completed the painting before Hillman's death. Besides, his body finished up in the sea, not on Mermaid's Grave.'

'Pure coincidence, then?'

'Yes and no.'

'I don't understand.'

'Look at how many people plunge to their doom from Beachy Head.' Rachel stared into the far distance. 'Some places attract death.'

'You think Hemlock Bay is one of them?'

'Everything I read about the place makes it sound too good to be true. Can somewhere so delightful have no dark side?'

Martha laughed. 'The Jekyll and Hyde of seaside resorts?'

A strange light came into Rachel's eyes. 'I wonder.'

'Why do you think it attracts death? Is it just because of the cliffs?'

Rachel shook her head. 'I wonder if some kind of serpent has slithered into Paradise.'

3

Jacob Flint peered at the letter, scanning it for clues like a philologist trying to decode the Rosetta Stone.

Written in a tidy hand on a single sheet of paper, the letter had arrived in an envelope bearing his business address: care of the *Clarion*, Clarion House, Fleet Street, London. As the chief crime reporter, Jacob was an easy target for anonymous letter writers with wild handwriting and a taste for capitals, underlinings, and exclamation marks. Their messages ranged from the risible and delusionary to the unpleasant and threatening. So did most of their claims about crimes and conspiracies.

Once in a blue moon, a nameless correspondent came up with a snippet of worthwhile information. His late predecessor Tom Betts had impressed upon him that even a madman has a story worth telling, so Jacob made a point of reading each letter before – in nineteen cases out of twenty – screwing it up and hurling it into the wastepaper basket.

This letter had arrived on Friday and survived the weekend simply because it differed from the usual nonsense. Not only were the contents commendably terse and devoid of literary flourishes, the sender hadn't remained wholly anonymous. At least he (or she) had appended initials. A sign of good faith? Or simply an attempt to tantalise?

Dear Mr Flint

A man is to be murdered at the summer solstice. The scene of the crime will be the cliffs at Hemlock Bay.

I wish to discuss the matter with you and seek your help to prevent this tragedy. I shall call at your London office at 11 a.m. on Monday next. If you are wondering why I have not spoken to the police, the answer is that I have, but they did not believe me. I am a regular reader of the Clarion and am confident that you have more sense.

Yours sincerely
T.G.H.

Now it was Monday, and the time was 10.45. The morning conference of the *Clarion*'s senior journalists had gone on longer than usual, thanks to an inconclusive debate about how to combat the summer slump in circulation. At this time of year, readers decamped to the seaside and were too busy enjoying themselves to bother about the news. Jacob had fifteen minutes to make sense of the letter before T.G.H. was due to turn up. Perhaps T.G.H. was a time-waster with no intention of visiting Fleet Street. However, something about the letter made Jacob think T.G.H. was serious – even if deluded. To admit that the police had shown no interest in what he said was admirably frank.

He frowned. In an ideal world, he'd reach a series of dazzlingly specific conclusions – for example, that his correspondent was a captain in the Grenadier Guards who had recently spent time in Spain and had a pet dog and a house in Canterbury, or alternatively that she was a vicar's wife with false teeth and a wonderful singing voice. Even if staggering feats of deduction were beyond him, he felt sure he could learn something about T.G.H.

Time to take a leaf out of Rachel Savernake's book. Rachel insisted that solving mysteries demanded a willingness to make creative leaps of imagination just as much as a meticulous attention to detail. Forensic evidence is all fine and dandy, she argued, but it's often open to more interpretations than scientists like to admit.

Very well, then…

The envelope in front of him was obviously cheap. Rather than using notepaper, the author had written on a sheet torn from an exercise book, probably from Woolworth's. Presumably the author was short of cash and accustomed to shopping in stores with a sixpenny price limit. Given the current state of the world's economy, mind you, that was true of almost everyone.

The handwriting was neat if unelaborate. There were no errors of spelling or grammar. This was the work of someone who had a certain level of education and wasn't pretending otherwise. There was no address, but knowing that Hemlock Bay occupied a tiny corner of the north-west coast, Jacob deduced that T.G.H. came from Lancashire.

Man or woman? The letter carried no hint of scent and there was nothing obviously feminine about either the script or phraseology. These points were, however, far from conclusive. The *Clarion* had become increasingly popular with women readers, many of whom hung on every pronouncement of the resident astrologer, Trewythian. T.G.H. talked about a forthcoming murder, so it wasn't much of a stretch to infer an interest in horoscopes. The police might be disinclined to lend a sympathetic ear to a woman with a strange story to tell. Their instinct would be to dismiss her as hysterical or a troublemaker. On balance, Jacob decided, T.G.H. was female.

Jacob's mind conjured up a picture of a bluff, busty matron who stood for no nonsense. A seaside landlady with a henpecked husband, perhaps, the sort familiar from a thousand saucy postcards?

Pleased with this exercise of his detective skills, he stretched out in his chair, luxuriating in his surroundings. He had a new office, a first-floor room befitting a senior journalist and commanding a view over Fleet Street but handy for a back staircase leading to a side door which gave on to an alleyway. The retirement of the newspaper's senior literary critic had given Jacob the chance to persuade his editor that he needed a suitable place to conduct confidential interviews with people who could come and go without being observed in the busy reception lobby. In truth, he'd continue to meet his sources in the pubs and clubs of the capital, but when he came down the corridor, the sight of the shiny brass plate bearing his name put a spring in his step. Over the past year or so he'd established himself, having acquired a reputation for an uncanny gift of being in the right place at the right time. In practice this meant keeping close to Rachel Savernake – although invariably several steps behind her.

The telephone rang and a bored female voice said, 'Visitor for you, Mr Flint.'

'Ah, yes,' he said, checking his watch. 'I do have an appointment in five minutes. She's early.'

'He's a man,' the girl said.

'Oh, really?' Perhaps it wasn't T.G.H. but someone else. 'What name did he give?'

'Hallemby.' She gave a derisive sniff. 'The *Great* Hallemby.'

'What can I do for you, Mr... Hallemby?' Jacob Flint asked.

His visitor nibbled at his fingernails. 'Actually, I'm known as The Great Hallemby.'

'Oh yes?'

Jacob wasn't sure what else to say. The man on the other side of his vast new desk was a scrawny individual with a sallow face and a limp handshake. His small eyes darted around the room, as if in search of something he'd mislaid. He looked a few years older than Jacob – early thirties, perhaps – but his greasy brown hair was already thinning. His shoulders were rounded, his tweed jacket threadbare, his shoes worn down at the heel. If greatness had been thrust upon this fellow, Jacob couldn't guess why.

'It's an anagram, see,' the man said, as if that explained everything.

His accent was as Welsh as bara brith. So much for interpreting character from a short letter, Jacob thought. At least the man's shabby clothes confirmed the assumption that he wasn't rich.

'I'm not sure I do.'

'My real name is Gareth Bellamy, but that wasn't exotic enough when I took up fortune telling.' He inspected his chewed fingernails sorrowfully. 'You'd never recognise me in my robes. Not to mention my wig. I cut quite a fine figure, if I say so myself.'

Jacob's heart was sinking fast. 'You tell fortunes?'

'It's a special gift,' the man said eagerly. 'Ever since I was a child, visions of the future have come to me. I can't control it and I haven't the faintest idea where they come from.'

'No?'

'Nobody in my family ever took me seriously, especially since I couldn't tip them the wink about who was going to win the Grand National or anything like that. I simply can't predict when I'll next be permitted a glimpse into the future.'

This sounded like a serious shortcoming in a fortune teller, but Jacob let it pass.

'I see.'

'Of course, I can always find something to say when clients pay for a reading. That's my job. I pride myself on being professional. A person only has to open their mouth to give something away about who they are and what's going on in their lives. Between you and me, it doesn't require exceptional powers to keep my customers satisfied. It's a knack. Just good, harmless family fun, see.'

'Of course.'

'The bigger things... they are different. When a vision comes to me, it may be as clear as day, or mysterious and incomplete. You never know.'

Jacob nodded sagely. 'So what brings you here, Mr Bellamy?'

'I'm a lifelong reader of the *Clarion*. Marvellous paper.'

'We pride ourselves on being the Voice of the People,' Jacob said, taking care to squeeze any hint of irony out of his own voice.

'Couldn't put it better myself. Over the past twelve months, I've read your own reports with enormous interest. Quite amazing. You've been Johnny-on-the-spot in some extraordinary murder cases.'

Jacob tried not to preen as the man waved at the large

noticeboard on the wall behind his desk. His first act on installing himself in his new home had been to cover the board from top to bottom with his favourite scoops. The bizarre crimes they chronicled all had two things in common. First, Rachel Savernake had played a crucial part in unravelling the truth. Second, her name didn't appear anywhere. This wasn't because Jacob claimed credit when it wasn't due. Rachel guarded her privacy with a ruthless zeal and he knew better than to infuriate her by parading in public either her fascination with extravagant mysteries or her genius for solving them.

'I've had my fair share of luck.' This was nothing less than the truth, but it sounded impressively self-deprecating.

'Very modest of you to say so. Those brilliant investigations are the reason I'm here. I was determined to speak to you rather than anyone else. Especially after the police sent me off with a flea in my ear.'

'Tell me more.'

Gareth Bellamy chewed a hangnail. A wary look came into his small dark eyes. 'You see, it's like this. I know that a murder is going to be committed at midsummer. I want to prevent the crime, but there's a huge problem.'

'Which is?'

'I've no idea who is going to be killed, or who is responsible. Like I said in my letter, all I know is when and where the crime is going to take place. The summer solstice in Hemlock Bay.'

It took twenty minutes of patient questioning for Jacob to get the story straight in his mind. In a nutshell, Gareth Bellamy hailed from Bangor in north Wales. After leaving school, he'd worked as a clerk, trying to better himself by moving from job to job. When the cold winds of economic depression blew across the Atlantic, the architects' firm which employed him was forced to shed most of its workforce and he was among the casualties. Out of work and unburdened by family commitments, he'd resolved to try his hand at something different.

Convinced that he had a knack of seeing into the future, he'd set up in business as a fortune teller. He bought a set of robes and a wig and set up as The Great Hallemby on the Victoria Pier at Colwyn Bay, next to the tea shop. Pickings were thin and the local police zealous, so he'd moved to the Lancashire coast, where the Vagrancy Act was less rigorously enforced. Business was brisker there. Maybe because the trippers who crossed his palm with silver were more credulous, or maybe they simply had more money to burn.

One evening, while getting ready for bed, Bellamy had one of those out-of-body experiences which, he insisted, came out of nowhere and for no apparent reason.

He had a vision of himself at dawn, strolling along the top of the cliffs known as Hemlock Heights. When he glanced out to sea, something stopped him in his tracks. Illuminated by the first streaky rays of sunlight, a body sprawled on the rocks below. The limbs were spreadeagled and the person was unquestionably dead. The head was bloodied and face down, and the corpse was dressed in a man's clothes. He must have plunged from the clifftop.

Bellamy was about to summon help when he heard someone whispering.

'So, it's finally done.'

'I... I can't quite believe...' The other voice was hoarse and breathless.

'I told you I could do it. We simply need to take care when the police ask questions.'

'Questions?'

'About his death. They'll speak to everyone in the neighbourhood. Just remember, nobody knows of any connection between him and me.'

'But…'

'Look at him! I did what I swore I'd do! And on the summer solstice. Everyone will think it was a simple accident. If we keep our nerve, nobody will ever suspect. Let alone be able to prove anything. Trust me.'

Shocked and bewildered, Bellamy glanced this way and that, desperate to see who was talking.

In vain. Within moments, the vision faded into nothingness. He was left on his own in the tiny bedroom in his lodging house, with the moonlight falling through a crack in the curtains on grubby whitewashed walls. Yet the sight of the dead man, stretched out on the unforgiving rocks, was imprinted on his brain. So were the words of the strangers on whom he'd inadvertently eavesdropped.

'After that, Mr Flint, I tossed and turned for the rest of the night, unable to get a wink of sleep. One thing I knew for sure: I couldn't live with my conscience if I didn't try to save a man from his terrible fate.'

Bellamy paused, as if awaiting a round of applause, before continuing. 'First thing the next morning, I caught a bus into Morecambe and headed for the police station. Believe me, I wasn't in the mood for shilly-shallying. I said to the desk sergeant that I wanted to report a murder. That made him sit up, Mr Flint, I can tell you.'

'I can imagine.'

'There was only one snag, see. When I said the crime hasn't been committed yet, he looked at me as if I was some kind of halfwit.'

Jacob made sympathetic noises.

'I insisted on seeing his superior and made such a fuss that a fellow called Inspector Young gave me a hearing. I explained the crime was due to take place on the summer solstice, but things went from bad to worse. When Young discovered that I'm a fortune teller, his manner changed. Instead of treating me like a lunatic, he became suspicious. As though I was some kind of fraudster.' Bellamy shook his head. 'It's a sad fact, Mr Flint. There's a lot of prejudice in this world.'

'Very true,' Jacob said.

'The inspector didn't believe a word I said. Even though I'd acted as any responsible citizen would. No wonder there's a crime wave and decent people aren't safe in their beds these days. Never mind enforcing the Defence of the Realm Act and stopping people from having innocent fun. The *Clarion* is right. This isn't Russia or Germany. The police aren't meant to be killjoys or petty bureaucrats. They should be keeping us law-abiding citizens safe from harm. I've handed them a serious crime on a plate. A man's life is in danger in Hemlock Bay. Yet they won't even lift a finger to save the poor devil.'

'I suppose they don't know where to start,' Jacob said. 'Is there anything more? Any flesh you could put on the bones?'

Bellamy spread his arms. 'What else can I say? I've told you everything.'

'The victim's clothes. Anything distinctive about them?'

He shook his head. 'I didn't take much in. It was a shocking sight and as soon as I realised he was dead, I had to look away.'

'The people you overheard. Were they both men?'

A shake of the head. 'Impossible to tell. One hardly said a word. They were speaking in whispers, so maybe one was a woman. Perhaps both of them.'

'Accents?'

Bellamy shifted in his seat. 'Hard to say, Mr Flint. I only caught a few snatches of conversation.'

'Did they sound as if they were local to the area?'

An evasive look flitted into the small eyes. With a touch of asperity, he said, 'I can't say, I'm afraid, and it's not right for me to speculate. Or to say anything that puts innocent people under suspicion. I wanted to lay the unvarnished facts in front of you.'

'I understand,' Jacob said. 'But there's so little to go on.'

'I don't agree,' Bellamy said. 'Hemlock Bay is a fraction of the size of Morecambe, let alone Blackpool. It can't be so difficult for an investigative reporter to find out what's what. Surely a scoop like this is meat and drink to a fellow like you?'

Jacob sighed. 'I'm not confident my editor would be happy for me to devote time and effort to researching the story.'

Bellamy glared at him. 'Because it's based on a fortune teller's vision, I suppose?'

'Well, you have to admit, the whole business sounds rather... fantastic.'

'I told you,' the other man said doggedly. 'I'm sensitive to atmosphere. There's something in the air at Hemlock Bay that is... stimulating to the senses. Including my sixth sense.'

'But all we have is a suggestion of a conspiracy between an unknown couple to kill an unknown third party.'

'I've also told you the victim is a man, as well as the scene of the crime and the date! Narrows things down, doesn't it?'

'What do you suggest? Should I prowl the cliffs at Hemlock

Bay at the summer solstice, keeping an eye out for potential murderers and warning solitary walkers not to get too close to the edge?'

An impatient flap of the hand. 'You're quibbling, Mr Flint. I'm not convinced you're taking me seriously.'

'Well...'

Bellamy's chin jutted out. 'I hoped you, of all people, would treat a forthcoming murder with the gravity it deserves.'

'Believe me,' Jacob said, 'I'm grateful for the information. The problem is that my editor is a born sceptic. If you could give me some red meat...'

'I've told you about a plot to commit murder, Mr Flint,' Bellamy snapped. 'If that isn't red meat, then I don't know what is. I thought you'd find the puzzle irresistible. The chance to investigate a murder that hasn't yet taken place! That's why I travelled all the way down from Lancashire to see you in person. At my own expense!'

Jacob shifted in his chair. 'I don't think we can reimburse...'

Bellamy waved his arms in agitation. 'I'm not looking for money! This is a matter of civic duty as far as I'm concerned. I've given you forewarning of a terrible crime. Let it never be said that The Great Hallemby didn't do everything in his power to save the life of a fellow human being!'

'Public-spirited of you,' Jacob said, 'but...'

'Speaking to the police was a complete waste of time. Guardians of law and order? Don't make me laugh!' Bellamy's bitterness was undisguised. 'If you ask me, they're constitutionally incompetent if not corrupt. When they sent me packing, I wasn't surprised. I hoped the *Clarion*, of all papers, wouldn't turn up its nose at an exclusive tip-off from a faithful reader.'

He got to his feet, evidently about to leave in a huff.

'Please don't misunderstand me,' Jacob said. 'I'd be very glad to speak to my editor. If he agrees to my becoming involved, I'll be glad to help.'

'You will?'

A watchful look came into the other man's eyes. Did he suspect he was being fobbed off?

'You have my word.'

'Let me give you my card,' Bellamy said. 'And perhaps I can take yours?'

'With pleasure.' Relieved that he'd managed to bring the meeting to a swift and amicable conclusion, Jacob felt able to indulge in a little bonhomie as they exchanged cards. 'You've acted very responsibly, Mr Bellamy. In the finest traditions of *Clarion* readers.'

'I'm obliged for your time.' The fortune teller consulted his watch. 'Now I mustn't dawdle. I need to get back to Euston in time for the next train. This morning was an early start for me, and I don't want to lose more earnings than I need. And I don't want my girlfriend hanging round the Rose Garden, either. She gets extremely jealous if I'm out of her sight for long.'

Privately, Jacob wondered if she might be glad to see the back of him.

'So what does she make of your premonition?'

The shiftiness returned to Bellamy's expression. 'I... I haven't discussed it with her.'

'Really?'

'Didn't want to upset her, see? A plot to commit a murder? Not very nice, is it? She's very sensitive, you know. Highly strung.'

Protesting too much, Jacob thought. He wondered why.

'Ah,' he said, trying to invest the syllable with maximum significance.

'Winifred works at Paradise; that's how we met.' Bellamy seemed keen to change the subject. 'Thanks to Skeleton Sue.'

'Skeleton Sue?'

'You must have heard of her.'

Jacob shook his head.

'One of the most popular puppets in the north of England. Mr Lescott, Winnie's father, made Skeleton Sue himself. The show is good clean fun. Very wholesome. Winnie operates some of the puppets and does front of house. Selling programmes and suchlike.'

'Well, you'd better get back before she starts fretting,' Jacob said. 'Thanks for coming to see me in person. It's good of you to take so much trouble.'

'I couldn't rest without doing my bit to make sure justice is done.'

They shook hands. Bellamy seemed eager to leave.

'Rest assured that I shall continue to read the *Clarion* with great interest.'

Jacob couldn't resist asking, 'Including Trewythian's horoscopes?'

Bellamy gave a wan smile. 'Never look at them, I'm afraid. Coals to Newcastle, see?'

The moment his visitor had left, Jacob swung his feet on to his desk and closed his eyes, trying to make sense of what he'd been told. It was facile to dismiss Gareth Bellamy as deluded. The man was articulate and intelligent. Nevertheless, the meeting had left him with an uncomfortable sense that he'd been told less than the whole truth. Did Bellamy know more than he'd admitted? Was he pursuing some kind of hidden agenda? Instinct told him that something about the fellow was off-key.

So what, if anything, should he do?

The first step was to dig into the man's background. How best to start? He looked up the number of a man called Harwood, an acquaintance from his early days in journalism who was now working for the *North Wales Weekly News*. After exchanging a few pleasantries, he got down to business.

'I'm interested in a man called Gareth Bellamy. Aged about thirty, give or take. Comes from Bangor and worked in clerical jobs before his employer ran into difficulties and let him go. After that he changed direction completely and took up fortune telling. His monicker is The Great Hallemby and he plied his new trade on the pier at Colwyn Bay before upping sticks and moving to Hemlock Bay.'

'What do you want to know?' Harwood asked.

'First, I'd like to check that what I've told you about his past is true. Then I'd be glad of any clues as to his honesty.'

'Fair enough. Give me twenty-four hours.'

'Thanks.' Jacob grinned at the telephone. 'I owe you a pint.'

'Yes,' Harwood said wearily. 'That's exactly what you said last time you asked me for a favour.'

'Double or quits?'

'You always were a cheeky young pup,' the other man said. 'All right, son. Leave it with me and I'll get back to you by this time tomorrow.'

Jacob put down the receiver. What next? Was there anything else he could do to make sense of The Great Hallemby's mysterious vision?

He didn't know where to start. Experience had taught him that when he was in a quandary of this kind, only one course made sense. He must consult Rachel Savernake.

4

'Time for a Bloodhound,' Rachel Savernake announced.

Martha Trueman laughed at Jacob's expression of bemusement. 'Cliff's latest experiment.'

Martha had brought him up in the lift to join Rachel in the roof garden of Gaunt House. Trueman was in the conservatory, mixing drinks at the bar. When Jacob had telephoned Rachel to say he'd come across a strange new mystery about a murder, she'd wasted no time in inviting him to dinner.

'If the rain holds off, we can dine al fresco,' she'd said gaily.

'I don't want to put you to any trouble. Let alone Hetty.'

'You don't need to be so timid where she's concerned. Her bark is much worse than her bite.'

'I'm still not sure she likes me. Or even trusts me.'

'Don't worry about Hetty. She has very high standards.'

Finding her reply less than reassuring, he'd squeezed the receiver in the palm of his hand. Typical Rachel. Reassuring people wasn't her forte.

'Mmmm.'

'With a lift as well as a dumb waiter, it's no trouble to

bring everything up to the roof. Besides, Hetty loves cooking for family and friends. You're more than welcome to join us. If you arrive by half past five, you'll be in time for a cocktail. A reward for your day of labour and a chance to savour Trueman's latest triumph.'

She'd rung off before he even had time to express his thanks. Rachel, he reflected, was the definition of an irresistible force. As for her mention of friends, it was a figure of speech. She and the Truemans kept themselves to themselves. To the best of his knowledge, he and Inspector Oakes of Scotland Yard were among the very few people they'd ever entertained. Did Rachel ever get lonely? He'd never dared to ask.

Trueman emerged from the conservatory, bearing a silver tray with blood-red cocktails in crystal glasses. Rachel clapped her hands in delight. Jacob found her guileless enthusiasm hard to reconcile with the sangfroid he'd witnessed more than once when she'd come face to face with callous and brutal murderers. She never blinked first.

'Your luck is in, Jacob,' she said. 'Finally the weather has been kind enough for us to enjoy preprandial cocktails in the open air. To celebrate, what better than a Bloodhound cocktail? Let's drink a toast to a new summer!'

Glasses were raised and Jacob inhaled the fruity aroma of the cocktail before taking a taste.

Martha threw him a smile. 'One Bloodhound sniffing another. Break it to us gently, Jacob. What's your verdict?'

'Delicious.' He had no reason to fib; it was a fool's game to try to pull the wool over these people's eyes, even about something as simple as a drink before dinner. 'Like a sort of strawberry martini, light and refreshing. Congratulations, Cliff, you've done it again.'

He rarely addressed Trueman by his Christian name.

The fellow's height and formidable physique made him an intimidating presence and Jacob usually felt it safer to keep a distance. Nominally Rachel's chauffeur, every now and then Trueman revealed an unexpected string to his bow. He'd developed a flair for mixing cocktails, and Harry Craddock's *The Savoy Cocktail Book* had become his bible.

Rachel's trust in Cliff Trueman was unyielding, but he was a man of few words and his demeanour made the Sphinx look like a quivering jelly. For a moment, Jacob thought he detected the faintest hint of a smile, but that was probably wishful thinking. Trueman kept his emotions buttoned up, but his physical strength was matched by the scale of his courage and devotion to Rachel. In a tight corner, there was no better man to have by your side.

'So you have a new puzzle to share with us,' Rachel said. 'Plenty of time for us to discuss it before dinner is served. Go on, Jacob. The floor – or rather, the roof – is yours.'

'Thanks.' Jacob cleared his throat. 'This is a mystery about a murder that has yet to be committed.'

Martha frowned. 'Like the death of Damaris Gethin?'

'No, this is very different from what happened at the Hades Gallery, thank goodness. I've been told when and where the crime is due to take place, but there's no clue to the identity of the victim, let alone whoever is planning the crime.'

Rachel pursed her lips. 'A good start. Carry on.'

As Jacob described the letter and his meeting with Gareth Bellamy, alias The Great Hallemby, he was conscious of her intense concentration. Impossible not to feel a warm glow. He admired Rachel, and there was no doubt that she was extremely good-looking. But something set her apart from other attractive women. Her sudden shifts of mood were unpredictable and occasionally disturbing. When provoked into anger, she was capable of being astonishingly ruthless. He hated to admit it, even to himself, but there were moments when she scared him.

'Hemlock Bay,' Martha said as he reached the end of his story. 'Well, well.'

'You know it?' he asked.

'None of us have ever been there,' she said. 'But we were talking about it only the other day.'

'Really?'

'Rachel has just bought a new painting called *Hemlock Bay*.'

Trueman made a scornful noise, making his sister laugh.

'According to Cliff, it's just a lot of random splodges of bright colour.'

'Let me guess,' Jacob said to Rachel. 'Another surrealist masterpiece?'

Rachel smiled. 'In my opinion, it's Virginia Penrhos's finest work. Trueman will tell you that's not saying much. But she does have talent. And she's not only painted Hemlock Bay, she's moved there from the south coast.'

'Is that so?'

'Yes, Hemlock Bay is fast becoming the most fashionable resort in the north of England. As for the painting, it's not quite as baffling as this pair would have you believe. After dinner, take a look for yourself and give us the benefit of your expert judgement.'

He laughed. 'You do love teasing me.'

'A girl must have some pleasure,' Rachel said. 'Don't you agree, Martha?'

'Definitely.'

Jacob grinned. 'There's a surrealist tinge to The Great Hallemby's mysterious vision. What do you make of it?'

'Eccentric fortune tellers make a change from spiritualists conducting dubious seances. His tale is thought-provoking, and your memory for detail is always excellent.'

'Thanks.' He tried to sound nonchalant, with limited success. Rachel never threw compliments around lightly.

'Did you bring the letter he sent you?'

He took it out of his pocket and handed it to her. She studied both letter and envelope with her customary attention to detail.

'The postmark is Hemlock Bay,' she said. 'So that part of his story seems to be true. A long way for him to travel, just to see you.'

Jacob couldn't help frowning.

'I don't mean to be rude,' she said, 'but it's quite an investment of time and money. Especially given your impression that he isn't well-off. And if his puppeteer lady friend is as jealous as he claims.'

'He's definitely not rich, if his clothes are anything to go by. I can't imagine why any girl would be jealous of him, but it takes all sorts.' Jacob hesitated. 'I suppose it's a sign of his bona fides that he took so much trouble to travel here and tell me his story.'

'Perhaps that's what he wanted you to suppose,' she said.

'You think he hoped to make a fool of me?'

'Unlikely.'

'What, then?'

'His professed devotion to the *Clarion* strikes me as excessive. Even if his scepticism about horoscopes does have the ring of truth.'

'Believe it or not,' Jacob said, 'reading our columnists' words of wisdom is a highlight of the day for thousands of readers.'

'Of course I believe it. What that says about human nature is a very different matter.' Rachel turned her attention back to the letter. 'The words seem to be carefully chosen. And quite specific. I wonder why.'

'Makes a pleasant change. Most of the people who write to me out of the blue take ten pages of semi-legible scrawl to get to the point.'

'He's also very frank about the rebuff he received from the police.'

'That impressed me, I must admit.'

'Yet he didn't mention the fact that he's a fortune teller. If he had, would you have refused to see him?'

'I might have found I was too busy and fobbed him off with an excuse,' Jacob admitted.

'So perhaps he's more canny than candid.'

'Fortune telling is nonsense as far as I'm concerned. And I'm not easily convinced by people who claim to have visions. I wouldn't put it past a man like Bellamy to lie through his teeth.'

'But?'

'Something about his story struck a chord.'

'So you don't think it was pure invention?'

'No. Even though I wasn't convinced by the conversation he claimed to have overheard.'

'Why not?'

'It seemed... too deliberate. Over-rehearsed.'

'As if he'd taken pains to learn a script?'

'Exactly.'

Rachel considered. 'He may simply have prepared what he was going to say with care, in order to make sure he didn't miss out anything important.'

'True. The story is wildly unlikely, but it was perfectly

coherent, not a rambling farrago. That's why I wanted to ask your opinion. I can't believe he made up the whole thing. What would be the point? It doesn't make sense.'

Rachel took another sip of her cocktail. 'What you mean is this: his motives are crucial.'

'Exactly.'

'So what have you learned about him?'

'After he left, I called a reporter I know from north-west Wales. He's digging around on my behalf.'

'Sensible to check on Bellamy's credibility. What exactly did you make of him?'

'He struck me as a curious mixture of straightforward and sly. When I asked him about the people he'd heard talking together, his manner was evasive. He even dodged a simple question about their accents.'

'Yes, I find that interesting.'

'Why? I can't see why he'd want to make a mystery of it. At this time of year, holidaymakers from all four corners of Britain arrive at the seaside.'

She gave a negligent wave of the hand. 'No matter. What do you make of his mention of the summer solstice?'

'It pins the prospective murder to a specific date.'

'When an unknown man will be pushed off a cliff by an unknown assailant. So in one respect the premonition is interestingly precise. Otherwise, it's vague in the extreme.' Rachel finished her cocktail. 'The cliffs at Hemlock Bay are dangerous. A few weeks ago, someone plunged to his death from Hemlock Heights.'

Jacob leaned closer to her. 'Really?'

'There is no doubt that it was a case of suicide. But now we know that if a similar tragedy happens at midsummer, the explanation will be foul play.'

Jacob stared. 'What are you driving at?'

'I wish I knew. But things often come in threes, don't they? And this is the third time in a matter of days that I've come across Hemlock Bay in strange circumstances. First, through Virginia Penrhos's decision to move there after painting a picture of a body on the rocks below her new home. Second, the inexplicable suicide of a young man with everything to live for and no apparent local connection. And now this bizarre tale about a premonition of death and a conversation about a plan to commit murder in the very same place.'

'Quite a coincidence,' Jacob said. 'Not that a good detective believes in coincidence.'

'On the contrary,' Rachel said languidly. 'Coincidences happen all the time. But when they come so thick and fast, I can't help wondering.'

'Me too,' Jacob said. 'I'm tempted to pay a visit myself. Tomorrow, I'll tell Gomersall about Bellamy's vision and see if he's happy for me to follow my nose.'

'Do your best to persuade him,' Rachel said.

'You think it's worth investigating?'

'Definitely. Not that I expect you to do all the hard work on your own.' She drained her glass and inhaled the perfume of the lilies. 'This is very pleasant, but I think we'd benefit from a change of scene. A breath of salty air, perhaps.'

Martha giggled and began to hum 'I Do Like to Be Beside the Seaside'.

'How very true.' Rachel's face lit up, as if she'd come to a decision that suited her. 'Let's pack our buckets and spades. Not to mention our bathing costumes. Time for us to take a trip to Hemlock Bay.'

5

'A fortune teller!'

Walter Gomersall, face screwed up in a pantomime of disgust, spat out the words as if uttering the foulest obscenity. The editor of the *Clarion* often proclaimed that he had no time for people who exploited the credulous. None of the senior reporters present at the morning conference were brave enough to ask how he squared this virtuous principle with hiring Fleet Street's most highly paid astrologer. But then, Jacob reflected, the life of a journalist is one long battle to reconcile truth and fiction.

'You have to admit, sir,' Jacob said, 'it's an intriguing story.'

'I don't have to admit anything. Sounds like hogwash to me.'

'I'm the first to accept it's an unlikely tale,' Jacob said meekly, 'but what if there is something in it? What if the *Clarion* managed to prevent a murder? To save a man's life after the police sat back and simply pooh-poohed the story...?'

His choice of words was no accident. *What if?* was a

question Gomersall often asked at these meetings; it was a favourite technique for inspiring his writers to come up with the ideas that kept the *Clarion* one step ahead of the competition.

'Visions of the future?' This was Bob Harley, a fresh-faced sports reporter with a flair for snaring scoops about soccer stars and Test cricketers. Gomersall had recently poached him from the *Witness*, although there were moments when Harley's juvenile sense of humour tested his editor's patience to breaking point. 'Trespassing into Percy's specialism, aren't we? Shouldn't we consult him for his expert opinion?'

Percy Jones was the amiable and inoffensive fellow who masqueraded as Trewythian, the astrologer. This morning he was conspicuous by his absence.

'He rang to say he won't be in today,' George Poyser said. 'Stomach ulcer playing up.'

'Shouldn't he have given us advance warning?' demanded Plenderleith, a puritan whose column about the City of London served as a pulpit from which he preached economic hellfire and damnation. The current state of the nation's finances suggested his apocalyptic warnings were as soberly factual as the shipping forecast.

The other reporters sniggered as Harley winced. His faith in Percy's gifts was being sorely tested by the astrologer's tips for filling in his football pools coupon. So far his predictions had failed to yield any winnings at all, let alone a jackpot.

'All right, gentlemen, you will have your little joke.' Gomersall put his thumbs in his lapels to indicate that he'd heard enough. 'Trewythian's horoscopes have brought us thousands of new readers. We need to make sure we don't lose them over the summer holidays.'

'Hemlock Bay is very popular these days,' Jacob was

determined to drag the discussion back to The Great Hallemby's premonition.

Gomersall's caterpillar eyebrows twitched. 'Never been there in my life, and I'm a born and bred Lancastrian. When I was a nipper, that part of the county was the back of beyond. Morecambe, now, I spent many a summer afternoon there. Riding donkeys along the beach or watching the miniature railway at the Figure Eight Park. Happy days.'

There was a moment's silence as the minds of those assembled boggled at the thought of the hefty figure of Walter Gomersall astride a donkey on the sands.

'My wife and I were talking about Hemlock Bay only last week,' Poyser said. 'Her sister lives a few miles away. Since the bridge and new road were built, it's developed into a smart resort.'

'Have you booked?' Jacob asked.

'No.' Poyser blushed. 'Once she heard about the nudist camp, it was out of the question. She says the place sounds like a den of iniquity.'

Harley said eagerly, 'Nudist camp?'

'Gymnosophists, they call themselves. They pride themselves on being pure in mind and body. Living in harmony with the environment. I tried to explain the health benefits to my good lady, but she wasn't having any of it.'

'Pity,' Harley said.

'As far as she's concerned,' Poyser said gloomily, 'nudism is just an excuse for immoral behaviour. So we've booked a week in Eastbourne instead.'

'Sin not Sun!' Gomersall tugged at his large ears, a habitual aid to thought. 'Damned good headline. The Naked Truth! Your missus has a point. It's a while since we ran a story about these cranks who parade around in the altogether. Spielplatz, isn't that what they call the place?'

Harley raised his eyebrows. 'Spielplatz?'

'Anyone would think it's a branch of the Weimar Republic. What self-respecting English holiday camp gives itself a German name?'

'Playground,' Poyser explained. 'Twelve acres of lawn and woodland, a few miles from St Albans.'

'Bizarre,' Gomersall said. 'Who in their right mind strips off in this climate? Last time I walked on the prom at Great Yarmouth, there was such a gale blowing that I kept my overcoat buttoned up to the neck. Makes you wonder how these folk survive.'

'Nudists are eccentrics.' Plenderleith was the eternal sceptic. 'Vegetarians, socialists, and heaven knows what. Behind the hedges that keep out prying eyes, who knows what goes on?'

'Isn't it more a question of what comes off?' Harley's cheeky grin prompted further merriment.

The editor raised his voice, sounding more like a soap box orator than chairman of a meeting. 'Gentlemen, please! Let's remember that the *Clarion* is a staunch upholder of traditional values and moral decency. We are a courageous and crusading newspaper or we are nothing. It's our bounden duty to shine a light on the dark corners of society.'

'Expose the nudists!' Harley murmured. 'There must be no cover up!'

Gomersall's glare was enough to silence a foghorn. 'We must find out more about what the nudists get up to. No smirking, lad! Tell me, Flint. I don't suppose there's any connection between this fortune teller of yours and these so-called nature lovers?'

Jacob swallowed. Knowing the way his editor's mind worked, he could see himself being despatched to join the sun worshippers. The very opposite of an undercover reporter.

'None that I know of, sir.'

'Shame.'

'We need a man on the spot,' Poyser said.

'Hoping to get up to Hemlock Bay without the missus?' Harley murmured.

Inspiration struck Jacob. 'I could become a Missing Man, like Lobby Lud!'

Heads turned towards him. There was a brief silence, broken by Gomersall.

'Tread on the *News Chronicle*'s toes, you mean?'

Jacob grinned. 'That's always a bonus.'

'We've never done anything like that before.' The editor gave his ear a fierce tug. One of these days, Jacob thought, it would come off in his hand.

'You mean, we've never nicked a gimmick from a competitor, sir?' Harley asked provocatively.

Gomersall's patience with him was wearing thin. 'The *Clarion* doesn't steal, lad. It doesn't even borrow. We make silk purses out of our rivals' sows' ears. Got that?'

'Absolutely, sir.'

'A Missing Man, eh? Not a bad idea,' Poyser said judiciously.

'It just came to me a moment ago.' Jacob's attempt to sound modest was an abject failure.

'You know,' Gomersall said, 'that might just be the ingredient we've been lacking for the summer season.'

'How about this?' Harley leaned forward and held his chin with his right hand in a parody of Rodin's *The Thinker*. 'Flinty could become our very own Clarion Charlie. Maybe we can circulate photos of him, riding a donkey on every beach he visits.'

Jacob was beginning to wonder if he'd made a big mistake. He took a breath but, before he could utter a word, his editor brought the conference to an end with a decisive wave of the hand.

'Thank you, everyone. Flint, I'm tempted by the idea of you posing as a Missing Man. Let me think on. I'll give you a shout within the next hour.'

Four years ago, the *Westminster Gazette* had scored a spectacular publicity coup by coming up with the notion of a Missing Man. The newspaper was struggling to survive, and summer's advent brought a new threat. Once northern workers began their season of wakes weeks – when between June and September one town after another closed its factories, shops, and mills so that local people could enjoy a well-earned holiday – newspapers invariably endured a period of sliding sales.

The inspiration for the Missing Man came from Agatha Christie's disappearance. Like the rest of Fleet Street, the *Gazette* had reported breathlessly on the nationwide hunt for the detective novelist after she vanished and abandoned her car near the Silent Pond in Surrey. The ensuing hue and cry had been a journalist's dream and it prompted some bright spark at the *Gazette* to invent Lobby Lud.

Agatha Christie had shown it was possible for a well-known individual, whose description was widely circulated, to remain at large even when hiding in plain sight in a well-frequented spa resort such as Harrogate. A *Gazette* reporter called Chinn was rechristened Lobby Lud, after the newspaper's telegraphic address for lobby correspondents based in Ludgate Circus, and tasked with making a tour of English seaside towns. Readers were given a photograph and description and told that the first to challenge him with a stipulated form of words would receive a handsome cash prize. All the fun of a manhunt coupled with the chance of a monetary reward.

The stunt proved a roaring success. It didn't save the *Gazette* from absorption into the *Daily News* and then the *News Chronicle*, but Lobby Lud survived the mergers unscathed. Chinn roamed the coast of England and Wales to this day, to the fury of countless men who bore a passing resemblance to him, and were constantly being accosted by eager readers who thrilled to the chase.

Jacob had no wish to squander his time by masquerading as a Missing Man. For a few days, however, it might make a change. If Gomersall was happy to pursue the idea, he'd have the perfect opportunity to sniff around Hemlock Bay without arousing suspicion. Perhaps he could spend time with Rachel and Martha. The shrill of his telephone broke into his reverie.

'Flinty? Harwood here. Traced your fortune teller for you.'

'Good work,' Jacob said. 'I definitely owe you a…'

'Several pints, I'd say. Anyway, here's what you need to know. Gareth Bellamy was sacked from his last job for pilfering.'

Jacob sat up. 'Tell me more.'

'He worked in the office of an architect in Bangor and dipped his hand in the till. Not the cleverest thief. He was found out within twenty-four hours. Said he was behind with the rent. He was adamant that he meant to reimburse his employer out of his next pay cheque.'

'Naughty, though.'

'Very. And it cost him his job. He did have one stroke of good fortune. His employer had a soft spot for him and was kind-hearted enough to beg the police not to prosecute. Said he felt sorry for Bellamy. The fellow must have a silver tongue.'

'I did find him quite plausible. As for the larceny, I suppose it was a first offence.'

'First time he'd been caught, at any rate. Bellamy didn't quite get off scot-free. The bobbies gave him a thick ear and told him to get out of town.'

Jacob's conversation with Bellamy was making more sense. The man had lied to him. An understandable lie, perhaps, but significant because it destroyed his credibility.

'I got the impression he didn't have much time for the police.'

'Now you know why. He skedaddled from his lodgings and nobody in the town has seen hide nor hair of him since. You know how hard it is to find jobs in this day and age. Without a testimonial from your old place of work, you don't stand a chance.'

'Which led him to tell fortunes on the pier at Colwyn Bay?'

'Exactly. Though if he was that good at seeing what the future holds, you'd think he would have avoided getting caught in the first place.'

'Thanks very much for your help. Forget about the pint, by the way, I'll send a bottle of bubbly. You deserve nothing less.'

'Think of it as an experiment, sir.' Jacob was in a breezy mood. 'A trial run. If I make a go of playing the part of a Missing Man at Hemlock Bay, you'll know it's worth asking a cub reporter to take on the role for the rest of the summer.'

Gomersall nodded. 'Makes sense. You can see for yourself whether there's anything in this wild story about a murder.'

'Absolutely, sir.' Jacob coughed. 'Getting back to the Missing Man, I'm not sure how long my inquiries will take. I'd hate one of our readers to identify me straight away. Build the suspense, that's my motto.'

'Fair enough. What do you have in mind?'

'How about a *Mystery* Man? You could print a photo of the back of my head, something that looks fascinating but gives little or nothing away.' Jacob felt himself getting swept along on a surge of enthusiasm. 'I could wear dark glasses as well as a hat. Perhaps glue on a moustache.'

Gomersall tugged his ear. 'We might publish your silhouette. Smoking a pipe.'

Jacob cringed inwardly. He loathed the smell of tobacco. But he sensed he was winning his editor over. 'The locals will love being in the national spotlight. Tourists will flood into town. Special coaches, traffic jams, jostling crowds. Countless *Clarion* readers in hot pursuit of a hundred-pound prize. The sort of money that can change your life.'

'Steady on, lad, I was thinking of a tenner a day, absolute maximum. Don't forget, there's a lot of people earning a shilling an hour, and that's if they're lucky enough to have a job.' Gomersall pondered for a moment. 'Five pounds might be plenty. I don't like to skimp, but in hard times, people are glad of any sort of money prize.'

Jacob waved a hand with the airiness of one to whom money is no object, at least when he isn't paying. 'Whatever the bean counters can justify to drum up publicity.'

'All right, when do you want to start?'

Jacob had given this some thought. It didn't make sense to wait until the summer solstice was upon him. Once he was at

Hemlock Bay, it wouldn't take him long to decide whether or not there was any truth in Bellamy's yarn.

'No time like the present, sir.'

'Very good. You may as well get cracking.'

As he left Gomersall's office, Jacob found himself whistling the same tune that Martha had hummed the previous evening. He could barely restrain himself from bursting into song.

So just let me be beside the seaside!
I'll be beside myself with glee
and there's lots of girls beside,
I should like to be beside, beside the seaside,
beside the sea!

6

Basil Palmer's Journal

5 June

I am settling into my new life at Hemlock Bay after arranging my business practice so that clients can be looked after by my assistant. My history of indifferent health offers a plausible excuse for deserting the office over the next few weeks. I have told people that my doctor has advised me to get plenty of exercise in the fresh air to build up my strength. Hiking in remote areas will justify an extended absence from home.

Shepherd's Cottage is an excellent find. Crucially, it is handy for Hemlock Heights, which loom one hundred and fifty feet above a mass of jagged rocks. The drop is sheer. Nobody who tumbled from the path that runs along the edge of the cliff would survive. That is, I anticipate, how Louis Carson will meet his end. A simple murder method, yes, to the point of being hackneyed. But I have learned from *Notable British Trials* that it's a mistake to over-elaborate.

Louis Carson's home is less than half a mile from my front door. My cottage stands on Beggarman's Lane, which meanders along before bending sharply to curl back on itself and, eventually, join the main road into the town. Open ground sloping from the lane to the coastline is crossed by well-worn tracks through the grass which zigzag towards the cliffs. At several points, they meet a path which runs along the clifftop. Turn left along that path, and you head to the lighthouse. Turn right, and the path dips down. For a hundred yards or so it occupies a shelf of rock below the highest point of the cliffs, before rising again on its way to the town.

Privacy has always been important to me, and never more so than now. Among the advantages of Shepherd's Cottage is its relative isolation. The lighthouse is the nearest dwelling, having been converted into residential accommodation. At present it is occupied by two women. One of them, I was told by the grocer when I stocked up with provisions, is a painter of some renown. When I asked what she painted, however, he admitted he didn't know. Her name – which he'd forgotten – meant nothing to him.

Yesterday, as I set out to explore my surroundings in a thin drizzle, I encountered the artist in person as she marched down the lane towards her home. Tall and ungainly, with wild, greying hair escaping from a shapeless beige hat, she wielded an umbrella like a sabre. I intended to give a civil nod of greeting and walk on by, but she stopped in front of me. Good manners made it impossible for me not to come to a halt.

'You must be our new neighbour!'

Her voice was gruff, her figure mannish, her gait awkward and quite unfeminine. Perhaps she is not forty, but she could pass for sixty. Such a contrast to the delicate grace of my beloved Alicia!

I bowed. 'Dr Seamus Doyle. How do you do?'

'A sawbones, eh? And you come from the Emerald Isle, if I'm not mistaken.'

Smiling in confirmation, I congratulated myself on my adopted accent.

'Splendid country. Almost as marvellous as the land of my fathers.' Giving a loud, discordant laugh, she extended her hand. 'Virginia Penrhos. I paint.'

She looked keenly at me, as if expecting a response, but the name meant nothing to me.

'Oh yes?'

'My friend and I have taken a tenancy of the lighthouse for the summer.'

'Ah.'

'The views from the lantern room are stunning, whatever the weather. Ideal for an artist, even a surrealist like myself. The colours of the water possess a unique quality. Always changing, almost impossible to capture. Just as well I don't bother painting conventional seascapes!'

I made polite noises, hoping they masked my profound lack of interest.

'Settled in yet, Doctor?'

'I only moved into the cottage yesterday.'

'We caught sight of you getting out of the taxi with your suitcases. Did you notice our curtains twitching?' She laughed again, showing large, crooked teeth. 'Only ribbing you. Ffion and I don't bother with curtains.'

The last thing I wanted to discover was that I had nosey neighbours, especially if they had the ability to conduct surveillance from fifty feet above ground level. My knees trembled. Knowing I dared not excite attention, I mustered a faint, if apprehensive, smile.

'What brings you here, Doctor?'

'I've come for a few weeks in search of rest and recuperation.' I cast my eyes down. 'I have suffered from wretched health for some time and my chest is weak. I decided that the sea breezes were the tonic I need.'

'Physician, heal thyself, eh?'

'I retired from practice a considerable time ago,' I replied.

I'm determined to discourage any suggestion that Dr Doyle might be willing or able to offer guidance in medical matters. In my experience, any man who admits to professional expertise, whether in the law, finance, or medicine, will be pestered for free advice. Annoying at the best of times, but positively dangerous when one does not actually possess the relevant know-how. It is so easy to give oneself away.

'Gentleman of leisure, eh?'

Conscious of the woman's scrutiny, I felt myself blushing. 'Nowadays, I simply seek solitude and the chance to appreciate nature's simple pleasures.'

A mischievous gleam came into her eyes. 'Ah, perhaps I understand why you chose Hemlock Bay. Nudist, are you?'

'Good heavens, no!'

She chortled. 'Don't look so horrified, man. This is 1931, when all is said and done. No harm in naturism. Ffion and I are keen to give it a try. They say that sunbathing is highly beneficial to one's health.'

'Really?'

'No need to be a stuffed shirt, Doctor.' My discomfiture seemed to entertain her. 'You're on holiday now. Once it's warm enough to disrobe in comfort, you might do worse than soaking up the sun. Do your chest a power of good.'

Clearly, this woman delights in her ability to shock. Resolving not to play her game, I raised my hat.

'I'm grateful for your advice, Miss Penrhos. Ah, I see the rain is easing, so if you'll excuse me, I shall continue to familiarise myself with the neighbourhood.'

'Good to meet you, Doctor. Come and take tea with us one day. If you fancy climbing up a great many steps, you can feast on the views. On a clear day, you can see the Isle of Man.'

She gave me a cheery wave as I hurried on, determining to have as little to do with her as possible. Quite apart from the fact that I haven't the faintest desire whatsoever to contemplate the Isle of Man from afar, I'm wary of the woman. I don't know much about artists, but presume they are more perceptive than most of their fellow human beings. Most people would regard Virginia Penrhos simply as an eccentric, but someone so inquisitive represents a threat.

Our conversation left me in pensive mood. I must be careful not to do anything suspicious within sight of her eyrie at the top of the lighthouse, but at least the only time I became flustered was when she teased me about nudism. I was confident that my Irish accent hadn't faltered.

On reflection, then, so far, so good.

As yet, I haven't met anyone else apart from a few locals. There are clusters of old terraced dwellings and a tiny, ramshackle pub called the Fisherman's Arms, which caters for locals rather than tourists. It's one of the few businesses in Hemlock Bay other than the farms which isn't owned by the development company.

I was told this by Mrs Stones, the widowed lady engaged by the land agent to come in and 'do' for me (with the stern proviso that she wouldn't get involved with 'the rough'). Mrs Stones is a stout party who lives in the end terrace house nearest to my cottage. She makes breakfast for me and pretends to dust, but otherwise I prefer to fend for myself. I have plenty of experience of the bachelor life and I don't want a stranger noseying around my possessions. Far less finding this journal.

A modern bungalow stands in extensive grounds on the way into town. As I passed by, workmen were dismantling a *To Let* sign outside the garden gate. The setting makes the bungalow a superb vantage point, and I considered taking a short-term lease, but the rent demanded by the agent was exorbitant. I am far from impoverished, but my income has fallen sharply since Alicia's death, and no sensible accountant would spend so rashly. As I strolled on towards the bay, I wondered who had taken the bungalow. Evidently someone to whom money is no object.

Opposite the bungalow, a wrought-iron gate hangs between two stone pillars topped with pineapples. A large slate is emblazoned with the legend *Beggarman's Rest*. Peering through the gate, I can see there is more than a touch of satire about the name. Such a handsome, well-built home must have cost a pretty penny. But even in these straitened times, Louis Carson can afford it.

6 *June*

This morning I saw Louis Carson in the flesh for the very first time.

Unable to contain my curiosity any longer, I rose early. At last the sun was shining on Hemlock Bay, and I smelled salt in the air as I walked along the Heights towards the town. When I was within sight of the esplanade, I doubled back over the grassland towards Beggarman's Lane.

Tucked away at the back of McAtee's report was a brief but useful paragraph summarising Carson's everyday routine in Hemlock Bay. The man is – helpfully, from my point of view – a creature of habit. Each morning he leaves home at eight and goes to the Hemlock Hotel. Typically, in the late afternoon he repairs to the bar, often drinking with guests. I suppose they regard him as convivial. Of course, this feigned bonhomie is an essential part of his modus operandi.

I timed my stroll to perfection. Carson's maroon Lanchester Twenty Three was emerging from the gate to his mansion as I approached. Recognising him from the photograph McAtee had taken, I felt a thrill of excitement on my spine.

As he sped past me, I tipped my panama hat. His response was a wave with a gloved hand. I suspect Carson relishes playing the part of a country squire, surrounded by forelock-tugging admirers. He is complacent as well as arrogant. And blissfully unaware that he has just greeted his nemesis.

Later

After feasting on a thick ham sandwich at a café on High Street, which runs parallel to the esplanade, I returned to my cottage. Sitting on a deckchair in the tiny garden, I read a short book purchased from the grocer. *The Illustrated Guide to Hemlock Bay.*

Before the war, this was a tiny settlement of lush farmland and isolated homesteads; its name derives from the poisonous plant found in abundance close to the shore. In the past, lawlessness was commonplace in an area so remote from the civilised world – that is, Heysham and Morecambe. Shifting sandbanks caused many a ship to founder, but the guidebook claims – with disconcerting pride – that wreckers did far more damage. Tunnels beneath Hemlock Heights were used to smuggle ill-gotten gains to their homes.

When the authorities improved the road connections, a

man called Jackson spotted the potential for transforming Hemlock Bay into a destination for discerning tourists. After the war he set about purchasing land and within a few years he'd created a fashionable resort catering to the affluent middle class. One only has to glance at the pre-war map reprinted in the guidebook to see how much has changed so fast. Harold Jackson and his American wife enjoy a reputation for being munificent benefactors and generous hosts. Mrs Stones has made it clear that she won't hear a word said against them.

The visitors congregate around the sea front or at the amusement park. The latter rejoices in the name of Paradise and is on the slopes of Hemlock Head, which rises above the promontory separating the main bay from a cove which forms part of the so-called Sun and Air Garden. The nudist colony adjoins the grounds of Hemlock Hall, where Jackson and his wife live. Their home is the last building in the resort. The land agent told me they would be glad to invite me to dinner, a prospect that chilled me to the marrow. He was nonplussed when I said that because of my ill-health, I would have to decline.

The town itself is modest in size. A broad esplanade is dominated by a large modern hotel in the art deco style, flanked at a respectful distance by smaller guest houses. On two roads running parallel to the esplanade is everything you might expect in a compact seaside town: shops, a public house, a cinema, theatre, and cafés and restaurants aplenty. At night, Mrs Stones told me, the amusement park is lit up, but Hemlock Bay has no desire to compete with the Blackpool Illuminations. The aim is to attract those people who, even in these straitened times, still have money.

According to McAtee, Louis Carson has entered some kind of business arrangement with Sir Harold Jackson. The old man – I call him that, although he appears to be not much older than me – has enjoyed a decade of rich pickings here, but prosperity must have softened his judgment. Perhaps he is also feeling the pinch. The Wall Street Crash continues to have reverberations around the world, like aftershocks following a massive earthquake.

No doubt Jackson fears a further deterioration in the market and intends to spread financial risk by seeking capital investment from Carson. I wonder whether he realises just how unscrupulous a partner he has acquired.

Given that Carson and I have never set eyes on each other prior to our fleeting encounter this morning, I shall be able to keep watch on him without arousing suspicion.

The indifferent weather hasn't encouraged people to wander away from the resort's attractions and admire the beauties of nature. This may change as the days grow warmer. Time waits for no man.

The first phase of my preparations entailed creating a new identity. The second required me to trace the man I want to kill. The third was to ensure that I was in the right place to act. The initial foundations are now laid. Tomorrow I begin in earnest to plan Louis Carson's murder.

7

Basil Palmer's Journal

11 June

Today I came within a hair's breadth of discovery and disaster. To say that the best-laid plans of mice and men often go awry is a cliché, but nevertheless it is true. Although I have preserved the secret of my identity, the incident shook me to the core. How narrow is the gap between triumph and despair!

I spent this morning traversing the path along the cliffs. At one point, as I neared the lighthouse, I glanced up and spotted Virginia Penrhos at the lantern window. Relishing the sight of the ebbing tide? Or keeping an eye on me? Stifling my resentment as our eyes met, I lifted my hand in greeting.

Sited at irregular intervals along the path are half a dozen gaily painted timber shelters commanding views of the bay. Inside each is a wooden bench, from which one can look out at the sea in comfort when it is chilly or raining. Another virtue of the shelters is that – like some of the trees on Hemlock Heights – they obstruct the view of anyone scanning the path from the lighthouse. So there are blind spots, even before the cliff path twists and turns and is no longer visible from the inquisitive artist's home.

On reaching the heart of the resort, I spent a few minutes gazing at sands as golden as Alicia's hair, and then repaired to a tea shop to the rear of the Hemlock Hotel, washing down an egg and cress sandwich with a cup of Earl Grey. Refreshed and ready to explore further, I decided to walk past the esplanade to Hemlock Head and the far boundaries of the resort.

Strolling down a ginnel connecting High Street to the esplanade, I emerged close to the hotel. A 'Blower' Bentley, a convertible in battleship grey, was parked in front of the canopied entrance. The sight of such a majestic vehicle in a small town in Lancashire was a striking reminder that Hemlock Bay is no ordinary seaside resort. There is wealth here, beyond question, a great deal of wealth. As a lover of fine cars, I paused close to the entrance to appreciate the smooth lines of the vehicle, imagining its power and speed on the racing track.

A smartly dressed man walked out of the hotel. With a jolt I realised that I'd almost collided with Louis Carson. I was conscious of a strange, shivery thrill.

Taking off my glasses, I studied my quarry. At first glance, Louis Carson resembled a commercial traveller, amiable but obsequious. His smile displayed prominent, pointed upper teeth. With a sallow complexion and irregular bald patch on the crown of his head, he hardly looked like a vicious criminal. Perhaps that is why he has escaped justice. So far.

'Cheerio, then!'

Carson's tone was cloying. Hatred burned within me, and I had to make a huge effort of will to restrain myself from confronting him.

He was speaking to a couple who had followed him out of the hotel, a tall fellow with racing goggles in a gloved hand

and a well-dressed woman wearing dark glasses and a low-brimmed hat.

As the pair were saying their goodbyes to Carson, I passed within a few feet of them. They were of no interest to me but, as I glanced at the tall man, our eyes met for a split second. My heart missed a beat.

The tall man was my old friend Hooker Jackson!

There wasn't a scintilla of doubt in my mind, even though I hadn't seen Hooker since 1914. There was no mistaking his broken nose – legacy of a rugger injury – or dimpled chin. Let alone the scar above his left eyebrow, caused by a fencing accident at school when, with typical bravado, he dispensed with his mask.

For one insane moment, I was about to exclaim with delight and run over to pump his hand. And then I came to my senses and jerked my head away so violently that it's a wonder my neck didn't snap.

To be recognised by Hooker would destroy all the painstaking work I'd done in preparing to wipe Louis Carson off the face of the earth. I owed it to Alicia to avenge her. I couldn't allow a reunion with Hooker to ruin my plans.

Dazed and aghast, I crossed the esplanade. I'd barely broken stride, but when I reached the short flight of stone steps leading down to the beach, I put my glasses back on and looked back at the Jacksons.

Hooker was talking to his wife. Seventeen years had passed since my solitary conversation with Sadie Jackson as a delicate young bride. She must be in her mid-forties now, and although she'd acquired a tan, she was still as thin as a rake.

Hooker opened the Blower's passenger door for her and she caught my eye while taking her seat. I had no fear that she would remember me, but still averted my gaze. One cannot be too careful when contemplating murder.

I was shaking with suppressed emotion. Even if I'd been so foolish as to try to run, I'd have found it impossible. It was all I could do to keep putting one foot in front of the other, following the edge of the promenade, trying to put as much distance between myself and my old friend as possible.

Behind me, I heard the Blower's engine starting up. I risked a surreptitious backwards glance and saw the Bentley race off in the other direction. Within moments the car had vanished in a cloud of smoke.

My mind whirled. In that instant when Hooker's eyes met mine, did I detect a flicker of recognition? That would spell catastrophe. On second thoughts I realised my guilty conscience was working overtime.

The inescapable truth was that the passing years had been much less kind to me than to Hooker. I'd lost most of my hair as well as putting on two stone. What is more, I was wearing my glasses and sporting a panama hat. I assured myself that it would have been a miracle if Hooker had managed to identify me as his old pal from Cambridge in a wholly unfamiliar context.

In my heart of hearts, I could not deny that there was a further, compelling reason why he was unlikely to identify me. Quite simply, Hooker meant a great deal more to me than I ever did to him.

But what does this extraordinary encounter mean for my self-appointed mission to kill Louis Carson?

Later

I purchased a pair of binoculars before setting off for Hemlock Bay and put them to good use this evening. Having spent hours wrestling with the riddle of Hooker Jackson on either side of a dinner of liver and onions, I commenced a vigil in the box room shortly before sunset.

According to McAtee's report, Louis Carson often takes an evening walk along the cliffs. I had asked the detective for detailed information about Carson's routine, on the pretext that I needed to have a full picture of the man on whom I contemplated settling my fortune. Carson manages the hotel, but he and his wife – who oversees the female staff – don't live on site. The evening stroll is, if not a fixture in his diary, a favourite form of relaxation.

Crucially, his wife does not accompany him on these perambulations. McAtee told me little about her, except that they tied the knot seven years ago. My concern is her husband, not the fact that she was foolish enough to marry a blackguard. I have no doubt he is a plausible liar and I am inclined to feel a degree of pity for her. The loss of her husband will prove a blessing in disguise, liberating her from a union with a man who destroyed two lives to my knowledge, and probably many more.

The poor weather since I arrived in Hemlock Bay has deterred Carson from taking his walk. Perhaps he is afraid of slipping on the wet ground and plunging to his doom on the rocks below. This evening, as I hoped, the sun tempted him out. I followed his progress through the binoculars, watching him go all the way to the lighthouse before he began to retrace his steps. Once or twice he stopped on the very edge of the cliff to breathe in the salty air. No doubt he finds this invigorating. A useful habit! The eagle-eyed artist must have noticed this. She will be able to testify to his behaviour at the inquest and confirm how easy it would be to slip over. It would only require a moment of carelessness.

I'm reinforced in my belief that a simple shove over the cliff is the best course of action. So straightforward and yet, in the absence of eyewitnesses, so hard to prove.

When he disappeared from sight, I put down my binoculars with a sigh of satisfaction. My researches are making excellent progress and my ideas about how to achieve my objective are taking shape. So far there is only one fly in the ointment.

Hooker Jackson.

Later

Midnight draws near. I am ready to set down my thoughts about my encounter with Hooker Jackson in the hope of making sense of them.

Sir Harold Jackson! The man responsible for the metamorphosis of Hemlock Bay from obscure hamlet to fashionable watering hole! Who would have thought it? Hooker has done remarkably well for himself. While no doubt he benefited from marrying money, his personality and drive are characteristics that have taken him to the top. On combing through my guidebook, I noticed a pencil drawing of him which I'd disregarded when skimming the text previously. It was almost an affectionate caricature, emphasising his misshapen nose, but there is no question that it is my old friend. If I'd noticed this earlier, I wouldn't have risked suffering a seizure when I clapped eyes on him outside the hotel. However, I have concluded that if I'd known in advance of his presence in Hemlock Bay, it would have made no difference. Given that I am determined to kill Carson, I had no choice but to follow him.

Hooker and I met on our first day at Cambridge and became fast friends, although he cut such a glamorous figure that I often felt – and I'm sure our fellow students believed – I was little more than a hanger-on. We were chalk and cheese, leader and disciple, hedonist and puritan. He was reckless, I was irredeemably respectable.

Hooker read History whereas I studied Mathematics, and he was a dashing all-round sportsman while I merely coxed the college's third eight (chosen because my skinny frame wouldn't weigh down the boat). His prowess at rugby earned him a Blue; his nickname, dating back to his schooldays at Harrow, came from his favoured position in the front row. Hooker was a ladies' man, while I was tongue-tied in the presence of the fair sex. Occasionally he asked me to supply alibis on his behalf to disgruntled lovers from Newnham or Girton when he was out enjoying himself in the town with a lusty barmaid or shop girl. I was glad to help, because I adored him as much as anyone I've ever known. Except for dear Mamma, of course, and my beloved Alicia.

After Finals – naturally, he breezed to a First by dint of furious last-minute revision, while I barely scraped a Third – the two of us drifted apart. Hooker's people were dead and he went travelling. While I was serving my articles with an accountant in Guildford, my own parents died too. The money they left me made it possible to buy into the practice that is now my own. I found myself working long hours to build a clientele, with no time for a social life. I wrote to Hooker a few times over the years, but never heard back. He was one of those convivial people who is rotten at keeping in touch.

In December 1914, I received a telegram, completely out of the blue. Hooker announced without preamble that he was getting married on Christmas Eve. Would I be his best man? I didn't hesitate to say yes, flattered that he should single me out for this honour. Only later did it occur to me that I was perhaps the one person in his circle who was unlikely to have family or social commitments in addition to my usual office work on the day before Christmas.

The previous winter, I had been laid low with TB, and my feeble chest rendered me unfit to serve in the armed forces, a reprieve for which – although I'd never admit it to a living soul – I was profoundly grateful. When we met again for a fortifying drink shortly before the ceremony, Hooker explained he'd trained as a pilot in the RFC, and was taking advantage of a brief period of leave before returning to France. Sadie, his wife-to-be, was a Californian heiress with jet-black hair and skin so pale it was almost translucent. She was a shrinking violet, and seemed as fragile as a piece of Dresden china.

'I always was a lucky so-and-so,' Hooker admitted cheerily as Sadie and her cousin Josephine left us to powder their noses. 'Sadie is everything I ever dreamed of. We met in London days before war broke out. When I came back to England, I popped the question and, to my amazement, she was rash enough to say yes.'

'She's beautiful.'

'Isn't she just?' He gave a self-deprecating laugh. 'I can't believe my good fortune. Admittedly, she's not taking too much of a risk. There's every chance she'll never see me again after I go back to France on New Year's Eve. It's a case of *carpe diem*, old boy.'

I understood what he meant. When he returned to duty,

his life would be in extreme jeopardy. So many young airmen were being obliterated by enemy fire. Hooker was right, at Trinity College he was famous for being a lucky so-and-so. But even a cat only has nine lives.

He drained his glass and smacked his lips. 'Believe me, Basil, I moved heaven and earth to obtain this marriage licence.'

I laughed. When Hooker's mind was made up, he was quite unstoppable.

The wedding took place at St Matthew's in Finsbury. Apart from the happy couple and me, Josephine was the only other person present. Like Sadie, she was slender, dark, and pretty. I have a vivid memory of the last time I set eyes on Hooker. He and the new Mrs Jackson clambered into a taxi outside the church and waved merrily. As they drove off, Josephine let out a long sigh.

'I wonder if we'll ever see him again.'

Her tone was sorrowful. We both knew the original pretence that the war would be over by Christmas was balderdash. There was no end in sight to the endless death and destruction.

When I murmured some optimistic platitude, she said, 'Let's hope they make the most of the holiday season, huh? Sadie was always a sickly one. I don't give either of them more than six months.'

She was obviously the sort of modern young woman who likes to shock, but I could scarcely disagree. For all her loveliness, Hooker's wife looked as if a puff of wind would blow her away. Josie and I chatted for a few minutes before I plucked up my courage and asked if she'd like to join me for dinner. She made an excuse and hurried away. Perhaps it was just as well.

I'd only exchanged a few words with Sadie, but I

sympathised, knowing what it was like to be afflicted by indifferent health. In the immediate aftermath of the war I succumbed to the Spanish flu and it was touch and go whether I would survive. Recovery proved to be a long haul and I needed to devote all my limited energies to keeping my practice afloat. I heard no more news of Hooker. After meeting Alicia, the only child of a prosperous client, I began a long and assiduous courtship. Meeting her changed my life forever.

If I gave a thought to Hooker, it was to our carefree student days. I presumed he was dead. But in my heart of hearts, I understood that, even if he was still alive, I could not expect to hear from him. Our friendship had run its course and he had no reason to rekindle it. Hooker was spontaneous and bold, a man who lived for the moment. On one occasion he even forged a cheque from a rich uncle for a dare. If he felt in need of admiration, no doubt his wife – who plainly worshipped the ground he stood on – would be happy to oblige. Why saddle himself with the company of a stick-in-the-mud like me?

And now, it turns out, both the Jacksons have not only survived but prospered. The impetuous young lovers have metamorphosed into respected pillars of the community. Yet it is somehow characteristic that, as the guidebook makes clear, the idea for establishing the naturist camp came from Hooker. He was always mischievous as well as opportunistic. The chance to capitalise on the current fad for parading around with no clothes on probably seemed too good to miss.

As my eyelids droop at the end of a long day, my overriding emotion is one of disappointment. My first, long-awaited sighting of my enemy has been overshadowed in the most unexpected way.

My resolve to kill Louis Carson is undiminished. I only caught a glimpse of him outside the hotel, but for that brief instant I felt an almost overpowering urge to thrust my hands around his neck and squeeze the life out of him. It is an utter misfortune that, of all the places where he might have chosen to move, he picked the home town of my oldest friend.

I cannot breathe easily. Hooker always had a keen eye – that was why he became such a first-rate batsman, opening the innings for the University. If we bump into each other again, there is a real danger that he will see through my disguise.

I must remain vigilant. The smallest slip may yet prove fatal.

'Cliff, you're a marvel,' Rachel said. 'You picked the perfect spot for our summer holidays.'

She and the Truemans were eating sandwiches and drinking lemonade under blue skies in the garden of their new home. This was the unoriginally named Bay View, the bungalow on Beggarman's Lane. Trueman had found the place after coming up on the train for a quick reconnaissance. He'd wasted no time in putting down a month's rent by way of deposit.

At dawn the four of them had left Gaunt House for the long drive north. Trueman loved driving and Rachel's Rolls-Royce Phantom was built for speed, so they had made excellent time. Within smelling distance of their deckchairs was a rose bed full of fragrant yellow and pink blooms. To their left, they could see the top of the lighthouse above the trees. Beyond the rose bed and the timber fence, the ground rolled down towards the sea. The water was so calm it was hard to imagine ships being wrecked on these very shores.

The big man finished his drink. 'The agent bit my hand off.

You wanted a house by the cliffs and by a stroke of luck this place was available.'

'Close to where the murder in Bellamy's premonition is supposed to be committed,' she murmured. 'Good to be handy for the scene of the crime.'

'Load of bunkum. Now we know the fellow's a liar and a thief, we can be sure he made that story up.'

Jacob had telephoned before they left London with the news of Bellamy's embezzlement from his employer in Bangor.

Rachel shook her head. 'I agree there are holes in the story, but that doesn't mean everything he said was a complete fabrication.'

'Surely you don't believe he had some kind of vision?'

'I'm keeping an open mind. There's a reason why he went to see Jacob. I'd be extremely sceptical if he'd asked for money. But making a few pounds doesn't seem to be his motive.'

'You're not telling me Bellamy was simply trying to be a good citizen?'

'Unlikely, I agree, but we mustn't allow scepticism to lead us to jump to conclusions. He's playing a long game.'

'He's a charlatan.'

'Even so.' Rachel shaded her eyes from the sun. 'The sea is gorgeous, isn't it? To think we're so close to Paradise.'

Hetty paused in her study of the local guidebook. 'Ridiculous name for pleasure grounds.'

'Paradise is close to the nudists,' Martha murmured. 'Almost cheek by jowl.'

'You obviously find them fascinating,' Rachel said. 'Do you want to investigate more closely? Find out whether any of them have murder in mind?'

Martha put down her glass and gave a mischievous grin. 'I bet one or two of them have something to hide.'

Hetty shut the guidebook. 'Something that would be better off hidden, more like.'

'Doesn't everyone have something to hide?' Rachel said. 'Like The Great Hallemby and his questionable past.'

'I've never had my fortune told,' Martha said in a plaintive tone. 'It might be fun to have my palm read or peer into a crystal ball.'

'Stuff and nonsense,' Hetty said. 'Codswallop. Baloney. It's absolutely—'

Rachel laughed. 'But none of that means Bellamy can't have stumbled across something sinister.'

Trueman shook his head. 'I bet he just wants to see his name in the papers.'

'Why go to such lengths to talk to a chief crime correspondent? There's no shortage of journalists and newspapers in the north-west. If he is desperate to see his photograph in the press, he'd have a better chance if a reporter ran a story with a local angle.'

'The *Clarion* has a huge circulation,' Martha said. 'He claims to be a devoted reader…'

'Flannel. There must be more to it than that. His letter to Jacob was odd.'

'Of course it was. He was talking about a murder that hadn't been committed.'

'Not only that. The letter was carefully written and very much to the point.'

'He wanted to catch Jacob's attention.'

'I think he was trying to do something more. Setting out the basic facts in a concise and sober way.' Rachel ran a finger around the rim of her glass, an old habit when wrestling with a knotty problem. 'Almost as if there needed to be a record for posterity.'

'You think Bellamy's afraid someone will kill him to shut him up?'

'Possibly.'

'So the letter would be a kind of posthumous way of saying *I told you so?*'

Rachel laughed. 'Remember what Jacob told us. When he said he was willing to consult his editor about investigating further, Bellamy was less than overjoyed. Why?'

'Your guess is as good as mine,' Martha said. 'No, in fairness, it's bound to be much better.'

'Don't underestimate yourself.' Rachel smiled. 'You deserve to have your fortune told. Who knows what you'll discover when The Great Hallemby looks into his crystal ball?'

'Maybe I'll hear something about a tall, dark, handsome stranger coming into my life and sweeping me off my feet.'

Rachel laughed. 'How about an impetuous young journalist with floppy fair hair?'

'You will have your little joke,' Hetty muttered.

'You do like Jacob, Martha?' Rachel said.

Martha didn't blush. 'I know he has his faults.'

'You can say that again,' Hetty said. 'I never knew anyone with such a knack for turning up in the wrong place at the wrong time.'

'He's a lot of fun. And rather sweet, in a hapless sort of way.' Martha turned to Rachel. 'But you're the one he's got his eye on.'

Hetty shook her head. 'Now you are joking. Even that boy must have more sense than to set his cap at Rachel.'

'He's devoted to her, anyone can see. Follows her around like a faithful spaniel.'

'Because he wants to get headlines out of her. A front-page story, that's what he really cares about.'

'You're such a cynic,' Rachel said.

'And you're not?' Hetty demanded.

Rachel was amused. 'Jacob's heart is in the right place, even if his brain sometimes goes absent without official leave. It's not that he isn't bright. On the contrary. He's one of the smartest journalists in Fleet Street.'

'That's not saying much for the rest of them.'

'Jacob's trouble,' Rachel said calmly, 'is that he lets himself get carried away by the thrill of the chase for a scoop.'

'Bull in a china shop,' Trueman said.

'Yes, but he always treats Martha with sensitivity and respect.' She turned to her friend. 'That's why I wondered if you were in the mood to offer him some encouragement.'

Martha gave a faint shake of the head and touched the side of her face. When she was in her teens, a vicious man had thrown acid at her. Rachel's wealth, inherited from the late Judge Savernake, had paid for surgery with Europe's leading specialist in facial disfigurement. Although the treatment was pioneering and protracted, the results so far were better than any of them had dared to hope. The scars on her cheek were less obvious now and there was every reason to hope that further operations would continue to diminish them. For all Martha's natural vivacity, the damage done to her confidence had been at least as profound as the cruel attempt to ruin her beauty.

'It's impossible,' she said.

'Nothing's impossible.' Rachel subjected her friend to a piercing stare. 'Oh well, I won't harp on. But... don't dismiss the idea out of hand.'

'For a moment,' Martha said calmly, 'I thought you were going to say *but you know I'm right.*'

Hetty shifted in her deckchair, anxious to change the

subject. 'I'm glad to be out by the coast again. London is all very well, but pea-soup fog is nothing like threads of mist over the water. I miss the sea breezes.'

'You mean the gales howling across Gaunt?' Rachel asked. 'Waves lashing against the rocks? Torrential rain and gnawing cold?'

'I'm not saying it was Paradise,' Hetty replied.

'No, that's here in Hemlock Bay, remember?' Martha stretched out her arms. 'I like this place. It's so peaceful and pretty.'

'Everything in the garden is lovely?' Rachel asked with a faint smile.

Martha waved at the roses. 'The perfume is delightful. Why would anyone want to commit murder in a place like this?'

'Things are often not what they seem.' Rachel pointed towards the cliffs. 'See those wild plants?'

'The white flowers, clustering like an umbrella?' Martha nodded. 'Hetty is right. It's good to be surrounded by nature again.'

'Let's take a closer look.'

Rachel unbolted the gate in the garden fence. Martha followed her down a grass track that led towards the path skirting the top of the cliff. Rachel bent over to sniff the wild flowers. When Martha did the same, she recoiled in dismay.

'Not as pleasant as they look?' Rachel asked.

'No!' Martha coughed. 'They stink of dead mice!'

'Hemlock,' Rachel said. 'At a glance, you might mistake it for parsley and be tempted to have a nibble, but I don't recommend it. The flowers and leaves are poisonous. Hemlock grows here in abundance, but it's one of the deadliest weeds you can find.'

'It looks so innocent.'

Rachel indicated their surroundings. From here they could see a brightly painted shelter and the deserted cliff path. Gulls were flying overhead and fishing boats were visible in the distance. A scene so picturesque it might have featured on a railway advertising poster.

'Like Hemlock Bay?' She shook her head. 'There's something wrong here. Never mind the stench from the plants. Can't you smell danger in the air?'

'To live in a lighthouse! How utterly wonderful!' Rachel exclaimed. 'It really is like a dream come true.'

Her girlish exuberance prompted a smile from Virginia Penrhos. Rachel had walked along Beggarman's Lane to get her bearings and then doubled back to the cliff path. Close to the lighthouse, she'd sat down on a convenient boulder. Taking a sketchbook and pencil from her bag, she'd set about drawing the scene in front of her. Every now and then she stood up and made an ostentatious study of the view from a different angle. After a quarter of an hour, the door at the base of the lighthouse was flung open. Virginia emerged, clad in a navy blue smock splashed with paint, her curiosity provoked beyond endurance.

'Yes, we're very lucky.'

'You live here with your family?' Rachel asked.

'With my friend Ffion Morris. We've rented the lighthouse for the summer. It suits me perfectly. Such glorious views. I'm Virginia Penrhos, by the way.'

She thrust out a bony hand.

'Rachel Savernake, delighted to meet you.' A moment's pause, and then she put her hand to her mouth in astonishment. 'Not *the* Virginia Penrhos?'

The artist laughed. 'As far as I know, I'm the one and only.'

'How utterly marvellous! I can't quite believe my luck.'

'Goodness, Miss Savernake, you're a real tonic for my morale. Yesterday I met a chap who has just moved here and he made it plain that not only had he never heard of me, he had no interest whatsoever in my art.'

'How extraordinary!' Rachel gushed. 'To meet you in person is the most enormous thrill. And on my very first day in Hemlock Bay!'

'How long are you here for?'

'I've taken a short-term lease on Bay View.'

'Another splendid situation. And you're an artist too?'

'Oh no, I simply enjoy a little amateur sketching.' Rachel closed her sketchbook. 'I'm a dabbler, not a gifted painter like you.'

'You flatter me, Miss Savernake.' Virginia subjected her to a measuring gaze. 'I wouldn't have thought that such a handsome young woman would have much interest in a minor surrealist.'

'You're far too modest.' Rachel was all doe-eyed innocence. 'The fact is, I was drawn to this part of the world by your painting of this very bay.'

'Good Lord, that's extraordinary. *Hemlock Bay* is... well, let's say a personal favourite of mine. So you're familiar with it?'

'More than that,' Rachel said. 'I found it so irresistible that I bought it for my house in London.'

Virginia's eyes widened. 'Are you serious? I mean, I heard from the dealer that he'd sold it to a connoisseur...'

'I don't claim any sort of expertise,' Rachel said in a small voice, 'but I loved it so much I was desperate to add it to my collection.'

'Heavens, I wasn't doubting your word. I'm just taken aback that a young woman like you would—'

'As I say, I'm a devotee of your work.' Rachel bowed her head. 'I was more fortunate than I deserve to come into a large inheritance which meant I could afford to acquire such a sophisticated work of art.'

Virginia looked her up and down, and seemed to like what she saw. 'Would you care to come in, Miss Savernake? Ffion will shortly be making afternoon tea, and you're welcome to join us.'

'How very kind.'

The older woman turned and strode out towards the door of the lighthouse. Rachel skipped after her. So far, she thought, so good.

'On such a pleasant day, we ought to take tea outside,' Virginia said, 'but as you can see, one drawback of such a unique building is the lack of a garden. I can't recommend sitting on the rocks down below. The views are superb, but not worth risking your life for. Besides, you can see so much more from the top of the lighthouse.'

They were in the lantern room. Virginia had transformed the circular space into a tiny studio, taking full advantage of the light. A blank canvas rested on an easel in the middle of the room, where once the lamp had burned. The steps of the spiral staircase were steep and narrow and Virginia, panting from the exertion, had parked herself on a window seat beside a door opening out on to a tiny balcony. Years of exercise in the harsh conditions on Gaunt meant Rachel could take the steps two at a time. She'd hardly drawn breath while rhapsodising about the panorama.

'Now that you've found such a unique home, you'll never want to leave!'

A curious expression flitted across Virginia's face. 'I'll never find a finer vantage point, it's true. Whether I'd care to live in Hemlock Bay forever is a different question. When I had our fortunes told, I asked the palmist what the future held for us here, but the fellow didn't give me a straight answer.'

'A fortune teller?' Rachel clapped her hands in delight. 'How truly divine!'

'Frankly, he didn't divine very much at all,' Virginia said drily. 'Neither Ffion nor I were told anything he couldn't have guessed from weighing us up for two or three minutes.'

'This was at the amusement park?'

The artist nodded. 'A pleasant place to while away an hour or two, even if Sir Harold Jackson was pushing his luck when he named it Paradise.'

'And the fortune teller's name is…?'

'The Great Hallemby.' Virginia grunted. 'Claims to be from the mysterious Orient but if you ask me, he's about as sophisticated as a bowl of leek-and-potato soup. All these fellows are rogues, of course, but I suppose having your palm read is all part of the experience of being at the seaside. Why do you ask?'

'Oh,' Rachel said carelessly. 'It must be jolly good fun to learn what fate has in store for you.'

Virginia stroked her long jaw. 'Don't you think that sometimes it's better not to know, Miss Savernake?'

Rachel tittered. 'I suppose you're right. We should content ourselves with the here and now. Especially in such a lovely spot as this. Hemlock Bay is utterly idyllic.'

'You're in good company. Turner thought the same, though he probably knew nothing of Hemlock Bay's dark history.'

Virginia flung open the balcony door and a gust of wind sent her hair billowing.

'Goodness,' Rachel said. 'It seemed so still before…'

'We're a long way up. Would you like to step outside?'

'I'd love to!'

'Please take great care.' Virginia's smile was tinged with menace. 'The balcony is narrow and it's a tight squeeze. The railing is so low, you could easily go over the edge.'

Rachel joined her outside and gazed towards the Irish Sea. Even on such a clear day, there was no remote speck on the horizon marking the island where she'd grown up. Gaunt was far distant and often wreathed in mist when the weather everywhere else was glorious.

Crude steps had been hewn into the rock face close to the lighthouse. They led to a small patch of sand, hardly enough to qualify as a beach. At the bottom of the cliffs were several caves. On the other side of the town rose Hemlock Head, conspicuous thanks to the colourful razzamatazz of the amusement park. The grounds of the Sun and Air Garden were out of sight.

'Shall we go downstairs?' Virginia asked. 'Ffion will be ready to pour the tea by now.'

They made their way back to the living room. Half a dozen unframed pictures stood on the floor, propped against the curving wall, and several sketches were scattered across the table. Through an open window, Rachel heard the movement of the water against the rocky shore. On a calm afternoon, the sound was soporific but Rachel knew from winters on Gaunt that in the midst of a storm, the roaring waves would terrify anyone unfamiliar with their fury.

She pointed to the outcrop of rocks. 'So that is Mermaid's Grave?'

'Evocative name, isn't it? The surface of the rocks is treacherous at the best of times. Even in fine weather, they're as slippery as a skating rink. The currents are so strong that anyone who fell in would be tugged underwater in the blink of an eye.'

A dreamy look flitted over Virginia's face. Picturing the scene in her mind, a subject for a future painting? With a visible effort, the older woman jerked herself back to the present.

'Now, Miss Savernake, do you take sugar?'

Rachel was conscious that Virginia's companion was subjecting her to intense scrutiny. Ffion Morris was in her early twenties, fair-haired and pretty and wearing a short-sleeved summer dress. She had very little to say for herself, and a glacial smile of greeting hadn't touched her china-blue eyes. After being introduced, she'd made the tea and scones without demur, but Rachel was left in no doubt that her intrusion was unwelcome.

As they buttered their scones, Rachel heaped praise on the paintings. Most were opaque swirls of colour, but one pen-and-ink sketch was easily recognisable. A head-and-shoulders portrait of Ffion Morris, wearing an expression of uncompromising resolve.

'A wonderful likeness!' Rachel exclaimed. 'You have such lovely features!'

Ffion gave a curt nod of acknowledgment. 'Ginny calls it *The Vow.*'

'I dashed that off shortly after the two of us became close,' Virginia said. 'Since then, I've painted Ffion a dozen times. Each time, I find some fresh facet to her character, but this one still pleases me the most. I wanted to capture her... commitment.'

'How gratifying it must be to model for your friend!' Rachel said.

'I'm used to it,' Ffion said.

Virginia gave a crooked grin. 'I hope familiarity isn't breeding contempt, my dear?'

Ffion shrugged and bit into her scone.

Virginia turned to Rachel. 'Perhaps I should paint you, Miss Savernake.'

'Oh my goodness!' Rachel put a hand to her mouth. 'That would be such an honour. But I hardly dare—'

'Let's discuss it another time,' Virginia said lazily. 'We're sure to keep bumping into each other.'

There was a short, deeply uncomfortable silence. Rachel looked around the room. 'This is such a fascinating home.'

'Isn't it? Trinity House took the lighthouse out of commission when a harbour was built further up the coast at Heysham. Harold Jackson snapped it up for a song and renovated it for residential purposes. His shrewdness and opportunism earned him a fortune. Not to mention a knighthood.'

Rachel nibbled her scone. 'He still lives in the area?'

'Oh yes, both Sir Harold and his wife are genuinely devoted to Hemlock Bay. They own almost all the land around here. Including your bungalow, of course.'

'Yes, his name is on my tenancy agreement.'

'And on mine, too.' Rachel noticed she didn't say *ours*. She glanced at Ffion, but the younger woman's gaze was fixed on her cup of tea. 'Until Harold Jackson and his wife came along, there was nothing much here but sheep and seagulls.'

'By the sound of things, Sir Harold transformed this area out of all recognition. The development must have made him unpopular in some quarters. People always resent change, don't they?'

Virginia shook her head. 'Before the war, this was a lonely, impoverished part of the world. The Jacksons are very generous. I haven't found anyone with a bad word to say about them. There's even talk of erecting a statue of Sir Harold on the promenade.'

'Goodness me.' Rachel paused. 'Have you met him?'

'As soon as we arrived, he and his wife invited us to dinner at Hemlock Hall. I'm sure they will invite you too. They are extremely sociable. Lady Jackson is American, of course.'

Rachel nodded.

'When they bought the place, it was close to falling down. Now it's one of the finest country houses in Lancashire and Lady Jackson loves entertaining.' Virginia cast a glance at her friend. 'I had a delightful time, although poor Ffion found the evening a dreadful bore.'

'What did you make of the Jacksons?'

'Harold Jackson oozes charm, but I'd say his wife is the power behind the throne. She's from California and not in the least troubled by any innate British reticence about enjoying her wealth.'

'If Sir Harold has made pots of money since the war,' Rachel said, 'I suppose he's ready to put his feet up.'

Virginia took a breath. 'Perhaps, but nobody has escaped the consequences of the Slump, have they?'

'I hear he's brought in a new business partner?'

Virginia threw a quick glance at her friend, but it wasn't so quick that Rachel failed to notice. 'That's right. A man called Carson. His home is opposite your bungalow.'

A certain flatness in her tone prompted Rachel to say, 'You don't care for him?'

'No, no,' Virginia said hurriedly. 'I hardly know the fellow. We've nodded to each other in passing, but that's all. But I've heard he… likes a drink.'

Ffion was becoming restive. Rachel thought she was struggling to suppress a snarl of contempt.

'You must excuse Ffion,' Virginia said. 'Her current passions are Celtic culture and the Communist Party. She deeply disapproves of capitalism. Especially businessmen like Jackson and Carson.'

'Parasites.' Lifting her head for a moment, Ffion spat out the word.

There was an uncomfortable silence. Rachel drank some tea and said, 'This is a town of newcomers, it seems. Who lives in Shepherd's Cottage?'

'A retired doctor, name of Doyle,' Virginia said. 'An Irishman who has spent a considerable period of time in South Africa. Rather evasive, I thought.'

'Evasive?'

'Didn't want to talk about himself at all.' The crooked teeth flashed in a smile. 'Unusual for any man to be so bashful, don't you agree? Made me wonder if he'd been struck off or disbarred or whatever it is that happens to doctors who misbehave. But I'm letting my imagination run away with me. As well as being unkind and unfair.' She smiled. 'Accusations that are often levelled against me, I should add.'

Ffion banged her cup down on its saucer so hard it was a miracle they didn't break into a hundred pieces.

Rachel pretended not to notice. The younger woman was simmering, like a volcano about to boil over. What might happen if she did erupt?

'Has Dr Doyle lived here long?'

'Oh no, he's yet another incomer.' Virginia considered Rachel. 'You ask a lot of questions, Miss Savernake.'

Rachel giggled. 'Do forgive me. I'm naturally inquisitive.'

'So am I. You must tell me about yourself.'

'Not much to tell, I'm afraid.'

'I find that hard to believe.' The wolfish smile returned. 'You strike me as a young lady with hidden depths.'

Rachel could almost hear Ffion grinding her teeth in anger. And jealousy?

'I came to Hemlock Bay in search of something different.'

'New experiences?'

'If you like to put it that way.' Rachel breathed out. 'You see, until now I have led such a very sheltered life. I'm hoping for a little excitement.'

9

Martha opened the front door of the bungalow at the same moment as a small, dumpy woman bustled out through the imposing gates of the house opposite. They exchanged smiles and she waited for Martha to join her on the lane.

'You must be our new neighbour.' To Martha, she sounded like a Londoner. She extended a small gloved hand. 'I'm Pearl Carson.'

'Martha Trueman. How do you do? I'm only a housemaid. I work for Miss Rachel Savernake.'

'Please don't say that you're just a housemaid. My mother was in service and I've worked below stairs as well as behind shop counters. Where would the rich folk be without having people like us at their beck and call?'

Martha smiled. Pearl Carson was about ten years her senior and five feet tall at most. She had a small, heart-shaped face and black curls peeping from beneath a cloche hat made of straw. Her coat looked expensive and it would be unfair to say that her appearance was nondescript. Pleasant and inoffensive would be nearer the mark.

'You're right, Mrs Carson. Nice to meet you. I'm on my way to look at the pleasure grounds.'

'Paradise? It's lovely, and you won't be bothered by any riff-raff. Sir Harold Jackson is very particular about maintaining standards. You're sure to enjoy yourself.'

'I gather there's a fortune teller. I'd love to have my palm read.'

Pearl Carson laughed. 'You're braver than me. To be perfectly honest, I'd rather not know.'

'Really? You're not tempted to peek into what lies ahead?'

'Not in the slightest. As it happens, my husband Louis and I have had a run of good luck this past two or three years. I'm always afraid things will take a turn for the worse. So I'd rather make the most of today and leave tomorrow to take care of itself.'

'I can't help thinking these fortune tellers must know a thing or two.'

Pearl smiled. 'I hope he tells you everything you wish for. As it happens, I'm heading in the same direction. Shall we walk together?'

'That's kind of you.' Martha glanced over her shoulder. 'You have a lovely home.'

'Thank you, we're very proud of it. Especially since both of us know very well how the other half lives. Louis and I never imagined living somewhere so grand, not in our wildest dreams. As for Hemlock Bay, this time last year, the name meant nothing to us.'

'Where do you come from?'

'We lived in Brighton for a few years, but I was born in Hackney.' Pearl looked sheepish. 'I'll be quite honest. I never knew my father and my poor mama didn't have two pennies to rub together.'

'Goodness!' Martha indicated the imposing gates. 'And now you live in a mansion!'

'An old converted farmhouse, actually. The Jacksons lived there after the war, while Hemlock Hall was being rebuilt. Sir Harold has worked a miracle here. He's a remarkable man.' A faraway look came into Pearl's eyes, but quickly she pulled herself back together. 'And now Louis is in partnership with him.'

'How marvellous!'

'I still can't quite believe everything that has happened. When I met Louis, he was selling wine for a merchant with premises next door to the pharmacy where I worked. We both had tragedy in common. I'd lost my husband to the Spanish flu, and his wife died the same way.' Pearl hesitated. 'We both felt bitter about the hand Fate had dealt us.'

'I can't blame you,' Martha said. 'At least your luck finally turned.'

'Yes.' Pearl gave a nervous smile. 'After my childhood sweetheart died, I swore I'd never remarry, but when Louis popped the question, I had to say yes. He was born with the gift of the gab, you see. All he needed was some money behind him.'

They walked on the grass, following the course of the lane as it wound towards the resort. After a few moments, both of them began to speak at the very same moment.

Martha laughed. 'Sorry. Please go on.'

'I was only going to ask about the people you work for. They made a good choice. Bay View has such a lovely position.'

'I'm employed by Miss Rachel Savernake. So are my brother and sister-in-law.'

'Elderly lady, is she? Not a crotchety old spinster, I hope? Believe me, I know they can be very difficult.'

'Oh no, Miss Savernake is my age.' Martha paused. 'Rather like you, she came into money.'

'Lucky girl,' Pearl Carson said lightly. 'Inheritance?'

'That's right.'

'How lovely when money goes to the people who really deserve it.' Pearl paused, as if inviting a confidence. 'And you enjoy working for her?'

'She is very generous, I must admit. Not too demanding, either. Although...' Martha's voice trailed away.

'Yes?'

'I'm not sure money has brought her happiness. She still seems... to be searching for something.'

'Such as?'

'Oh, I don't know. New friends, new experiences. Anything out of the ordinary.'

'Then she's come to the right place, believe me. In some ways, this resort reminds me of Brighton. Hemlock Bay is much smaller, but it's exciting in its own way. And nicer. No dingy alleyways, no festering slums. There's plenty of fun of every kind here, as long as you know where to look.'

'And where should she look?'

Pearl laughed. 'I'm bound to recommend the Hemlock Hotel, aren't I? That's where I'm heading. You see, Louis is the hotel manager and I look after the female staff. To think I've worked as a chambermaid myself! Sometimes I have to pinch myself to realise I'm not in a dream.'

Her face shone and Martha found herself warming to the woman. She knew for herself the strange joy of embarking on a way of life that had once seemed impossibly far out of reach. Each day felt as surreal as one of Rachel's paintings.

'That must be very strange. But thrilling, too.'

'I'm determined not to get above myself,' Pearl said. 'Sometimes I give the maids a hand. I'm not too proud to tidy up bedrooms or make beds. To this day, I pride myself on my hospital corners!'

Martha laughed. 'What does Sir Harold Jackson make of that?'

'Oh, he… doesn't take much notice of me.'

'Stand-offish, is he?'

'No, no, quite the opposite,' Pearl said hurriedly. 'He's very good-natured, not at all like some rich folk who wouldn't give the likes of you and me the time of day.'

'I suppose he's hoping to retire? Does your husband hope to take over the business side of things eventually?'

Pearl hesitated. 'Louis is full of ideas,' she said slowly. 'He's keen to make all kinds of entertainments available.'

'What sort of entertainments?'

'Oh, there's dancing, some of it quite… exotic. And Louis has set up a bridge club. He's talked about introducing chemin de fer for those who fancy a little flutter. Of course, there are strict rules about gambling and Louis is scrupulous about keeping on the right side of the law.' She paused. 'But you must forgive me, my dear. If I'm not careful, I'll give the impression of touting for business and that would never do.'

'It sounds marvellous,' Martha breathed. 'Between you and me, Miss Savernake is quite daring. I mean, to look at her, she seems quite demure. Butter wouldn't melt in her mouth, and so on. But beneath the respectable surface…'

The older woman giggled. 'We all need a chance to let our hair down. Especially when we're living in such troubled times. Everyone deserves a spot of pleasure, if you know what I mean.'

'You never said a truer word, Mrs Carson.'

'Please, dear, call me Pearl. I hate to stand on ceremony. Just because I live in a big house, it doesn't mean I've forgotten what it's like to scrub floors and kowtow to my betters. I always dreamed that one day I'd escape.'

'And so you did... Pearl.'

Martha saw the older woman's eyes flicker as she noticed the scars on her face. But she regained her composure in an instant, and her expression was kindly.

'Who knows, my dear? One day, you may drop as lucky as me.'

'Oh, I don't know. I'm happy as I am. Most of the time.' Martha hesitated. 'Though now and then I get the urge to kick over the traces.'

'Perfectly natural, and definitely nothing to be ashamed of. We all know what it's like to be tempted to behave in a way that is... out of the ordinary.' Pearl caught hold of Martha's wrist and leaned towards her. Speaking in a whisper, even though there was no one else within earshot, she said, 'Don't be shocked, but I adore sitting out in the Sun and Air Garden.'

Martha stopped in her tracks. 'You don't mean...?'

'Nudism, yes. Sir Harold's a strong believer in it. As he says, there's no shame in the human body. Believe me, the garden couldn't be more private or discreet. And it's incredibly decent. All about purity. In fact, some of the regulars can talk the hind leg off a donkey about their beliefs. They call themselves gymnosophists and preach the benefits of a truly classless society. The Dean of St Paul's himself has spoken about the new freedom of the body sweeping across Europe. He says it's a splendid omen of increasing health. So Sir Harold reckons that God is on our side!'

'My goodness,' Martha said.

Pearl roared with laughter. 'Sorry, my dear. For a moment, I was right up on my hobby horse, wasn't I? Take no notice. I don't want to embarrass you. Perish the thought!'

'I'm not in the least embarrassed,' Martha said stoutly. 'It all sounds fascinating. I had no idea.'

'Your mistress sounds quite delightful. And I'm sure she values discretion. A wealthy young lady needs to be careful, doesn't she? There are so many people out to take advantage these days.'

'How very true,' Martha said sadly.

They reached the esplanade and continued walking until they reached the forecourt of the elegant palace that was the Hemlock Hotel.

'I'd better say goodbye,' Pearl said. 'I must see how Louis is feeling. He's been under the weather lately, so he needs to take it easy.'

'Sorry to hear that,' Martha said. 'What seems to be the trouble?'

'Gastric influenza, the doctor says. Once we get some better weather, a few more days like this, he'll be as fit as a fiddle. Now, if you turn right at the end of the esplanade, you'll find Paradise in front of you. The Sun and Air Garden is on the other side of Hemlock Head. If ever you did want to pop in for an hour or two, you'd be most welcome. A chance to absorb the sun's healing rays will do wonders for you. No charge, of course. Be my guest.'

'Oh… that's extremely generous of you.'

'Think nothing of it. Us working girls have to stick together, don't we?' With a merry laugh, Pearl opened her handbag and fished out two small red oblong cards. 'Here you are. Just make sure you show this at the entrance to prove you're a member. Obviously they have to take great care about who is allowed in.'

'Obviously,' Martha agreed.

'Nobody in the least bit unsavoury. Sir Harold and Lady Jackson are very proud of the garden's reputation and rightly so. In this day and age, you simply can't be too careful.'

'Thank you very much.' Martha handed back one of the cards. 'You gave me two by mistake.'

'No mistake, my dear. Keep it. Just in case your Miss Savernake wants to come along. She sounds like just the sort of respectable young lady Louis likes to encourage in Hemlock Bay.'

'I'd best be on my way,' Hetty Trueman said. 'My husband wants to go for a walk along the cliffs before supper.'

'Might as well,' Mrs Stones said dismally. She was an angular woman in her fifties with a forehead creased in a permanent frown. 'Tomorrow, it will be raining cats and dogs, you mark my words. Mind you don't fall over the edge. It's quite dangerous. They've never put up any railings.'

The two women were sitting outside, on ancient metal chairs which wobbled nervously on uneven slabs of York stone. For the moment at least, the garden of End Terrace was bathed in sunlight, but throughout the half-hour span of their acquaintance, Mrs Stones had displayed an outlook so gloomy that even Hetty felt like a devil-may-care optimist.

She'd contrived to bump into the older woman and wangle an invitation to come in for a cuppa. Mrs Stones explained that she enjoyed a bit of company, but Hetty soon discovered this was a euphemism for having a captive audience to hear her litany of complaints. Hetty rapidly acquired an in-depth knowledge of Mrs Stones's various ailments as well as her opinion on everything that was amiss with the state of the modern world.

When negotiating with the land agent over the tenancy of the bungalow, Cliff Trueman had declined the offer of Mrs Stones's services as a housekeeper. Hetty was at pains to make it clear that this was not in any way a personal slight and was told bluntly that it was just as well Miss Savernake had her own servants, given the state of Mrs Stones's varicose veins. Not to mention the rheumatism in her knees and hips. It was a wonder she could manage to make breakfast for that retired Irish doctor and do a little light dusting. Not that he showed much gratitude. Mrs Stones got to her feet and flapped a scrawny hand in the direction of Shepherd's Cottage.

'That's where the doctor lives. Not that he'll take any interest in you.'

'Airs and graces, has he?' Hetty asked.

'Doesn't care for company, that's for certain.' Mrs Stones sniffed. 'And do you know, he refused to even look at my bad back! I've never known anything like it.'

Hetty made sympathetic noises. She'd discovered that this phrase and its variants were recurrent features of Mrs Stones's conversation.

'Even said I was better off consulting someone who was up to date with modern medicine!'

'I suppose that's reasonable,' Hetty ventured. 'Nothing worse than a wrong diagnosis.'

'It's the principle of the thing,' Mrs Stones said, deploying another favourite phrase.

'You don't do for the ladies in the lighthouse, then?'

'Ladies!' Mrs Stones scoffed. 'I could think of another choice word, believe me. I don't want anything to do with that sort. One of them's an artist, you know. I've never heard anything like it. Disgusting!'

'Oh dear.' Hetty got to her feet. She was gaining more respect for detectives like Inspector Oakes. The trouble they had to go through to prise information out of people. 'Anyway, thanks so much for tea and the chat. Lovely to be out in the sunshine after such a damp spring.'

The garden amounted to a patch of grass speckled with daisies and dandelions, bordered by a row of lacklustre geraniums and pansies. Mrs Stones had fallen out with her neighbours, and a thick hawthorn hedge provided a formidable barrier to prying eyes. Between a circular well hole and a wire fence separating her property from farmland stood a black corrugated shed, where she kept the rusting chairs on which they'd sat while drinking their tea.

'Far too much work for me,' Mrs Stones said. 'Looking after the outside was Stones's job, not mine. Ever since he died, I've not had the heart to do anything with it. Just as well Sir Harold sends one of his gardeners over every now and then, to do the necessary.'

'That's very good of him.'

'Oh, he's decent enough, Sir Harold. Keeps his eye on things. We could do a lot worse.' By Mrs Stones's standards, this struck Hetty as positively effusive. 'Mind you, I dread to think what will happen here if that fellow Carson takes over.'

'Is that in the offing?'

'You never know,' Mrs Stones said darkly.

'You don't care for Mr Carson?'

'That fellow's nothing like Sir Harold, I can tell you that for nothing.' Mrs Stones sniffed. 'He's certainly no gentleman, you can tell that a mile off. As for that wife of his, she keeps going on about how she was a servant once upon a time.

Pretends the sun shines out of her husband's posterior, if you'll pardon my French, but she doesn't fool me for one minute.'

'No?'

Mrs Stones shook her head. 'I caught sight of her once outside the Hemlock Hotel, when she thought nobody was looking. She and her husband were with the Jacksons, but Carson was doing all the talking, as per usual.'

She paused, and Hetty leaned towards her. 'Yes?'

'I saw the way she looked at Sir Harold Jackson.'

This woman, Hetty thought, was as skilled as Rachel when it came to building up the suspense.

'Go on.'

'If you ask me, she's besotted with the man.'

'Goodness!'

'Shocking, isn't it?' Mrs Stones demanded.

'Very.' Hetty hesitated. 'And how did Sir Harold react?'

'Oh, if you ask me, he didn't even notice. Anyway, her ladyship is a beauty, even if she is American. Not like Mrs Carson, that podgy little thing.' Mrs Stones tutted her disapproval. 'Ideas above her station. I've never known anything like it.'

'What about Mr Carson? Did he cotton on?'

Mrs Stones was, for once in her life, less than definite. 'Hard to say with that one. But I'll tell you this.'

Again the cliffhanger pause. Hetty was sorely tempted to scream at her to get on with it.

'Yes?'

'I don't trust him an inch. If he ever does find out that she's making eyes at Sir Harold, I wouldn't like to be in her shoes. Not for all the tea in China.'

10

Within five minutes of parting from Pearl Carson, Martha was walking through the gates of Paradise. St Peter was conspicuous by his absence, his place at the ticket booth occupied by a diminutive old man in a flat cap. He insisted on stamping Martha's hand with *PARADISE* in purple italics, so that she could re-enter before closing time (half an hour before sunset) if somehow she managed to tear herself away briefly from all the marvels at her disposal.

Paradise sprawled over steep ground. Martha followed looping pathways to the top of the hill, where the vista took her breath away. Hemlock Bay in all its glory, the long sweep of sand and the glittering water. Beyond the cliffs in the distance stood the lighthouse. On the other side of Hemlock Head, the view was obscured by clumps of trees, masking the Sun and Air Garden, which extended from the lower slopes on the far side of the head and encompassed the small cove separated by the promontory from the main resort.

She made her way back down the slope, this time examining more closely the pleasures of Paradise, starting with the Rose Garden. A brawny gardener in a purple string vest paused in the act of deadheading faded blooms to give her a salacious wink, followed by a tuneless whistle. It was like being serenaded by a Neanderthal, she thought, and kept on walking.

Divided into four sections, the garden had a cherub fountain in the centre and overlooked a small bandstand. From shelters in the Swiss chalet style, people could listen to music and inhale the perfume of the flowers while they recovered from the climb. Not a sprig of hemlock in sight.

Overlooking the bay was an open-air dance floor, with a huge loudspeaker shaped like a funnel clipped to a stout wooden pole. Further down the slope, she caught a sugary whiff of candyfloss in the air. Deckchairs encircled a marionette show, where puppets chattered and gyrated on a covered stage beneath a proud banner proclaiming *Showtime With Skeleton Sue*. A buxom young woman with coffee-coloured skin wandered between the rows of seated spectators, calling out as loudly as one of those new-fangled Tannoy speakers.

'Buy a souvenir programme for a penny! Have your pictures taken with Skeleton Sue! Only threepence for half a dozen, memories to last a lifetime!'

This must be Winnie, lady friend of The Great Hallemby. She had a forthright manner which, to judge by the coins changing hands, worked wonders when it came to selling puppet-related memorabilia.

While parents parted with their hard-earned cash, small children whooped with delight at the puppets' antics. Their excitement was almost drowned out by screeching from an aviary full of parrots and a hundred and one other brightly coloured birds from all four corners of the globe. There were creatures on display to suit every fancy, from budgerigars and cute little rabbits to glamorous peacocks and a large tank of pythons, curled up yet menacing. The kiddies' playground had a see-saw, roundabout, and half a dozen swing-boats flying through the air.

Martha passed through an arched doorway into the gaudily painted Penny Arcade. Inside she could barely move for people cramming their hard-earned money into solid oak slot machines on cast-iron feet. When someone started the Band Machine, it was impossible to hear herself think, thanks to the cacophony of drum, cymbals, trumpet, and organ playing together in less than perfect harmony.

At the end of the corridor, another door led into the Mirror Maze, a winding passageway which distorted Martha's appearance in so many different ways that by the time she emerged into the open air, she felt quite dizzy. She found herself outside a building guarded by a wizened old woman with ragged hair. A large signboard bore the promising disclaimer: *Exclusively for Adults! Warning: Do Not Enter if You are of a Sensitive Disposition or Easily Shocked!!!*

Who could resist such a challenge? Not Martha, and she was by no means alone. Even on a sunny afternoon at the beginning of summer, the cramped interior was packed with people eager to discover precisely What the Butler Saw. The butler had evidently spent most of his working hours peeping through keyholes at ladies of the house in various states of undress. Tiring of the gauze-veiled parade of plump breasts and buttocks, Martha headed for the exit.

The Great Hallemby plied his trade in a wooden hut tucked away in a secluded corner of Paradise, and separated from a fish pond by a wall of vast rhododendron bushes. Behind the hut, the sharp leaves of a tall, thick holly hedge sheltered denizens of the Sun and Air Garden from the gaze of those whose voyeurism wasn't sated by discovering What the Butler Saw. Curiosity impelled Martha to take a closer look. One patch of lower hedging had died away; a determined intruder could wriggle through, but she heard a dog barking. The guard was evidently doing his rounds, making sure there were no trespassers. She strolled back to the front of the hut.

The Great Hallemby was emblazoned on a noticeboard above the door in a lurid flourish of orange and purple which described the wonders Hallemby had foretold in the course of a career taking him from Cairo to China. No mention of Colwyn Bay; just artful disclaimers to guard against the risk of prosecution, making clear that he traded in character readings, not foretelling the future.

A bell hung beside the door, alongside a sign warning the unwary not to enter unless they were bidden. To disturb The Great Hallemby otherwise was presumably to court disaster. On the bright side, the cost entitled customers to a hand reading as well as a peek into the crystal ball.

Martha rang the bell and waited.

'Enter and sit!'

A sonorous voice of command. She glanced up and saw above the door a flared metal opening, an inch wide. The Great Hallemby communicated with his prospective customers through some kind of speaking tube contraption. No trace of a Welsh accent, she thought.

She put sixpence in a box craftily marked *Voluntary donations* and stepped inside. Drawing aside a black velvet curtain, she entered a claustrophobic antechamber painted with mystic symbols. She took a seat on a wooden bench, facing a second black curtain. Above it was another flared tube opening.

A minute passed before the fortune teller's voice issued another instruction.

'Step inside!'

Pulling back the curtain, she found herself in a small, windowless cubicle. She could hear a faint Indian chant, but she was on her own. Rush matting covered the timber floor, except for a small area in the centre where a pentagram was chalked on the wood. There was a shelf on either side of the room; a single candle flickered on one, while on the other a small porcelain burner infused the air with incense. On the far wall hung a painting of a cross-legged fakir wearing a turban. Beside it hung a pair of black curtains, this time embroidered in gold with the signs of the zodiac. A record player sat in a corner of the room and as she set eyes on it, the chanting stopped. The principal furnishings comprised a green baize table and two chairs with high backs. On the table was something large and round and covered in green felt. She didn't need to be a seer to guess it was a crystal ball.

'Welcome!'

With a dramatic flourish, The Great Hallemby pulled apart the curtains and strode into the room. Martha had paid close attention to Jacob's account of his meeting with Gareth Bellamy and it was safe to say there was no comparison between the shifty fellow he'd described and the formidable figure now facing her. His flowing gold and black gown hung around him in billowing folds and she saw he was wearing a silk scarlet blouse and black trousers. His enormous moustache was surely glued on and he wore a fez matching his blouse. In the feeble light, Martha couldn't be sure, but she suspected his cheeks were powdered white, and that he'd put on a dab of lipstick to emphasise the contrast with the red of his lips.

He bowed deeply.

'How do?' Martha said in her broadest northern accent.

A pained expression flittered across his face. 'Please be seated, my child. You may remove your hat and coat.'

He'd opted for a sonorous boom, with a dash of paternalism and a vaguely foreign intonation. Martha did as instructed. When getting ready to go out, she'd taken a strategic decision to leave the top buttons of her blouse undone and she was conscious of him inspecting her figure. Apparently satisfied with what he'd seen, he gathered up his gown and sat down facing her.

'What is it that you seek from The Great Hallemby?'

'I'd like to know what the future has in store for me.'

'My child, do you understand the importance of this matter?'

'Well, I...'

'No!' He held up his hand. 'Listen to me. You stand on the brink of an experience which may change your life.'

'Good heavens!'

'You need to be prepared, Miss...'

'Trueman,' Martha supplied.

'Yes, Miss Trueman, gazing into the future carries with it both rich opportunity and the potential for disaster. Are you content to proceed?'

'I paid my sixpence,' Martha said in a small voice.

'A modest investment, my child, for the untold wealth of possibilities that may be on the very cusp of unfolding around you.'

He contemplated the ceiling, as if lost in thought, perhaps overcome by the elegance of his own rhetoric. Martha kept very still and waited for him to speak again.

'It is remarkable. You possess an aura, a definite aura.'

'I do?'

He glanced at the side of her head and his eyes opened very wide. Before entering this inner sanctum, Martha had made sure to push her hair back so that even in the shadows he could see the acid scarring. She was conscious of him shifting in his chair, and she suspected he'd had to force himself not to let out a gasp of dismay.

'Your... your aura tells me much more than words could ever explain. I divine that you have endured great troubles, my child.'

Martha looked down. 'You are right.'

'Better days lie ahead,' he said. 'Let me examine your hands and see what further truths they reveal.'

Obediently, she extended her hands, palms up. He ran his fingertips lightly across them.

'Your palms are taut with nerves. Sit back and concentrate, ridding yourself of any mental distraction. The palms need to be concave, so that you do not smooth away the scoring. That's where the truth lies. In the lines of head, heart, and life.'

He launched into a flatteringly embellished description of the most appealing parts of her personality and the welcome news that she could expect to enjoy prosperity and good health in years to come. Martha liked what she heard so much, she wished it were true. Whatever his faults, this man had a talent for telling stories.

'You are a young woman of immense character and fortitude, Miss Trueman. In the coming weeks, you will find you are asked to make a choice on which your future happiness depends.'

'Is it... is it to do with a man?'

The fortune teller inclined his head. 'More than that, your palms do not disclose.'

'What a pity!' Martha dabbed the corners of her eyes with a lacy handkerchief.

'My child, there is no cause to distress yourself. The time is ripe to see what the crystal has to say.'

The Great Hallemby spread his hands over the cloth in a gesture of reverence before whipping it off with a panache worthy of a matador making a pass with his cape. In the gloom, the sphere's soft glow was hypnotic. He picked it up and turned it around in his hands again and again.

For fully half a minute he hummed a strange tune, as if in a trance. Martha was conscious of the woody aroma of the incense. Finally he fixed his unblinking gaze on her and presented her with the crystal ball.

'Take it,' he ordered. 'As you hold the crystal, close your eyes and keep them shut tight. Empty your mind. Forget about the passage of time. Breathe deeply. This will allow me to peer into your future.'

She cupped her hands to receive the crystal and shut her eyes as required. The ball felt heavy and cold in her grasp. In her head she began to count. The only sound was The Great Hallemby's heavy breathing. She had a shrewd suspicion that he was paying more attention to her bosom than to any vision in the crystal.

When she'd counted past five hundred and fifty, she heard a catarrhal clearing of the throat. In a muffled whisper, he said, 'You may open your eyes and return the crystal to me.'

She did as he asked and then sat back and listened as he expounded what he'd seen. Stripped of the flowery metaphors, it amounted to a picture of contented tranquillity. Martha was seated and pregnant, knitting tiny mittens for the new baby while surrounded by affectionate, pretty children. In the background, a handsome, well-dressed older man smoked his pipe and smiled at his family with genial benevolence.

'How wonderful!' Martha explained, when the fortune teller leaned back in his chair, a gesture that indicated the session was about to end. 'But what about the choice you said I'd have to make?'

'You will meet someone. A stranger who will show you kindness. Through his good offices, you will meet the man of your dreams.'

'My goodness!'

The Great Hallemby inclined his head. 'That is all I can see in the crystal, my dear.'

'Thank you. I don't know what to say.'

'I wish you well, my child.'

She began to rise from her seat. 'Oh, there is just one more thing.'

'I fear I have told you everything revealed to me by your palms and by the crystal ball.'

'It's just about the man who did this to me.' She touched the scar tissue on the side of her face. 'I had this picture in my head of him lying dead. I thought you would see the same vision.'

'A vision?'

'Yes, it was a bright new dawn on the summer solstice and his body was sprawled across the rocks beneath the cliffs.'

He stared at her, appalled, but she refused to flinch. 'You're saying he was dead?'

'That's right. His face was hidden, so I couldn't be sure it was the man who hurt me, but I thought you would know.'

'What... what are you talking about?'

'Can you explain what it means?'

'No, I can't.' His voice had risen and the foreign accent had slipped. One of his eyelids had developed a twitch. This was undoubtedly Gareth Bellamy the Welsh clerk rather than an exotic seer. 'You'd better leave, Miss Trueman.'

'But I—'

He made a shooing gesture, his vast sleeves flapping like the wings of a giant bird.

'Enough! Go now!'

She took a step back. 'Thank you, anyway, Mr Bellamy. I'll be sure to look out for that kind stranger.'

As she spoke, he froze in horror.

It came to Martha with a sickening jolt that she'd committed a dreadful blunder. In a moment of sheer carelessness, she'd given away the fact she knew the man's real name.

Bellamy's face contorted with rage. He shoved the table out of the way and lunged forward. Clamping his hands around Martha's neck, he began to squeeze.

Martha's upbringing had been anything but sheltered. She clawed at his face with fingernails as sharp as razors, and kneed Bellamy between his legs. As he reeled, she ripped his hands away.

He yelped in pain, arms flailing. There were livid scratches on his face. She'd drawn blood. With minimal backlift, she delivered a kick to his groin with the point of her shoe as he crashed to the floor with a wild scream.

Without even looking, she grabbed hold of the curtain behind her. Ripping it off its hooks, she hurled it over the man's prostrate form.

As she bolted through the opening, she glanced back into the room. The Great Hallemby lay in a heap on the floor with the black curtain on top of him. It looked like a crumpled velvet shroud.

Even as she threw herself out of the fortune teller's hut and into the safety of the open grounds, even as she berated herself for her stupidity, one consolatory thought flitted through her mind.

I bet he didn't see that coming.

II

Arm in arm, Cliff and Hetty Trueman strolled along Hemlock Heights, luxuriating in the sea breeze, following the twists and turns of the path towards the town.

'Who would have thought it?' she said as the beach came into view. 'The four of us on holiday at the seaside. As if we don't have a care in the world.'

Her husband pondered before replying. 'Let's make the most of this. You never can tell what the future may bring, however many crystal balls you gaze into. Rachel is right; life is for living. No need to worry about what might go wrong.'

For Trueman, this was a long speech, verging on a personal manifesto. A nod from his wife acknowledged this.

'I know, I know.' She sighed. 'That's just the way I am. I can't help myself.'

He was too wise to argue, so they walked on in silence as the path wound gently down the slope to the resort. Soon they came to the Shore Gardens, which boasted a bandstand and a boating lake as well as neatly tended beds of pansies and an ice cream kiosk doing a roaring trade.

A 'reflex man' in his early twenties approached them from the esplanade. His shirt sleeves were rolled up and he was wearing khaki shorts, plimsolls, and a smile as big as the camera slung around his neck. Hetty protested that she didn't like having her picture taken, but her husband slung his arm around her shoulder as the photographer snapped away.

'Here,' the young man said, handing them a docket. 'Walking pictures are my speciality. That's a good 'un. Take a look at my stall on the beach and see if you don't agree. I develop and print the negatives each night and keep them available for sale. For seven days only, mind.'

With a cheery wave, he moved on to his next victims. Trueman bought Hetty an enormous cornet from the kiosk and scanned the esplanade while she sat on a bench and feasted on three scoops of vanilla.

'The Hemlock Hotel looks posh,' he said. 'Best leave that to Rachel. There's a big pub on the main street. I'll chat up some of the locals, get an idea of the lie of the land here.'

Hetty swallowed the last fragment of cone. 'While you're boozing, I'll buy meat and potatoes and then get back to the bungalow and make a start on dinner.'

The sea front teemed with people making the most of an early glimpse of summer. The sound of their merriment was carried by the breeze. There was no shortage of passers-by whose taste in clothes was not merely smart but expensive.

His wife followed his gaze. 'Hemlock Bay is quite swanky for a Lancashire resort, wouldn't you say?'

He grunted. 'Seems too good to be true.'

'This is a seaside town, built for people's enjoyment.' Hetty paused. 'Nothing like Mortmain or Blackstone Fell.'

'On the surface, that's true enough. All the same...' He

shook his head. 'I'm not a man for flights of fancy, but... I'd say Rachel's right about this place.'

'I'm not fey either, but I know what you mean.' She exhaled. 'Hemlock Bay looks so lovely in the sunshine, but it gives me the creeps.'

'Me too,' he said. 'There's a worm in the bud.'

A burly uniformed commissionaire, brass buttons gleaming in the sunlight, stood on guard outside the imposing glass entrance of the Hemlock Hotel. Just in case any undesirables were foolish enough to mix with the well-heeled residents, Rachel thought. She bestowed her sweetest smile and was rewarded with a tap of his peaked cap.

Sashaying through the revolving doors, she found herself in a light and airy lobby filled with hothouse plants. It was like straying into the Palm House at Kew Gardens. The smell of freshly watered leaves mingled with the aroma of beeswax polish. Huge gilt pilasters supported the reception hall's high domed roof, and a vast curling staircase led up to the bedroom floors. Her feet almost vanished in the luxuriant depths of carpet. A notice next to the desk unapologetically displayed the tariff for accommodation. Full board for a week cost as much as a month at most seaside hotels, but Rachel supposed that people got what they paid for. If they could afford it.

She surveyed her surroundings. As well as a private lounge, a large smoking room, and a sea view conservatory closed for renovations, there was a large American Bar open to non-residents. A small orchestra was playing 'Puttin' on the Ritz' as two couples twirled around on the parquet floor. In each case, the woman was in her fifties and bejewelled, and the man guiding her with a fixed smile was half her age and light on his feet.

At least, Rachel thought, a woman could drink here on her own and not be pigeonholed as a flibbertigibbet or a courtesan. Yet was it so much better to be regarded as a meal ticket? She made a performance of seating herself on a stool at the end of the bar and shrugging off her cape, so as to reveal her chiffon party dress, sleeveless and daringly cut.

A young barman who had been talking to a middle-aged couple wasted no time in moving towards her.

'What can I get you, miss?'

His accent was broad Lancashire and he was rather handsome. Although he lacked the sophistication she associated with the Hemlock Hotel, she suspected it wouldn't take him long to acquire the same slick charm as the gigolos on the dance floor.

'A glass of Bollinger.' She treated him to a dazzling smile. 'And please do have one yourself.'

'Thank you very much, miss, that's very generous.'

'Like it here?' she asked as he popped a cork.

'You won't find me complaining, miss. Mind you, I've only been here a week.'

'What brought you to Hemlock Bay?'

A wary look came into his eyes. 'Friend of a friend said it was a good place to work.'

'Oh yes?'

'My last situation was in Blackpool. This hotel is different. They aren't slave drivers here. Don't make you work all the hours that God sends.'

'Glad to hear it. Sir Harold Jackson has an excellent reputation.'

'So I hear, miss, though I haven't met the gentleman myself.

Mr Carson runs the show.' He lowered his voice. 'Speak of the devil, the gaffer just walked in.'

Rachel turned her head as Carson caught sight of her. One appraising glance later, he was striding towards the bar, nodding affably to right and left as he approached. A sallow-faced man who had lost quite a lot of hair, he wore a fulsome smile that failed to disguise the calculation in his gaze.

'Good evening, madam.' He introduced himself and she did likewise. The barman poured him a gin and tonic without being asked. 'Champagne, eh, Miss Savernake? You're in a celebratory mood?'

'I'm simply thrilled to get away from it all.' She gave a coquettish smile. 'I'm looking for something different. A chance to open myself up to new experiences.'

'Whatever you're hoping for,' Carson said, 'you'll find it here in Hemlock Bay.'

'How exciting!'

He gestured to the barman. 'Young Albert here is looking after you, I hope?'

'We're getting on like a house on fire,' Rachel said. 'Your hotel is splendid. I'm beginning to wish I'd booked in here for the summer, instead of renting a bungalow. Although the situation is lovely, on top of the cliffs.'

'You're at Bay View?' He nodded as Albert handed him a gin and tonic. 'My wife and I live across the road at Beggarman's Rest.'

'A modest name for such a grand home.'

'We've been very fortunate.' He probably intended his smile to be humble, but it struck Rachel as triumphalist. 'A few years ago, I'd never have dreamed... but anyway, it's an absolute pleasure to meet you, Miss Savernake. What brings you here, may I ask?'

'I was recommended to come to Hemlock Bay. A distant relation of mine waxed lyrical about it. Said I'd have a lot of fun.'

'Delighted to hear it!'

She smiled. 'As a matter of fact, he stayed in this very hotel. I don't know whether you came across him? His name was Edward Hillman.'

For a fleeting moment, Carson's expression betrayed a mixture of consternation and bewilderment. Yet he was quick to compose himself.

'I'm afraid I don't recall.' He forced a self-deprecating cough. 'Of course, each week a great many guests come and go. But we're always grateful for an enthusiastic testimonial.'

'Edward said he found happiness here,' Rachel murmured.

Carson knitted his brow, as if trying to solve a crossword clue.

'Good to know. Nice to see you, Miss Savernake. I must be getting along, but do enjoy your stay in our little town.'

He wasted no time in leaving the bar. He hadn't even touched his gin and tonic.

'Your very good health!' Trueman said, lifting his tankard of foaming beer.

'Cheers,' said his companion, whose tipple was Scotch whisky. 'Grand to meet you.'

'Likewise.'

Trueman took a swig and then wiped his mouth. They were standing by the counter in the Select Bar of the Mermaid, the only pub in the centre of town. At least, Trueman thought, he wouldn't need to traipse around half a dozen hostelries in search of snippets of useful gossip. In every other seaside resort, a pub lurked around every corner.

Hemlock Bay was different. One of a kind. Because the place had been pretty much built by one man, he'd been able to ensure that his business interests were not disrupted by aggressive competition. As a result, the Mermaid was packed to the rafters from opening time to last orders, thick with the fug of smoke and ale.

'Just arrived?'

The other man had stood behind Trueman in the queue and they'd fallen into conversation about the prospects of England's cricketers in the forthcoming battle with New Zealand. His accent suggested Cockney origins, but the fact he wasn't a local didn't stop Trueman standing him a drink. You never knew who you might bump into, or what interesting titbits they might disclose.

Trueman nodded. 'Thought I'd take a look at what's what.'

'Where are you staying?'

'Other end of town. Not far from the lighthouse.'

'Didn't know there were any guest houses out that way.'

'The lady I work for has taken a bungalow. Bay View, it's called. Apparently they were going to build four of them, until the stock markets went mad and land values collapsed. Nobody has much money these days.'

The other man wiped a line of sweat from his brow. 'There's always a few with cash in the bank.'

Trueman took a swig of his beer. 'Or under the floor-boards.'

'You're dead right,' the other man said. 'So what do you do?'

'I'm only a chauffeur.'

'Thought you might be a heavyweight boxer.' The other

man was six feet tall, but Trueman dwarfed him. 'Bet you'd be handy in the ring.'

Trueman shrugged. 'I can look after myself.'

'I bet you can. My name's Joe, by the way.'

'Cliff Trueman.'

They shook hands. 'Chauffeur, eh? So what brings you here, then?'

'I work for a young lady who came into an inheritance.'

His companion guffawed. 'Do you, now? Rich young spinster, eh? Not looking for an older bloke who can teach her a thing or two, is she?'

Trueman shrugged. 'Some people reckon she's a bit on the cold side.'

'Is that right?' A ribald laugh. 'Sounds like she needs warming up.'

'She keeps us busy, I know that. My wife does the cooking and my sister's a maid.'

'Nice to keep things in the family. What's this young lady's name? Anyone famous? I've not heard of film stars coming to Hemlock Bay, but it's only a question of time.'

'She's not famous and you haven't seen her on the silver screen. Name of Savernake. Rachel Savernake.'

A frown. 'Rings a faint bell.'

'Miss Savernake keeps herself to herself. You must be thinking of someone else.'

The other man scratched his head, as if to stimulate his memory. 'Going back before the war, wasn't there a judge by that name? Never came across him; it was before my time.'

'Mine too.' Trueman became thoughtful. His rugged features didn't give anything away, but he'd never expected anyone in Hemlock Bay to have heard of the late Judge Savernake.

'Had a hell of a reputation. Got a thrill out of hanging people, according to whispers I heard.'

Trueman shrugged. 'There are a few Savernakes up and down the country. They pronounce the name in different ways, but Miss Rachel comes from this part of the world, only further up the coast. Cumberland way.'

'Oh aye? The Lake District is worth seeing, so I've heard.'

'Take your umbrella when you go, that's my advice.' Trueman placed his glass on a beer mat. 'So what do you do when you're not propping up a bar, then?'

'Oh, nothing special. This and that.'

'Very mysterious.' Trueman waited a few moments, but the other man wasn't the feeble sort who felt compelled to fill any lull in a conversation. 'You knew about this judge, did you? Not in the legal profession, by any chance?'

A mocking grin. 'Do I look like one of m'learned friends?'

Trueman considered his companion's broad shoulders and formidable jaw. He was pasty-faced and his breathing was strangely laboured, but nattily attired in a three-piece suit, silk tie, and shiny black leather shoes. Gold cufflinks twinkled on his wrists. His voice wasn't uneducated, but neither was he a toff. Working class, yes, but not doing too badly for himself by the look of things.

'Londoner, eh? Not a Scotland Yard man, by any chance?'

The man laughed. 'You're quite a detective yourself, chum, but you're out of date. Once upon a time I was a bobby, for my sins, but it's many a long year since I last walked a beat.'

'What do you get up to these days?'

He tapped the side of his nose. 'Let's just say I'm a businessman, and leave it at that, eh?'

'Fair enough. You're based in Hemlock Bay?'

A shake of the head. 'Came up here for a change of scenery.'

'Aye, they say a change is as good as a rest.'

'You never said a truer word, chum.' The man turned towards him, close enough for the whisky fumes to warm Trueman's cheeks. 'There's money to be made here, and there's not many places you can say that about.'

'Very true. But doesn't one bloke own most of the town? Sir Harold something or other?'

'Jackson, yes, he's made a fortune here. But he's getting past it, from what I hear. Time for others to get their fair share.'

'Oh yes?'

The other man finished his drink and belched. There was a faint bleariness in his eyes and he winced as he gave his stomach a quick rub. Leaning forward, he tugged Trueman's lapel.

'Believe me, chum. Sir Harold's not the man he was. The good life has made him too comfy. So there are opportunities to be had, for those smart enough to snaffle them.'

'Such as?'

The other man put a finger to his lips. 'Ask no questions, and I'll tell you no lies. But I'll buy you a pint, how's that?'

'Joe, you're a gentleman.'

While his new friend queued for service, Trueman cast his eye around his fellow drinkers. At this end of the bar, half a dozen middle-aged men were talking loudly about golf. One member of the group caught his eye, a sandy-haired fellow, who was paying no attention to his colleagues' boasts about birdies and eagles. He seemed more interested in the freckle-faced young man who was busy serving behind the bar. As Trueman watched, the barman glanced at the golfer, before looking quickly away and smoothing his rather long hair. A faint smile slid across the sandy-haired man's face.

Joe returned with the drinks. 'Here you go.'

Trueman lifted his glass. 'These opportunities you mentioned…'

'Mum's the word,' the other man interrupted. 'Forget I said anything.'

It was as if he'd got a grip of himself and resolved to stop boasting, for fear of letting a confidence slip.

'So where are you staying?' Trueman asked.

'The Hemlock Hotel. My room's right at the front on the first floor. Lovely sea view. Not to mention a balcony.'

'Very nice. Surprised you're not drinking there.'

A shrug. 'I had a couple in the Hemlock before I popped round here. Decent hotel, but full of people who are rich and posh. Thought I'd try a proper pub.'

Trueman grinned. 'And I'm not rich or posh.'

'Your Miss Savernake sounds as though she's not short of a few bob. What's she going to do with herself in Hemlock Bay?'

After a moment's pondering, Trueman said, 'You know, I think she's looking for excitement.'

'Is she now?' The man drained his tumbler. 'I bet she'll find it in Hemlock Bay. I'd best be getting along, but it's been good to meet you, Cliff. We must have another drink together in the not too distant. Maybe you can even introduce me to your Miss Savernake.'

'Fair enough, Joe,' Trueman said warmly. 'I'll see you around. By the way, I didn't catch your surname.'

The other man rubbed his stomach again.

'McAtee.'

'A busy day,' Rachel said, stifling a yawn as she poured the coffee. 'We need a shot of caffeine to keep awake.'

Hetty had rustled up a cottage pie, one of her specialities. Now they were in the living room, whose bay window looked out across the garden and towards the sea. The temperature had dropped three or four degrees since afternoon and clouds were gathering over the water, as if in mutinous conspiracy against the holidaymakers.

'Tomorrow is Sunday and the forecast is for heavy rain. We can draw breath and decide what to do next.'

'Didn't Jacob say he's driving up tomorrow?' Hetty asked. 'I suppose he'll want to be fed and watered.'

'The *Clarion* booked him into the Hemlock Hotel.'

'Typical. Always falls on his feet, that young man. Even if he relies on you to make sure he has a soft landing.'

'With luck, he'll be able to tell us something about the unfortunate young man from Liverpool who threw himself from the cliff.' Rachel shook her head. 'Meanwhile, I'm itching to hear how you all got on.'

'I didn't get very far with Mrs Stones,' Hetty said mournfully.

'Tell me everything!' Rachel commanded. 'Remember, leave nothing out, however trivial. I'm sure you discovered something of interest.'

When Hetty had finished describing her tête-à-tête with Mrs Stones, she shook her head in sorrow and said, 'Told you I wasted my time.'

Rachel laughed. 'Nonsense. Why are you always so hard on yourself? Thanks to you, we know that Mrs Carson has taken a fancy to Sir Harold, and that if her husband learns about it, he might resort to drastic measures.'

'Mrs Stones loves to look on the dark side. You can't take her word as gospel.'

'She sounds more likely to be guilty of malicious glee rather than malicious invention. Cliff, how did you fare?'

Rachel listened intently to Trueman's account of the conversation in the Mermaid before saying, 'This man McAtee, who is so anxious to make my acquaintance. What do you make of him? Is he my type?'

The big man allowed himself a laconic smile. 'I daren't think what your type is. All I can say for certain is, McAtee's not it.'

'A common or garden womaniser?'

'Amongst other things. He's not on the straight and narrow. What his game is, I can't tell you.'

'He admitted to being a former policeman.' Rachel was thoughtful. 'Do you think he regretted telling you?'

Trueman nodded. 'Stone cold certainty. He got carried away for a minute or two. The drink was talking. I understand why. He's away from home, taking it easy on a Saturday night and trying to get over a bad stomach. But he was annoyed with himself for confirming my guess.'

'I wonder why McAtee left the police. Did he jump or was he pushed?'

'He wanted me to think that he resigned to go on to greater things,' Trueman said. 'I'm not convinced.'

Hetty said to Rachel, 'Why not ask Inspector Oakes if he can use his influence and find out why McAtee left? The inspector's sweet on you; he'll be glad to help.'

'Good idea. I'll telephone him,' Rachel said, refusing to be provoked. 'You've been very quiet, Martha. Tell us about your trip to Paradise. What delights did The Great Hallemby foresee for you in his crystal ball?'

Colour rose in Martha's cheeks. 'I have a confession to make.'

'You're destined to fall in love with a Fleet Street journalist?'

'Even worse than that. I'm a rotten detective. I made an utter hash of things.'

Rachel gave her a searching glance. 'What went wrong?'

Martha recounted her conversation with Pearl Carson and her visit to Paradise. 'So you see,' she concluded. 'Not only did I fail to learn whether Mrs Carson really does care for Sir Harold, I gave the game away with Bellamy. When I called him by his real name, I wanted the ground to swallow me up. You should have seen his face. For a few moments, he really did want to strangle me.'

She lifted her head so they could see the marks left on her neck by Bellamy's bony fingers.

Trueman swore. 'He'll regret that.'

Martha patted her brother's hand. 'Don't worry, Cliff. You know I can look after myself. My knee hurt him much more than he hurt me.'

Rachel nodded. 'He must have been beside himself with rage. Talking about the body on the rocks shook him, just as we hoped. But finding out that a stranger – and a young housemaid at that – knew his real name obviously shocked him to the core. So the red mist descended.'

'It was more than anger,' Martha said. 'He was scared.'

'As if he didn't know what *you* were capable of?'

'Exactly. Though he found out when I scratched his face and made him bleed,' Martha said grimly. 'The marks will take a bit of explaining to the jealous girlfriend.'

'Serves him right. Do you really think he meant to kill you?'

Martha considered. 'Until he became agitated, he didn't strike me as the violent type.'

Rachel's tongue passed over her lips. 'Who knows what any of us might do when driven to extremes?'

'I'd say his instincts are more... insidious. He's a born schemer. Just not as clever as he likes to think.'

'You did everything I asked.'

'I made a mess of things by putting him on his guard. Now he knows I'm as much of a fraud as he is. What's more, I've let Jacob down. He'll find it harder to investigate if Bellamy suspects...'

'You know Jacob. Nothing can stop him once he's on the scent of a story.'

'Bellamy's up to no good, I swear. The minute I mentioned a body on the rocks, he became a bag of nerves. Even his eye started to twitch. I wouldn't trust him an inch. But I still don't understand why he invented the so-called premonition.'

Rachel shrugged. 'Was it entirely an invention?'

Martha stared at her. 'What do you mean?'

'I wish I knew.' Rachel sighed. 'That story of his has a significance we haven't understood.'

'So what's he plotting?' Martha couldn't hide her frustration. 'I wish you'd been there. You'd have wheedled him into letting something slip.'

'Don't be hard on yourself. We only arrived here a few hours ago. I'm the first to admit my plan was vague. Simply to put the cat among the pigeons and see what happens. Sometimes life is too short for subtlety. We're learning as we go along. In a few short hours, we've already made a lot of progress.'

'Did you manage to make an impression with your artist?'

Rachel laughed. 'The two of us got on famously. Like most creative people, Virginia Penrhos loves to bask in the glow of admiration. I gushed so much, I made an enemy. If looks could kill, her companion would have disembowelled me with a glare.'

She described her visit to the lighthouse. 'Ffion Morris

strikes me as volatile. She is a deeply unhappy creature, so much is clear. What I want to know is why.'

'Some people are miseries by nature,' Hetty pronounced. 'Like Mrs Stones.'

'True, but Mrs Stones is an ageing busybody whose best years are behind her. This young woman is very different. The death of Virginia Penrhos's cousin hurt her badly, and she had no success on the stage, but she and Virginia aren't short of money and the lighthouse is a magical place to live. Yet she's tense and angry, and the relationship is strained. I encouraged Virginia to take an interest in me and Ffion couldn't hide her jealousy. Something has gone wrong between them.'

'What exactly?'

'I've no idea.' Rachel frowned. 'I thought I was familiar with the outlines of Virginia's life and career, but it's an incomplete sketch. Ffion Morris is a blank canvas. As soon as I got back here, I telephoned an art dealer who happens to be in my debt. With any luck, he'll paint a fuller picture.'

'You think Virginia is bored with Ffion?' Martha asked.

'There's a genuine tenderness in the way she looks at the girl, but I think she finds her deeply frustrating. Perhaps that's why she deliberately tormented her by making a fuss of me. Especially when she talked about my posing for her.'

Hetty grunted. 'She'd probably paint you as a geometrical shape.'

Rachel laughed. 'I'd rather be portrayed as an enigmatic swirl of colour.'

'Be careful what you wish for. This so-called artistic temperament covers a multitude of sins. You'll probably end up as a streaky blob of black paint, dripping on to the floor.'

Martha said, 'Perhaps Virginia simply enjoys goading her friend. Unkind of her.'

Rachel nodded. 'And very unwise. Provoking jealousy is a dangerous sport. Did you know Ffion is Welsh for foxglove? A plant whose flowers are delicate and pretty. And quite as deadly as hemlock.'

12

'Dr Seamus Doyle, I presume?'

Rachel Savernake had spotted a slightly built, round-shouldered figure emerging from Shepherd's Cottage and changed course to intercept him on the lane. The sky was a dark shade of sepia and the wind was getting up. She'd seized the opportunity to take a brisk walk along the cliffs before the heavens opened. Back in Gaunt House, she had a large and well-equipped gym, but while on the Lancashire coast, she was determined to keep fit enough to be able to enjoy Hetty's dinners with a clear conscience. Clear so far as her figure was concerned, at any rate.

The man was wearing his Sunday best, walking with his eyes fixed on the ground, as if hoping not to catch anyone's eye. When Rachel hailed him, his head jerked up. For a moment, he seemed to contemplate walking past her with barely a nod of acknowledgement. But there was something about Rachel that was impossible to ignore. Especially when she stood right in front of you.

'Ye… es.' Mechanically, he doffed his hat, revealing sparse brown hair turning grey at the temples. 'How do you do?'

'I'm Rachel Savernake. I've taken the bungalow down the road.'

She opted for a hearty tone, guessing that if she gushed as she had with Virginia, this little mouse of a man would run a mile. Perhaps he'd feel less alarmed by the jolly hockey sticks type. As Hetty liked to say, it's easier to catch flies with honey than vinegar.

'Oh yes?' He was evidently torn, wanting to get away, yet itching with curiosity. Surrendering to temptation, he scratched the itch. 'How… how do you know who I am?'

'I called on Miss Penrhos yesterday afternoon. The artist, don't you know? She mentioned you to me.'

'She did?'

'Yes, I was enquiring about my new neighbours. Always good to get acquainted, don't you think? I've arrived in these parts not knowing a blessed soul. She mentioned your name. I gather you're a medical man?'

'Retired,' he said hastily. 'Long retired.'

'Yours is such a fine profession. Dedicated to healing. And you see so much of human nature in the raw. Were you in practice in this part of the world?'

'It's a very long time since I last held a stethoscope,' he said as soon as he had the chance to get a word in edgeways. 'For many years, I was in South Africa.'

'Marvellous country,' Rachel pronounced. 'Not Jo'burg, by any chance? Cape Town? I once knew someone who—'

Interrupting with an unexpectedly decisive shake of the head, he said, 'I was many miles inland, in a tiny village. Very remote. You wouldn't have heard of it.'

'Sounds like a long, long way from Tipperary,' she said

with a roguish grin. 'Which part of the Emerald Isle do you hail from?'

'I spent longest in County Mayo,' he said. 'Off the beaten track. The middle of nowhere, really.'

'Sounds delightful! You obviously have a taste for out-of-the-way places. What brings you to this part of the world?'

'I'm recuperating from a long illness.' He looked this way and that, as if searching for an escape route. 'Now if you will excuse—'

'I can't imagine a better place to recuperate! Hemlock Bay is grand, don't you think? So very peaceful.' As she spoke, a faint rumble of thunder in the distance mocked her encomium, but she rattled on regardless. 'I was thrilled to meet Miss Penrhos. Her friend is rather quiet, I must say, but so very pretty. Have you met our other neighbours yet? Do you know the chap who lives in the manor house? I'm told his name is Carson.'

He flushed a deep red. Opening his mouth, he seemed about to fire an angry retort, but she saw him thinking better of it.

'As... as it happens, I'm on my way to church. I don't want to be late for the morning service.'

'Mustn't keep you!' Rachel boomed. 'Delighted to make your acquaintance, Dr Doyle. You must come round for tea tomorrow!'

Lifting his hat, he said, 'Good day to you, Miss Savernake.'

With that, he scuttled off down the lane. Feeling the first drops of rain on her cheeks, she contemplated his retreating back. What sins, she wondered, might the little man have to confess?

'I didn't believe a word he said,' Rachel said, after describing her encounter with Dr Seamus Doyle.

She and the Truemans were in the living room at the rear of the bungalow. Outside, the rain was teeming down. The roses were bending under the weight of water. They looked as miserable as bullied children.

'Why not?' Martha asked.

Rachel ticked off the points on her slim fingers. 'First, his accent slipped whenever he got nervous. If he's an Irishman, I'm the Queen of Sheba. Second, I doubt he's ever set foot in South Africa. He was obviously terrified at the prospect of my poking into his background, so he claimed he'd lived and worked in obscure places I was unlikely to know anything about. I'd say he comes from the south of England. Maybe London.'

'You think he really is a doctor?'

'Let's just say I wouldn't want to take anything he prescribed. I doubt he knows his arsenic from his embrocation.'

'Why do you think he's lying?'

'Why does anyone assume a false identity?' Rachel asked.

There was a thoughtful silence before Hetty coughed and said, 'Because they have something they don't want other people to know about.'

'Exactly. Something in their past or something they want to do. Or both.'

'Any idea what he's up to?' Martha asked. 'Is he a criminal on the run and lying low?'

Rachel's brow furrowed. 'Can you be on the run and lie low at the same time? Whether or not, I'm sure the last thing he fancies is a cup of tea and a chat. What interested me most was his reaction when I mentioned Carson. He just about managed to clamp his mouth shut, but his expression gave him away. He couldn't hide a look of sheer contempt. Perhaps Carson is simply another troublesome neighbour who stuck his oar in where it wasn't wanted. Whatever the truth, there's some history between them.'

'What do we know about Carson?' Cliff Trueman asked.

'Mrs Stones suggests he's the jealous type. And he must have a good head for business if he's persuaded Sir Harold Jackson to give him a share in the development company.'

'I rather liked his wife,' Martha said.

'You think the so-called doctor is smitten with her?' Trueman asked.

'I've no idea.' Rachel smiled. 'Wouldn't it be interesting to find out?'

'Who in their right mind loves to be beside the seaside?' Jacob gasped.

As Martha opened the front door of Bay View, he was trying to control a broken umbrella that had acquired a mind of its own in the wind. In this weather, the bungalow's location seemed lonely and exposed. Rain hammered down from charcoal clouds and the air was filled with the howls of the gale. Jacob was panting with exertion as he wiped the rain out of his eyes. Water was dripping off his hat and raincoat.

'I've seen drowned rats that looked more cheerful,' Martha said.

Grabbing hold of his skinny wrist, she yanked him inside and banged the wooden door shut on the storm. He pulled off his hat with a loud groan.

'Stop moaning,' she said. 'Yesterday was gorgeous. Sunlight gleaming on blue water and golden sands. I could feel my skin tanning. Such a pity you missed it.'

'That's summer over and done with,' he grumbled. 'Hope you made the most of your time lazing on a deckchair.'

'I wasn't entirely idle. I had my palm read and Bellamy tried to strangle me.'

He gaped at her. 'You're joking!'

She pointed to her neck. 'The marks are fading, but all ten of his fingers squeezed my throat. For a moment, I thought he was going to kill me.'

Aghast, he said, 'Good grief, are you all right?'

'Never better. With any luck, Bellamy is feeling very sore today. I kicked him hard in a very painful place.'

He shook his head in disbelief. 'You've only been here twenty-four hours and someone already tried to murder you. What on earth is going on?'

'All in good time, Jacob. Bellamy's frenzy was like this squall. Something and nothing.'

'You think so?'

'This storm feels like an April shower to anyone who grew up on Gaunt.'

'Remind me not to go there for my next holiday.'

He shrugged off his wet coat and she hung it on the hall stand before folding her arms and considering his dripping frame.

'You're drenched to the skin. Better take off your trousers as well. You don't want to catch a chill.'

Flushing, he said, 'Thanks, but I'll manage. I've already changed once in the hotel. Because the lane is so narrow, I was stupid enough to park in the lay-by down the road, instead of stopping at your gate. The storm worsened in the time it took me to run here. So much for the road sign saying *Welcome to Hemlock Bay*.'

'Pleased with your room?'

'They say it has a sea view. I can't even see the esplanade at present, the window panes are so wet and blurry. At least they left some chocolates on my pillow. A special treat, I thought, but apparently they give them to all the guests. No wonder a room costs so much. Glad the *Clarion* is paying, not me.'

Martha peered at him. 'Have you been scalped? I've never seen you with your hair so short.'

'Part of my disguise as Clarion Charlie.' He mustered a grin. 'Like the new look?'

'Don't let it make you feel self-conscious or embarrassed,' she said. 'With any luck, your hair will grow back again, thick and strong.'

He frowned. 'Don't you—?'

'Come and have a nice cup of tea. You'll soon be as right as… well, rain. Hetty's made chocolate cake. Behave yourself and she might give you a slice.'

Her prediction was spot on. It took more than vile weather to subdue Jacob for long. Once he had some tea and cake inside him he regaled Rachel and the Truemans with a lurid account of his drive up from London, making it sound as though he'd raced through a series of miniature Windermeres with the aplomb of a Malcolm Campbell.

'What do you make of Hemlock Bay?' he asked when he'd run out of anecdote. 'Stumbled across any murderers yet? Not counting The Great Hallemby. I hear he's already tried to strangle Martha.'

'All in a day's detective work,' Rachel said breezily. 'At least you can tell we haven't been idle. And I've just received an invitation, asking me to dinner with Sir Harold Jackson and his wife.'

Jacob whistled. 'Quick work. Here five minutes and already you're hobnobbing with the man who made Hemlock Bay what it is.'

'He's probably curious about who can afford the extortionate rent he charges for this bungalow.'

'Looks pleasant enough to me,' Jacob said. 'Dare I ask what you're paying?'

When she told him, he whistled even more loudly. 'I see what you mean. The least he can do in return is offer a little hospitality. Anyway, what have you all been up to?'

'We'll build the suspense by leaving Martha's tale of woe till the end,' Rachel said. 'Cliff, tell us about your friend from the Mermaid.'

Jacob listened to each of them in turn. When Martha described her experience in the fortune teller's hut, his face turned pale.

'That's terrible. He didn't strike me as the violent type. Sounds like you had a narrow escape.'

She shook her head. 'He attacked me in a panic. I bet he regrets it now. What bothers me is that I gave away that I knew his real name. I feel as if I've let you down.'

'Don't give it another thought. Rachel is right. Bellamy is as weak as dishwater. Shake his confidence, and he's more likely to give the game away. Whatever the game is.'

'Thanks.' She gave a shy smile and patted his hand. 'Now, what have you found out about the lad who jumped from the cliffs?'

'A chap I know on the *Liverpool Daily Post* came up trumps. He attended the inquest on Edward Hillman, whom everyone knew as Ted.'

'Excellent,' Rachel said. 'We're all ears.'

'Hillman was a pleasant young man. Intelligent, nice-looking, industrious. Well-mannered and quiet. After leaving school he went to work in the accounts department of the Mersey Docks and Harbour Company. He worked his way up the ladder and at a Christmas party thrown by the firm, he met the chief accountant's daughter. One thing led to another and last autumn the couple became engaged. The wedding was due to take place this summer. He was still living at home with his widowed mother and offered to take her on one last holiday before getting married.'

Rachel leaned forward. 'His young lady and her family didn't come along too?'

'Oh no. It was just Ted and Mrs Hillman. She was due to celebrate her sixty-fifth birthday the day after their arrival and he wanted to make it a special occasion. A kindly gesture on his part, and entirely typical. Everyone agreed he was a good son. He was also an only child – or at least he had been since two older brothers were killed in the war – and she was a doting mother in poor health. They came to Hemlock Bay.'

'Had they ever come here before?' Rachel asked.

'Apparently not. Mrs Hillman had a soft spot for Rhyl, but her son persuaded her to go up the coast for a change. Reckoned the air here would agree with her.'

'Where did they stay?'

'The Hemlock Hotel. An expensive choice, but Ted had just won on the pools and wanted to do his mother proud. She enjoyed her birthday, but that night she went down with a heavy cold that turned into a bout of bronchitis. They had to cut their trip short and after they got home, she struggled to recover. It didn't help that she detected a change in her son. People at the office noticed too. So did his fiancée, Monica. He became increasingly morose and short-tempered. Started making silly mistakes at work. Nobody could understand, it was so out of character. When Monica tried to get him to talk about whatever was wrong, he bit her head off. Even threatened to break off the engagement, though that would have landed him with a breach of promise suit. The following day, he didn't turn up at the office. No message, no explanation. Instead he drove up to Hemlock Bay. Several passers-by saw him wandering up and down these cliffs and said he seemed distraught. Nobody spoke to him. Eventually he found a suitable spot and threw himself over the edge.' Jacob paused. 'A hundred yards from this bungalow, at a guess.'

'How dreadfully sad,' Martha said. 'Did he leave a note?'

'Nothing. His death was a mystery to everyone. Including the coroner. Inevitably the verdict was suicide while the balance of his mind was disturbed.'

'Did anyone speak to his mother and find out exactly what happened here at Hemlock Bay?' Rachel asked.

Jacob shook his head. 'The consensus was that he'd had a good time here. His mother said he seemed in good heart, although she was poorly and not paying much attention. The coroner suggested that he came back to end it all because this was the scene of his last happy memories. According to my pal, people speculated that he changed his mind about marrying Monica and couldn't face up to the implications. It wasn't just a matter of losing a prospective wife. His job was in jeopardy, his whole career. The chief accountant would be incandescent about such brutal treatment of his beloved daughter. And if Ted was sacked by the Dock Company, he'd find it hard to get another position elsewhere.'

'I wonder,' Rachel said. 'Your friend in Liverpool sounds as though he has a knack for smelling out a story. Could you persuade him to talk to Mrs Hillman and try to find out what Ted got up to while she was in her sick bed at the hotel?'

'He always does his best to help,' Jacob said. 'However, it won't be possible this time, I'm afraid.'

Rachel gave him a quizzical look. 'Because…?'

'Because the wretched woman never got better. She died shortly after the inquest. Bronchial pneumonia.'

She nodded, as if a point had been proved. 'So much for the medicinal qualities of Hemlock Bay's air.'

As Hetty cleared the tea things away, Jacob wondered aloud about Virginia Penrhos's picture of a body stretched out over Mermaid's Grave.

'Do you think she foresaw his death?'

'Another premonition?' A touch of mockery sharpened Rachel's voice. 'I think one is plenty, never mind two. For a start, Edward Hillman didn't die in that precise spot.'

'A surrealist might not bother about details like that.'

Rachel shook her head. 'It's a mistake to think that surrealists don't care about accuracy. On the contrary, they are fascinated by what some call "the fury of precision". What intrigues me—'

She was interrupted by the shrilling of the telephone.

'Let me guess,' Jacob said. 'Virginia Penrhos wants you to sit for her.'

Rachel laughed. 'That would be fun. For me if not for Foxglove Morris. Actually, I'm expecting a call from Scotland Yard.'

'Who else?' he said, feigning a yawn of ennui.

'Feel free to eavesdrop,' she said.

'I need no second invitation.'

'Of course not, you're a journalist.' She lifted the receiver. 'Yes?'

'Miss Savernake?' Inspector Philip Oakes' voice was crisp yet civilised.

'Good afternoon, Inspector. Kind of you to spare me a few moments on a Sunday. But how many times have I asked you to call me Rachel?'

'Thank you... Rachel.' He didn't, she noticed, reciprocate by inviting her to address him by his Christian name. Stiff upper lips only softened so far, presumably. 'No trouble. Though I'm hoping that when I've answered your question, you may be prepared to answer one from me.'

'You've had some luck?' she said, taking care not to commit herself. 'Was McAtee in the police force?'

'More than that, once upon a time he was an up-and-coming sergeant in the Metropolitan Police.'

'A capable detective?'

'I never met him, but I'm told that if a good nose for crime and criminals is all it takes to be a good detective, he'd have made it to the top. Joe McAtee's trouble is that he cuts corners. He was happy to turn a blind eye to villainy if someone made it worth his while. In the end he was shown the door for taking bribes. But none of the charges could be made to stick, and he didn't wind up in chokey like some of his bent colleagues who weren't quite so smart.'

'Tell me more about him.'

'He had a common-law wife, but left home to live with a woman who was married to a burglar he'd put behind bars. When the cuckold got out of the nick, he and McAtee had a violent bust-up. Did I mention McAtee has a wicked temper? As well as fists that really carry a punch? At least one of the villains he beat up in the cells when forcing out a confession was never able to walk again.'

'Did the husband get his wife back?'

'Yes, but his left arm was so badly broken in the fight that he lost the use of it permanently.'

'I hope the marriage was worth it.'

'Three months later, his body was fished out of the Thames at Greenwich. Maybe he fell in after drinking himself into a stupor, maybe someone gave him a shove. Nothing could be proved. If he was murdered, the killer was never found. McAtee was questioned, but he produced a cast-iron alibi. Given by a bunch of fellow poker players.'

'How convenient. I suppose they were all decent, God-fearing souls?'

'Only one of them had been in prison, if that's what you're wondering, and all of them probably had good reason to do McAtee a favour.'

'Surprise, surprise. What did he do for money after leaving the police?'

'Set up as a private detective. In fairness, he's a good one.'

'You've not come across him personally?'

'No, but I'm told he'll take any job as long as it pays well. Investigating suspected thefts when the victims don't want to involve the police or our boys have given up because of a lack of leads. Spying on people to get evidence that will stand up in a divorce court. I'm told he's doing very well for himself.'

'Even in these straitened times?'

Rachel pictured the inspector shrugging at the other end of the line. 'The word is that he's never short of cash.'

'What about his business interests?'

'I can't help you there, Miss... um, Rachel.' He coughed. 'All I know is that recently he put his inquiry agency on the market. His nice little semi-detached in Wimbledon, too. Seems he's thinking of making a move up north.'

'To Hemlock Bay?'

'So it seems. I'd never even heard of the place until you called me.'

Rachel was pensive. 'Does he have any personal connections to this neighbourhood?'

'Said he fancied a change of scene, but Joe McAtee isn't given to whims. He has an eye for the main chance. I'll guarantee he's found a line of work that pays well.'

'Lucky man,' Rachel said. 'Thank you so much, Inspector. You've been an enormous help. When we get back to Gaunt House, you must come round for dinner and let us spoil you.'

'I'd enjoy that,' he said. 'Meanwhile, perhaps you can satisfy my curiosity. What makes you ask about McAtee?'

'Trueman bumped into him in the pub last night. He sounds like a braggart, but even with a few drinks inside him, he wasn't so stupid as to give away what he was up to.'

'Why does he interest you? And what brought you to Hemlock Bay in the first place?'

Rachel was amused. 'You're presuming, Inspector, that there is always a dark and sinister motive for my actions.'

'No offence,' he said, 'but that's my experience.'

'I'm not in the least offended,' she said lightly.

'And you're not answering my question, either.'

'Sorry, Inspector. I don't mean to be evasive.'

'Really?'

'Believe me, it's a long story.'

'With you… Rachel, it always is,' he said heavily. 'I never met anyone quite so… hard to pin down.'

'Thank you. I take that as a compliment.'

He grunted. 'To satisfy my curiosity, I've already checked and as far as I can tell, nobody has been murdered in Hemlock Bay for many a long year.'

'Long may that peaceful state of affairs continue.' Rachel's tone sharpened. 'My fear is that it won't.'

There was a pause while Oakes digested this. 'Who do you think is about to get murdered?'

'If only I knew.'

After replacing the receiver, Rachel turned to Jacob. 'Ready to metamorphose into Clarion Charlie?'

He frowned. 'We've put out a few teasers over the weekend, but the campaign begins in earnest tomorrow. My main aim is not to be spotted too quickly. I don't want Gomersall to insist I move on before I've had time to make sense of Bellamy's—'

He was interrupted by the piercing cry of the telephone. Rachel picked up the receiver.

'Yes?... Good afternoon, Doctor.' Her voice became coy. 'How absolutely lovely. Shall we say three o'clock?... Marvellous... Thank you so much. I do look forward to seeing you again. And you know where to come!'

When the call was over, she treated her friends to a dazzling smile. 'Wonders never cease. Doctor Doyle has accepted my invitation to come here for tea tomorrow.'

'Perhaps you underestimated his nerve,' Martha said.

Rachel laughed. 'Or overestimated his survival instincts.'

13

Basil Palmer's Journal

14 June

M urder isn't easy.

It has dawned on me why so many intelligent people finish up on the gallows, with their crimes pored over and their blunders analysed within the pages of *Notable British Trials*. The challenge, I've discovered, is to expect the unexpected – and then to handle things without giving oneself away.

I've done my utmost to learn from the misadventures of men who have something in common with me. Respectable, God-fearing individuals who were perfectly law-abiding until they found it necessary to kill a fellow human being.

Crippen is the fellow for whom I have greatest sympathy. A generous man whose kindly nature earned him the love of a good woman, even if regrettably she was not his wife. He made his share of mistakes, changing his story about Mrs Crippen's disappearance at the drop of a hat. It was foolish to allow his mistress to dress in his wife's favourite furs. Yet if it hadn't been for the inquisitiveness and persistence of busybodies in his social circle, he would have lived happily ever after. Instead, he was hanged, a fate I am determined to avoid. I refuse to give Louis Carson's ghost such satisfaction.

Major Armstrong had only himself to blame. To commit one successful poisoning is an achievement in itself. He should have rested on his laurels. To attempt to repeat his crime was inviting disaster. Inconceivable that I would do likewise. Once Carson is dead, I shall retire from murder.

Even Harold Greenwood blundered. His wife was poisoned, and I have no doubt he was responsible, but somehow he managed to secure an acquittal. The secret of his success was that he never panicked. He did, however, attract attention by marrying a much younger second wife shortly after disposing of her predecessor. There is no danger of my following his example. For me, there will never be any other woman than Alicia.

This is where I differ from the criminals. They wanted to get rid of their wives. What I long for is very different – to avenge the death of mine.

I keep urging myself to look on the bright side, but I confess to feeling daunted. Seeing Hooker Jackson again after so many years was a heart-stopping reminder of the risks I run. At least he lives on the far side of the resort. I shall do my utmost to keep out of his way.

I worry about my neighbours. Virginia Penrhos's powers of observation – for even a surrealist is presumably observant – trouble me. The old lighthouse is a perfect vantage point for a snooper.

The Savernake girl may also prove a threat. True, she is young and naïve, and I was able to brush away her questions. But did I fail to conceal my loathing of Carson when she mentioned his name? Looks can give one away as easily as incautious words.

A nosey young flibbertigibbet with time on her hands is the worst kind of nuisance. I don't wish to spend another moment in the girl's company, but her manner suggests she won't take no for an answer.

I must take the bull by the horns. Hence my acceptance of her invitation to tea. Perhaps I can turn her curiosity to my advantage.

Later

Time is not on my side. This chilling reality is becoming more obvious by the day. I have arranged to visit Miss Savernake tomorrow afternoon, but even if I shake off my inquisitive female neighbours, there is no guarantee that something else won't interfere with my plans.

Today's dismal weather deterred Louis Carson from taking his usual walk on the cliffs. His unwillingness to venture out on a wet evening typifies his cowardly nature, but narrows my options. No murderer wants to rely on the English climate, but I have no choice. I dare not dither.

As soon as the chance comes to kill him without being caught, I shall seize it.

15 June

Tea at Bay View was at best a qualified success. I was pleased by the ease with which I maintained the deception about my identity, but disheartened by news that further complicates my plans.

I arrived at the bungalow sniffling loudly and explained

that I was going down with a heavy cold. I made clear I was fulfilling a social obligation to call, but that my visit would be brief.

'What a shame!' Miss Savernake cried. 'Did you catch a chill when you went to church? The weather was so rotten yesterday. Thank goodness today is brighter. As it happens, you're in luck!'

'I am?' I asked in a hoarse whisper.

'My housekeeper keeps some marvellous home remedies. Take one of her powders, and you'll be raring to go in no time!'

In between hacking coughs, I reminded her that I was a doctor and quite able to deal with my symptoms.

'Oh yes, of course! I quite forgot you're a medical man.'

A glint in her eyes made my spine prickle with apprehension. Did she doubt my credentials? Then she smiled again, and I reproached myself for letting my imagination run away with me. When all is said and done, she is a genteel young filly, no doubt with limited experience of life. Why should she question my account of my past?

I'd established an excuse for saying as little as possible, while trying to discover how much they know about the Carsons. Was it too much to hope that I might learn something that would help me to remove my enemy?

The answer, unfortunately, was yes. The housemaid, a girl with a scarred cheek but otherwise handsome, has bumped into Carson's wife and found her most agreeable. She confirmed what McAtee's report said, that Mrs Carson helps her husband to look after the hotel staff. Typical of the man that he involves the wretched woman in his dubious activities. Alicia never worked and never wished to.

The Bay View ménage is peculiar. The maid is sister to Miss

Savernake's chauffeur, a hulking brute who didn't utter a word in my presence, and whose wife acts as housekeeper. They seem to be on remarkably familiar terms with their employer. I suppose her youth and naïveté means they can take liberties.

Miss Savernake herself remains, despite my cautious but repeated efforts to draw her out, peculiarly enigmatic. She has a knack of deflecting questions and although this is no doubt due to admirable modesty, I found it frustrating. Her dress sense is immaculate and, although I know little of women's fashion, I have met enough wives of wealthy clients to recognise the hallmarks of voguish Continental design. She is obviously worth a great deal of money, and I am surprised there is no sign of a young man in her life. She is attractive, if you like dark hair and a trim figure. Not that anyone could compare to dear Alicia and her golden tresses.

During a lull in the conversation, my hostess asked if I read that dreadful rag, the *Clarion*. The fervour of my denial seemed to amuse her. She told me about a publicity stunt that the newspaper has dreamed up. One of their reporters has arrived in Hemlock Bay and there is a generous cash prize for anyone who can identify the man and address him with the correct form of words.

'They call him Clarion Charlie!' the maid interjected. 'I went down to the beach earlier to see if I could spot him. Not that it will be easy to recognise him from the picture they printed in the paper. He's wearing a trilby and smoking a pipe. You can hardly see his face at all.'

'I expect he's horrid and ugly,' Miss Savernake said, with a disconsolate pout. 'Like something dreamed up by the Brothers Grimm.'

The maid was strangely entertained by this, but my reaction was one of irritation, coupled with foreboding.

It is now clear that I need to act at the very earliest opportunity. Not today; my nerves are simply not up to it. But, if the weather holds, tomorrow. The simple truth is that the longer I wait, the more difficulties I'm likely to encounter. The *Clarion* crams its columns with deplorable tosh, but its readership runs into millions. I envisage this absurd new competition prompting people to flock to Hemlock Bay in the hope of earning a reward. Money talks, but the last thing I need is to find the clifftop path filled with visitors in hot pursuit of an itinerant newspaperman.

Later

Disaster!

Just when I thought I had dealt with the obstacles to my plan to the best of my ability, and was readying myself for the decisive moment, something has occurred to stop me in my tracks.

McAtee is here. In Hemlock Bay. Even as I write the words, I can hardly believe my own eyes. Or my wretched luck.

But for my own regrettable curiosity, I would still be in blissful ignorance. However, immediately after my visit to Bay View, I saw Carson walk out through the gates of his home. I wondered if he'd brought forward his evening stroll on the cliff, but he turned in the direction of the resort.

In a split second, I decided to follow him, taking care not to attract his attention. I wasn't desperate to know his destination. I guessed he was heading to the Hemlock Hotel. If venturing further afield, he would have travelled by car.

The truth was that I'd become excited by the thought that sprang into my mind.

I am pursuing the man whose life I shall shortly bring to an end. And he doesn't have the faintest idea that he is about to die.

Reprehensible, perhaps, but I'd defy anyone who has suffered as I have suffered not to experience a savage delight in the knowledge that he is on the verge of achieving a form of wild justice.

Carson moved at a brisk pace. Initially I aimed to keep twenty yards behind him, but the gap between us increased until we reached the esplanade.

As I walked beside the low sea wall, it dawned on me that my impulsive pursuit had been an unwise act of self-indulgence. What if he spotted me? While there was no risk of him recognising me, I didn't wish to provoke his curiosity. As I come up behind him on the cliff path when about to do the deed, I need to take him unawares.

On reaching the Hemlock Hotel, he marched straight in. As I contemplated the hotel's revolving doors, a broad-shouldered fellow came out. At the same moment a young woman who was about to enter the hotel paused to allow him to step past her. He lifted his hat and gave a courteous nod before striding off in the direction of Hemlock Head. But his genial good manners were lost on me.

I recognised him with a stab of horror and disbelief. Joseph McAtee, whose report had brought me here, had come to Hemlock Bay.

Later

This is wretchedly bad luck. First Hooker Jackson and now McAtee! Fate is hurling endless obstacles into my path.

Try as I might, I cannot fathom why McAtee has turned up here. Can it be a mere coincidence? Naturally, I'd like to think so. It isn't impossible that, after tracing Carson to the Lancashire coast, he decided to spend a few days here, relaxing after his labours. Given the amount he charged for his services, he could afford to spend the whole summer on holiday.

But I can't help fearing that there is a more sinister explanation for his presence.

14

'You've been extremely helpful,' Rachel said into the telephone. 'I'm much obliged. And yes, please do send me your new catalogue as soon as it arrives in from the printers.'

She put down the receiver and returned to the living room, where Trueman and Martha were leafing through the *Daily Mail* and the *Clarion* respectively. Having ordered half a dozen newspapers, Rachel had risen at the crack of dawn so as to be outside the bungalow, planting geraniums in the window box, when the boy came to deliver them.

Young lads with their wits about them were a valuable source of information. They were also putty in the hands of an attractive and chatty woman a few years their senior. By the time Rachel let the boy go on his way, she'd learned as much about their new neighbours as she'd have gained from a week's surveillance.

She turned to Martha. 'What news of our friend the Mystery Man?'

'The *Clarion* can scarcely contain its excitement. Look at this.'

She held up the paper so they could see the full page feature headlined *Clarion Charlie Coming to Hemlock Bay!*

'*Can you spot our Mystery Man when he arrives in north England's swishest resort? This is a great opportunity for testing your powers of observation and deduction,*' Rachel read. 'I think that's pushing it, don't you?'

There was a large photograph of Jacob, taken in profile, with a trilby hat slung low on his head. Thanks to the brutality of his haircut, he appeared to be bald. He was wearing rimless spectacles and had a pipe clamped between his lips.

'His own mother wouldn't recognise him,' Trueman grunted.

'They certainly haven't flattered the poor lad,' Martha said. 'And that's not the only obstacle to winning the prize. People who spot him need to be word perfect.'

Rachel read the text. '*Give the right challenge! When you recognise our Mystery Man, present him with a copy of the* Clarion *and say, "You are Clarion Charlie, and I claim the handsome reward offered by the country's most popular newspaper!" If your challenge is correct, Clarion Charlie will immediately acknowledge it, but a single mistake will forfeit the prize.*'

'Anyone who accosts a perfect stranger and comes out with all that malarkey deserves more than a fiver,' Trueman muttered.

'What about that art dealer you were talking to?' Martha asked. 'Did you learn anything new?'

'Yes, I've pieced together the story of how Virginia became involved with Ffion. Virginia had a cousin called Nerys who was married to a leading theatrical producer, Miles Horne.'

'That name sounds familiar.'

'Yes, last spring he was involved in a sensational story

which made headlines in the popular press. Does Fifi Garcia ring a bell?'

Martha nodded. 'She was mixed up in it somehow.'

'Yes. And it turns out that Fifi Garcia was a stage name taken by Ffion Morris. She dreamed of making a career as a singer, but never got any further than a small part in the chorus of *Show Boat*. However, during its run at Drury Lane, she met Nerys and they became... very close.'

'They were lovers?'

Martha liked to call a spade a spade. Hetty gave a sceptical grunt.

'Yes. They went to enormous lengths to keep their relationship hush-hush. Unfortunately, Horne found out and created a dreadful scene. Not content with threatening a divorce, he made it clear he wouldn't rest until both women were destitute. Nerys Horne was a highly-strung woman at the best of times. The intimidation was too much for her and she drank a bottle of bleach.'

Martha made a face. 'A horrible way to go.'

'Yes, a shocking business. No wonder it's stuck in your mind. Nerys was a popular woman, while Horne was a short-tempered bully. You may remember that the adverse publicity after her death was so ruinous, he took an overdose of sleeping pills.'

'Quite a tragedy.'

'Fifi survived, but the scandal killed off her career. Such as it was. The only ray of light was that at the inquest on Nerys, she met Virginia. Over the years, Virginia has had many female companions, none of whom have lasted long. She was living with a French concert pianist, but in her own way, she's as fickle as her cousin. She fell head over heels for Ffion. Within a week of Nerys's funeral, the concert pianist was back in Paris and Ffion had moved in with Virginia.'

'Was Ffion equally smitten?' Martha asked. 'Or was she more interested in Virginia's money?'

'How cynical you are.'

'I spend too much time in your company, that's why.'

Rachel laughed. 'I always wanted to be a bad influence. As for Virginia, her father was a cotton broker and she inherited enough to live in style even before her paintings started to sell. Ffion's Aunt Bronwen was a reclusive spinster who had made her a generous allowance.'

'So she's not dependent on hand-outs from Virginia?'

'Unfortunately, the aunt was a puritanical conservative who was horrified by the scandal and cut off the allowance. For good measure, she summoned her solicitor and altered her will. Apart from a few minor legacies to servants, she bequeathed her entire estate to the Royal Society for the Prevention of Cruelty to Animals.'

'Wills can be changed. Some old people are constantly adding new codicils.'

'Gives them a sense of power,' her brother murmured.

Rachel nodded. 'I'm afraid the aunt dropped down dead of a heart attack before the ink was dry on her signature. The RSPCA profited to the extent of more than one hundred thousand pounds.'

Trueman whistled. 'As a Communist, would Ffion mind?'

'People who have met Ffion suspect her political principles are barely skin deep. Not that it matters in the short run, given that Virginia isn't short of cash. But life must be very difficult for Ffion. She lost the love of her life and her dreams are in tatters. Meanwhile, Virginia's artistic career is finally blossoming.'

'And if Virginia's roving eye turns elsewhere...' Martha suggested.

'Exactly. Ffion strikes me as neurotic and vulnerable. I suspect she's casting around to find some sort of meaning in life, and not having any success. If someone else supplants her in Virginia's affections, she'll also be looking for a new home and means of financial support. A marriage of convenience to a wealthy man would be one solution, but she hates men even more fervently than she despises capitalism. So her options may be limited.'

Martha considered. 'Is there a risk of her seeing you as a rival for Virginia's affections...?'

'When I joined them for tea, Virginia certainly did nothing to ease her fears. Quite the opposite. She likes playing games with people's emotions.'

'Watch out,' Trueman said. 'Sounds like Ffion Morris has a good motive to eliminate you.'

Rachel smiled. 'She's not the first to want me out of the way. No wonder she kept glowering. The newspaper boy says he's heard the two of them screaming at each other from behind closed doors.'

'So early in the morning?' Martha asked.

'Not a sign of a healthy relationship. Both women have a short fuse.'

'Might one of them turn violent?'

A shrug. 'Anything is possible.'

'Why did they move here? Did they hope to make a fresh start? Or is there more to it than that?'

'I keep coming back to the same question – why Hemlock Bay? Is that body on the rocks in her painting a clue?'

Trueman had been mulling things over. 'If Ffion and

Virginia's cousin kept their relationship so quiet,' he said slowly, 'how did Horne find out about it?'

'Good question,' Rachel said. 'And all the more interesting given that I've asked it myself, and nobody I've spoken to seems to know the answer.'

On his first morning in Hemlock Bay, Jacob took advantage of the improved weather to explore. Might as well enjoy mooching around the resort at his leisure before being forced to look at the world through unbecoming spectacles while sucking on a pipe. Martha had sketched two maps for him, one of the whole resort, the other of Hemlock Head, highlighting points of special interest.

As he ambled through Shore Gardens, he spied the unmistakable bulk of Trueman, striding away from the beach. The big man was clutching something in his shovel-like hand.

Jacob gave him a cheery wave. 'A very good morning to you! What have you got there?'

Trueman flourished a photograph for Jacob's inspection. A crisp image of him and Hetty, marching along the esplanade as if they owned the whole of Hemlock Bay.

'A walkie!' Jacob couldn't resist parading his knowledge of the professional lingo. 'Excellent. You both take a good picture.'

'Always full of flannel, aren't you? Anyway, Hetty will be pleased, even if she'd never admit it. You may think she hasn't got a sentimental bone in her body, but it isn't true.'

Jacob nodded. He was acutely aware that he was privileged to be granted these occasional glimpses of the human side of the curious ménage which had become a surrogate family to him. The true nature of Rachel's relationship with the Truemans still baffled him, but he'd learned to curb his itch to ask intrusive questions. They'd tell him what they wanted, when they wanted, and not before. He'd learned to break the habit of a lifetime and exercise patience.

Trueman looked towards the beach. Something had snagged his attention.

'What is it?' Jacob asked.

'The lad I mentioned, the barman at the Mermaid. He's looking at the photos right now.'

Jacob followed his gaze. The reflex man in khaki shorts was standing behind a little stall on the sand, displaying the snaps he'd taken over the past few days. A handful of people were congregated around the photographs. One of them was a skinny young fellow with freckles.

'The young chap who was exchanging coy glances with the sandy-haired golfer?'

For some reason, this individual interested Rachel. She'd asked Jacob to go to the pub this lunchtime and try to chum up with him. If Jacob pretended to be one of the idle rich, that might help the conversation to flow. More than that, she wouldn't say, and Jacob knew better than to demand information before she was ready to share it.

'That's the bloke.'

He and Trueman watched as the barman exchanged a few words with the photographer before moving away without making a purchase.

'I'm surprised a barman would be looking at a bunch of beach photographs. It's not as if he's on holiday himself.'

Trueman nodded, like a teacher encouraging a pupil as he gropes for the right answer. 'So?'

Jacob considered. 'So he's gone over there because he's

pally with the photographer. Two young chaps, both earning a few bob in the summer season, and they have a chinwag. Nothing unusual in that.' He paused. 'Is there?'

'It's all information, isn't it?'

The barman was crossing the esplanade now, no doubt on his way to work. Jacob checked his watch.

'I've got time to kill before I go to the pub for lunch. Thought I'd walk up to Hemlock Head before turning back.'

'Not venturing as far as the Sun and Air Garden?'

'Too shy to go in on my own. Maybe with friends?' Jacob grinned. 'If Rachel and Martha want to invite me along…?'

The big man said slowly, 'I wouldn't put anything past that pair.'

Jacob waited. He guessed there was more to come.

'You won't ever hurt them, will you?'

A vigorous shake of the head. 'Never.'

'Because if you did,' Trueman said softly, 'I'd make you regret it to the end of your days.'

Jacob arrived at the Mermaid as the ornate clock on a tower halfway down High Street struck twelve noon. He repaired to the Select Bar for a pork pie and a pint.

Stationing himself at the bar, he breathed in the beer fumes while waiting to be served. Behind the counter was the freckle-faced barman. Jacob invited him to have a drink, and pressed half a crown into his damp palm.

'Keep the change.'

'Thanks very much for your kindness, sir.' His smile was broad, his manner full of boyish charm. 'Extremely generous of you.'

Jacob rested his elbows on the oak counter. 'The name's Jake.'

'Nice to meet you, Jake. I'm Laurence, but my pals call me Laurie.'

'Cheers, Laurie.' As he raised his tankard, Jacob glanced around. The pub was busy but nobody was taking any notice of them. 'Good place to work?'

'Can't complain,' the boy said, smoothing his hair. 'You meet some interesting people.'

'I bet you do. Live on the premises?'

'They've given me a cubbyhole on the top floor.' A wry smile. 'All right, but barely room to swing a cat in. Let alone do anything much more exciting. This isn't exactly the Hemlock Hotel.'

'Yes, the Hemlock's fine as far as comfort goes.' Jacob loosened his collar. 'A bit stuffy for me, though, that's why I came here.'

The lad considered him. 'You're staying there?'

'For my sins,' Jacob said breezily.

'Very nice. Not that I believe you're the sinful sort. You look like a very respectable gent to me.'

'Oh, well, we all have to let our hair down once in a while, don't you think? After all, this is the seaside.'

'All work and no play makes Jake a dull boy, eh?'

Jacob rewarded the barman's wit with an appreciative snigger.

'You never said a truer word.'

'What do you do, then?'

'Odds and ends,' Jacob's shoulders gave a modest twitch. 'Actually, I don't have a proper job. To tell you the truth, I've led a charmed life. Or so my dear mama used to say. I don't need to sweat night and day to keep body and soul together.'

The barman's eyebrows lifted. 'Lucky you. Winning ticket on the Irish Sweep, was it?'

'Not me.' Jacob winked. 'Though I do enjoy a flutter when I get the chance.'

'Do you now?'

The young man pulled a few more pints for his customers before drifting back to where Jacob was drinking.

'Member of the landed gentry, are you?'

'Not me, Laurie. My old man owned a woollen mill in Bradford. That's how he made his pile. Not that it did him much good. Dropped dead of a heart attack before he was fifty.'

'Sorry to hear that.'

'Don't worry. He was in bed with his secretary at the time, so you could say it served him right.'

The barman chortled. 'Nice way to go, eh?'

'If you like that sort of thing. Personally, I think it's sordid. The girl was the brassy type and poor Mama never got over the shock. She's always been religious and now she's taken up with some hellfire crowd.' Jacob mimicked a street preacher. 'Repent now, or your sins will find you out!'

'Better make sure you don't go around sinning, then.'

Jacob smirked. 'I've decided to concentrate on not getting found out.'

The boy laughed. 'On your own here, then, Jake? Or have you brought a lady friend?'

'Not me. Girls nowadays are just out for what they can get from a chap. Thought I'd enjoy a few days by the sea and discover what pleasures Hemlock Bay has to offer.'

'We've got all sorts here. Everything from open-air dancing to a nudist camp. Depends what you fancy.'

Jacob returned the barman's smile. 'Actually, I'm in the mood for adventure.'

★

'How did it go, Mystery Man?' Rachel asked.

'You were right,' Jacob said, adding cheekily, 'For once.'

'Laurence Bishop has a penchant for men with money?'

'Yes. Whether he's simply looking for a rich sugar daddy to pamper him, or something more sinister is going on, I can't say.'

A gull keened overhead. She'd waited for him in a shelter on Hemlock Heights. He joined her on the covered bench as if on a momentary impulse.

After giving a brief résumé of his conversation with Laurie at the Mermaid, he described the young man's encounter with the beach photographer.

'Interesting,' she murmured. 'So you made a new pal?'

'I promised to drop in again towards closing time. Laurie gave me the impression he couldn't wait. If it's not pouring down, we might go for a walk on the front.'

'How romantic. The pair of you can lick your Raspberry Ripples under the stars.' She consulted her watch. 'I'd better get back to the bungalow to help Martha prepare for tea with Dr Doyle. Not that I believe he is a doctor.'

'What is the man playing at, do you think?'

'Nothing to do with medicine. Beyond that, I'm guessing. He's not short of money and he's not come here to improve his social life. I almost had to poke him in the eye before he agreed to drop in. Whatever his motives, he's up to something, and it must be important. His false identity is too transparent for him to have made a career out of crime. My guess is that as a general rule he's hopelessly strait-laced.'

'You don't think he has any connection with any of the other people who have turned up here? The artist and her friend? Joe McAtee? The Great Hallemby?'

'Too soon to say.' She smiled. 'Perhaps you'll find out more when you consult your other new chum, the fortune teller.'

Jacob wandered around Paradise for half an hour, filling his lungs with the smell of fish and chips and trying not to be deafened by the screams of overexcited children. He was curious about Winnie, the woman in Gareth Bellamy's life, and wondered if she'd agree to talk about him. But the deckchairs in front of the puppet theatre were empty. A sign said Skeleton Sue would not be appearing in any shows today, 'owing to a family indisposition'.

An interesting euphemism. Martha said she'd scratched Bellamy's face violently enough to leave some damage. Presumably this meant the fortune teller had a lot of explaining to do as soon as his beloved saw the scratches. Given that she was – if Bellamy was to be believed – fiercely jealous, Jacob wondered how he'd allayed any suspicion that he'd been attacked by an angry woman. Someone he'd pestered beyond endurance, perhaps. If the scratches had caused a rift between the couple, Winnie might be willing to speak freely about Bellamy. Perhaps she'd cast a light on whatever lay behind his so-called premonition about murder.

But she was nowhere to be found. He came across an elderly gardener who was trimming the lawn edges around a nearby flower bed and asked if he knew where she might be.

'Winnie Lescott?' The gardener spat on the ground, as if to help him think. 'Nah. I keep my distance from that one. Not like some I could mention. If you've any sense, you'll give her a wide berth. Hard as nails and mouth like a sewer. It's the foreign blood, y'know.'

Not the most glowing testimonial. Skeleton Sue's admirers

would be shocked to hear it, but Jacob wasn't surprised. He couldn't see Bellamy enjoying much success with the ladies, however credulous they were. If Winnie was a termagant, perhaps they were well suited.

He made his way to the fortune teller's hut and rang the bell, but there was no answer. Bellamy was probably reading someone's palm. He went to inspect the hall of mirrors and enjoyed pulling demented faces in front of the glass. After tiring of that, he succumbed to the temptation to ascertain exactly what the butler had seen. Half an hour later, he returned to the hut. Again he rang the bell. Again there was no reply.

Bellamy must be doing a roaring trade. Jacob imagined people earnestly asking him whether they would manage to spot Clarion Charlie. Or perhaps they simply wanted to be told they'd meet the love of their life before their annual break by the sea sped to an end.

This time he decided to keep a watchful eye on the hut. As soon as Bellamy's latest client emerged, he'd seize his chance and march in through the door before anyone beat him to it.

He loitered beside the rhododendrons. In this tranquil enclave, the spreading bushes were dense enough to deaden the noise from the rest of the grounds. As he inhaled the pleasing lemony fragrance from a cluster of bell-shaped white flowers, he was almost able to persuade himself that he had indeed found Paradise.

From here he had a direct view of the entrance to the hut. During a quick reconnaissance, he'd noticed a padlocked door at the back of the hut. Yet even if Bellamy used that for a quick exit, he'd come into view as soon as he moved away from the building. Surely he wouldn't crawl through that small gap in the hedge into the Sun and Air Garden? Presumably he'd return to the main park via the network of pathways.

As Jacob waited, he ran through his meeting with Bellamy in his mind. The more he thought about it, the less plausible that bizarre premonition sounded. Yet if it was a figment of the man's imagination, why bother the police and the *Clarion* with it? And why seem disconcerted when Jacob promised to raise the matter with Gomersall?

Minutes ticked by. Jacob was easily bored and he soon tired of waiting. He convinced himself that if he waited until midnight he'd see nothing more, because the fortune teller wasn't inside. Perhaps he wasn't working today. Had he gone off somewhere with Winnie, hoping to attempt a reconciliation after a quarrel?

If so, was it worth taking a look inside the hut to see if there was any clue as to what Bellamy was really up to?

As usual with Jacob, the thought was father to the deed. He marched up to the hut, rang the bell and, after a short precautionary wait, stepped inside.

Martha had given a vivid description of the interior of The Great Hallemby's lair. It was dark in the antechamber and he took a moment to allow his eyes to adjust. As he moved forward, he smelled the incense and candle wax. So someone had been here quite recently.

Swishing aside the velvet curtains with a cavalier's flourish, he marched into the small room at the back.

The Great Hallemby had been waiting there all the time. His body was sprawled on the floor, close to an upturned table and a scarlet fez. Blood leaked on to the rush matting from a terrible wound in his temple. A few inches away was the murder weapon, streaked with dark stains.

Gareth Bellamy had been battered to death with his own crystal ball.

15

'So what did you make of our visitor?' Martha asked as the clock on the living room mantelpiece struck five.

'Apart from the fact that he isn't suffering from a cold, isn't a doctor, and isn't called Doyle?' Rachel said. 'He definitely has mischief in mind. Look at the determined way he tried to pump me, in between those hopeless attempts to pretend he had a genuine cough.'

'He didn't have any joy questioning you.'

'Whatever he is, he's certainly not a barrister. The man couldn't cross-examine a child with sticky fingers and smears of chocolate all over its mouth. Perhaps he's more at home with numbers than people. A banker, an actuary. Possibly an accountant.'

'He looked unhappy when I mentioned Clarion Charlie.'

'Yes, he's obviously desperate for peace and quiet, that's why he's rented one of the properties furthest from the main resort. The publicity about Jacob's Mystery Man stunt will bring crowds of people flocking into the resort, and he's afraid they may interfere with his plans.'

'Whatever they are.'

'Yes, he's still keeping a few cards close to his chest.'

In the hall, the telephone rang and Martha skipped away to answer it.

'Rachel!' she called through the open door. 'Jacob needs to speak to you.'

Rachel got to her feet. 'Don't tell me he's managed to worm out the truth behind the sinister premonition?'

Martha's expression was bleak. 'Bellamy has been murdered. Smashed over the head with a crystal ball.'

Hetty said what they were all thinking.

'None of us predicted this.'

Trueman drove Rachel to Hemlock Hall. The Jacksons had bidden her for six thirty. It was a short journey from the bungalow but, as they approached the promontory at the far end of the esplanade, their progress was slowed by a hubbub outside the gates of the amusement park. The gates were closed and an ambulance and police car were stationed nearby. Hundreds of people milled outside, noisy with excited bewilderment. A hapless constable was trying to persuade everyone to disperse, but the crowd kept growing. Nobody wanted to miss the chance of being a bystander at a tragedy. Out of a clear blue sky, death had come to Paradise.

'I suppose the police are hunting a Mystery Man,' Rachel said. 'Let's hope they don't arrest Jacob.'

'I wouldn't put it past him to finish up in clink.'

Rachel smiled. 'He swore to me that he'd restrained the urge to pick up the murder weapon. When he rang off, he was about to call Gomersall. There's nothing he loves more than telling the *Clarion* to hold the front page.'

Trueman steered the Phantom past the throng and turned into the long, sweeping drive of the Jacksons' home.

'This trouble at Hemlock Bay,' he said. 'The Hillman boy's suicide. The weird painting. A meek little man pretending to be a doctor and an inquiry agent with a history of corruption. A premonition of a murder and the killing of a fortune teller. Sir Harold Jackson is supposedly the man who pulls the strings around here. Do you reckon he is behind it all?'

'I wonder,' she said. 'That's one of the reasons why I was eager to accept his kind invitation. But he's done very well for himself over the years. Why would he suddenly orchestrate all this mayhem? Isn't it the last thing someone in his shoes would do? The Jacksons have everything they could wish for. Why court disaster?'

They pulled up outside a gabled porte cochère. The manor house was suitably imposing, brick-built to a late Georgian design, obviously renovated and maintained to the highest standards.

'Knowing you,' Trueman said, 'you'll soon find out.'

'I'm afraid my husband will be a little late this evening,' Lady Jackson said in a warm drawl as she escorted Rachel into the sitting room. She was smoking a cigarette in a holder apparently made of solid gold. The furnishings and decor supplied ample evidence that the Jacksons had sophisticated taste and the funds to indulge it. 'He was called off the golf course to deal with... an unfortunate incident. Can I offer you a cigarette? It's a Marlboro, my favourite brand. "Red tips to match your pretty lips," you know?'

'Thank you, but I don't smoke.'

'A shame, but young women are so often indoctrinated into

believing it's a masculine pleasure that should be denied to the fair sex. Personally, I deplore the way so many busybodies discriminate against us.'

Rachel admired her sturdy feminism, although she was tempted to say that she hated the taste or smell of cigarettes. Perhaps because the late Judge Savernake had smoked like a chimney. But this wasn't the moment to allow herself to be distracted.

'I saw people swarming outside the gates to Paradise. Nothing is seriously amiss, I hope?'

Her hostess, very dark and very thin, was wearing an evening gown of lace and tulle with a ruffled skirt. Rachel recognised the hallmarks of Chanel. Yet for all her elegance and the sophistication of her make-up, Sadie Jackson looked gaunt.

In a sombre tone she said, 'I'm afraid it couldn't be much more serious. A man has been found dead and it looks as if he was murdered.'

Rachel put her hand to her mouth, but resisted the temptation to overindulge in histrionics. Gushing might lure someone as eccentric as Virginia Penrhos or as naïve as Dr Doyle into lowering their guard, but the Jacksons would be shrewd enough to see through an excess of blather.

'My goodness, how shocking. Not one of the holidaymakers?'

A shake of the head. 'The victim worked at the park. A man called Bellamy.'

'How sad. Did you know him?'

'I only met him once.' Sadie Jackson compressed her lips. 'The man was a fortune teller. He plied his trade as The Great Hallemby.'

'Fascinating!'

'That was my reaction when he arrived in Hemlock Bay. I thought it would be amusing to have my palm read.'

Rachel studied the older woman's expression. 'Do I gather the reading wasn't a success?'

'The man was a fraud.' Sadie Jackson frowned, as if dismayed by her own credulity. 'Sorry, I don't mean to be unkind. At the time, paying him a visit seemed like harmless fun. He assured me and my family of a long and healthy life.'

Rachel waited.

'A week later, I went for a routine medical examination. Doctor Sowden said I was as sound as a bell, but I was worried by a persistent cough and so I persuaded him to seek a second opinion. He referred me to a Harley Street specialist, who found a tumour had reached an advanced stage,' Sadie Jackson said. 'I spent my forty-fifth birthday undergoing an operation to remove one of my lungs.'

'I'm so sorry to hear that.'

A wan smile. 'I should thank my lucky stars that I survived. The same disease killed my mother. In those days it was rare and seldom diagnosed until it was too late.'

'How dreadful.'

Sadie Jackson's eyes were misty, as if she'd drifted far away. 'Birthdays are bad news in my family. Mom died on my sixteenth. As if that wasn't enough, a fortnight after my operation, our older son – both our boys are away at school – was seriously injured. A freak accident, while Bobby was playing rugby. A sport he loves, just like his father. For weeks it looked as though he'd never walk again. He's recovering, thank heaven, but he'll limp like an old man for the rest of his life. And would you believe it, the accident happened on Bobby's thirteenth birthday. Unlucky, huh?'

On a large mahogany sideboard stood half a dozen family

photographs in silver frames. Several showed two young boys, strongly built for their age, laughing for the camera. In one shot, the older son, wearing a striped rugby shirt and shorts, stood next to his proud father. The likeness was unmistakable.

Rachel bowed her head. 'I'm so sorry.'

'Wrong of me to blame the fortune teller, isn't it? Unfair. The cancer, the accident, they came out of the blue. But I was angry with him. It was as if by misleading me, somehow he'd tempted fate and ruined my life. The good news he invented meant I had to be taught a lesson.'

'Human nature,' Rachel said softly.

'Foolish, though. I'm not proud of myself, believe me. I like to think I'm strong, but for ages I was terrified about what would happen next. Disasters so often come in threes, don't they? Or is that just another piece of nonsense, like reading palms?'

'It's so hard to see what lies ahead for any of us,' Rachel said.

'Maybe Bellamy's own murder is the third calamity. A sensational crime can ruin a thriving tourist trade. Adverse publicity deters holidaymakers, especially when money is tight. I only hope the police soon solve the crime.'

During their conversation, Sadie Jackson had seemed almost to be speaking to herself, as if Bellamy's death had knocked her sideways. Suddenly, she pulled herself together.

'I'm sorry, Miss Savernake, you must forgive me. You've caught me at a bad time, but that's no excuse for neglecting my duties as a hostess. I shouldn't be burdening you with our personal misfortunes.'

'Please don't dream of apologising, Lady Jackson. You've had a harrowing time, and I'd have understood if you'd cancelled my invitation after this latest appalling tragedy.'

'Not at all, I'm delighted to meet you. Dinner with a charming guest is the best possible way to put aside this wretched business for an hour or two. We love offering hospitality to people who take summer tenancies of the properties over at Hemlock Heights. We want them to feel welcome. In fact, we invited one of your neighbours to join us this evening, but unfortunately he sent word that he is indisposed.'

'Oh really?'

'He's a doctor, and he lives in Shepherd's Cottage.'

'Dr Doyle? Yes, we've met.' Rachel smiled. 'He did have a bad cough, poor soul.'

'Glad to hear he wasn't simply avoiding our company. I did wonder. His reply was brusque, rather rude. At least he should know what medicine to take for a cure.' There was a touch of mockery in her voice. 'May I take you on a tour of the house while we wait for my husband?'

'That would be lovely.'

'My pleasure. We're so proud of the place. It's very precious to me. As a callow American, I can't get over the fact that I'm living in a house that's three hundred years old. Not that it's recognisable from the ruin we bought at the end of the war.'

'You've transformed the whole town, not just the Hall.'

Sadie laughed. 'Hemlock Bay was a collection of scattered cottages and a couple of beaches when we arrived.'

'What brought you here?'

'Harold and I were desperate to get away from it all. We were luckier than most, because he'd got through the war without a scratch and we had plenty of money to invest. Harold dreamed of creating somewhere special for people of discernment.' She gave an apologetic laugh. 'Forgive me, I sound like an advertising brochure.'

'Please go on. I'm fascinated.'

'We drove over here one day. A diversion while we were touring in the Yorkshire Dales. The new bridge had been built and Harold spotted an opportunity. He felt the place had potential as a seaside resort, but it would take all our capital to make it a big success. Thank the Lord, I trusted his judgment. Land was dirt cheap and so was labour. So we took the plunge and we've never had a moment's regret since. Watching a dream become reality. Building the hotel, converting the lighthouse, developing Paradise...'

Her voice trailed away, and Rachel guessed that she'd remembered the death of Gareth Bellamy.

'Was the Sun and Air Garden part of your dream?'

Sadie Jackson looked her in the eye. 'Can you keep a secret?'

Rachel's expression was demure. 'Cross my heart and hope to die.'

'I trust my instinct, as well as Harold's. I feel I can rely on your discretion, Miss Savernake.'

'Please call me Rachel.'

'And I'm Sadie.' The older woman laughed. 'I've never got used to British formality. Or the title. Lady Sadie! Sounds like something from a nursery rhyme or a bawdy song you hear in pubs.'

Rachel giggled. There was something wry and self-deprecating about her hostess that she found attractive. Despite the woman's wealth and social standing, she hadn't lost her humanity.

'Here goes.' Sadie took a breath. 'Harold and I are nudists. We were one of the first couples to spend a weekend at Spielplatz in Hertfordshire when it opened two years ago. The idea that nudism is somehow immoral or uncivilised is repugnant to both of us. We always dreamed of creating our own private place to enjoy nature, that's why Harold never developed the land between Hemlock Head and this house. The Sun and Air Garden embodies our beliefs.'

'Weather permitting, of course?'

Sadie's face creased with amusement. 'We're not so fanatical that we're happy to suffer frostbite. Lancashire isn't San Diego. We created a place to enjoy simple pleasures, not to suffer cruel and unusual punishment.'

'I'd no idea the Sun and Air Garden represented some form of crusade.'

'We're giving more people the chance to live as nature intended. To realise that we're not cranks or cultists, as some newspapers like to suggest. That's why we haven't broadcast our personal views. Bear in mind, most of our money is still tied up in Hemlock Bay. Harold's knighthood binds us even more closely to the establishment. Over the years, the press has been good to us and given the resort some wonderful publicity. But they can turn against you in a flash. The popular prints are the worst. They'd betray their nearest and dearest to sell a few more newspapers. I wouldn't trust some of them an inch.'

'You're thinking of the *Clarion*?' Rachel suggested mischievously.

'Dreadful, aren't they? Though we're delighted by their latest initiative. Clarion Charlie, a sort of Lobby Lud character, is coming to Hemlock Bay.'

'That should draw the crowds.'

Sadie Jackson's smile faded. 'This murder will drown out everything else. I only hope the police don't upset innocent holidaymakers.'

'I shall have my alibi ready for inspection,' Rachel said

lightly. 'Fortunately, I've been at Bay View most of the day, and the servants can vouch for me.'

'I spent this afternoon resting in the garden, sipping lemonade and then having tea. Doctor Sowden assured me I'll live to be a hundred, but I still lack energy.'

'It's very good of you to take the trouble to invite me here. Are you sure it's not too much…?'

Her hostess raised a hand. 'Please don't worry. I never meant to suggest I was too tired to entertain you. Your visit is very welcome and the staff do all the hard work. Before I take you on a tour, may I tempt you with a glass of sherry? Harold recently acquired a cask of amontillado. I'm no expert, but I must say it's exquisitely smooth to taste.'

'I find it impossible to resist temptation,' Rachel said gaily. 'Even though I've read my Edgar Allan Poe.'

Sadie Jackson hesitated before bursting into laughter. For the first time since Rachel's arrival, she seemed entirely at ease.

'Me too. But your teeth can stop chattering, Rachel, there's nothing to fear. We don't have catacombs and I've no intention of walling you up in the cellar.'

16

'Hillman?' Sir Harold Jackson frowned. 'The boy who killed himself?'

Since Rachel's host had returned from the scene of the crime, the conversation had ranged widely. By tacit consent they had steered away from the subject of murder until the main course, a magnificent chateaubriand, had been washed down with a first-rate claret. The Jacksons had waxed lyrical about the charms of Hemlock Bay and in return Rachel gave them a highly selective account of her life in London. When they asked what had brought her to the resort, she said a distant relative called Edward Hillman had recommended her to come here.

'That's right. It was very sad.'

'And inexplicable,' Sadie Jackson murmured. 'To be so depressed that you feel you can't go on must be awful.'

'He obviously loved Hemlock Bay,' Rachel said.

'At least that is a small consolation, I suppose. Were you and he close?'

'I'm afraid not. His death was a complete mystery. Rather like this terrible business with the fortune teller.'

'Rotten show.' Sir Harold put down his knife and fork. 'The fellow was bashed over the head with his own crystal ball.'

'I feel so sorry for the poor soul who found the body,' Sadie said. 'Such a horrific experience. Enough to scar anyone for life. Don't you think so, honey?'

'You can spare your sympathy, my dear. The person in question is a journalist. Name of Flint. A reporter with the *Clarion*, believe it or not.'

His wife stared at him. 'Something to do with this Clarion Charlie campaign?'

'Supposedly, he's here on holiday.'

'But why in Hemlock Bay? Surely he didn't just stumble upon the body by chance? A fortune teller bludgeoned to death with his own crystal ball? It's crazy, the story of a lifetime. Did he have a tip-off?'

'Not as far as I know. However, I presume Inspector Young didn't tell me everything.'

'He's in charge of the investigation?'

'Yes.' A sigh. 'I know him in my capacity as chair of the bench. Not the sharpest brain, I'm afraid. He'll find this case taxing.'

'Is Flint a suspect?' Sadie considered. 'Maybe he battered Bellamy to death in a fit of rage and then covered up his crime by pretending he discovered the corpse.'

'The police haven't arrested him,' Sir Harold said. 'On the contrary, he's thrilled to have stolen a march on his rivals in Fleet Street and he's taking full advantage. Buzzing around like a gadfly, questioning all and sundry.'

'Are the police allowing him to behave like this?' his wife asked.

'Oh, he's got the gift of the gab. Young is eating out of his hand.'

Sadie shook her head sorrowfully. 'The man is probably desperate to see his name in the papers.'

'I had the bad luck to bump into Flint as I finished talking to Young. Believe it or not, the impudent young pup had the brass neck to ask for an exclusive interview.'

His wife frowned. 'I hope you didn't say yes.'

A pink tinge came to his cheeks. 'I did speak to him.'

'Harold! It's one thing to court the press when we're seeking a free advertisement. But with a tragedy like this...'

'Flint is a cocksure young fellow. If I gave him the cold shoulder, he'd fill his column with sly innuendoes at our expense. It could be very damaging to the resort's reputation. I must admit, I'd almost forgotten the tragic death of that poor fellow Hillman, but I suppose the press may rake over the coals again. And remember the fuss that papers like the *Witness* made when we opened the Sun and Air Garden?'

Sadie murmured, 'Actually, I've got a confession of my own. I told Miss... I mean, Rachel about our interest in... healthy living.'

'Ah.' Her husband raised his eyebrows. 'You'll keep mum, Miss Savernake?'

'You can depend on me.' Rachel wore her butter-wouldn't-melt expression. 'And I hope you'll call me Rachel, too... Sir Harold.'

Smiling, he said, 'Harold, please. Neither of us cares for stuffy conventions, as you've gathered. As for Flint, it made sense to give him my point of view before his imagination ran away with him.'

'I suppose you're right, honey,' Sadie said, 'though he'll twist your words to make a more exciting story.'

'I took the precaution of asking Louis Carson to join us.'

Sadie raised her eyebrows. 'He was at Hemlock Head?'

'Not at the time of the murder. He and his wife have been in the hotel all day. The conservatory roof sprang another leak in the heavy rain on Sunday and, among other things, he was supervising the emergency repairs. When he heard the news, Carson rushed round to see if there was anything he could do to help.'

'Decent of him.' But Sadie sounded sceptical. 'Did Flint interview him too?'

'Whatever you may think of the man, Carson is as sharp as a tack. He and I acted as witnesses for each other and he made it clear to Flint that if I was misrepresented in any way, he'd live to regret it. Of course, he expressed himself in his silkiest manner.'

'Of course.' Sadie drained her glass. 'I don't wish to be unkind, honey, but you don't think the culprit might be one of Bellamy's dissatisfied customers?'

He glanced at Rachel. 'My wife has told you about her encounter with The Great Hallemby?'

'I was sorry to hear about the troubles you've endured.'

'Ah, well. "Into each life some rain must fall." Isn't that Longfellow?' He finished his claret. 'We've enjoyed great good fortune in this family, Miss Savernake. One can't expect everything to keep going swimmingly forever. I hate to sound selfish, but Bellamy's death came as a blow to morale as well as a dreadful shock. The last thing you want in a seaside resort is any suggestion that there's a murderer on the loose. Bad for business. Thankfully, it looks as if Young will soon be in a position to make an arrest.'

Rachel's eyes widened. 'Really?'

The conversation paused as the waiter came in to clear the plates and replenish their glasses. Once the door closed behind him, Harold Jackson drank some more wine and leaned over the table.

'I can speak off the record? You are the daughter of a judge, after all. You understand the importance of keeping certain matters confidential.'

'Judge Savernake was a great one for secrets.' Rachel ran a slim finger over the rim of her glass, but didn't raise it to her lips. The Jacksons were drinking freely and, although she had a good head for alcohol, she had no intention of keeping pace with them. 'Naturally I'm curious. If you feel able to share some information, I shan't breathe a word.'

Except to the Truemans, she thought. And possibly Jacob, provided he behaves himself.

He nodded. 'The prime suspect is Bellamy's lady friend. Winnie Lescott.'

'*Crime passionnel*?' Sadie asked.

'Apparently, Bellamy got mixed up with some other woman who scratched his face. Made a mess of his looks. Not that he was Rudolph Valentino to start with, God rest his soul. The Lescott girl took umbrage, and the more vehemently Bellamy protested his innocence, the angrier she became.'

'How sad.'

'Indeed.' He turned to Rachel. 'Winnie helps her father with the puppet show. One of the biggest draws in Paradise over the past three summer seasons. Ron Lescott is the salt of the earth, but his daughter's a rum one.' He coughed. 'Matter of fact, she isn't white. Ron met her late mother in South Africa during the Boer War. Fine figure of a woman, Petronella, but temperamental. She died of a stroke shortly after they came to Hemlock Bay, so Winnie had to take her place. Good head for business, but a real firebrand. She's fallen out with almost everyone who works in Paradise. If it wasn't for Ron's popularity, we'd have asked her to leave.'

Rachel considered. 'So the police theory is that Winnie and Bellamy had a violent quarrel and she hit him over the head with his own crystal ball?'

'There's no doubt they had a heated row. Several witnesses heard them ranting at each other. Bellamy claimed a client was upset by a pessimistic reading and raked him down the cheeks with her nails, but Winnie didn't believe him. She raved about what she'd do to him if she found he was... um, misbehaving with another woman.'

'Has Inspector Young arrested her?' Sadie asked.

Harold Jackson shook his head. 'The woman has vanished. First thing this morning, she told her father she wouldn't be able to help with the puppet show. He had to cancel the performances. When he looked for her later, she was nowhere to be found.'

'So the police are in hot pursuit?'

'She has a head start, but I can't imagine she'll get far.' He sighed. 'I only hope she hasn't done something foolish, like throwing herself off a cliff.'

As she savoured the mint chocolate accompanying her after-dinner coffee, Rachel considered the Jacksons. The alcohol had not only helped them to recover their equilibrium after the shock of Bellamy's murder but also loosened their tongues.

'So you hope that Inspector Young will wrap up the case quickly?' she asked.

'He seems confident.'

Rachel detected a note of caution. 'But?'

'Between you and me, I wonder if he's jumping to conclusions. But then, I must beware of making simple things complicated. It's a bad approach in business and the same must be true of police investigations. With any luck, the fuss will soon blow over. That's Carson's view.'

'And you trust his judgment?'

Harold Jackson eyed her warily. 'Louis Carson has done very well for himself. That says something about his acumen. Any fool can prosper when times are good. Not so easy when the chancelleries of Europe are in utter turmoil.'

'How long have you and Mr Carson been partners?'

'A few months. He and his wife came here on holiday last year and fell in love with the area.'

'As you and Sadie did after the war?'

'Yes, something about this place exerts an irresistible appeal.'

'Like the mermaid of the old legend?'

A shadow crossed his face. 'Except that Hemlock Bay doesn't lure people to their doom.'

Other than Edward Hillman and Gareth Bellamy, Rachel thought.

Perhaps the same reflection occurred to her host, who hurried on. 'I wonder if you'll decide to make your home here? Escape from the grime and smoke of London?'

Rachel smiled. 'The Carsons came up from the south of England, didn't they?'

'Brighton, yes. Carson had made his money there, and after discovering Hemlock Bay, he was keen to invest. At first I was doubtful. We've built this town up on our own. But Sadie's illness and young Robert's accident came in quick succession and our thinking changed. I'm not far short of fifty. The clock is ticking and we need to look to the future. Neither of our boys have the faintest interest in coming into the business, so I need to consider how to take out my capital without damaging the financial stability of Hemlock Bay.'

'In other words, it made sense to spread the risk?'

'Certainly. Before the Wall Street Crash, I'd never have given Carson's approach the time of day. But in times as hard as these, I had to swallow my pride. I love this place, but nothing stays the same forever.' He glanced at his wife. 'Not that I warmed to Carson at first. His wife, on the other hand, is friendly and down to earth.'

Sadie Jackson laughed. 'Behind every successful man is an extremely determined woman.'

'Martha, my maid, met Mrs Carson,' Rachel said. 'She found her very approachable. Not in the least high and mighty.'

'Yes, I enjoy her company. She's been a great support while I've been feeling fragile. We exchange recipes and she's encouraged me to take up knitting. Because we're both dark-haired, with similar colouring, she asks me for advice about the latest American cosmetics. I've introduced her to Max Factor make-up and Koremlu Cream for removing superfluous hair. We get on like a house on fire. If you ask me, her husband would never have got so far without her.'

Harold Jackson nodded. 'Mrs Carson confided in me that Brighton was going downhill. The racecourse attracts undesirables. Razor gangs rule the slums. She persuaded her husband to move somewhere more respectable.'

'You'll have gathered,' Sadie said, 'that we're very proud of Hemlock Bay. We wouldn't do anything that would jeopardise everything we've achieved. But the Carsons were willing to relieve us of significant financial and management burdens. Louis Carson made us an offer we could hardly refuse.'

'So everything has worked out for the best?' Rachel asked Sir Harold.

'You won't hear me complaining. The Carsons run the hotel with the utmost efficiency. Despite the economic woes, Hemlock Bay continues to attract the right people.' He beamed at Rachel, subjecting her to the full force of his charm. 'Judges' daughters, for example.'

'Famous artists, too.'

'Miss Virginia Penrhos, you mean?' He exchanged a smile with his wife. 'Neither of us can make any sense of her paintings, but she's pleasant enough, if a little eccentric.'

'And her friend, Miss Morris?'

'Quiet as a mouse when she came here for dinner,' Sadie said. 'I got the impression that she doesn't care for people who make money from business. Not that she's ever earned money from the sweat of her brow, as far as I can make out. She'd rather be kept by someone.'

'Miaow,' her husband said affectionately. 'The girl was bored, that's the top and bottom of it.'

'Harold prefers to thinks the best of people, Miss Savernake. Not like me.' Sadie sounded languid, but her gaze was thoughtful. 'But that's more than enough about the two of us. I notice you've been drinking rather cautiously, but do let your guard down, just a little. You've cross-examined us very subtly, while dodging most of our questions about you. I'm fascinated. Were you not tempted to follow in your father's footsteps and go into the law?'

'The judge and I could hardly be more different,' Rachel said calmly. 'But I do admit to a burning passion for justice.'

17

'Young of the Yard,' Jacob said to himself, rolling the words off his tongue as he sauntered along High Street in the gloaming. 'Definitely has a ring to it. Pity he'll never reach the giddy heights.'

Discovering Bellamy's body had shocked him to the core. This wasn't the first corpse he'd set eyes on. No crime reporter – especially not one who consorted with Rachel Savernake – could hope to avoid sudden and violent death. Yet his work hadn't hardened him to the point of callousness. Seeing the Welshman sprawled across the floor, battered to death with the main tool of his trade, had sickened him.

Jacob was rarely knocked off balance for long. His method of dealing with the sheer horror of the crime was to throw himself into the business of talking to the police and anyone else he could find. He set himself the goal of creating a memorable front page splash. A story to take pride of place on the wall of his new office.

Inspector Young's ill-concealed ambition to see his name in print was a welcome bonus. The constable who was first to arrive at the hut had proved disconcertingly suspicious, but once the inspector arrived, Jacob convinced him of his bona fides so quickly that he wondered whether the detective was too gullible for his own good. It certainly helped that an obvious suspect had emerged as soon as questions were asked of people who worked at Hemlock Head.

Winnie Lescott's temper was as notorious as her jealousy. The crystal ball was heavy enough to be an effective murder weapon, but not too heavy for a woman to bludgeon an unsuspecting victim with it. Winnie was strong enough to have committed the crime without breaking sweat. The fact that she'd vanished from Paradise was widely regarded as a compelling reminder that there's no smoke without fire.

Inspector Young, a stocky man brimming with energy as well as unfulfilled ambition, had firm ideas about his priorities when conducting a murder investigation. Within an hour of his arrival, he'd announced that he would make a public statement to members of the press 'and other interested parties' at twelve noon the following day. The conference would be held, by kind permission of Sir Harold Jackson, in the smoking room of the Hemlock Hotel.

Jacob could read Young's mind. The inspector hoped to inform the assembled pressmen that Winnie was already under lock and key, thanks to his fast work and the untiring efforts of the officers he'd sent to pursue her. 'We've alerted all ports,' he told Jacob. 'There's no hiding place.' These were obviously phrases he loved. If she was still on the run tomorrow, no matter. He'd have the perfect platform to explain his methods of detection as well as the futility of his suspect's flight from justice, while making an impassioned public appeal for fresh information.

Like the detective, Jacob had a clearly defined set of

priorities. His first move had been to call Rachel. Next, he broke the news to Gomersall, and his editor's amazement was a reward in itself.

'So your fortune teller was hoist with his own petard?'

'That's… one way of putting it, sir.'

Jacob could almost hear his editor rubbing his hands. 'What if it's not the man's girlfriend who killed him? What if the killer nurses a grudge against people who look into the future?'

'Better ask Trewythian to check his life insurance, sir.'

'Is anyone safe?' Gomersall demanded rhetorically.

'Probably not, sir.'

This was the right answer. Jacob's editor had a penchant for stories that alarmed his readers. This sprang not from some form of journalistic sadism but from a determination to give people what they wanted. For some unaccountable reason devotees of the *Clarion* liked nothing better than to feel afraid that they were all about to be murdered in their beds.

Gomersall chortled. 'I'll be honest, lad. I simply don't know how you do it. If I sent you to a church service, you'd stumble over a dead chorister the moment you left your pew. Positively uncanny. Anyone would think you've made some sort of Faustian pact. Not in league with the devil, are you?'

No, Jacob thought. Only Rachel Savernake.

It didn't take him long to write his story. The raw material was sensational and for once there was no call for his skills in lurid embellishment. The picture of Bellamy's head crushed by the crystal ball would haunt him forever. He even indulged himself by allowing a few hints of his genuine sense of horror to seep into the staccato sentences demanded by the *Clarion*'s house style.

Even as his competitors from Fleet Street and the local

stringers assembled in the hotel, his breathless account of discovering the crime would festoon every news stand in town. Rival attempts to find interesting and original angles were doomed to seem hapless and irrelevant at best, tacky and salacious at worst. Jacob suspected that some of his colleagues would stoop to cramming their reports with sly references to unspecified but disgusting antics at the nudist camp. He'd only mentioned the Sun and Air Garden twice. And then only in passing.

As the town clock struck ten, there was a spring in his step. Things could hardly have gone much better since his rain-drenched journey to Hemlock Bay. Except for Bellamy and Winnie Lescott, of course. Gomersall had been forced to agree that there was now no earthly point in Jacob pretending to be Clarion Charlie. He must concentrate on reporting the murder and its investigation. Bob Harley would come up on the first train tomorrow. The coupling of murder story and Mystery Man competition was sure to be a winner. The editor was salivating at the prospect of the *Clarion*'s circulation soaring to stratospheric heights.

In high good humour, Jacob sauntered into the Mermaid. The Select Bar was packed and the smell of excitement was as palpable as the beer fumes. Bellamy's name was on everyone's lips. So was his exotic alias, although now that he'd been battered to death with his own crystal ball, it seemed more ridiculous than ever. Everyone in the pub was claiming to have inside information about what had *really* happened. Rachel Savernake hadn't been in town for seventy-two hours, Jacob reflected, and already nobody was talking about anything but murder.

At the far end of the bar, Laurie was deep in conversation with a middle-aged man with sandy hair. Presumably the golfer Trueman had seen on the night he met McAtee. As Jacob watched, another man approached the bar. He was middle-aged with patchy dark hair and a half-empty tankard in his hand. Laurie made his apologies to the golfer and turned to the other man. From Rachel's description, Jacob felt sure this was Louis Carson. Interesting. But the pair only spoke briefly; in fact, Carson did all the talking. Laurie nodded and Carson put his tankard down on the counter before heading for the door.

The golfer seemed to be nonplussed by this exchange, and Laurie was evidently keen to mollify him. Jacob couldn't understand what was going on, but he didn't want to be part of it. In a few hours' time, his name would be all over Hemlock Bay, and he'd be fully occupied keeping one step ahead of the other reporters.

Catching Laurie's eye, he assumed a sorrowful expression. The barman gave a quick shrug and turned back to the sandy-haired golfer, who responded by placing his hand on the young man's arm.

'So you were denied a romantic tryst with young Laurie?' Rachel asked.

Jacob took another sip of Glenmorangie. He'd hurried to Bay View to find that she'd arrived back from Hemlock Hall half an hour earlier and was enjoying a nightcap with the Truemans. He'd given a breathless account of the day's events and Cliff Trueman had already refilled his glass.

'I'll get over it,' he said. 'Why are you so interested in a barman? Or do you still insist on being mysterious about him?'

'He forms a tiny part of a bigger pattern, like a stitch in a

Fair Isle jersey.' She gave him a teasing smile. 'When I puzzle over what's going on in Hemlock Bay, I keep thinking about Humbug Billy.'

He considered this as he breathed in the honey fragrance of the whisky. 'You do love to tantalise me.'

She smiled sweetly. 'I deserve a little fun every now and then.'

'All right, who was Humbug Billy?'

'First things first. Do you know when Gareth Bellamy was killed?'

'I spoke to the doctor who examined his body. He was reluctant to commit himself, naturally.'

'Naturally. However?'

'When pressed, he said Bellamy died a few hours before I found him. No later than two o'clock. Maybe one.'

'So that's why the inspector didn't treat you as a serious suspect. I did wonder.'

'I like to think my upstanding character and transparent sincerity were decisive factors.'

'Do you now?' Rachel sighed. 'Martha described the hut's setting. I gather it's at the back of the amusement park. Easy to sneak in and out unobserved?'

Jacob nodded. 'A risky place to commit a murder, but you'd be unlucky if someone caught sight of you. If you want to know what I think…'

He allowed himself a theatrical pause, prompting Rachel to burst out laughing. 'Now you're tantalising me. Go on.'

'I'd say the killer was either bold or desperate. Or both.'

'The crime might have been committed on the spur of the moment.'

'Someone who didn't like what Bellamy saw in the crystal ball?'

'Or something that he said or did.'

'Inspector Young is confident Winnie Lescott fits the bill. He might just be right.'

'Did you tell him that Bellamy came to see you in London?'

'Yes, I needed to explain why I called on him. I didn't want Young to think I was just a naïve tripper, anxious to find out if I was going to win the football pools or meet the girl of my dreams.'

'Heaven forbid. What did Young say about the premonition?'

'He thought it was nonsense. Bellamy spoke to him before he contacted me, remember. In the inspector's opinion, fortune tellers are charlatans and Bellamy made up a tissue of lies.'

'Why would he do that?'

'He was simply chasing free publicity.'

'From what you've told us about the inspector, that sounds like the pot calling the kettle black.'

Jacob grinned. 'Inspector Young is a man of strong opinions.'

'That's not always a bad thing,' Hetty said.

'No, but I'd say he's blinkered. As far as he's concerned, Winnie Lescott murdered her lover. So he'll brush aside any evidence that doesn't fit with his pet theory.'

'I hope to God he's wrong!' Martha blurted out.

She had been subdued ever since he'd walked through the door. Apart from a mumbled greeting, she'd kept her mouth shut. He knew her well enough to realise that she was brooding, and he was shrewd enough to realise why.

'You're not blaming yourself in any way, I hope.'

She shrugged and said nothing.

'Come on, Martha, you've nothing whatsoever to feel guilty

about. Bellamy attacked you, remember? You scratched him in self-defence. Perfectly natural. And entirely reasonable in the circumstances.'

'But don't you see?' she demanded. 'You've confirmed my worst fears. Winnie Lescott's temper was wicked and she had a stand-up row with him. Because of the scratches, she accused him of messing about with another girl. The policeman's right. The obvious assumption is that they had another quarrel in the hut and it ended with her battering him with the nearest thing at hand. His crystal ball. The fact she's made herself scarce straight away is damning.'

'There could be an innocent explanation,' Jacob said. 'What if the person who killed Bellamy has harmed Winnie as well?'

'Leaving Bellamy's body to be found by any Tom, Dick, or Jacob, but successfully concealing hers?' Rachel asked.

'It might be worse than that,' Martha said. Jacob realised to his dismay that she was struggling to fight back the tears. 'What if Winnie turns up and is able to prove her innocence? They will turn their attention to whoever scratched Bellamy's face. Someone provoked into doing that might just as easily be provoked into murder. What happens if they question me?'

'Please, Martha,' he said. 'It's not like you to get upset. Nobody's going to accuse you of murder. You didn't kill him, and even if someone was stupid enough to suggest you did, Cliff and Hetty can give you a cast-iron alibi anyway.'

'That's not the point,' she said in a muffled voice. 'I'm not worried about being hanged. I'm upset that I made a mess of things when I talked to him. It's made things much more difficult for the rest of you.'

'Honestly, Martha, that's nonsense. You've got things out of proportion.'

Hetty Trueman cleared her throat. All eyes turned to her.

'I never thought I'd say this, Martha, but Jacob is absolutely right.' Jacob gaped at this admission, but she ignored him. 'Haven't I told you often enough this evening? You've got nothing to apologise for. Bellamy hurt you and it would have served him right if you'd done some real damage. Not just a few marks that would soon heal.'

'If he were still alive,' Martha said quietly.

Her brother said, 'No reason to torment yourself. None of us have forgotten what you went through all those years ago.'

Martha touched her cheek. 'The scarring isn't as bad as it was.'

'On the outside, that's true. But inside…'

Rachel leaned forward and rested her hand on Martha's for a moment. 'His death isn't your responsibility. If you want to blame anyone, blame me. It was my idea that we come here and start poking our noses into other people's business. It was me who encouraged you to have your fortune told. Selfish of me, and self-indulgent. I'm the guilty one. Not you.'

Martha dabbed at her face with a handkerchief. 'I don't mean to make a fuss.'

There was a long pause as Rachel savoured her whisky. 'You're not. We've said everything that needs to be said. What matters now is what we do next. There's more to this case than meets Inspector Young's eye. I hoped Bellamy might give us a lead about whatever is going on in Hemlock Bay. I thought he'd stumbled across something, perhaps without realising exactly what it was.'

'You didn't expect him to be murdered?' Jacob asked.

'If I had,' she said patiently, 'I'd have given you fair warning.'

'So what do you make of it? Was he killed on the spur of the moment?'

'The fact the killer didn't bring a weapon suggests the

answer is yes. On the other hand, if it was someone familiar with the inside of the hut, they'd know the crystal ball would make a handy weapon.'

'So you think Winnie Lescott is the likely culprit?'

'I'd be surprised if she turns out to be the killer.'

'You would?' Martha's shoulders slumped.

Rachel turned to Jacob. 'Do you know if anyone else who works at Paradise has gone missing?'

'No idea. There was a lot of confusion after word got round that Bellamy had been murdered. Why do you ask?'

'Think back to your meeting with him. And remember what happened when Martha visited Paradise.'

Martha blurted out, 'I don't understand.'

Rachel flicked a stray hair out of her eye. 'Don't worry, it may be a complete red herring. What still fascinates me is that yarn Bellamy spun about the premonition.'

'I don't believe he ever had a premonition,' Jacob said.

'Certainly he lied to you, but I think there is something in the farrago about the body on the rocks that explains why he was murdered. It's so frustrating. At present, I can't see the wood for the trees.' She put her tumbler down on a side table before adding quietly, 'But believe me, I will.'

Hetty drummed her fingers on the arm of her chair.

'There's something rotten in Hemlock Bay,' she pronounced.

'It's one of the prettiest resorts I've ever seen,' Jacob protested. 'Bellamy's murder doesn't change that.'

'On the surface it's lovely, I grant you. But what lies beneath?'

Rachel nodded. 'Good question. The Jacksons are understandably proud of everything they've achieved. Yet I sense a lurking sadness. They mask it well, but my impression is that they are surprisingly insecure.'

'Don't tell me they're strapped for cash.' Jacob couldn't hide his lack of sympathy.

'The economic crisis has affected them, like almost everyone else.'

Except you, Jacob was tempted to retort. Instead, he said, 'But?'

'They are strong, intelligent people, but personal misfortunes have dented their confidence. Not so long ago, I suspect it was almost invincible. Now it's as if they're tormented by a sense of doom. They are fighting against it, but are terrified of being overwhelmed.'

'What makes you think that?'

Trueman refilled Jacob's glass, but Rachel covered hers. It took her less than five minutes to give a concise but comprehensive account of her evening at Hemlock Hall.

Jacob shook his head in wonder. A smile spread across his face. 'Incredible!'

Rachel stared at him. 'What is?'

'Sir Harold and Lady Jackson are nudists! A knight of the realm in the altogether! Who would have guessed?'

Trueman shifted in his chair. Hetty's brows knitted. For a moment nobody spoke. Suddenly Jacob felt cold, as if someone had opened the door and an Arctic gale had blown through the bungalow.

'You will treat everything said between these four walls as under the seal of the confessional?' Rachel asked pleasantly.

Jacob swallowed. 'Of course, of course.'

Her smile vanished. For a moment her bleak and uncompromising expression made him think of a hangman contemplating the gallows.

'I have your promise? I wouldn't wish there to be any misunderstanding.'

'Absolutely, no... no need to ask the question.' He was almost stammering. 'I definitely won't breathe a word about it in the *Clarion*.'

'Or to anyone else outside this room?'

'Never,' he said fervently. 'You can trust me.'

'Thank you.' Rachel leaned back in her chair. 'I'm sure I can.'

He gulped down the last of his whisky. Trueman offered a top-up, but he shook his head. He felt dizzy, as if he'd clung on to a cliff face and clambered back to safety after risking a plunge into an abyss.

Taking a breath, he said, 'What did you learn from the Jacksons?'

'Plenty, but there's an anomaly which I need to check. I agree with Hetty. There's something wrong here.' She allowed herself a faint smile. 'That's why I mentioned Humbug Billy.'

'Who was he?'

'A stall-holder in Bradford market, back in the 1850s. His real name was William Hardaker, and he sold sweets. His peppermint humbugs were especially popular. In those days, sugar was an expensive luxury, so the humbugs were flavoured with a tasty white powder, delightfully known as daft. Due to a catastrophic mix-up, arsenic was used instead of daft. At least twenty people died and hundreds fell sick. Humbug Billy himself was paralysed.'

'Fascinating, but what has this got to do with Hemlock Bay?'

A dreamy look came into her eyes. 'Don't you see? The humbugs were harmless until the arsenic was added. A pleasant sweet acquired a curious taste. A little treat became deadly. The question is this. What is the lethal ingredient that has poisoned the delights of Hemlock Bay?'

He'd lost the thread. 'You tell me.'

'My best guess is that he's called Louis Carson.'

18

Basil Palmer's Journal

16 June

I hope I can be forgiven for thinking that, ever since I arrived in Hemlock Bay, my every move has been opposed by a malign fate. At every turn, obstacles have confronted me. Inquisitive neighbours were bad enough, but now both Hooker Jackson and Joseph McAtee present threats to my enterprise. What is more, the Mystery Man campaign will flood the resort with prize-hunters. And now, an appalling calamity. A man has been brutally murdered on my own doorstep. Or at least within a couple of miles of it.

Mrs Stones broke the news to me when she arrived to make my breakfast and flick a duster this morning. I can't imagine she has been so animated since the Armistice.

'Would you believe it?' she demanded, waving her copy of the *Clarion* under my nose. 'A clairvoyant, killed with his own crystal ball! And in Hemlock Bay, of all places!'

A chill ran through my body. 'What? You mean someone has died here?'

'The Great Hallemby, he called himself! Bludgeoned to death in Paradise!'

'Good Lord.'

'Whatever next? We'll all be murdered in our own—'

'May I see?' I asked, desperate to dam the torrent of exclamations.

She handed the newspaper to me. In the past, I've seldom spared the *Clarion* anything more than a cursory glance. The tone of its reporting is excitable and sensationalised, with little factual information of any kind, let alone details of interest to a chartered accountant. The story occupied almost the whole of the front page and covered many column inches in the rest of the paper.

Astonishingly, the reporter – a man by the name of Flint – stumbled across the body himself. Flint claims to have been staying in the Hemlock Hotel on holiday. If that is true, it is a remarkable coincidence, given that he appears to be the newspaper's chief crime correspondent. But I suppose even representatives of the gutter press are entitled to have holidays. The deceased, whose real name was Bellamy, was killed in the hut where he told people's fortunes. Why Flint was there in the first place is unclear. Presumably he is embarrassed to admit to wanting to have his palm read. His description of the scene of the crime was melodramatic, but I was particularly interested to read the comments attributed to the detective in charge of the investigation.

'We have made rapid progress with our enquiries,' Inspector Young insists. 'I anticipate that we will soon be in a position to make an arrest. Perhaps even within the next twenty-four hours.'

Flint is coy about the prime suspect's identity, but only a dunce would fail to read between the lines. The report makes frequent references to the dead man's 'close friend', a woman named Lescott who works at a puppet show. Flint quotes several people connected with the pleasure grounds, but not her. Indeed, he makes a point of mentioning that she was not available for comment, and leaves his readers to put two and two together.

Is she on the run?

Hooker Jackson is quoted as confirming that Paradise will reopen today as usual. He was obviously concerned to dismiss any criticism that he had been insensitive. 'Mr Bellamy's death is a dreadful tragedy,' he told Flint. 'However, it is in the finest traditions of family entertainment that the show must go on. This is certainly what poor Mr Bellamy himself would have wanted.'

Is it? I'm not convinced, but the implication is clear. Patrons of the pleasure grounds are not at risk because the culprit's identity is known and she is about to be apprehended. I can only presume that the murder was sparked by some kind of lovers' tiff, and that the woman picked up the nearest weapon within reach, namely the crystal ball.

'Extraordinary,' I murmured as I handed the newspaper back to Mrs Stones.

'Isn't it?' she breathed. 'Whoever would have thought? In Hemlock Bay, of all places!'

If Mrs Stones had not been present, I would have had my head in my hands. Policemen will no doubt mill around the town today, hoping to find the missing woman. I can only pray that the inspector's optimism is not misplaced.

I am beginning to wonder whether Providence has taken a hand in my humble affairs. Is it possible that all these setbacks have a deeper significance, and that I should reconsider my resolution to rid the world of Louis Carson?

And yet, wouldn't that be a betrayal of Alicia?

As soon as Mrs Stones has gone, I shall retrieve that

crumpled letter from its hiding place. Reading it will stiffen my resolve and give me the courage to keep on.

8 July 1930

Dear Basil

By the time you read this note, I shall be dead. I hope you will forgive me for what I have done. I have not been a good wife, and now I am about to commit a mortal sin.

I fell in love with Neville Carrington the evening you brought him home for dinner. Every other client of your practice had proved deadly dull. Neville was not only handsome, but wonderful company. He expressed a burning desire to read my poetry, the same verse that you once, in a fit of pique, derided as flowery tosh. That he also appeared to be extremely wealthy was neither here nor there. It was only later that I learned that he earns very little at the Bar and that the little poetry publishing press he runs as a sideline is hopelessly unprofitable, an avocation rather than a business. Its survival is entirely dependent on funding from Lavinia, his dreadful wife, whose claws have always kept a tight grip on the purse strings.

To say that I was infatuated with Neville does not do justice to the enduring power of my emotions. All my life I had dreamed of true love, and finally I had found it. I won't beat about the bush. Neville and I began a torrid affair. It was wild and passionate, everything that our marriage is not. You are not a bad man, Basil, far from it. In many ways you are too good for me. You dote on me, rather as a lepidopterist admires a butterfly trapped in his collection. But I have long yearned to spread my wings.

Neville was desperate to marry me. He said so many times. I have no doubt that you would refuse your consent to a divorce, but that is the least of our problems. I would be happy to live in sin, even though Neville is unwilling to see my good name tarnished. But the stumbling block is Lavinia. She is vindictive by nature and her solicitor – who has served the Henderson-Halls for forty years and is principal trustee of the family trust – is a wily bird. If Neville walked out, she would cut him off without a penny and make sure that he was ruined as a professional man. Neither of us could bear that. Neville insists that he wouldn't care a jot, as long as we were together, but I know in my heart that isn't true. He is too accustomed to his creature comforts. And so, for that matter, am I.

We were wrestling with our dilemma when disaster struck. Neville received an anonymous letter, a disgusting blend of cowardice and menace. The author revealed that he was in possession of one of the letters I had sent to Neville. His extensive quotation from one purple passage proved the point. By some unfathomable means he had got hold of the letter when we were staying in Brighton, snatching a blissful weekend together while you were visiting your Aunt Maud in Ludlow and Lavinia was having an old school friend to stay.

For the return of the letter, he demanded an absurdly high sum. The money was to be sent to an accommodation address in Kemptown, close to the shore at Brighton. The name he used was Nap Moth. As Neville said, this was transparently an anagram for phantom. Just one more means of tormenting us, another twist of the screw.

Lavinia could have paid without a second thought, but Neville assured me there was no chance of his persuading her to give him such an amount, whatever the pretext. As a result, I had to beg you for the money which I said was needed for my cousin's emergency operation.

The compromising letter was returned to Neville, and we prayed that would be the end of the matter. But forty-eight hours later came another demand, accompanied by a quotation from an even more extravagant expression of my physical desires. This time he wanted twice as much as before.

At this point, Neville admitted that half a dozen letters of mine – 'the juiciest', he said – had been stolen from him in Brighton. He'd brought them in his suitcase because he was afraid that Lavinia might stumble across them during his absence from home. Meanwhile you had discovered that my cousin was fit and well and were refusing to believe my frantic lies about how I'd spent five hundred pounds in addition to my usual allowance. At that point, you and I were barely on speaking terms. I begged Neville to talk to Lavinia, but his forecast proved correct. She refused to give him one pound, let alone a thousand.

Neville decided to play a risky game. He said we must call the blackmailer's bluff. I was too distraught and frightened to argue. Perhaps he was right, and we had no choice. His letter refusing to pay another penny was magnificently disdainful. But we knew we were courting disaster.

Neville received a telephone call at his office – from the blackmailer himself. He sounded oily, Neville said, a regular Uriah Heep. The vile creature gave us forty-eight hours to produce the money. Otherwise, the remaining letters would be sent to Lavinia. Neville said he would make payment by instalments. He has an interest in prizefighting and hired a muscular fellow to accompany him to Kemptown.

The accommodation address proved to be a chemist's shop close to the Sassoon Mausoleum. At first the chemist was unwilling to disclose the true identity of Nap Moth, but Neville's hireling soon managed to knock it out of him. The chemist sailed on the windy side of the law and was crafty enough to make sure he knew something about his customers. He'd discovered that the name of our blackmailer was Louis Carson and that the man lived somewhere in the locality, but that was all.

The money was never collected. Carson had got wind of Neville's determination to fight back. He retaliated with the most powerful weapon at his disposal. He did not bother with you, Basil, because he guessed that you would forgive me anything. Like an anarchist hurling a bomb, he sent my letters to Lavinia.

She threw Neville out of the house. He could go and live with his slut for all she cared. That was me, Basil, a slut! One thing he could be sure of, she said. He'd never receive a farthing from her, as long as she lived.

Can you imagine our despair? I know you've always prided yourself on your lack of imagination, but I swear that even you, Basil, must in your heart understand at least something of the pain of true love.

Neville was distraught. Not even my adoration was enough to console him. He is a man of wild emotions, as I am. That is why we are soulmates.

There is no easy way to say what I need to say, so I shall be brief.

On this earth, we are doomed. We have resolved to follow the precedent of Mayerling. Like those other star-crossed lovers, Crown Prince Rudolf and his beloved Mary Vetsera, we shall both go blissfully into the uncertain beyond. As Mary said of Rudolf, 'If I could give him my life I should be glad to do it, for what does life mean for me?' I feel the same.

Do not think unkindly of me, Basil. You are, by your own lights, a decent man.

I have not behaved as a respectable wife should, and although I cannot regret yielding to my passions, I apologise for any distress that I may have caused you.

Please do not blame Neville for what has happened. There is only one person who is guilty of cruelty and wrongdoing.

His name is Louis Carson, and I hate him with every fibre of my being.

Goodbye, Basil.

Your respectful wife
Alicia

Later

Neville Carrington oozed charm from every pore and my dear Alicia was susceptible to the admiration of a handsome bounder. She was always headstrong and inclined to act on impulse rather than after the meticulous weighing of pros and cons. I can quite see why she fell in with his absurd and utterly selfish proposal that the pair of them should die in a suicide pact.

Of course, he was a weak-willed coward. Having shot Alicia, he lost his nerve and could not face turning the gun on himself. I don't believe he had any sort of coherent plan, for in such circumstances he would inevitably be convicted of murdering my wife.

Perhaps he realised this, I cannot say. All that is certain is what happened. The pair of them had met for their final, fatal tryst in his basement room in chambers. After shooting Alicia, he ran out of the building in a panic. A passing Alvis (the 12/50 model) knocked him down on the Embankment. For the next forty-eight hours he lay in a coma, with a police constable at his bedside. He died without regaining consciousness. Plainly a merciful release. At least he was spared the gallows.

Alicia's death prostrated me. I was already at my wits' end with grief when, the following day, I received her letter. I revealed its existence to nobody and shortly before the inquest I was admitted to a nursing home. People described me as a broken man.

Thankfully, the coroner was sympathetic and discreet. As a result of his concern for the well-being of the bereaved, the scandal was hushed up as well as Lavinia Carrington and I could have hoped. Neville Carrington was said to have suffered a temporary derangement. He had fallen head over heels with a beautiful woman and lured her to the flat on a pretext. When she resisted his overtures, he killed her in hot blood, before meeting his end as he rushed from the scene of his crime in a fit of horrified remorse. A tragedy for all concerned. Thankfully, the eyes of the nation were fixed on the Test Match at Headingley, where Bradman was putting English bowlers to the sword. I was profoundly grateful for our national obsession with the summer game.

As I began my slow recovery to health, my thoughts began to crystallise.

Carrington's extravagance and lack of judgment meant he would always need money and could never have kept Alicia in the style to which she was accustomed. They would have quarrelled. The so-called passion would have faded. His eyes would have wandered in other directions as he looked for some other rich woman to take Lavinia's place.

In the meantime I would have remained patient and shown forbearance. Alicia would have come back to me. She would have learned her lesson. We should have been reunited forever.

Despise Carrington as I do, I have never entertained the slightest doubt about who is the real villain of the piece.

Louis Carson.

That man is responsible for everything that has gone wrong in my life. Alicia's blood is on his hands, and I shall not rest until I have avenged her.

19

'Mon Repos?' Jacob repeated, scribbling on his notepad. 'Number Seven, Tower Mews?'

'Isn't that what I said?' demanded the querulous voice at the other end of the telephone. 'You'd best set off right away.'

'Absolutely. And if you can find a way to detain them until I arrive, there's an extra fiver in it for you. Don't arouse their suspicion, whatever you do.'

'Tall order, that. Very tall.' There was a momentary pause. 'How about another ten pounds if I manage to pull it off?'

'You drive a hard bargain, Mr Hennessey.'

'Listen, chum, I'm doing you a big favour here. I don't know how these people will react when they find out I've blown the gaff on them. They could turn nasty. But I'm public-spirited, see?'

'In the finest tradition of *Clarion* readers, yes.' Time was short and Jacob wasn't in the mood to haggle, so he contented himself with a touch of satire. 'All right, you've twisted my arm. Done.'

The man coughed. 'You will bring payment in full? In cash? I don't believe in cheques.'

'You can trust the *Clarion*,' Jacob said. 'I'm on my way.'

He bounced out of the telephone booth into the vast and gleaming lobby of the Hemlock Hotel. The call meant he'd have to sacrifice the hotel's bacon, eggs, and fried bread, but the surge of joy he felt when receiving an exclusive tip-off offered rich compensation. That tingling thrill of keeping one step ahead of the police never palled.

His front page story about the Crystal Ball Killing had reaped an immediate dividend. He'd taken care to mention that he was staying at the Hemlock Hotel, hoping that anyone with valuable information would have the nous to contact him there. On his way in to breakfast he'd been intercepted by a flunkey and directed to the telephone. A boarding house owner in Blackpool was on the line.

According to Hennessey, two guests had arrived at his desk without a prior booking the previous evening. They looked shifty, in Hennessey's opinion, although Jacob didn't regard that as significant. Couples arriving at hotels with minimal baggage usually looked shifty, for reasons that were predictable and seldom criminal. The man had registered them as Mr and Mrs John Smith, with an address in Gas Street, Manchester. His companion answered the official police description of Winnie Lescott.

Hennessey might be mistaken, but Jacob was optimistic. The boarding house owner sounded sly but shrewd – ideal qualities in an informant. And how many brown-skinned women in their twenties would be checking into a seaside hotel within fifty miles of Hemlock Bay on the same day the prime suspect in the Crystal Ball Murder disappeared?

As Jacob headed for the revolving doors, he almost collided with the man he'd seen talking to Laurie in the Mermaid the previous night. Louis Carson.

'I'm so sorry, sir. Please excuse me. And a very good morning to you.'

In fact the near-collision was Jacob's fault, but he accepted the apology with a gracious flap of the hand.

'Morning. Mr Carson, isn't it?'

'Indeed. I have the honour to be the manager here. I do hope you're enjoying your stay.'

'Lovely, thanks.'

As Jacob moved away, the other man caught him by the sleeve. 'It's Mr Flint, isn't it? The newspaperman?'

'That's me.' Jacob felt a surge of pleasure at being recognised. Was this the sign of a growing reputation, something to mention to Gomersall next time his salary was reviewed? 'So you're a *Clarion* reader?'

'I'm afraid I don't have much time to read newspapers, but the girl on the desk just pointed you out to me. You arrived on Sunday, she said. And you had the misfortune to be involved in that dreadful business up at Paradise?'

'That's right. Did you know the victim, by any chance?'

'This man Bellamy?' Carson shook his head. 'Never met the poor fellow. I don't believe in fortune telling.'

Unctuous as the man was, Jacob was inclined to believe him.

'So you've no idea if he had any enemies?'

Carson shook his head. 'I spoke to Inspector Young and offered him a room for the night with my compliments. My impression is that he suspects a domestic tragedy. With any luck the matter will soon be cleared up and everyone will be able to get on with their lives.'

Everyone except Bellamy and Winnie Lescott, Jacob thought. 'The inspector won't be staying here long, then?'

'No, he seems confident, thank goodness. He assured me he wouldn't need the room for a second night.'

Jacob nipped back to his room to collect his notebook, pen, and a couple of sheets of *Clarion* letterhead and was soon bowling along the road to Blackpool in his nimble little Riley 9. The skies were grey and miserable, and desultory spots of rain toyed with the holidaymakers' emotions by hinting at a cloudburst which never quite materialised.

He made good time and had little difficulty in finding Mon Repos. As he'd anticipated, it was the most dilapidated of all the guest houses in Tower Mews. He presumed it was also the cheapest, hence the appeal to a couple who were short of money and on the run. In case he needed to make a quick getaway, he parked in front of the door and rapped the rusty knocker.

'Mr Hennessey? I'm Jacob Flint.'

The man wore a grubby vest, ancient trousers and a pair of carpet slippers. A Woodbine dangled precariously from a small, mean mouth. He reeked of smoke and avarice.

'They're upstairs.' Hennessey's grin revealed more gaps than teeth. If he was concerned about harbouring a brutal murderer, he showed no sign of it. 'Went straight back up there after breakfast and locked the door. Last night I had a complaint from the people in the next room about the noise they were making. Worse than newlyweds, they said. I suppose if she gets sent to the gallows, they never will be wed. Ah well, at least she's had some fun. Live and let live, that's what I say.'

Jacob didn't attempt to unravel the contradictions in this philosophy. 'Which room?'

Hennessey stood directly in front of him, barring his way into the building. He extended a grubby hand stained yellow by tobacco. 'Money first. Nobody puts one over on Dick Hennessey.'

Jacob pulled out his wallet and peeled off the notes. The other man counted them ostentatiously to ensure that he wasn't being cheated and then shuffled to one side.

'Number Nine. Two floors up. Watch that loose board after the first landing. Wouldn't want you to break your neck, would we?'

Jacob hurried up the steps. A foetid aroma hung over the staircase, a charmless blend of overcooked sausages and cheap cigarettes. A different world from the polished magnificence of the Hemlock Hotel, he thought. How the other half holidayed.

He reached his destination without mishap and put his ear to the keyhole. There was the sound of heavy breathing and a woman's muffled laughter. He banged on the door.

Inside the room, a man swore violently and told the unseen intruder what he could do.

'Miss Lescott!' Jacob shouted through the door. 'My name is Jacob Flint and I'm a reporter with the *Clarion* newspaper. We want to pay for your story.'

There was a short silence.

'What are you talking about?' A woman's voice, breathless.

In the course of his short career in Fleet Street, Jacob had lost most of the illusions about human nature he'd once cherished. When chasing a scoop, there wasn't room to indulge in finer feelings. He'd learned to concentrate on what people cared for most.

'Twenty-five pounds in cash for exclusive rights to your story. In other words, you don't talk to anyone else from the press but me. Half the money the moment you sign the contract. The other half when we publish the first instalment tomorrow. Better be quick, before my editor changes his mind.'

He heard muffled whispering, but couldn't make out what they were saying.

'Twenty-five pounds?' the woman demanded.

'I've got the contract in my pocket.' This wasn't quite true, but he'd scribble a few words on a sheet bearing the *Clarion* letterhead to keep the bean counters happy. 'The moment you sign, I'll put the cash in your hand.'

There was another pause.

'I'm not decent.'

Jacob clenched his fist in triumph. As usual, money talked.

'I can wait,' he said cheerfully.

An hour later, Jacob had a signed contract in his pocket, a notebook full of hasty scrawl, and two bemused passengers in the back of his Riley 9. Hennessey had, on payment of another pound, permitted Jacob to interview Winnie and her companion, whose name was Johnny Gratrix, in the dingy cubbyhole he called the 'guest lounge'. He'd even stumped up refreshments, in the form of stewed tea and dry custard creams.

Johnny, a hulking labourer, was a native of Hemlock Bay who had worked as a farmhand prior to starting work at Paradise two months ago. He assisted the head gardener and was more at ease wielding a shovel than explaining himself to the press. Winnie, much brighter and more opinionated than her lover, did all the talking. Jacob guessed that, in her relationships with men, she wore the trousers.

Jacob was an adept cross-examiner and a patient listener. Despite Winnie's taste for digression, he soon pieced her story together. Her father's puppet show was, she claimed, the biggest attraction at the pleasure grounds, and since her mother's death, he'd relied on her help to keep the show going. As far as Jacob could judge, the old man was the one person in the world she really cared for, but she hated feeling that, like Skeleton Sue, she was just one more puppet on a string. A woman of strong passions, she possessed a quaintly old-fashioned romantic streak. She longed to escape to a better life, but one disastrous relationship followed another as she searched in vain for the man who could give her everything she wanted. Jacob suspected he didn't exist.

Johnny had taken a shine to her from the moment he'd set eyes on her, she explained, but she'd given him short shrift because he was like so many men: Only Interested in One Thing. He was, she said, 'a ladies' man', a genteel euphemism which Jacob enjoyed so much he underlined it three times in his scribbled notes. Besides, she added virtuously, when she met Johnny, she was already spoken for. She'd always been fascinated by things mystical, and when Gareth Bellamy arrived to ply his trade in Paradise, he entranced her with his ability to read her palm and see a rosy future unfolding for her in the crystal. Before long, they embarked on a tempestuous affair. But her hair-trigger temper had scared off Bellamy's numerous predecessors, and it didn't take much to rouse her to fury. Most of all she hated Bellamy even looking at another woman.

'I needed to be his one and only, Mr Flint,' she said, taking a slurp of tea. 'A lady has her pride.'

'Of course,' Jacob said. 'Quite right, too. And did Bellamy…
I mean, Gareth, actually misbehave with other women?'

Winnie lifted her chin. 'He led them on. Same as he did
with me. Dropped hints about what he saw in the crystal.
Told me he was just trying to keep his clients satisfied, but
that was flannel. I gave him what for, believe me.'

Jacob did believe her. She was a big woman with thin skin.
No doubt a frightening prospect when provoked.

'Can you tell me about your final quarrel?'

'His face was badly scratched. Someone had really got her
claws into his left cheek. He must have tried it on once too
often, maybe got carried away. I gave his other cheek a smack.
No more than he deserved.'

'What was his explanation?'

'Some woman had gone berserk because she didn't like
what he'd seen in the crystal. Rubbish! I didn't believe a word
of it. As if Gareth ever gave anyone bad news. He always said
it was unprofessional to upset the punters, see?'

Jacob could think of another word, but he let it pass.
Bellamy was a born liar and he'd forfeited any sympathy by
attacking Martha. Jacob understood why Winnie had hit the
man, even if he didn't approve. The question was: had she
gone so far as to kill him? She denied it, and he believed her.

According to Winnie, Bellamy tried to make it up to her
by swearing that he'd seen a vision of a wonderful future. He
was about to come into a good deal of money and would be
able to set them up in comfort far from Hemlock Bay. Maybe
on the east coast: Scarborough, Bridlington, or Whitby.

Winnie didn't believe a word he said. None of his promises
ever amounted to anything, and the scratches on his face were
the last straw. In her mind, they proved he was never going to
change. She told him she never wanted to see him again.

So she'd turned to Gratrix for comfort, and together they hatched a hare-brained scheme for running away together. Gratrix had nothing, but she'd saved some money of her own for a rainy day, and she told her father she needed to get away for a while. She and Gratrix had been drinking in the Fisherman's Arms, not far from the lighthouse – where the landlord, Johnny's uncle, interpreted the licensing laws with extreme flexibility. The two of them were fantasising about what to do next when one of the locals arrived, agog with the news of murder in Paradise. Winnie's lover was dead, his head crushed to a pulp by his own crystal ball.

The news threw her into a panic. She was terrified the police would treat her as the obvious suspect. Her fellow workers at Paradise had never liked her and would be quick to point the finger. Someone who looked different from everyone else was always a convenient scapegoat. Johnny Gratrix and the landlord of the Fisherman's could provide her with an alibi, but she didn't believe their word would cut any ice with detectives looking for a quick arrest. The sad thing was, Jacob reflected, she was right.

Johnny had begged a farmer he knew to smuggle them out of the village in the cab of his tractor. From the main road they'd thumbed a lift to Blackpool. Winnie was shrewd enough to realise they'd be found sooner or later, but she thought that in the meantime, someone deranged enough to murder Bellamy in the heat of the moment was sure to give themselves away. She'd never even heard the term 'forensic science', but even she realised the killer was likely to be covered in blood. Bellamy's hut wasn't overlooked, but how would the killer get away from the pleasure grounds without being seen?

How indeed? If Winnie wasn't guilty, who was? She'd

convinced herself that Bellamy had been killed either by the woman who had scratched his face or by a vengeful lover of hers. Jacob knew that wasn't true, but by the time she'd reached the end of her story, he was persuaded of her innocence. Her account of the naïve and reckless way she and Gratrix had behaved had the ring of truth. What they'd done was stupid but entirely believable. No tissue of lies, however devious, could carry quite as much conviction.

'You don't think they're going to arrest me, then?' she demanded as he turned on to the road that led to Hemlock Bay.

'Don't worry about a thing. You can trust me. The *Clarion* is right behind you.'

He spoke with such cheery assurance that she didn't seem to realise it wasn't a direct response to her question.

In the smoking room at the Hemlock Hotel, Inspector Young was relishing his public address. He was standing on a makeshift podium, complete with lectern. Those present might have mistaken his solemn demeanour for that of an archbishop preaching a sermon if not for his habit of stealing glances at the large gilt mirror to check that he looked as commanding as he sounded. Over the years, the inspector had seldom been presented with any opportunity to soak up the limelight. Now he had the good fortune to be investigating a sensational crime, he was intent on making the most of it.

He'd taken the trouble to vet the list of people attending in addition to members of the fourth estate. First and foremost there was the chief constable. Major Busby was a purple-faced old soldier who had never held him in high regard. The major had a long-standing gripe that the local force failed to show the same standards of discipline as his old battalion. When Young had incautiously pointed out that the war was over, the major retorted that the war against crime was never-ending. Their relationship had been strained ever since and the inspector blamed old Busby for standing in the way of his further advancement. With any luck, a successful conclusion to this case would make it impossible to deny him promotion.

Sir Harold Jackson was also there, of course. He chaired the local bench and it was almost as important to impress him as to satisfy old Busby. A good word from Sir Harold would go a very long way. Those present also included the hotel manager Carson and his wife, and two women Sir Harold vouched for as distinguished visitors to the resort. One was an artist, apparently renowned, even if the inspector had never heard of her. The other was a demure young woman called Savernake, daughter of a late Old Bailey judge. People with connections, people who could hardly fail to admire the dynamism with which he'd conducted his investigation.

Thanks to extensive repetition and a series of long and meaningful pauses, his statement took much longer to deliver than the assembled hacks had expected. As he embarked on his peroration, there was an audible muttering and shuffling of feet.

The reporters were desperate to put questions of their own, acutely conscious that Jacob Flint had stolen a march on them. It was bad enough that he was the first newspaperman on the scene, but the fact that he'd actually discovered the dead fortune teller was salt on the wound. His breathless first-hand account had described the melodramatic nature of the killing at exuberant length. The inspector, for all his rhetorical flourishes, had added nothing new. Meanwhile, as the pressmen were uneasily aware, Jacob himself was nowhere to be seen. Nobody knew what he was up to, but all his competitors felt unhappily certain that he was up to *something*. The whiff of frustration in the air was almost as pungent as the stench of tobacco.

'In short,' Inspector Young said, 'I am confident – *absolutely* confident, I might emphasise – that we will shortly be in a position to make an arrest. As I've already said, my men are leaving no stone unturned in their determination to bring the murderer to justice. Let me repeat that, so there isn't a shadow of doubt. No. Stone. Unturned.'

He coughed, and allowed himself yet another pause. Although he hadn't quite reached the last of his somewhat superfluous cue cards, a reporter in the front row, a burly fellow with a bulbous red nose, could restrain himself no longer.

'Can you assure us that by the end of today, Mr Jacob Flint will be under lock and key?'

The speaker was a crime reporter for the *Daily Slogan* who bitterly resented being dragged from the hostelries of central London to this outpost of what passed for civilisation in the north of England. His intervention prompted an outburst of merriment which had Inspector Young on his feet and calling for order.

'Mr Flint has been interviewed,' the detective announced, 'and I can tell you that he is not at present helping us with our enquiries.'

'Hope you're keeping close tabs on him,' said the man from the *Witness*, deadliest rival of the *Clarion*. 'Always said one day that lad would go too far.'

Inspector Young took a breath. 'You gentlemen of the London press will have your little joke.'

'This is no joking matter,' the *Witness* man said. 'Have

you any idea of the number of murder scenes where young Flint has been present before anyone else got a whiff that something was up? Bears close investigation, if you ask me. All we're asking as citizens and ratepayers is that the police do their job.'

Inspector Young frowned and cleared his throat so menacingly that even the noisiest journalists were subdued.

'I can tell you all that Mr Jacob Flint...'

His voice trailed away as the heavy door at the rear of the smoking room swung open and Jacob's head appeared. The first person he caught sight of was Rachel. He gave her a cheeky wink before treating Inspector Young to a triumphant grin.

He marched in and, as he approached the podium, he was followed by Winnie Lescott, her head held high. Johnny Gratrix lumbered along in their wake.

There was a momentary stunned silence before the man from the *Daily Slogan*, unable to contain his emotions any longer, uttered a loud groan of defeat. He was expressing the collective misery of all his colleagues.

'Afternoon, Inspector,' Jacob said breezily. 'Sorry to butt in, but better late than never. The *Clarion* brings good news to Hemlock Bay.'

The inspector stared at Winnie Lescott. He opened his mouth to speak, but when she glared, words failed him.

Jacob jumped up on to the podium and beamed down at his professional colleagues.

'I'm delighted to announce that Miss Lescott here is ready and willing to talk to the police. She is absolutely determined to clear her good name and to give the authorities whatever help she can in bringing the culprit to justice. The death of such a close companion as Mr Bellamy has come as a shocking blow. No wonder she needed to take time with a caring friend to come to terms with the tragedy. She will describe in an exclusive interview with the *Clarion* the personal nightmare she has experienced during the past twenty-four hours.'

'But...' Young began. His face was red and he was gripping the lectern in order to remain steady on his feet. He looked like a man who has been clouted with his own truncheon.

'Thankfully,' Jacob interrupted, 'Miss Lescott has a cast-iron alibi. Mr Gratrix here can tell you exactly where she was throughout the course of yesterday. Other witnesses are available if his word alone will not suffice. Full details for the wider public will appear on tomorrow's front page. The lady is, of course, innocent of this heinous crime.' He turned to the detective. 'Rest assured, Inspector. The *Clarion* stands ready to give you every possible support in the hunt for the real Crystal Ball Killer.'

20

'Extraordinary,' Virginia Penrhos said. 'Can you believe it?' Inspector Young's conference had broken up in disarray ten minutes earlier. After calming herself with a stiff drink, she'd bumped into Rachel again in the lobby.

'Where Jacob Flint is concerned,' Rachel murmured, 'I've learned to suspend my disbelief.'

Virginia's bushy eyebrows shot up. 'You know him?'

'Our paths have crossed in London. An impetuous young man.'

'So I gather.' Virginia frowned. 'Did he follow you up here?'

Rachel smiled sweetly. 'He carries a torch for my maid. A very pretty girl, Martha. Far too good for him.'

'Have you any idea why he's so convinced that this man Bellamy wasn't murdered by his mistress? It seems utterly ridiculous. The detective made it as plain as a pikestaff that she committed the crime in a fit of jealous rage.'

'He did,' Rachel admitted.

'The woman had the motive and presumably plenty of opportunity.' Virginia was warming to her theme. 'Not only that, she fled the scene in the company of another man. Highly incriminating.'

'True.' Rachel sighed. 'I suppose the police are bound to make further inquiries. I don't even have a complete alibi myself. Not for the whole of yesterday afternoon.'

She gave Virginia a rueful smile. The artist responded with a decisive shake of the head.

'Inspector Young is fond of his own voice, but that doesn't mean he's such an idiot that he'd suspect you, my dear. What motive could you possibly have for bludgeoning Bellamy to death? You never met him, did you?'

'Never,' Rachel said. 'Not even to have my fortune told.' She put her hand to her mouth, as if she'd committed a faux pas.

Virginia smiled grimly. 'Don't worry, my dear. Nothing he claimed to see in our palms or in that crystal provoked me into bashing him over the head.'

'Honestly, I wasn't suggesting that you—'

'Of course. And you're right. Until the killer is safely behind bars, there will be endless stupid speculation.' She took a breath. 'The question is this. Why would anyone want to kill the man? Revenge, jealousy, greed. Those are the reasons why one person takes another's life. This Lescott woman is the obvious candidate. A fiery character, by all accounts. The journalist must be barking up the wrong tree. He looks very young. Wet behind the ears, frankly.'

'Very wet,' Rachel said. 'As I understand it, Bellamy came to Hemlock Bay recently. Any of us might have crossed paths with him in the past...'

Her voice trailed away, as if she'd been struck by an embarrassing thought. Virginia gave her a searching look.

'I know what's crossed your mind,' she said quietly. 'Ffion

and I are Welsh. So was Bellamy. Apparently, he came from Bangor, not far from Llangefni, where I grew up. But I swear to you, neither of us had ever heard of Gareth Bellamy, let alone his wretched nom de plume, until we arrived in Hemlock Bay. In case you're wondering, we certainly didn't recognise him when he told our fortunes. Because we'd never seen him before. The man meant nothing to us. Nothing.'

As she spoke, her voice had become increasingly strident. Rachel bowed her head.

'Please forgive me. I didn't mean to imply... it's just that I'm sure the police will ask us all questions. Whether we knew him, where we were yesterday afternoon...'

Virginia snorted. 'The good inspector may be in for a shock. Ffion and I were taking advantage of the lovely weather. Relaxing on the terrace in the Sun and Air Garden. Making friends with the watchman's Alsatian. We miss not having a dog of our own here. Are you a dog lover, Rachel?'

Before Rachel could answer, Louis Carson and his wife emerged from the smoking room. On catching sight of the two women, Carson seemed eager to get on his way but Rachel intercepted them.

'An astonishing turn of events, Mr Carson! What do you make of it?'

'Indeed it is. Remarkable.'

He tugged at his tie. After their previous brief encounter, Rachel guessed he was wondering whether to indulge in polite conversation or come up with an excuse to escape. She made the decision for him by addressing his wife.

'And you must be Mrs Carson! My maid met you the other day.'

Pearl Carson smiled. 'Martha, isn't that her name? A very pleasant girl.'

Carson surrendered to the inevitable. 'Dearest, this is Miss Savernake, our neighbour from Bay View.'

As the two women shook hands, Rachel said, 'Martha told me you gave her complimentary tickets to the Sun and Air Garden.'

Pearl Carson laughed. 'I thought you might both enjoy yourselves there. It's very discreet. Don't you agree, Miss… Penrhos, isn't it? You live in the lighthouse, don't you?'

Virginia nodded. 'The Sun and Air Garden is an oasis of calm. Given what happened yesterday at Paradise, any opportunity of peace and quiet is to be relished.'

'The inspector seems flummoxed,' Pearl Carson said.

'Out of his depth, I fear,' her husband said.

'I hope this ghastly business is soon cleared up. The longer the police allow it to drag on, the worse it will be for everyone.'

Virginia Penrhos was brusquely unsympathetic. 'You'll get more visitors, not fewer. People flock to a crime scene like vultures to carrion.'

Before either of the Carsons could reply, Sir Harold Jackson emerged from the smoking room. He nodded to Louis Carson and exchanged a smile with Carson's wife. Was it her imagination, Rachel wondered, or did the man's very presence cause Pearl Carson to brighten?

'The chief constable has asked Young for a word in private,' Sir Harold said. 'The inspector's detective work isn't up to snuff, that's painfully obvious. He spotted a simple explanation for the crime and swallowed it hook, line, and sinker, without bothering to check whether it stood up to scrutiny.'

'Is it definite that the Lescott woman didn't kill Bellamy?' Carson asked.

'Apparently she and her beau were drinking at the Fisherman's Arms when the crime was committed.'

'Can the medical people be precise about the time of death?'

'They don't need to be so far as Winnie Lescott is concerned. There was hardly a moment yesterday when she was out of sight of at least one other person.'

'Among that class of person,' Carson said sorrowfully, 'alibis can be bought and sold like a packet of cigarettes. Surely she is still the most credible suspect?'

'Unfortunately,' Sir Harold Jackson said, 'these things don't arrange themselves for our convenience.'

'Where does that leave us?' Pearl Carson asked.

'In some difficulty, my dear Mrs Carson, I'm sorry to tell you,' he said grimly. 'You see, the unpalatable truth is that if Winifred Lescott didn't kill Bellamy, someone else did.'

'Which means...' she began before he finished the sentence for her.

'... that unless the culprit has gone on the run, we have a murderer in our midst. Here in the heart of Hemlock Bay.'

'May I offer you a lift home, ladies?' Sir Harold asked.

He'd followed Virginia and Rachel through the revolving glass doors. Outside the drizzle was getting heavier. He indicated his Bentley, parked in a reserved space next to the main entrance.

'Kind of you,' Virginia said, 'but I don't want to take you out of your way.'

'No trouble at all. I'm heading in your direction. Sadie is resting this afternoon and I don't want to get under her feet. It'll do me good to take a walk and fill my lungs with sea air. Even in damp and blustery weather, an hour or two roaming around the countryside always does me a power of good. Who knows, it may even help me to make some sense of this rotten mess about Bellamy.'

'In that case, thank you. Ffion is under the weather herself, so I intend to spend the afternoon painting.'

Sir Harold squinted at the leaden skies. 'Not the loveliest outlook today, I'm afraid.'

Virginia laughed as he held open the rear door for her. 'So much the better. One of the many advantages of surrealism is that I can conjure a tantalising work of art from the most unpromising visual material.'

'I'll take your word for it.' He turned to Rachel. 'Care to join us, Miss Savernake?'

'You're very kind,' Rachel said as he ushered her into the back of the car. 'Do you have a theory of your own about the murder?'

'I'm at a complete loss, I must confess. The whole business seems unfathomable. Thankfully, the chief constable realises the time has come for decisive action.'

'What sort of action?' Virginia asked.

Sir Harold coughed. 'I'm sure neither of you ladies would betray a confidence…'

'Perish the thought,' Rachel said.

'Major Busby spoke to me off the record, in my capacity as chairman of the local magistrates. He wants Young to step back from leading the investigation. The poor devil has done his best, but this is a different kettle of fish from arresting drunken youths on Morecambe promenade. Young lacks experience of a complex murder investigation carried out in the glare of national publicity.'

'Does the chief constable believe the case is complex?'

Virginia asked. 'Sordid, yes. Such a crude act of violence. It's not as if the murderer concocted an ingenious plan.'

'Whoever it was vanished from the pleasure grounds without a trace.'

'Paradise is always busy. With any luck, witnesses will soon come forward.'

'Let's hope so. At present, all the signs are that this crime isn't as straightforward as Young led everyone to believe. Murder is too serious a crime for anyone to stand on ceremony. Let alone be distracted by parochial pride. So the chief constable has decided it's time to call in expert help.'

'Scotland Yard?' Rachel asked.

'Correct.'

'Isn't that premature? Not to mention harsh?' Virginia shook her head. 'Bellamy was murdered only twenty-four hours ago. Even if the local man did fasten on to the Lescott woman too quickly, it's foolish to panic.'

Sir Harold started the car. There was plenty of room in the back, but Rachel was conscious of Virginia's bulky frame pressing against her.

'It's imperative not to let the trail go cold. The first twenty-four hours of an investigation are vital. If Lescott's daughter didn't kill the fortune teller, a great deal of valuable time has already been lost. The real culprit has been allowed to commit a savage crime and get away with it. Scot-free.'

'You're assuming the killer is a man?' Rachel said quietly.

'What?' He glanced over his shoulder. 'Oh yes, indeed, Miss Savernake. That's my theory, for what it's worth. I don't regard this as a woman's crime.'

He turned his attention back to the road as he navigated

the slight bend at Shore Gardens. They left the esplanade and turned into Beggarman's Lane.

'You don't?' Rachel asked.

'No. The killing was too brutal. Too impulsive.'

'You suppose a woman would be subtler?'

'Certainly. That's why so many poisoners are female. This is a different sort of crime.'

'Unpremeditated?' Virginia suggested.

'Looks to me as if the fellow had a row with Bellamy, and in a fit of uncontrollable rage picked up the crystal ball because it was the weapon nearest at hand. What he did may have been entirely out of character. Good afternoon, Mrs Stones!' He waved a gloved hand as they passed a woman on her way into town, canvas shopping bag in hand. 'If so, perhaps he is gathering the courage to confess.'

'I hope so too, Sir Harold,' Virginia said. 'Although frankly someone capable of extreme violence may not have such a tender conscience. As long as bringing in someone from London doesn't cause further delay. The uncertainty is crippling, especially for anyone who is naturally sensitive. Like Ffion, for instance. She has been in a state of extreme nervous tension ever since we heard the news.'

'Quite so. This morning I impressed on the chief constable the need to ensure that our peaceful community isn't condemned to live in fear a moment longer than necessary. Between you and me, he spoke to the Metropolitan commissioner even before today's public meeting. Frankly, that took me aback, but he's never had great faith in Young. The man doesn't recognise his own limitations. Reinforcements from London should arrive later today. With any luck this whole messy business will soon be sorted out and all of us can get back to normal.'

'Except for the murderer, of course,' Rachel said pleasantly.

He shot her a curious glance. 'Indeed. Ah, here we are.'

The car eased to a halt outside the front gate of Bay View and Virginia said she'd get out as well. After saying their goodbyes, the two women watched the Bentley glide off down the lane.

'The murder has upset you, as well as Miss Morris,' Rachel murmured.

Virginia looked at her sharply. 'Yes, perhaps more than it should have done.'

'If the two of you are unhappy in Hemlock Bay, might you cut short your stay here?'

There was a pause. 'You're very shrewd, aren't you? There's more to you than meets the eye, I'm certain of it. And yes, I don't mind admitting that I've thought about leaving.'

'Why?'

'The first time I ever set eyes on this place, it seemed idyllic. Lovely and tranquil, a real haven. A welcome escape from the real world.'

'Just as your art offers a means of escape,' Rachel said.

'Exactly. The murder has ruined everything. Perhaps above all, it's destroyed my illusion. The trouble is, I'm skilled in one particular art. Deceiving myself.'

Virginia seemed almost to be talking to herself. Rachel said nothing, and after a few moments the older woman straightened, as if coming to a decision.

'No, I won't allow myself to be stopped by the death of a man who meant nothing to me.'

'I'm glad.'

'Are you?' Virginia clasped Rachel's hand. 'Your features really are striking, my dear. So very feminine, yet strong. Fine cheekbones, firm jaw. Have you ever modelled for an artist?'

'Never.'

Virginia smiled. 'Perhaps you'd be kind enough to sit for me?'

'For you?'

'Yes, my dear girl. Don't worry, I shan't interfere with your holiday, and it won't take up too much of your time. Once I get a fuller sense of your character... I can let my imagination roam. If you're willing to take the risk of inspiring a surrealist, that is.'

'Are you serious? I mean, I have no experience...'

'No modesty, now! I demand a straight yes or no. Please don't make me beg!'

Rachel laughed. 'You flatter me, Virginia. To be honest, there's nothing I'd love more.'

'Splendid! That's settled, then.' A pause. 'My closest friends call me Ginny.'

'You're sure Miss Morris won't mind... Ginny?'

Virginia's tone sharpened. 'Ffion is a delightful girl, but she is in no position to complain. I choose my subjects, no one else.'

'How marvellous! Would tomorrow afternoon be convenient? Four o'clock?'

'Perfect!'

'I'll look forward to it.' Rachel smiled. 'Even if you paint me as a dark, mysterious blur.'

The other woman considered her. 'Do you know, my dear girl? That might be the perfect way to capture your air of mystery.'

21

'Congratulations, Jacob,' Rachel said. 'That was quite a *coup de théâtre*. Poor Inspector Young looked as if he'd need reviving with smelling salts when you waltzed in with the prime suspect and her fancy man in tow.'

Jacob made a token attempt to look modest, failing hopelessly. He'd arrived at Bay View as the others were finishing tea. Having missed breakfast and lunch in the cause of the *Clarion*, he was ready to make up for lost time by devouring what remained from Hetty's latest batch of scones.

'Winnie Lescott isn't an easy woman. She flares up at the slightest provocation and always insists on having the last word. When I left the hotel, she was threatening to ring Gomersall and demand twice as much money for her story. When she's got me to thank for making sure she won't spend the night in a prison cell.'

'Poor Jacob,' Martha said. 'Such ingratitude. At least we appreciate your public spirit and sense of duty.'

'Unlike your colleagues in Fleet Street,' Rachel said. 'If looks could kill, you'd have keeled over the moment you walked into the smoking room. At least you made sure there was no miscarriage of justice.'

Jacob looked at her. 'You didn't think Winnie was guilty, did you?'

'No. Why would she visit his fortune telling hut to confront him? It didn't make sense. Surely the time for a homicidal outburst was when she first saw his scratched face, and promptly put two and two together to make five?'

He nodded. 'Her big mistake was running away. Highly suspicious.'

'Martha gave us a hint, don't forget. She mentioned the gardener – this man Gratrix – who winked and whistled at her while she was walking through the Rose Garden. A lecherous labourer sounded like the sort of man Winnie might turn to if she fell out with Bellamy. On the principle of any port in a storm. That's why I asked if anyone who worked at the pleasure grounds was missing.'

'Guesswork, surely?'

Rachel shrugged. 'Yes, but with a foundation in evidence.'

'Such as?'

'You reported your conversation with Bellamy faithfully, didn't you? Remember what he said?'

Light dawned in Jacob's eyes. 'He mentioned that he didn't want Winnie hanging around the Rose Garden.'

'Precisely. He knew what Johnny Gratrix was like.'

Jacob looked hopefully at the last scone on the tray. Hetty nodded and he swooped on it as if he hadn't eaten in a week.

Rachel said, 'This leaves us with two questions. Who did kill him? And why?'

'Care to make a stab in the dark?' he mumbled, mouth full.

Martha clicked her tongue. 'A carefully reasoned deduction, you mean?'

'Sorry,' he said, gulping the rest of his scone. 'Of course that's what I meant to say.'

He sounded unrepentant, but Rachel's expression didn't flicker. 'I had the glimmering of an idea but, on second thoughts, I was on the wrong track.'

'Try us.'

'I was struck by the fact that Bellamy hails from Bangor, while Virginia Penrhos – or Ginny, as she wants me to call her – grew up on Anglesey. An island across the Menai Straits from Bangor. She's older than him and when she left that part of the world to pursue her artistic interests in England, he would probably still have been at school. But it's an interesting coincidence and I wondered if their paths had crossed in the past.'

'Plausible.'

'So I thought. Unfortunately, Virginia raised the Welsh connection herself without any prompting. She claims she'd never heard of Bellamy before she came to Hemlock Bay.'

'She might be lying.'

Rachel gave him a cool look. 'Strangely enough, that possibility had occurred to me. The snag is that I believed her.'

'Feminine intuition?' he asked with a mischievous grin.

'Living dangerously, Jacob,' Martha whispered. 'You've had a successful day; don't push your luck.'

'I might be mistaken,' Rachel said unexpectedly. 'I like to think I'm good at judging when someone tries to pull the wool over my eyes, but it's not an exact science. However, Virginia made the point with quiet confidence and a minimum of fuss. I'm strongly inclined to accept that she was telling me the truth.'

'What about her young pal?'

'Ffion, who is apparently so frightened by a murderer

on the loose that she's taken to her bed? She comes from Machynlleth in mid-Wales, but Virginia claims Bellamy was unknown to her as well. At least until they had their fortunes told.'

'Maybe Bellamy said something while reading their palms that provoked Ffion to murder. She sounds as though it wouldn't take much to knock her off balance.'

'Bellamy's fortune telling was deliberately bland. It seems unlikely that he would have antagonised either of them. Let alone cause one of them to come back several days later and attack him in a frenzy of violence.'

He sighed. 'All right. Let's suppose one of the ladies from the lighthouse didn't commit the murder. Who is left?'

'We may get further by asking ourselves a different question. *Cui bono?*'

'Who benefits from the crime,' Jacob said smugly. He didn't know much Latin, but that phrase had lodged in his mind.

'Do we know who inherits under Bellamy's will?' Martha asked.

'The chances are, he hasn't made one,' Rachel said. 'People his age often don't. In which case his estate will be distributed to his closest family members. I doubt it makes any difference. All the signs are that he was short of money.'

'Winnie said he was hoping for some sort of windfall,' Jacob said. 'She didn't know how much cash was involved and she didn't know where it was supposed to be coming from. In fact, she didn't believe a word of it. I can't blame her. Poor old Bellamy found lying came more easily than telling the truth.'

'He had a vile temper,' Martha said, touching her neck. 'If he flew off the handle again, perhaps someone hit him on the head in self-defence.'

'Perhaps,' Jacob said. 'Although who and where the murderer might be, I can't imagine. Maybe the Scotland Yard man will pick up a lead.'

Rachel consulted her new diamond watch, purchased from Cartier a fortnight ago. 'Inspector Oakes should arrive in the next two or three hours. Why don't you stay and have dinner with us? Afterwards, we might pop over to the Hemlock Hotel this evening to say hello.'

Jacob stared at her. 'There's no guarantee that the Yard will send Oakes. He's a busy man.'

'After you rang this morning, I called to let him know that events might take an unexpected turn. Unexpected by Inspector Young, at any rate. After your performance in the smoking room, I sent a quick telegram suggesting that he speak to the assistant commissioner at the Yard and advise him that this case is anything but open and shut. I received a reply shortly after I got back here. He was on his way to Euston Station.'

'We really must stop meeting like this.'

Inspector Philip Oakes sipped the froth off his beer and wiped his mouth before leaning back in his chair with a sigh of satisfaction. Officially, he'd finished work for the evening at nine o'clock. Major Busby had briefed him and his sergeant, a man called Wagstaffe, and he'd also spoken at length with Inspector Young. Wagstaffe, a firm believer in early-to-bed-and-early-to-rise, had retired to his room on the hotel's top floor, leaving his superior free to relax in the American Bar in the company of Rachel Savernake and Jacob Flint.

Rachel laughed. 'Worried about your reputation, Inspector? I don't blame you. No young woman with any claim to respectability should find herself mixed up with as many murders as me.'

Oakes laughed. 'It's all right, Miss Savernake. I'm accustomed to consorting with shady customers.'

'Rachel, please. No need for formality when there's nobody else around.'

He shook his head. 'Easier if we keep things strictly professional, Miss Savernake. I'm up here on official duty and I wouldn't want to forget myself when other people are about.'

'Of course,' she said quickly. 'I quite understand.'

Jacob stared moodily at the ceiling. He liked Oakes and enjoyed his company. More than that, he respected his intelligence and integrity. Yet although he hated to admit it – even to himself – he felt a pang of dismay at any hint that Rachel was attracted to the man from Scotland Yard.

Absurd, he knew. Rachel was hopelessly out of reach as far as he was concerned, protected from lesser mortals – including himself – not only by the Truemans but also by her restless mind and scathing sense of humour. Sometimes she seemed so cold and distant that he was convinced she didn't have a romantic bone in her body. Yet there were fleeting moments when he wasn't quite so sure.

Suddenly he realised the detective's eyes were on him.

'Penny for 'em.'

Jacob tried not to blush. 'I wonder if anything Gareth Bellamy told me gives a clue to his death.'

'I didn't know he visited you in Fleet Street.' Oakes took another drink. 'You two had better spill the beans.'

'There are quite a lot of beans,' Jacob said.

'Better get on with it, then, before the bar closes for the night.'

Jacob and Rachel took it in turns to tell their tales. Oakes listened, intent yet expressionless, resisting any temptation to interrupt with questions.

'You've been busy,' he said at length. 'And you've had a head start, given that Inspector Young couldn't imagine anyone other than Winnie Lescott as the culprit.'

'Is Young co-operating with you?' Jacob asked. 'Or has his demotion thrown him into a great sulk?'

'Naturally he's upset that the chief constable called in the Yard, but he seems a decent enough fellow. With any luck, I'll be able to make sure he comes out of the case with enough credit to soothe his battered pride. With great reluctance, he's accepted that Winnie didn't kill Bellamy, but he hasn't a clue about who else might be responsible.' He exhaled. 'So what do you two make of it all?'

Jacob cleared his throat. 'Rachel has persuaded me that Louis Carson is up to no good.'

Oakes gave her an appraising glance. 'Because events in Hemlock Bay have taken such a macabre turn since he and his wife moved here?'

She nodded. 'It seems a good working hypothesis. Unfortunately, I can't supply you with a shred of evidence linking Carson to Bellamy's murder. He seems to have spent yesterday here in the hotel.'

'Hardly a cast-iron alibi,' Oakes said. 'My understanding is that the scene of the crime, on the other side of Hemlock Head, is only ten or twelve minutes away from here.'

'True,' Rachel said. 'But he'd need to get there and back, having committed the crime without witnesses and disposed somehow of any bloodstained clothing. That would take half an hour as an absolute minimum. Conceivable, but a very tall order.'

Jacob said, 'I've been asking around. As far as I can tell, Carson was fully occupied with hotel business. Plenty of people saw him at different times during the day. So far, I've not heard anything that implicates him. Nobody has mentioned anything unusual about his behaviour. The same goes for his wife.'

'Carson is the sort who might get someone else to do his dirty work,' Rachel said. 'But that begs the question. Why would he want Bellamy dead?'

'Something to do with this mysterious premonition?' Oakes asked.

Rachel shrugged. 'We need to look at other potential suspects. Trueman has gone to the Mermaid in search of McAtee.'

'What brought McAtee here, I wonder? Did he have some sort of link with Bellamy, for instance?'

'I can't imagine what it would be. I wonder if he's come here in pursuit of the mysterious Dr Doyle, but again I've no idea why.'

Last orders had been called, and no one else was left in the American Bar. The barman threw them a meaningful glance and as the inspector drained his tankard, Rachel checked her watch.

'Time to go. You'll be busy tomorrow, Inspector, but I hope we can catch up when you have a spare moment.'

'I hope so too,' he said.

He smiled so shyly he might have been a schoolboy, and Jacob felt another pang of jealousy.

'Any joy?' Rachel asked.

Resplendent in his chauffeur's uniform, Trueman was

standing beside the Phantom in the hotel car park. His buttons
gleamed in the moonlight. The rain had stopped and despite
the lateness of the hour the temperature was remarkably mild.

'No sign of McAtee in the Mermaid. Don't know where he's
got to. I finished up gossiping with a pair of crime reporters
from London.'

'Learn anything?'

'Only that if there's another murder in Hemlock Bay,
there's a good chance the victim will be Jacob Flint.'

Rachel smiled. 'Surely they don't hate him that much?'

The big man shrugged. 'They don't dislike him on a
personal level. He's good company and stands his round. But
they're afraid they'll never get another scoop as long as he's
around, he's such a lucky bastard.'

Rachel couldn't help laughing. 'He makes his own luck.'

'With a helping hand from you.'

'Jacob will always drive people to distraction. It's his way.'

'Any moment now, you'll be telling me he's got a heart of
gold.'

'I know he can be bumptious, but there's no malice in him.
Whenever something knocks him down, he bounces straight
back up again like a jack-in-the-box. It's easy to forget there's
a good brain hidden beneath all that floppy fair hair. And, not
that it matters much in Fleet Street, he writes well.'

'I'll take your word for it,' Trueman muttered, and opened
the car door.

The roads were deserted at this hour and they were back
at Bay View in next to no time. While Trueman manoeuvred
the Phantom into the tiny garage, Rachel lingered outside the
bungalow, breathing in the night air.

Somewhere in the trees, an owl hooted. In an uncharacteristic
flight of fancy, she imagined the unseen bird giving her the

benefit of its wisdom. Hinting that the truth about Hemlock Bay was within touching distance. An idea began to form in her mind.

Trueman joined her. 'How is your handsome policeman friend?'

'Inspector Oakes?' she asked carelessly. 'On good form, I'd say. I suppose he is quite nice-looking. I've never given it any thought.'

'No?'

As usual, Trueman's craggy features gave nothing away. Rachel frowned.

'Jacob and I told him everything we know. He's a first-class listener.'

'Of course. All three of you speak the same language.'

'You're right,' she said softly, gesturing towards the moon. 'And I'm grateful for the illumination.'

The warm smell of frying bacon and freshly made coffee wafted through Bay View, as Rachel emerged from the bathroom in a salmon pink kimono. Her black hair was tousled and her feet bare. She'd had a restless night, tossing and turning as her unconscious mind strove to untangle the secrets of Hemlock Bay. She was padding across the landing when a frantic knocking at the front door stopped her in her tracks.

The metal flap of the letterbox lifted with a clang. The anguished voice of an older woman shrieked through the gap in the door.

'Come quickly! You must come quickly!'

Rachel raced downstairs, taking the steps two at a time. As she lifted the keys from a hook, she heard the Truemans rushing up behind her.

'Let me answer!' Hetty called. 'You're not decent!'

Taking no notice, Rachel flung open the door. An angular woman stood on the step. Her pallid features were wrinkled with distress and her whole body seemed to quiver.

'Mrs Stones!' Hetty cried over Rachel's shoulder. 'Whatever is the matter?'

'Please! You must come to Shepherd's Cottage at once!'

'What's happened?' Rachel demanded.

'It's Dr Doyle!'

'What about him?'

'I think he's dead!'

22

'I've never seen anything like it,' wailed Mrs Stones as they awaited the arrival of the police.

For once in her life, this was no exaggeration. She'd told her story in between gulping sobs. On arriving at Shepherd's Cottage to make the doctor's breakfast, she'd found the kitchen door was locked. There was a faint whiff of something in the air, but a bout of pneumonia in childhood had left her with a poor sense of smell and she thought nothing of it.

Normally, Dr Doyle was out of bed and pottering around by the time she reached the cottage. His habit was to take in his pint of milk from the doorstep. Today the milk was still waiting, and he was nowhere to be seen. When she stood at the foot of the stairs and called his name, there was no reply. It was a bright morning and she wondered if he was in the garden, but when she tried the back door, she found that too was locked.

Puzzled, she went outside. The kitchen was cramped and had a solitary window. The curtains were drawn, but imperfectly, and she was able to peer through a chink. What she saw made her heart lurch. A man's stockinged feet and lower legs – in twill trousers – were visible on the stone-flagged floor. The rest of him was out of sight, but the feet were immobile and at an angle which suggested he was unconscious or dead.

Terrified, she'd stumbled down the lane to seek help at Bay View. Pausing only to throw a mink cape over her kimono, Rachel raced along the lane to the cottage with the Truemans in hot pursuit and Mrs Stones bringing up the rear. When they looked through the gap in the curtain for themselves, the feet were still lying where Mrs Stones had seen them.

None of them was in any doubt that Doyle was dead.

The others stood back as Trueman picked up a large stone and smashed the window, knocking out the whole pane. The stench of gas from the kitchen was overpowering.

Covering her mouth and nose with a handkerchief supplied by Hetty, Rachel poked her head through the opening and rested her elbows on the top of a sizeable wooden window seat. A few seconds were all she needed to take in the scene.

'Doyle's head is inside the oven.' She held back Hetty and Mrs Stones. 'No, I'm afraid there's nothing we can do for him. He's probably been dead for hours. Martha, can you go back to Bay View and call the police? Better not touch the telephone in the cottage. Or anything else for that matter. I'd love to have a quick snoop, but I'd better resist temptation. They will need to check for fingerprints.'

'You don't think…?'

'Right now,' Rachel said slowly, 'I don't know what to think. Last night, I persuaded myself that I'd made a breakthrough, but Doyle's death puts a different complexion on things. Suicide or not, this is something I never expected.'

Martha's face fell. She wasn't accustomed to seeing Rachel at a loss.

'Shall I ring the local station?'

'Inspector Oakes won't thank us if we give Young further cause to resent him. The danger is that the local men may decide this isn't any of Scotland Yard's business. We don't want them to miss vital evidence. Call the hotel and ask to be put through to Inspector Oakes. Leave it to him to decide how many toes he's prepared to tread on.'

'You think he'll want to come here? Is Doyle's death connected with the murder of Gareth Bellamy?'

Mrs Stones moaned softly behind them. Hetty murmured words of comfort in her ear.

'We can't rule out coincidence,' Rachel said. 'But two unconnected and rather terrible deaths inside little more than twenty-four hours would raise eyebrows in Whitechapel or Limehouse, never mind Hemlock Bay.'

Martha nodded. 'I'll let Jacob know too. He'll never forgive me if I don't give him the chance of another scoop. And it can't do any harm.'

'Except,' Rachel said softly, 'for giving his rivals in Fleet Street an even stronger motive to murder him.'

'Such a dreadful tragedy, Doctor!' Rachel exclaimed as the front door opened and a middle-aged man marched out, black bag in hand.

She'd waited patiently for the chance to intercept Dr Sowden as he emerged from Shepherd's Cottage. The little house remained a hive of activity, with Inspector Young and his sergeant buzzing around inside while a burly young constable patrolled up and down the lane, ready to send any nosey passers-by on their way. Inspector Oakes and Sergeant Wagstaffe had put in an appearance before returning to the Hemlock Hotel, Oakes to make a report to the chief constable, and Wagstaffe to enquire into the dead man's background.

Young's sergeant had taken statements from everyone present at the time the body was discovered. Two sombre attendants had just left the cottage bearing a stretcher with the blanket-shrouded corpse to a waiting ambulance.

The doctor, a well-fed man with thinning hair and pink cheeks, looked Rachel up and down, as if checking for symptoms of an ailment. Or perhaps he was simply agog at the sight of a young woman without make-up, wearing a mink cape and not much else. She was even barefoot.

'Miss Savernake, is it? The neighbour who found the body?'

'It was Mrs Stones raised the alarm,' she said shyly. 'Of course we all rushed over here without a second thought.'

'Indeed, indeed. Not easy for you, my dear young lady. Wretched business. Very upsetting for all concerned.'

'It's so terribly sad.'

'Please don't distress yourself. These things are hard to bear, but you mustn't dwell on what you saw. Especially if you have no one to lean on.'

She responded with a doleful smile. Hetty had accompanied Mrs Stones back to her house to make her a consolatory cup of tea, while Martha had returned with her brother to Bay View.

'You're very thoughtful, Doctor.'

Sowden exuded the genial assurance of one whose patients constantly shower him with thanks for his kindness and wisdom.

'I can prescribe a sedative, if you wish.'

'Thank you, but I think I can manage,' she murmured.

'Plucky of you, Miss Savernake. If you're quite sure…'

Rachel looked at the ground. 'I suppose there is no doubt that the poor man… took his own life?'

'A matter for the inquest, my dear young lady. But I think I can safely say that the coroner and his jury will not be unduly troubled. I fear it's a straightforward matter. Asphyxia by coal gas poisoning.' He clicked his tongue in disapproval. 'In my youth, it was unknown. Nowadays it's commonplace as a cause of death. Especially in cases of *felo de se*. A regrettable consequence of technological advances in the field of domestic heating. The march of progress, Miss Savernake, all too often takes us backwards.'

His eyes twinkled as he uttered this aphorism, his self-satisfaction no doubt reinforced by Rachel's rapt gaze.

'You… you don't think it could have been an accident?'

His smile was tolerant. 'Indeed not. You see, the evidence points to a simple conclusion. The poor fellow had been drinking brandy. There is an empty bottle on the kitchen table, together with a single glass tumbler. There was also an empty bottle of Veronal.'

'Isn't that a sleeping powder?'

Sowden nodded. 'I prescribe it to my own patients but, like any barbiturate, it must be used with discretion. My impression is that he took a little of the powder, whatever was left in the bottle, to dull his senses. Then he swallowed brandy as a means of plucking up enough Dutch courage to end it all.'

'How awful! If only someone else had been with him last night.'

'Or earlier in the day. Pending a post-mortem, my preliminary view is that he died yesterday afternoon. Beyond doubt, he was alone. The kitchen door was locked on the inside and so was the window until the glass was broken. As if that wasn't clear enough, the poor devil seems to have left some kind of scrawled message.'

'He did?'

'Inspector Young tells me it was lying underneath his body, which suggests he dropped it as he prepared to... well, end it all.'

Rachel put a hand to her mouth. 'My goodness! What on earth did the note say?'

Dr Sowden shook his head. 'I'm afraid I really cannot divulge that, my dear young lady. The facts will come out soon enough at the inquest.'

'Please forgive me,' Rachel said in a small voice. 'Naturally I'm consumed by curiosity.'

'I quite understand.'

'I'd hate you to think I was encouraging you to disregard professional etiquette. Especially since I've heard such wonderful things about you from Lady Jackson.'

'You have?' He beamed. 'That's very good of her ladyship. You're a friend of hers?'

'I had a delightful conversation with dear Sadie – I mean, Lady Jackson – the evening before last. She and her husband invited me to dine with them.'

'Splendid, splendid. Marvellous hosts, aren't they? Indeed, I've had the honour of dining at the Hall on many an occasion.'

'Sadie couldn't stop singing your praises. She says she owes her very survival to your care.'

'Oh, dear me, I wouldn't go as far as that. Indeed, it really is too generous of her ladyship to say so, especially given that she is experiencing...' He coughed, as if to cover embarrassment. 'Lung cancer is a truly pernicious disease. When I was a boy, tumours on the lung were a rarity, but now they have become increasingly common. I put it down to the prevalence of asphalted roads, polluting the very air that we breathe. Yet another example, I regret to say, of the malign consequences of a modern industrial process.'

'How alarming.'

'There is so much so-called progress that is anything but. I fear for the younger generation.' He gave a sorrowful smile. 'People of your age, Miss Savernake, alas. But you must put these things to the back of your mind. In my opinion...'

'I suppose,' Rachel interrupted, 'that as a medical man, Dr Doyle would know exactly how to... do what he did in as efficient a manner as possible. I like to think that he passed away painlessly.'

Sowden shook his head. 'I really shouldn't breathe a word about this, but it will come out at the inquest anyway. The police don't believe the man was a qualified doctor.'

'My goodness!' She put her hand to her mouth. 'Can that really be true?'

He gave a decisive nod, unable to disguise his delight at provoking such amazement. 'This is strictly between ourselves, of course, but I know I can rely upon your discretion. Yes, they have found documents indicating he was actually an accountant called Basil Palmer.'

'You mean... he was living under a false identity?'

'So it seems. They found his diary.'

Her eyes opened very wide. 'They did?'

'The diary gives his real name. It seems that he lost his wife recently. Looks like the calamity unhinged the poor fellow's mind.'

'You... you think he came to Hemlock Bay... to die?'

'A dismal thought, is it not?'

'Unspeakable!'

Sowden leaned closer, and she caught the faintest whiff of

antiseptic. 'Believe it or not, Palmer wouldn't be the first. We had a young fellow only a few weeks ago who threw himself off the Heights, just over there.' He pointed in the direction of the cliffs, prompting Rachel to gasp in dismay. 'Please don't upset yourself, Miss Savernake. The poor wretch had previously enjoyed a happy holiday here and coming back seems to have afforded him some solace at the very end. Indeed, I regret to say this is what happens when people develop a passion for going to the seaside. When their lives take a dark turn, they come back like lemmings, rushing headlong to disaster.'

'So-called progress?' Rachel murmured.

'Indeed, my dear young lady. You took the words right out of my mouth.'

'Rachel!'

As she walked along Beggarman's Lane towards the bungalow, Rachel heard footsteps pounding behind her and the sound of a woman panting. She composed her features into an expression of surprised pleasure before turning round.

'Ginny!'

Virginia Penrhos was out of breath by the time she caught her up. Her hair and clothes were in even more disarray than usual. She wasn't remotely handsome, Rachel thought, and yet there was something compelling about her presence. Should she give Ffion Morris the benefit of the doubt and accept that the attraction was not merely financial?

'Rachel, goodness me, you've got nothing on your feet! What on earth is going on at Shepherd's Cottage?'

'I've just left there.'

'Yes, I've been watching from the lantern room. I went up there to continue work on my painting and saw people coming and going as if there's been some sort of catastrophe. Policemen, an ambulance, a person on a stretcher. You appeared to be in the thick of it.'

Rachel bowed her head. 'It's rather dreadful. Dr Doyle is dead.'

Virginia Penrhos stared at her. 'Good God! Don't tell me there's been another murder?'

'Apparently not. Mrs Stones raised the alarm when she found the kitchen door was locked. My chauffeur broke a window and we found the poor man lying on the floor with his head in the oven.'

'You mean he's killed himself?'

'So it seems.' Rachel paused. 'Unless, I suppose…'

Her voice trailed away.

'What?' Virginia came up close, as if to shake her by the shoulder, before thinking better of it at the last moment.

'After Sir Harold dropped us off yesterday afternoon, did you do some painting?'

'I did, as it happens.'

'So after we parted company,' Rachel interrupted, 'you were in the lantern room?'

'I spent some time with Ffion, making sure she had everything she needed. After that, I went upstairs and stayed there. When I'm in the mood to paint, I hate any break in my concentration, whatever the reason. Since Ffion was unwell and resting, I was able to work uninterrupted until about eight o'clock, by which time I was famished. But why do you ask?'

Rachel gave a guileless smile. 'I simply wondered if you'd seen Dr Doyle? Or anyone else, going to and from the cottage during the afternoon?'

'No. The lane was quiet, as usual. A few people on bicycles, the occasional passing car. There was one youngish chap in a trilby, out on a stroll. Otherwise I don't think I saw anyone on foot until Mrs Stones came back from the town, laden with shopping, sometime after five. Does it matter?'

'Dr Sowden thinks that poor Dr Doyle died yesterday afternoon.'

Virginia looked startled. 'You mean the poor fellow's been lying there since then?'

'So it seems.'

'Good Lord.' Virginia turned her head and stared out to sea, evidently racking her brains. 'Of course, if the doctor popped out into the garden, for instance, I may not have noticed. I was intent on my canvas. As you know, my dear Rachel, aiming for photographic realism is a bad habit that I broke several years ago.'

'This man in the trilby, can you tell me anything about him?'

'Never seen him before. He was wearing a tan gabardine macintosh and was about six feet tall. I had the impression that he was killing time, wandering aimlessly rather than with a set plan. I first caught sight of him as he was coming from the direction of the cliffs.'

'As if he'd branched off from the clifftop path to cross to the lane?'

'Exactly. He had a good look at the lighthouse, as most sightseers do, then made his way along the lane in the direction of the Fisherman's Arms.'

Rachel smiled. 'Trust an artist to have an excellent eye for detail! Did he pay particular attention to Shepherd's Cottage?'

'As far as I can recall, he walked straight past.' Virginia frowned. 'Surely you don't think...?'

'I don't know what to think,' Rachel said.

'I saw you talking to that smarmy fellow Sowden. What does he make of it?'

Rachel made a performance of being torn by indecision. 'Oh dear, I did promise Dr Sowden that I wouldn't say a word about this. But you won't breathe a word to anyone else, I'm sure. I feel I can trust you.'

'With anything,' Virginia said softly.

'Dr Sowden is under the impression that the... the deceased wasn't a doctor, and his name wasn't Doyle.'

'Good grief!' Virginia's eyes opened very wide. 'Mind you, I thought there was something odd about the fellow. Something that didn't quite add up.'

'Adding up was one thing he was good at,' Rachel said. 'I gather he was actually an accountant by the name of Palmer.'

'How extraordinary! What on earth was he playing at?'

'Dr Sowden doesn't have a clue.'

'As usual,' Virginia grunted.

'You don't have a high opinion of him?'

'His reputation rests on a comforting bedside manner and medical knowledge that's twenty years out of date. I persuaded Ffion to consult him a fortnight ago, to see if he could do something to calm her nerves. Complete waste of time. He prescribed Veronal, which I gather is his remedy for almost every complaint under the sun.'

'Is that so?' Rachel said thoughtfully.

'Frankly, it's nothing more than a glorified sleeping draught. Taking it made no difference to poor Ffion.'

'Does she still take it?'

Virginia shook her head. 'She finished the bottle, but didn't bother to get another. Or to see old Sowden again. As for Dr... I mean Mr Palmer, I understand now why he was so determined to shy away from giving medical advice. What a miserable end.'

'I wonder what drove him to take such a drastic step,' Rachel murmured.

'He had no family?'

'I gather he lost his wife recently.'

'Alone in the world, eh?' Virginia clapped a hand to the side of her head. 'Of course! It's just dawned on me – I can guess what has happened!'

'You can?'

'Blindingly obvious, isn't it?'

As Rachel watched, the older woman's lips moved soundlessly for a few moments as she worked out in her mind the sequence of events.

'That's it!' she exclaimed. 'Nothing else makes sense of what's been happening in Hemlock Bay.'

'Tell me,' Rachel urged.

'This man Palmer went to have his fortune told and something Bellamy said caused him to suffer some kind of derangement. Perhaps a misguided prediction connected with his late wife? In a wild state, he hit Bellamy with the crystal ball and made good his escape. At first he thought he'd got away with it. But with this Lescott girl cleared of suspicion, he realised it was only a question of time before the police caught up with him.'

'So Palmer committed murder and then killed himself?' Rachel said.

Virginia Penrhos nodded emphatically. 'He must have been tormented by a mixture of guilt and remorse. The poor devil had nothing left to live for.'

23

'So the man from Shepherd's Cottage murdered Bellamy in a fit of rage and then killed himself?' Jacob let the words hang in the air, as if working out whether they made sense. 'A plausible theory, I suppose.'

He and Martha were reclining in deckchairs in the garden of Bay View, soaking up the sun and talking about murder. The morning newspapers lay at their feet. He'd enjoyed his own front page story in the *Clarion* so much that he'd already read it three times. Rachel had joined them a few minutes earlier after changing into a summer frock. She'd recounted Virginia Penrhos's explanation for the latest death.

'Don't sound so grudging,' Martha said. 'You two can't solve every mystery.'

'What on earth could Bellamy have said to provoke a mild-mannered accountant into a homicidal frenzy?' Jacob asked.

'You never met Palmer – as I suppose we must call him. How do you know he was mild-mannered?'

'Are you seriously suggesting he was ready to fly off the handle the moment anyone spoke out of turn?'

Martha shook her head. 'He was obviously pretending to be someone he wasn't. Deceitful, then, but you're right. Not the passionate type.'

'You never know with human beings,' Rachel said. 'Wild emotions seethe beneath the most serene of surfaces.'

Jacob wrinkled his brow. 'That still doesn't explain what Bellamy said or did to drive him into some kind of homicidal frenzy.'

Martha turned to Rachel. 'Did Virginia Penrhos convince you?'

'No, but at the moment I'm struggling to find a better explanation for what has happened. When she mentioned Veronal to me, I did wonder if the bottle found in Shepherd's Cottage belonged to Ffion Morris.'

'You've only got Virginia's word that Ffion used all the stuff up.'

'That's right, but the stumbling block is this. If Virginia did have something to hide, why refer to Veronal at all?'

'Criminals often give themselves away by mistake,' Jacob said, with the breezy confidence of an expert. 'That's why so many of them get caught.'

'Perfectly true. The trouble is, I felt she was telling me the truth about the Veronal.'

'I bet Virginia doesn't know everything that Ffion gets up to, even if she is supposedly at death's door,' Jacob said.

Martha sat up. 'You think Ffion's illness isn't genuine?'

'It's certainly convenient,' Jacob said airily.

'Rachel, do you agree there's nothing wrong with her?'

'No,' Rachel said.

Jacob looked put out. 'You haven't set eyes on her for several days.'

'When I did meet Ffion Morris, I felt that she is a deeply troubled woman.'

'Feminine intuition again?' he asked.

'Virginia was telling the truth about Ffion consulting Dr Sowden, I'm sure of it. So I doubt the illness is feigned. The interesting question is, what is really wrong with her? And what caused it?'

Jacob made a sceptical noise. 'Aren't you letting your admiration for Virginia's art affect your judgment?'

Rachel raised her eyebrows. Martha was watching them like a spectator at a duel between two opponents who were unevenly matched. Jacob hesitated for a moment before continuing.

'I mean, Ffion sounds highly suspicious to me. What if she slipped out of the lighthouse and hurried over to Shepherd's Cottage, in order to drug Palmer and shove his head in the oven?'

'While somehow making sure that the kitchen was locked from the inside?' Rachel said.

Jacob's brow knitted. 'I suppose when you put it like that...'

'If you're right, that raises many more questions than answers. Including motive – why on earth would Ffion kill Palmer?'

'Homicidal mania?'

Rachel gave him an old-fashioned look, but it wasn't enough to take the wind out of his sails.

'You got the impression she's unstable,' he said. 'Who knows what she is capable of? Maybe that's why she's taken to her bed. The shock of committing murder has left her prostrate.'

'Perfectly plausible. However, when Virginia waylaid me, I wondered if in some way she was implicated in Palmer's apparent suicide. Or if Ffion was. Or both of them. I half-expected bluster and lies. But there's no doubt the news of his death came as a complete shock to her.'

'Perhaps that proves how astute she is at pulling the wool over people's eyes.'

Martha winced, but Rachel responded with a shrug of the shoulders. 'I'm not infallible. And nothing's impossible.'

'Except for someone to have murdered Palmer?' Martha asked.

'So it seems.'

'Virginia might easily not have noticed someone going in or out of the cottage. Murderers take care not to draw attention to themselves.'

'In principle, yes. Unfortunately, I found her very lack of certainty convincing.'

Jacob was a picture of scepticism. 'Really?'

'Yes, really.' Rachel's smile was full of charm. 'And Jacob, please bear in mind that if you utter the phrase "feminine intuition" one more time, I'll ask Trueman to pick you up and drop you over the edge of the cliff.'

'The thought never entered my head,' Jacob said virtuously.

She shook her head sorrowfully, like a teacher whose star pupil has developed a delinquent steak. 'Your inventions, on the other hand, are hopelessly transparent. As for Virginia, the lantern room commands an unrivalled view of Hemlock Heights.'

'There must be plenty of blind spots,' Jacob objected.

'Agreed. Much of this garden is concealed by the trees, the clifftop path dips out of sight, and so on. But Shepherd's Cottage is closer to the lighthouse and I'd expect Virginia to spot anyone going in or out.'

'Not if she glanced in another direction at the vital times.

The woman was painting, not conducting a surveillance operation.'

'It's not as simple as that. I can't believe that someone popped into Shepherd's Cottage, killed Palmer in the heat of the moment, and then managed to get away without leaving any trace of his – or her – presence and with nobody any the wiser.'

'What if it was a premeditated crime?' Jacob demanded. 'Suppose Palmer was the victim of a cunningly conceived plan?'

'Very well. Let's assume someone went to the cottage, determined to kill the man for some inexplicable reason. Whether or not they realised Virginia might be in the lantern room, they'd be taking a huge risk. What if someone saw them?'

'There weren't many people around.'

'So someone visiting a known recluse would stand out even more.'

'They might have a perfectly reasonable explanation for turning up at the cottage.'

'Maybe, but if their visit coincided with the presumed time of death, they'd have tricky questions to answer.' Rachel shook her head. 'Besides, I still believe the theory falls at the first hurdle. If someone approached or left the cottage, on foot, on a bicycle, or in a car, it's unlikely that Virginia missed it.'

'Virginia didn't go up to the lantern room immediately after coming back with you from the hotel.'

'True,' she admitted.

'Let's go back to the idea that Ffion killed Palmer. Virginia would have a powerful reason for pretending to you that she saw no one.'

'I agree, although their relationship is reaching a crisis point. Never mind Palmer, I suspect the person Ffion is keenest to get out of the way is me. But would Virginia resist the temptation to give evidence that put Ffion in the clear more conclusively? In my opinion, she can lie through her teeth when it suits her, but if she was fibbing to me about what she saw – or rather, didn't see – then she is a better actress than Gladys Cooper.'

'That doesn't mean she's right to suspect Palmer of murdering Bellamy.'

'No, but even if she was trying to throw me off the scent, her explanation for his suicide wasn't rehearsed. It sprang into her mind as we were talking, I'd swear to it. And because she's an intelligent woman, it's a theory that fits with the available evidence and makes a great deal of sense.'

'Might the deaths of Palmer and Bellamy be entirely unconnected?'

'Yes, it would be stupid to rule out that possibility. A man may kill himself for a wide variety of reasons, many of which seem irrational to an outsider. We can only hope this message Sowden mentioned casts light on what was in Palmer's mind.'

Martha reached out to squeeze Rachel's hand. 'You sound frustrated.'

Rachel gave her a rueful smile. 'You know me too well. Last night, when Trueman brought me home, I persuaded myself I was on the verge of unravelling the webs of deceit that people have been spinning in Hemlock Bay. Now they seem more tangled than ever.'

The back door of the bungalow opened to reveal Hetty Trueman. She didn't seem to be in the best of humours.

'Back from your errand of mercy?' Jacob asked cheekily. 'Made a friend for life?'

Hetty rolled her eyes. 'That Stones woman could talk the hind legs off one of those donkeys down on the beach. She spouts more nonsense than you do, young man, and that's saying something.'

'Did she give you any clues to Palmer's state of mind?' Rachel asked. 'Any reason why he might want to kill himself?'

Hetty sighed. 'She kept talking about seeing the poor man with his head in the gas oven. Saying she'd never witnessed anything like it in her life. Apart from that, she kept repeating that he was a queer one.'

'In what way, exactly?'

'Secretive. Always glad to see the back of her each morning. Not that I blame him. She's the sort who would much rather natter than work. He told her he didn't want her dusting his precious books or photographs. And he hated her asking questions. Especially not about her arthritic fingers and the pain she keeps getting in her back. She never forgave him for that, I can tell you.'

'Presumably she didn't find out much about him?'

'He kept the photographs in his bedroom. One of them was taken at his wedding. All the others were of his wife. A pretty girl, according to Mrs Stones, and she's not one for scattering compliments. Much younger than him.'

'Did she ask him about his wife?'

'Only once, and it brought a tear to his eye. He told her she was dead, but he wouldn't say any more. She's not the kind who gets embarrassed easily, but even she realised it was best to leave well alone.'

'Any reason to believe someone held a grudge against him?'

'He wasn't a good listener, and Mrs Stones didn't like that, but it's hardly a reason to kill someone, is it?'

'Nobody else?'

Hetty shook her head. 'He kept himself to himself. According to her, he became gloomier with each passing day. When they first met, he seemed quite jaunty, but that didn't last. As if the death of his wife preyed on his mind.'

'Until he decided to end it all?'

'What else? We all saw that the kitchen was locked. I can't see how anyone could have got in there.'

'Virginia Penrhos saw a stranger wandering around nearby yesterday afternoon,' Rachel said. 'A man in a trilby and tan gabardine macintosh.'

'What if he was up to something?' Martha asked. 'Suppose Palmer was a crooked accountant who had stolen money from a client before running off to Hemlock Bay? Suppose the victim found out where he was hiding and…'

'Ingenious,' Jacob said, 'but you're barking up the wrong tree.'

'Because I can't explain how he got in and out of the locked kitchen?'

'Not only that.' He beamed, like a conjuror about to produce a missing ace of spades from an unsuspecting onlooker's pocket. 'If the chap is the man I think he is, his only crime is being in the wrong place at the wrong time.'

'Isn't that your speciality?' Martha asked.

Jacob laughed. 'Not guilty – for once.'

'Go on, then. The suspense is unbearable.'

'I know a chap with a tan gabardine macintosh. His name is Bob Harley and he's one of my colleagues at work. His mistake was catching our editor's eye at the wrong moment. Just after Gomersall agreed that while I'm up here, I should concentrate on crime reporting.'

'So when Virginia saw him wandering around the Heights, he was simply familiarising himself with the neighbourhood?'

Jacob nodded. 'If she'd been quick off the mark, she could have nipped out of the lighthouse to make the challenge. And won five pounds for being the first person in Hemlock Bay to spot Clarion Charlie.'

24

'Warmest day of the year so far!' Jacob said cheerily. 'God's in his heaven, and all's well with the world.'

'Give or take the occasional violent death,' Rachel murmured.

The sun was beating down as they strolled into the resort together with Trueman. Salt seasoned the fresh air and even the squeals of the seagulls sounded like a catchy melody rather than a litany of complaints. Shore Gardens blazed with colour. Butterflies flitted from flower to flower, bees hummed smugly, and small children raced around the paths, whooping with excitement and spilling ice cream from their cornets.

Shading his eyes from the glare, Jacob scanned the crowded beach and the swimmers splashing through dappled water. 'Bellamy's murder hasn't deterred people from coming to Hemlock Bay.'

Trueman followed his gaze. 'No sign of the reflex man or his stall.'

'Lying low,' Rachel said.

'On a day like today?' Jacob shook his head. 'Doesn't make sense. The visitors are out in droves. If he was snapping away on the promenade, he'd do a roaring trade.'

'Maybe he's meeting up with his chum Laurie,' Trueman said. 'I'll nip round to the Mermaid and have a look.'

'Keep an eye out for Joseph McAtee,' Rachel said. 'I'd love to know what brought him here. I'd also like to hear what he makes of Bellamy's murder.'

'Will do. Though you may have a better chance of spotting him in the hotel. He is staying there, after all.'

She gave a brisk nod of assent and he strode across the esplanade without another word. Jacob pointed to the promenade, where a news vendor with a Woodbine in his mouth was leaning against a large placard which bore the masthead of his newspaper.

Can YOU *spot Clarion Charlie?*

'Looks like this morning's edition has almost sold out,' he said with undisguised jubilation. 'I'd better make the most of the sunshine. Once word gets out that Bellamy's murderer has been found dead, Gomersall will tell me to pack my bags and get back to London. Not to worry, I don't envy Bob Harley his job. Who wants to be a Mystery Man?'

'Palmer did,' Rachel said, as Jacob bought the vendor's last copy. 'I wonder why. So you agree with Virginia's solution to the puzzle?'

'There are a few loose ends,' Jacob said judiciously, folding the paper and putting it under his arm. 'Palmer's death does feel like a bit of an anticlimax.'

Rachel tutted. 'Not for him.'

'You know what I mean. I've been spoiled by the high melodrama of places like Mortmain Hall and Blackstone Fell. I think your artist friend is right. Palmer killed Bellamy in an inexplicable moment of madness, and couldn't cope with the guilt. If the gas oven seemed like the only way out, he must have been in a dreadful depression. Doesn't bear thinking about.'

'We must think about it if we're to make sense of everything that's happened. As for loose ends, there are more than you'd find in a heap of spaghetti.' Rachel heaved a sigh. 'Much as I like spaghetti, this case has a sour taste.'

'I don't suppose we'll ever know the meaning of Bellamy's mysterious premonition. Perhaps we should take it at face value? Maybe he really did believe he could look into the future.'

'Last night I thought I'd worked out a viable explanation,' Rachel said, 'but Palmer's suicide suggests I was on the wrong track.'

'Care to share your thinking?'

She shook her head. 'If Palmer was driven to take his own life because he couldn't cope with a tormented conscience after murdering Bellamy, then I was miles off the mark. Even if someone else was responsible for Palmer's death...'

'You sound doubtful.'

'For the very good reason that, right now, I fail to see how anyone could have entered Shepherd's Cottage and then murdered Palmer and arranged matters to make it look as if he'd killed himself, before getting away from the scene of the crime without leaving any trace. Unless I've missed something, the inevitable conclusion is that nobody did anything of the sort, and Palmer's death is what it seems. A self-inflicted tragedy.'

A Tin Lizzie thundered past them and they watched it swing abruptly to the right, narrowly missing a stone pillar as it jolted into the car park of the Hemlock Hotel.

'The local police,' Rachel said. 'The sergeant's driving reminds me of Inspector Young's detective work. Full of vim, but not quite as reliable as he'd like to believe. Come on, Jacob. Shall we see if the inspector has cracked the mystery of the locked kitchen?'

Jacob made a derisive noise. 'He's sure to have made a meal of it.'

'Inspector Oakes is in the smoking room.' The chief receptionist was a woman whose austere manner seemed to Jacob better suited to the Dorchester or Ritz than a seaside hotel. Not that he'd ever stayed in the Dorchester or Ritz. 'He's in conference with colleagues and has given strict instructions that he is not to be disturbed.'

'Fair enough,' Jacob said. 'We'll wait.'

'As you wish.'

The woman wrinkled her nose. She and Jacob hadn't hit it off from the moment he'd registered on arrival and dripped all over her polished rosewood counter. Discovering that he worked for the *Clarion* hadn't helped. She'd made no bones about telling him she never read anything but the *Daily Telegraph*, and regarded newspapers whose front pages favoured bold headlines and even bolder photographs as no better than children's comics.

Jacob and Rachel stationed themselves in armchairs commanding a view of the lobby and lifts. Rachel was hoping to spot Joseph McAtee. Jacob, a firm believer in the principle that it pays to advertise, was content to hold the *Clarion* open in front of him while he read his horoscope.

'What do the stars foretell?' Rachel murmured.

'*Some changes will come into your life,*' Jacob read aloud.

'However, this will not take you by surprise, since they will have been of your own making.'

'Such insight.'

'I hope he doesn't mean the bloke from the *Witness* is plotting to murder me. Can you guess what Fate has in store for you?'

'Break it to me gently.'

'If there is any way you can persuade others that your ideas are realistic, start working on them now. Someone is reluctant to agree with you and this is frustrating. Do not lose heart. You will gradually break down their defences.'

'Wise words, I'll keep them in mind. Ah, here comes Inspector Young.'

As the inspector, accompanied by his own sergeant and Wagstaffe, bustled out of the smoking room, he caught sight of Rachel and the *Clarion* concealing Jacob's face. The headlines made him wince, but he managed a weak smile for Rachel's benefit.

'Good day to you, Miss Savernake. I trust you've recovered from your shocking experience at Shepherd's Cottage?'

'Yes, thank you,' she said meekly. 'That poor man. I suppose…'

Young considered her. 'I gather you and Inspector Oakes have met before? It's obvious he holds you in high regard. You're something of an amateur criminologist, I understand.'

'A dabbler,' she murmured. 'Human nature is so extraordinary, don't you think? The psychology of murder I find irresistibly fascinating. What impulse drives a seemingly decent person to commit a terrible crime?'

'Yes, well, I'm sure that's all very interesting. Unfortunately, I have to concentrate on hard facts and evidence I can bring before a court. At least we can be confident that this sorry state of affairs has come to a conclusion. The good folk of Hemlock Bay can get back to life as usual.'

'You're satisfied that Mr Palmer died by his own hand?'

'While the balance of his mind was disturbed, as the inquest will no doubt conclude. What exactly Bellamy did to provoke him isn't quite clear, but he obviously wasn't thinking straight. In any case, establishing motive isn't the be-all and end-all. The case is cut and dried. I've had a word with Inspector Oakes, of course, as a matter of courtesy. You'll be glad to hear that he's of the same mind as me.' He threw a triumphant glance at Jacob, or rather the *Clarion*. 'A bad business, but at least we've been saved the palaver and expense of a trial.'

'And justice has been done?'

'Rough justice, perhaps, Miss Savernake. But justice nevertheless.' He gave her a brisk nod of farewell. 'Now if you'll excuse me, I must call on the coroner.'

As he made his way through the revolving doors, Jacob lowered his newspaper. 'Cut and dried,' he said. 'Makes a change from open and shut, I suppose.'

'Yes, Inspector Young is probably a real bloodhound when it comes to solving bicycle thefts, but with serious crimes, he has the opposite of a Midas touch. He's so confident this is a case of murder followed by suicide that I'm strongly tempted to revise my own opinions about what happened in Shepherd's Cottage.'

'You still face the same stumbling block. How could anyone have murdered Palmer?'

'Unfortunately, I've no idea. First things first. Let's consult the oracle. Or at least Scotland Yard.'

★

'You're satisfied that Palmer took his own life?' Rachel asked.

Inspector Oakes exhaled. He'd invited them to join him in the smoking room and rung for coffee and sandwiches. They were sitting around a small circular table on which lay a buff document folder.

'Frankly, I don't see any alternative explanation that stands up to scrutiny.'

'You searched the cottage?'

He shifted in his chair. 'As you know, I had a quick squint, but this is Young's bailiwick. After the Winnie Lescott debacle, I'd prefer not to tread on his toes unless absolutely necessary. In fairness, he's just given me a detailed report.'

'Oh really?'

Philip Oakes settled his gaze on Jacob. 'I'm afraid there's nothing I can say to the press at present. It's a matter of protocol. You'll understand how important it is to observe the niceties.'

'Absolutely right,' Jacob said fervently. 'Please don't worry about me. My lips are sealed, my hand is stilled. And I've lost my pen.'

He threw Rachel a wary glance. She responded with a smile that verged on maternal.

'You've already gathered enough sensational material today to fill the whole of tomorrow's *Clarion*. Besides, Inspector Oakes knows he can rely on your integrity.' There was a faint tinge of menace in her tone. 'And so do I.'

'Understood,' Jacob said quickly. 'Imagine I'm not here.'

'I'll do that with pleasure,' Oakes said. 'Very well. I'm speaking entirely off the record?'

Rachel nodded. 'This is extremely good of you. I do appreciate it.'

There was a knock on the door and a waitress came in

with their refreshments. When she'd made herself scarce, Jacob stirred sugar into his coffee, reflecting moodily that the detective wouldn't dream of granting such a favour to anyone other than Rachel. Beneath that smoothly professional exterior, Oakes was undoubtedly as dazzled by Rachel as... well, as Jacob himself.

The inspector cleared his throat. 'Let me take things in order. First, the scene. As you know, the door to the kitchen was locked. What is more, the key was in the lock, meaning that no one could have opened it from the passageway. Your statement makes clear, Miss... Rachel, that the window was closed prior to Trueman breaking in, and it's hard to see how anyone could have prised it open from the outside.'

'Yes, I did wonder if someone got out that way, shutting the window behind them, but I can't see how it could be managed.'

Oakes nodded. 'If there was any jiggery-pokery, I'd expect to see scuffing around the window frame, but there was none. The same is true of the door.'

'Locked doors can be opened by surreptitious means,' Rachel said.

'In theory, but I saw no sign of that at Shepherd's Cottage. Nor did Young, and his examination was less cursory than mine. The stone flags of the floor appear not to have moved since the day the cottage was built. The ceiling is solid. Above the kitchen is a lumber room which was also kept locked. The interior is full of cobwebs, as if nobody's been inside for years. Mrs Stones never bothered to clean it.'

Rachel drank some coffee. 'There's a fireplace in the kitchen.'

'At my request, Inspector Young told Sergeant Hamilton to investigate it thoroughly. They are convinced that it would be impossible for anyone to escape up the chimney. The sergeant's build is as slender as mine, which is why he had to get himself covered in soot, rather than the constable. He says he'd have got completely stuck if he'd tried to climb up any further.'

'What about fingerprints?'

'A check has been made, with particular emphasis on every surface in the kitchen. There are plenty of prints which appear to belong to the dead man and Mrs Stones. As you'd expect, there are also a few blurred patches, but nothing out of the ordinary. There's precious little else to say about the physical evidence.'

'Did they find anything else which suggests Palmer took his own life?'

'Yes, although most of the evidence is circumstantial.'

'For example?'

'Palmer kept a diary. It was on his bookshelf in the living room.'

'So he was a keen reader?'

'Doesn't look like it. Apart from well-thumbed copies of *Rob Roy* and *David Copperfield*, there was an ancient copy of *Gray's Anatomy*, presumably there just as window dressing, a handful of musty accounting ledgers going back years, and the diary.'

Rachel put down her cup. 'Tell me about the diary.'

'Not much to tell. It's a leather-bound journal, with his name and a home address in Guildford tucked away at the back. Hardly a treasure trove of helpful detail. The whole book only contains half a dozen scattered entries, and all of them relate in some way to his late wife. For example, he writes a line or two about her on her birthday, their wedding anniversary, and the anniversary of the day they first met.

No question, the man was besotted with her. From the photographs in the cottage, she was undoubtedly attractive and her early death seems to have left the poor devil beside himself with grief.'

'What does he say about Bellamy?'

'Bellamy's name never appears.'

'Hemlock Bay?'

'Hardly gets a mention. He jotted down the address and telephone number of the property agent who acts for Sir Harold Jackson, but that's about all.'

'There's no possibility that the diary entries were in some form of code or cipher?'

Oakes stared at her. 'The idea never crossed my mind. But I'd need a great deal of persuading that was the case. The wording of the sporadic entries doesn't seem contrived. Palmer just scribbled a few words, every now and then. Perhaps he found it therapeutic. As far as I can tell, he dwelt in the past, not the present. As if his life ended when his wife died.'

'What do we know about her death?'

'Wagstaffe has done some quick work. His enquiries have already yielded a good deal of interesting information. Above all, the fact that the poor woman was murdered by a love-crazed admirer.'

Jacob, who had been bursting to speak for several minutes, could no longer restrain himself.

'Gareth Bellamy?'

Oakes turned to him and said quietly, 'I'm still imagining you're not here.'

For once in his life, Jacob looked abashed. He bit savagely into a ham and mustard sandwich before subsiding into silence.

'Alicia Palmer,' the inspector said, 'was shot by one of her husband's clients, an unsuccessful barrister and even less successful part-time publisher called Neville Carrington. Carrington was married to a wealthy older woman, but Mrs Palmer was a regular visitor to his room in chambers in the Temple.'

'Were they lovers?' Rachel asked.

'So it seems, but they must have had an almighty bust-up. Having shot her, Carrington promptly ran out of the house and fell under the wheels of a passing car. He died of his injuries.'

'A double tragedy,' Rachel said thoughtfully. 'There's no connection between Carrington and Hemlock Bay?'

'Nothing known at present.'

'What about the widow, Mrs Carrington?'

'A wealthy woman in her own right. The scandal must have been bruising for her. After the inquest she decamped to Monaco. There may be more to the case, of course, and we'll do our best to dig deeper. So far, it looks like a straightforward story of two lives destroyed for no good reason.'

'Not counting Palmer's own life,' Rachel said.

'Yes, and that brings me to the most compelling piece of evidence of all. The note found beneath his body.'

Oakes opened the buff folder and took out a sheet of notepaper. It was very creased and appeared to have been screwed up prior to being straightened out again. He laid the sheet face up on the table and watched as they craned their necks to read the scrawled words.

I am responsible for the fortune teller, so it is only right that I should pay the price.

Basil Palmer

25

Rachel examined the message for some time, as if trying to decipher Egyptian hieroglyphics.

Oakes said quietly, 'Are you all right?'

'Can we be sure this is Palmer's handwriting?' she demanded.

'Young checked it against the entries in his diary. Difficult to form a definitive view, with so little to go on. Even experts in calligraphy tend to hedge their opinions with caveats in such a case.'

'But?'

'But there's a strong similarity, to say the least. The letter *f* in particular is distinctive. And the signature tallies.'

Rachel frowned at the sheet of paper. 'The wording made me wonder if there was some clue hidden in the message. But if there is, at the moment I'm defeated by it.'

'A complicated anagram?' Jacob suggested.

She shook her head. 'If so, it's beyond me.'

'I don't think we need to overcomplicate matters,' Oakes said. 'For practical purposes, what happened looks tolerably certain. Palmer drank alcohol and a sleeping draught to steady his nerves before putting his head into the oven. He also wrote this suicide note, which looks like a confession to murder into the bargain.'

'He doesn't explain why he killed Bellamy,' Jacob objected.

Oakes hesitated, perhaps wondering whether to maintain the fiction that Jacob was invisible, before grasping the nettle. The question had to be answered sooner or later.

'Nothing unusual in that,' he said curtly. 'You can't expect a fellow who is at the end of his tether to supply a logical analysis of his thought processes.'

'What do we know of Palmer?' Rachel asked.

Oakes shrugged. 'Our initial enquiries suggest there isn't a great deal to know. He has no criminal record and his practice is said to be eminently respectable.'

'How boring. Is it possible he was dipping into his clients' funds?'

'If he was, I expect it will soon come out. But there's no hint of disreputable conduct.'

Rachel raised her eyebrows. 'A model citizen?'

'If there is such a thing. Even the tax authorities haven't put a black mark against his name. Wagstaffe reckons the most exciting thing that ever happened to the poor man was having his wife murdered. Sad epitaph, eh?'

'Very sad,' Rachel said. 'What about the time of death? Dr Sowden seems to think Palmer's head has been in the oven since yesterday afternoon. What do you make of the doctor?'

Oakes shrugged. 'Strictly between you and me, Dr Sowden reminds me of Inspector Young.'

'So, an affable man whose abilities are limited as well as being compromised by complacency?'

The detective allowed himself a rueful smile. 'Harsh but fair. By the way, I never said that.'

'Of course you didn't, Inspector.'

'As the resort has developed, Dr Sowden has prospered. He's built up a lucrative practice, but I detect a strong preference for a quiet life. He said he likes to get his morning surgery over and done with quickly so he can nip off to the golf course. Examining Bellamy's corpse was more than enough professional excitement for him. Now he's had to cope with a second sudden death. However, Young assures me that Sowden has the Jacksons' full confidence. When Lady Jackson was sick recently, he made sure she had the very best treatment and care.'

'He certainly knows which side his bread is buttered,' Rachel said grimly. 'I presume he has no doubt that Palmer committed suicide?'

'None whatsoever. I find it hard to argue.'

'In the spirit of full disclosure, I need to tell you about my conversation with Virginia Penrhos. Her evidence bears out your thinking.'

She gave a brief account of what Virginia had said. Oakes listened with an intent expression, but as Jacob finished the sandwiches, his mind wandered. Was there any serious prospect of the cordial relationship between his two friends blossoming into a romance? He had no doubt the policeman found Rachel at least as much of an enigma as he did. In the eighteen months he'd known her, he'd learned a great deal but there was still a great deal more that he didn't understand.

Her moods fluctuated with such bewildering rapidity. One moment she was cold, ruthless, and sardonic. The next she became witty, kind, and generous. Her single-mindedness was as frightening as her loyalties – to Jacob personally, as well as to the Truemans – were fierce. Like Oakes, she had a burning passion for justice, but their ideas of what constituted justice, and their methods for achieving it, could hardly be more different. Whereas the Scotland Yard man believed in rules and order, Rachel cared nothing for protocol. To her, all that mattered was the end result. While Oakes did his utmost to follow the letter of the law, Rachel behaved as if she was above it.

Was this because she was the daughter of a tyrannical judge? Jacob had never been able to make any sense of their relationship, but he'd noticed that Rachel never spoke directly of her father. She only referred – coldly and impersonally – to Judge Savernake. He was curious, but she and the Truemans had made it clear that their past life on Gaunt was not a topic for discussion. A mystifying taboo, but he dared not break it. Whatever the truth, he was convinced Oakes didn't realise quite how far she was prepared to go to make sure malefactors got their just deserts.

So the two of them were chalk and cheese. Could such differences ever be reconciled? Unbidden, a strange thought slid into Jacob's mind, as he listened to Rachel explaining what Virginia could see from the lantern room.

There's hope for me yet.

'For what it's worth,' Rachel said a few minutes later, 'I don't believe Virginia Penrhos was lying when she said nobody approached Shepherd's Cottage yesterday afternoon. But perhaps she missed something.'

Turning to Jacob, Oakes said, 'Caught up with your colleague yet? There's an outside chance he may be a useful witness.'

Jacob shook his head. 'Harley will be out and about, dodging the eager bounty hunters. I can leave a message that you'd like to speak to him.'

'Thanks. I'm happy to leave him to the tender mercies of the local men. Inspector Young deserves a change of luck.'

'Am I right in deducing, Inspector,' Rachel asked, 'that your work here is nearly done?'

'Yes, there's a limit to how long my superiors will allow me to enjoy the sea air when there's no doubt that Basil Palmer committed suicide.' Oakes relaxed in his chair. 'We can't be sure why he killed Bellamy, but his note accepts responsibility for the fortune teller's death. Bizarre, yes, but when a man is so emotionally unbalanced...'

'You've reported your views to the chief constable?'

'My provisional conclusions pending the inquest, yes.'

Philip Oakes was invariably so precise, Jacob thought. Verging on prim. Rachel, he'd guess, was by instinct drawn to Cavaliers rather than Roundheads, but in the inspector's case, she seemed happy to make an exception.

'What does Major Busby have to say?'

'His priority is to wrap up the case quickly. I gather he's coming under pressure from Sir Harold Jackson to draw a line under recent events at the earliest opportunity. The major believes in doing the Right Thing. Keeping Sir Harold happy is a crucial ingredient of the Right Thing.'

'Of course, you'll have checked the whereabouts of people at about the time Bellamy was murdered. Are you sure that Louis Carson's alibi holds water?'

Oakes nodded. 'It's clear that he – and his wife, for that matter – were kept busy with hotel business throughout that afternoon. We'd soon find out if they'd been absent without leave for any significant period of time.'

'I'm sure you're right,' Rachel said meekly.

'In case you're wondering about other pillars of the local community, Dr Sowden happened to mention that he was playing golf with Sir Harold Jackson, the local vicar, and the manager of the Hemlock Bay branch of Martins Bank.'

She smiled. 'I suppose we have to exonerate them from suspicion. Going back to Louis Carson, is he keen for the police to wrap up their inquiries?'

'I doubt his opinion cuts much ice with the major. Sir Harold may be preparing for retirement, but his is the voice people listen to in Hemlock Bay.'

'Did Major Busby actually say that Sir Harold is about to retire?'

'That's his belief. He says Sir Harold's decision is perfectly understandable. The man has transformed this place. Until he came along, there was nothing here but sheep, sand, and sea. Unfortunately, his wife has been unwell.'

'So I understand.'

'These are hard times for entrepreneurs, but Sir Harold is lucky to have found someone who is capable of taking over the reins and has the financial means to buy him out.'

'In due course, Louis Carson will become lord and master of Hemlock Bay?'

Oakes allowed himself a wry smile. 'Perhaps he deserves your sympathy. Any more violent deaths in this neck of the woods, and he may find Sir Harold has sold him a rather expensive poisoned chalice.'

'Not that you're expecting any more deaths?'

'Fingers crossed,' he said grimly.

Jacob was getting bored. He coughed loudly and said, 'I assume you don't think this so-called premonition of Bellamy's warrants further investigation?'

Oakes grimaced. 'What do you suggest? Getting in touch via the spirit world?'

'Not advisable,' Rachel said. 'That didn't work too well for Jacob the last time he tried it.'

'I don't like loose ends,' Jacob said in a mulish tone. 'Why would a man travel all the way from Lancashire to London to spin such an unlikely yarn?'

'Every investigation has loose ends,' Oakes said. 'If such a trivial oddity even qualifies as a loose end.'

'Have it your own way,' Jacob muttered.

'Don't be sulky,' Rachel said. 'If Bellamy hadn't come to see you, you'd still be slaving over a hot typewriter in London and you'd have missed all the excitement.'

Sergeant Wagstaffe's return brought the conversation to an end and Jacob went to leave a message for Harley with the formidable receptionist. Rachel was settling back into her armchair when Trueman came in through the revolving doors.

'Any luck at the Mermaid?' she asked.

He shook his head. 'No sign of either McAtee or the beach photographer. The barman was so fully occupied with customers trying to figure out if Clarion Charlie was in there having a quiet pint, he paid no attention to his golfing pal. Maybe they've had a tiff.'

Pearl Carson entered the lobby from the direction of the offices. Catching sight of Rachel, she raised a hand in greeting, and Trueman stepped away, the very model of a discreet chauffeur who knows that his place is in the background.

'Good afternoon, Miss Savernake! I hope you've been making the most of the sunshine?'

Rachel's expression was doleful. 'A lovely day, isn't it? Such a shame that...'

Her voice trailed away and Pearl placed a warm hand on hers.

'You're referring to the tragedy at Shepherd's Cottage?'

Rachel nodded, but seemed lost for words.

'I never actually met the poor man, but I heard the news just before lunch. How dreadful, to be in such a state of mind that you can't bear to carry on. I simply can't imagine it.' Pearl shook her head. 'I gather Mrs Stones raised the alarm?'

'Yes, she came to Bay View to let us know that the kitchen was locked and she'd glimpsed him through the curtains. He was... lying on the floor.'

'How awful.'

'As if that wasn't enough,' Rachel said, 'it turns out that his real name wasn't Doyle, and he wasn't a doctor at all.'

Pearl Carson's jaw dropped. 'Good Lord! That's astonishing!'

'You didn't know?'

'Certainly not. As I say, I never even met the man.'

Rachel dabbed her eyes, as if anticipating tears. 'It's... quite extraordinary.'

'It certainly is. What was his real name, do you know?'

'The police say his name was Palmer.'

'Palmer?' Pearl's expression was quizzical.

'Basil Palmer. Apparently he was an accountant from Guildford. Makes you wonder, doesn't it? What brings a man on his own from Guildford to Hemlock Bay? And what drives him to suicide?'

'It's... incredible.' If Pearl's bafflement was feigned, Rachel thought, she deserved to be on the stage. 'I heard a whisper that Dr... I mean, this man Palmer, is the one who murdered The Great Hallemby.'

'The fortune teller, yes,' Rachel said. 'I heard that story too.'

'It... it doesn't make sense.'

'No,' Rachel agreed. 'Nothing seems to make sense at the moment.'

Out of the corner of her eye she saw Jacob strolling towards her, having done battle with the chief receptionist. She gave an almost imperceptible shake of the head. Catching her eye, he promptly took a close interest in the foliage of the potted plants.

Pearl Carson took a deep breath. 'You must forgive me for sounding so distressed. My husband and I are working day and night to make a success of things here. Buying into Sir Harold's business took up all our savings. The dreadful things that have happened here lately are a devastating blow. If visitors feel unsafe, they will give Hemlock Bay a very wide berth.'

'Judging by the crowds on the beach, the resort is more popular than ever.'

The older woman sighed. 'On the principle that there is no such thing as bad publicity? Perhaps it's true, but I'm not sure. Nothing has ever come easily to me, you see. I don't mind hard work, but I understand why Sir Harold is ready to take a step back, after all he's achieved over the past few years.'

'I presume he's confident that the present... difficulties will soon blow over?'

'Oh yes.' Her expression softened. 'I spoke to him a few minutes ago. The chief constable has assured him that the police have everything in hand. The murder of The Great Hallemby was ghastly, but it seems clear the man responsible has... finally done the right thing.'

Her words lingered in the air for a few moments before Rachel said, 'I wonder if you can help me?'

A bright, professional smile. 'Ask away.'

'I was hoping to have a word with a gentleman who is staying here. I haven't seen him around and I wonder if you might know where he is?'

If Pearl Carson was tempted to retort that she wasn't her guest's keeper, she gave no sign of it. A twinkle in her eye indicated that she suspected a budding romance.

'And who might that be?'

'His name is Mr Joseph McAtee.'

The twinkle vanished. 'Mr McAtee?'

'That's right.'

'I'm afraid you're out of luck.'

'He hasn't left Hemlock Bay, has he?'

'Yes, he's... in Lancaster, and I don't think he will be back in the next few days.'

'Oh dear. He didn't leave a forwarding address, by any chance? I am quite anxious to get in touch with him.'

'I'm afraid that won't be possible.'

'Really?' Something in Pearl's voice snagged Rachel's attention. What wasn't she saying? 'Surely he didn't leave without paying his bill?'

A decisive shake of the head. 'No, no, there's no question of that. I mean...'

'Yes?'

Pearl Carson lowered her eyes. 'He left here in the most unfortunate circumstances. He was under the weather a couple of days ago but yesterday morning he took a turn for the worse. We called in Dr Sowden, a very good man, and he insisted on whisking him off to the hospital at Lancaster.'

'My goodness! What on earth is wrong with him?'

'At first it seemed like flu. A bug has been going around. My husband Louis has been affected himself. But this appears to be more serious. Dr Sowden says it's a form of ataxia, whatever that is.'

'It sounds worrying,' Rachel said thoughtfully.

'I'm sorry to say it is. I called the hospital this morning, to see if there was any improvement, but they told me it had deteriorated. He isn't responding to treatment. It does sound rather as if... it's touch and go whether he'll survive.'

20

'Curiouser and curiouser,' Trueman said.

With lunchtime over, he had repaired to the American Bar with Rachel and Jacob. They had the place to themselves. The barman had tired of polishing glasses and retreated to a back room. Everyone else was out seeking the sun. Or Clarion Charlie. Or both.

'How sick was McAtee when you met him in the pub?' Jacob asked.

'Hard to say. He's the sort who thinks it's unmanly to admit to feeling off colour. With hindsight, he did look seedy. Pasty-faced and sweating a bit. He rubbed his stomach, as if he had a pain in his guts. He probably put it down to a bout of holiday indigestion. Overindulging in booze and rich food.'

'That doesn't usually land you in hospital. Let alone leave you fighting for survival.' Jacob turned to Rachel. 'Looks like he's been poisoned.'

She nodded. 'People can be poisoned accidentally, of course. Even in Hemlock Bay.'

'Hemlock!' Jacob exclaimed. 'Why didn't I think of that before? Do his symptoms suggest that he's taken hemlock?'

A dreamy look came into Rachel's eyes. 'The late Judge Savernake had an extraordinary library, one of the finest in private hands. I studied accounts of famous trials and books about murder by every method known to man. Poison was a favourite of mine. I devoured Alfred Swaine Taylor's textbooks like other children read penny dreadfuls.'

'Nothing beats a misspent youth,' Jacob said. 'What's your diagnosis?'

Rachel pursed her lips. 'The symptoms Trueman noticed might be due to a wide variety of causes.'

When he had a bright idea, Jacob was like a dog with a bone. 'Including hemlock poisoning?'

'It's possible.'

'Likely, don't you mean? Hemlock grows around here like a weed.'

'That begs the question. McAtee had his wits about him. He wouldn't consume a fatal dose of hemlock by mistake.'

'Didn't strike me as the suicidal type, either,' Trueman growled.

'No. Deadly poisons affect people in different ways but, even if someone else administered poison to him, his condition has worsened more gradually than you'd expect if he'd consumed a significant amount of hemlock.'

'Palmer pretended to be a doctor. What if he dosed McAtee with something supposedly medicinal—'

'Aren't you forgetting something?' Rachel interrupted. 'Palmer went out of his way to emphasise that he was long retired and unable to offer any medical advice, never mind prescribe a dangerous toxin. Leaving that aside, there are other questions. Why would he do such a thing and when would he have the opportunity?'

'Just drawing a bow at a venture.' Jacob tutted. 'Surely you can't believe McAtee's illness has nothing to do with everything else that's happening here?'

Rachel was pensive. 'If I wanted to be fanciful, I'd say his sickness is a metaphor for everything that's gone wrong in Hemlock Bay.'

Jacob's brow furrowed. 'You mean there's a curse on the place?'

'Conjuring up a newspaper headline, Jacob? No, by all accounts everything here was sweetness and light until a few months ago. All the calamities have occurred since the Carsons arrived. I can't believe it's a coincidence.'

'Oakes told us they have alibis for Bellamy's murder. What's more, they seem to have been here in the hotel again yesterday afternoon, when Palmer died.'

'I don't dispute any of that,' Rachel said. 'I'm not saying they have murdered anyone. Pearl Carson swears she had no idea of Palmer's deception, and I believe her. But even if she's innocent, I'm convinced all this mayhem has some connection with her husband.'

'Can't imagine why.' He was about to tease her about losing her touch, but a glance at Trueman's expression made him reconsider. 'Anyhow, this area has a long history of rum goings-on. Remember Mermaid's Grave! Think of all those poor souls who were shipwrecked on the rocks, before the lighthouse was built. While they drowned in the briny, the rascally shepherds and farm folk of Hemlock Bay were scuttling off with the contraband.'

Rachel looked at him. 'You're absolutely right.'

He hadn't expected that. 'You agree?'

'Of course, Jacob.' She laughed, her mood transformed in an instant. 'If you will keep hammering nails, every now and then you're bound to hit one on the head.'

'Ouch.'

'No need to look hurt.' She sprang to her feet. 'As a sounding board, you're invaluable.'

'Glad to be of service,' he muttered, but she was already racing for the door.

In the hottest hour of the day, Rachel strode along Beggarman's Lane as purposefully as a soldier on a quick march. Her mood was exuberant. This was the sensation she craved above all others, the knowledge that she was on the brink of solving a knotty puzzle. A physical thrill of pleasure coursed through her body. For too long, she'd kept turning down blind alleys. Finally she was confident that she was on the right track.

She broke her stride as Mrs Stones approached from the other direction, head bowed, shopping bag in hand. A stroke of luck, Rachel told herself.

'My dear Mrs Stones,' she said. 'How are you?'

The older woman mopped sweat off her brow. 'I had to get out of doors. I couldn't stop thinking about… that awful stench of gas.'

'You'll feel better after a nice cup of tea and a cake,' Rachel said.

'I just can't forget what's happened,' Mrs Stones said. 'I've never seen anything like it. Put me right off my lunch, it did.'

'I'm not surprised. You need to relax, take some care of yourself. Once you've got some tea inside you, why not sit in Shore Gardens and feed the ducks in the pond or look out at the sea? An hour's rest will do you a world of good. It's the very least you deserve, after everything you've been through.'

'I've never...' Mrs Stones began, but Rachel had already given her an encouraging wave and set off again.

At Bay View, she found Martha and Hetty lazing in deckchairs and browsing through the latest issues of *Woman and Home* and *Film Weekly* respectively.

'Any luck with the keys to Shepherd's Cottage?' she asked.

Hetty nodded. 'Mrs Stones put them down on the kitchen table when I brought her here before we went to End Terrace. I slipped the tea caddy over them. She was in so much of a dither, she didn't even notice she hadn't picked them up again. I've taken impressions in a bar of soap, in case she remembers before you've made any use of them.'

'Wonderful. We'll make a criminal of you yet.'

Hetty gave her an old-fashioned look. 'The things I do for you.'

'You're indispensable, we all know that.'

'You never said why you might want to sneak into the cottage.'

'Because I didn't know. Palmer's suicide caught me off guard. I couldn't make head nor tail of it.'

'But now you've had one of your ideas.'

'Long overdue, but yes.' Rachel turned to Martha. 'The constable keeping watch over Shepherd's Cottage looks like a callow youth. He must be bored stiff, having so little to do on such a warm afternoon. It's not as if anyone is likely to break in.'

Martha looked at her. 'Except you?'

Rachel smiled. 'This morning I caught him giving you a surreptitious glance when he thought you weren't looking.'

'You're letting your imagination run away with you.'

Rachel shook her head. 'You trust me on everything else, why won't you believe me when I assure you that red-blooded young men go weak at the knees at the sight of you?'

'She's always been too modest for her own good,' Hetty said.

'Exactly. If you happen to go out for a walk and bump into him, I'm sure he'll be thrilled if you stop for a word.'

'He didn't look like a sparkling conversationalist,' Martha said.

'Don't judge by appearances. Who knows, he may pluck up the courage to ask you out to the pictures.' Rachel smiled. 'If he's a dull dog, well, you only need to distract him for a quarter of an hour. Give me a start of ten minutes. I need to call at End Terrace first.'

'You're onto something, aren't you?'

'Am I so transparent?'

'When you're in this kind of humour, yes.' Martha smiled. 'All right. Ten minutes?'

'Perfect, thank you.'

With a quick wave, Rachel was on her way again, pausing only to collect the keys and a small Eveready torch from the kitchen. She gave the constable a brisk nod when he saluted her outside Palmer's cottage. He looked at her with undisguised interest, but she didn't say a word. His luck would turn when Martha came along.

She continued along the lane until she reached End Terrace. With Mrs Stones safely out of the way, she gave a perfunctory knock on the front door before slipping around the side of the house into the rear garden. Picking up a pebble, she lobbed it into the old well.

There was no splash.

A smile played on Rachel's lips. Even on a lovely summer's

day, the interior of the well was dark. She shone the torch into the opening and peered down.

As she'd anticipated, it wasn't really a well at all. Iron grips had been driven into the rocky sides at intervals. Twenty feet down, she saw an entrance that looked like an underground passageway.

Two minutes later she was back on the lane. This time she followed the path leading to the cliff before diverting towards Shepherd's Cottage. There was no one around, but a prickling at the back of her neck told her that someone up at the top of the lighthouse was watching.

So be it.

There was a gate in the low privet hedge separating the cottage garden from the grassland. Rachel entered the little garden and hurried to the back door. It was out of the line of sight from the lantern room. She let herself in and found herself in a passageway connecting the kitchen with a wash house.

The police had left the kitchen door open and the smell of gas was nothing more than a nauseating memory. The smashed glass had been tidied and a board propped up on the window seat as an inadequate cover for the gaping hole Trueman had made when breaking in.

The music of Martha's laughter filtered into the kitchen. She and the constable were getting acquainted outside the front door. Rachel had watched her friend's confidence grow in leaps and bounds ever since they'd arrived in London. The self-doubt that had plagued her ever since the acid attack surfaced every now and then, but absorbing herself in the mysteries that fascinated Rachel had done her morale far more good than any help a psychiatrist could offer.

Getting down on her hands and knees, Rachel examined

the stone flags of the kitchen floor. Oakes was right; none of them had been moved since the day they were laid. She took another look up the chimney, and confirmed that there was no underground access to the fireplace.

She stood up and dusted herself down before prowling around the room, testing every surface. There was no give anywhere but when she ran her hand beneath the lip of the window seat, her fingers touched something. Dropping to her knees she saw a simple catch concealed within a tiny recess. She flicked off the catch, and lifted up the top of the window seat.

The space below was ten feet deep. Trueman might struggle to squeeze in there, but anyone smaller could manage. Again, there were iron grips to enable the occupant of the cottage to climb below.

Rachel's spine tingled. Her hunch had been vindicated. Shepherd's Cottage was connected to the old network of smugglers' tunnels.

27

Rachel's work at Shepherd's Cottage wasn't finished. She moved from the kitchen to the parlour at the front of the house. The curtains had been drawn as a mark of respect for the dead, which was fortunate, given that Martha and the young constable were standing outside the window.

Martha gave a throaty laugh in response to some risqué remark. Rachel should have enough time to find what she was after. Even though she wasn't quite sure exactly *what* she was looking for.

There was a bookcase with three shelves. As well as the books Oakes had mentioned, she saw the Bible, a complete Shakespeare, a copy of *Jane Eyre* and an old book about the history of Morecambe. On the bottom shelf stood a row of old leather-bound accounting ledgers, with dates on their spines. The first was marked *Financial Year 1919–20*. Rachel plucked it from the shelf and leafed through it quickly.

The clerk who had written up the records had a neat, easily legible hand. The entries began on 6 April, the start of the tax year. They related to the business of Palmer's accounting firm.

To Rachel's irritation, they appeared to be exactly what they seemed. She was a fast reader and on a quick skim she spotted nothing untoward. Even the travel expenses didn't seem to be inflated.

At the back of the ledger were several blank pages. A wild thought occurred to her. Might something be written there in invisible ink? She'd need a bag of some kind to carry all the ledgers back to Bay View for detailed examination if she couldn't find anything soon.

She leafed through the second journal, paying particular attention to the blank pages at the back. Nothing caught her eye. The same was true of the third book.

With the fourth, she flicked straight to the end of the tax year. Persistence earned its reward. On the first page after the final entry for 5 April 1923 was a mass of closely written text which looked like some kind of diary.

The handwriting was different and she had no doubt that it was the work of Basil Palmer himself. He'd taken an old office ledger, no longer relevant as regards the Inland Revenue, and made use of the space at the back to set down his private thoughts. No doubt he'd reasoned that the chances of anyone bothering to pore through the minutiae of his firm's historic finances were negligible. Working on the old principle, Rachel thought, of how to hide a leaf. In a forest, of course.

She only needed to read the first line to know that she'd discovered exactly what she'd hoped for.

1 January 1931

My New Year's resolution is to murder a man I've never met.

★

Brisk and decisive as ever, Rachel left the cottage by the way she'd entered, locking the back door again after her. The ledger containing Basil Palmer's private journal was tucked under her arm. She didn't care about leaving fingerprints. The police would hear from her soon enough. But first things first. She had no intention of missing her appointment to sit as a model for Virginia Penrhos.

She took the clifftop path rather than the lane. They'd arranged to meet at four, and that was still twenty minutes away, but as she approached the lighthouse, Virginia came out and waved.

'I watched you going up to Shepherd's Cottage.' The older woman was in her paint-smeared smock. 'I was so curious, I couldn't concentrate on my work. Your maid was passing the time of day with that young policeman outside the front door. I lost sight of you once you went round the side of the building. Did you actually go inside?'

'Yes,' Rachel said insouciantly. 'Trespassing, I suppose, but I needed to take another look around.'

'Really?' Virginia's brows knitted. 'May I ask why?'

'Of course you may, Ginny.' Rachel looked her in the eye. 'I don't believe that Basil Palmer committed suicide.'

'Good grief! Are you serious?'

'Never more so.'

'I can't make any sense of it. You're suggesting that he was murdered?'

'I'm certain of it.'

'But… I mean, as I told you, I didn't see anyone going to the cottage yesterday afternoon.' A shadow crossed her face. 'I hope you're not suggesting that…?'

'Oh, I believe you,' Rachel said. 'Basil Palmer was involved with something that doesn't concern you at all. Or Ffion, for that matter.'

Virginia's mystification was obviously unfeigned. 'I can't pretend to understand.'

Rachel held the accounting ledger aloft. 'You don't need to. I think there will be enough information in this book to explain the poor man's death.'

Virginia shook her head. 'I'm sorry, my dear girl, you're talking in riddles. I'm completely lost.'

'There have been plenty of strange goings-on in Hemlock Bay and I'm happy to discuss one or two of my ideas while you paint. If you don't mind talking while you work, that is?'

Virginia stared at her. 'You're an extraordinary young woman.'

'Please forgive me, I'm in danger of getting overexcited. As I told you, I've never modelled for an artist before.'

'What I mean is, there's a great deal more to you than meets the eye.'

'Perhaps your painting will uncover it.'

Virginia laughed. 'I wonder. Would you like to sit outside? It's such a lovely day. My smaller easel is downstairs. Let's fetch it out and two canvas chairs. We can talk as I paint.'

Five minutes later, they were sitting out on the headland. Rachel had her back to the sea, a few yards from the edge of the cliff, close to Mermaid's Grave. Basil Palmer's ledger rested on her knees, open at the first entries. Virginia sat facing her, paintbrush in hand.

For a little while, neither of them spoke. Virginia worked

quickly, while Rachel studied the journal until she was ready to break the silence.

'How is Ffion today?' she asked.

'Still under the weather,' Virginia said.

'I hope she doesn't mind my posing for you.'

Virginia's brush sketched a dismissive gesture. 'I paint whom and what I like, my dear Rachel. An artist can't trouble herself with the whims of others.'

'But if she objects...'

'Ffion is a dear in many respects, but she's also a fragile creature. Dreadfully fragile. The shock of... recent events has hit her extremely hard.'

'I suppose anyone might be upset when a neighbour dies suddenly,' Rachel said calmly, 'but why has she been so badly affected?'

'It's not simply a matter of the death of Dr Doyle, or Palmer, whatever his real name is. The man who told our fortune was brutally murdered, remember.'

'I haven't forgotten,' Rachel said crisply.

Virginia paused for a moment before resuming work on the picture. Rachel concentrated on the diary. At one point a middle-aged couple who were following the clifftop path took an interest in what was going on and came over to speak to them.

'We're searching for Clarion Charlie,' the husband said in a broad Yorkshire accent.

'There's a jolly good prize for the first one to find him,' his wife added eagerly.

'You won't find him here,' Virginia said curtly, without pausing in her brushwork.

The husband looked at the canvas, then at Rachel, then

back again at the work-in-progress. He shook his head sorrowfully and led his wife away without another word.

Rachel stretched languidly. She was relishing the experience of sitting for an artist. This felt like a brief respite from the darkness of murder. She was acutely aware that what she had discovered would destroy several lives. Not everyone affected was, in her eyes, equally deserving of their fate. Her idea of justice didn't coincide with what the law of the land prescribed.

Virginia's concentration had been disturbed by the interruption. She made a disgruntled noise before stepping back and peering at the canvas.

'Hopeless,' she muttered under her breath.

Rachel's hearing was sharp enough to catch what she said. 'Isn't that the nature of creativity? The artist must keep pushing herself to achieve perfection, even though she knows it's unattainable?'

Virginia's expression was bleak. 'Everything I've produced in my life was a masterpiece until I started work on it. I spend a long time thinking about what I'm aiming for – I've done the same with this painting of you – before I start. I've learned from bitter experience that the longer I take to execute the idea, the further the result will be from what I hoped for. That's why I work fast. But from the first brushstroke, everything goes rapidly downhill.'

'I love *Hemlock Bay*.'

'Thank you, dear girl.'

'I'm curious about how you could bear to part with it.'

There was a long pause. 'You're right. It's one of the few pieces where I came vaguely close to achieving what I set out to do. And yes, it was a wrench to let it go.'

'So why did you?'

Virginia gave her a sharp look. 'An artist cannot live on praise alone.'

'My understanding,' Rachel said gently, 'is that you're very far from destitute. I paid a fair price for *Hemlock Bay*, but after the dealer took his commission, I doubt the money can have made any meaningful difference to you.'

Virginia pushed a hand through her straggly hair. 'When we first met, I thought you were a simple young thing. A gushing ingénue, if you will pardon my candour. I was mistaken, wasn't I?'

Rachel nodded. 'I was keen to make your acquaintance, so I will admit that I wasn't entirely frank.'

'You knew I'd come to live in Hemlock Bay?'

'Yes. Several distinct snippets of information came to my attention at around the same time that made me curious about the place.'

'And now,' Virginia said drily, 'the resort's misfortunes are headline news from Land's End to John o'Groats.'

'True.'

'What are you, Miss Savernake? You're not connected with the police, and yet you behave...'

'I'm a nosey parker,' Rachel said lightly. 'Mysteries fascinate me. That's common enough. But where other people are content to borrow detective novels from the library or read the latest sensation in the popular press, I take a more... personal interest.'

'But you came here before Bellamy was killed. Let alone the other fellow.'

Rachel breathed out. 'Let me take you into my confidence.'

Virginia gave her a cold stare. 'Please do. I think it's about time.'

'If you hear me out, you'll understand why I was... diffident about speaking bluntly until now.'

'Go on.'

'My friend Jacob Flint is a journalist with the *Clarion*. He's a crime reporter and a short time ago a visitor called at his office in London. Gareth Bellamy.'

Virginia's eyes opened very wide. 'Good Lord.'

'Bellamy claimed to have had a premonition about murder.'

'What?'

Rachel outlined the story, keeping a close watch on the other woman as she did so, but Virginia's face was a mask.

'Extraordinary, don't you think?'

'Very,' Virginia muttered. 'Of course, the man was a charlatan. You simply couldn't believe a word he said.'

'Jacob thought there was something very odd going on. Bellamy's story raised more questions than answers.' Rachel ticked the points off on her fingers. 'First, why did he take so much trouble to write to Jacob and then call on him in Fleet Street, without waiting to see if Jacob would be interested in what he had to say? Second, when Jacob promised to take the matter up with his editor, why was Bellamy less than enthusiastic? Third, was it mere coincidence that he talked about someone being thrown over the cliffs and you'd painted a picture of a body on the rocks of Mermaid's Grave?'

'I've already told you,' Virginia said. 'Until Ffion and I went to have our fortunes told, we'd never heard of Bellamy, let alone met him. In fact, we didn't know his real name until the news of his murder.'

It was as if Rachel hadn't heard her speak. 'Fourth, was he truly public-spirited or did he have a less honourable motive? Jacob discovered that Bellamy had lost his job as a result of dishonesty, so it seemed unlikely the man was acting out of a pressing sense of civic duty. He was up to something. What could it be?'

'And your answer?' Virginia demanded.

'Bellamy was down on his luck. No doubt his earnings here were better than in Colwyn Bay, but he was a man on the make. So I asked myself this. How could a second-rate fortune teller improve his reputation?'

'You tell me.'

'Isn't the answer obvious? What if he came up with a prediction of some kind that seemed utterly outlandish, but turned out to be true?'

'How could he do that?'

'Suppose he eavesdropped on a conversation about a plan to murder someone. He might pick and choose from what they said and fashion it into a supposed vision of the future.'

'Far-fetched,' Virginia said. 'When people conspire to commit murder, surely they take great care not to do so in public?'

'They might not realise they were being overheard.'

'Even so. It's quite a risk.'

'Not if they were speaking in some form of code.' Rachel paused. 'Or, perhaps, an unfamiliar language.'

Virginia stared. Rachel leaned back in her chair and folded her arms.

'What if, for instance, the individuals concerned were talking in Welsh?'

28

Virginia's expression gave nothing away. This was rather like playing poker with an expert card sharp, Rachel thought. A duel of wits. A seagull circled overhead, as if keeping a watchful eye on proceedings.

'Welsh isn't an easy language to learn. Outside Wales, I can't recall ever having heard anyone conversing in Welsh. So I suppose if two people are Welsh speakers, and they don't want anyone to know what they are discussing, using Welsh must seem quite safe.'

'There's still a risk, surely,' Virginia objected.

'Not in England. Not if it seems that nobody is listening.'

Virginia's eyes narrowed. 'What exactly are you suggesting?'

'There was a small antechamber outside the room where Bellamy was killed. He kept people waiting deliberately, so that he could listen to anything said, and make use of it when he pretended to read palms or gaze into the crystal. His methods weren't elaborate. He'd set up an air pipe, rather like the speaking tube in my motor car, and even if he couldn't hear everything said, especially if his customers were whispering, he'd learn enough to make it seem that his skills were genuine.'

'I'm still not clear what you're getting at.'

Rachel leaned forward. 'The outlines of what happened are clear to me, even if the precise details are obscure. It's like seeing a building through a veil of mist.'

Virginia shrugged. 'You have a vivid imagination.'

'I take that as a compliment, Ginny, thank you. If you want to mark my homework, I'd say that Ffion fell in love with your cousin Nerys and while they were holidaying in Brighton they had the misfortune to encounter Louis Carson.'

'Louis Carson?'

Rachel jerked a thumb towards the lane. 'Yes, the same fellow who lives in the house opposite mine. Carson is a ruthless blackmailer. He demanded money in return for his silence about Ffion's relationship with Nerys. When she told him to go to hell, he retaliated by making sure that puritanical old Aunt Bronwen found out about what her niece was getting up to. Ffion was ruined and left in a state of deep distress. Might falling victim to a vicious blackmailer have contributed to Nerys's death, I wonder?'

'My cousin was beautiful, but as fragile as Ffion,' Virginia said quietly. 'Carson's actions were tantamount to murder. He caused her to take her own life.'

'I see. You found Ffion attractive, and after Nerys's death, you offered her solace and financial security. But it wasn't a love match on quite the same scale.'

Virginia gave a thin smile. 'I'm made of sterner stuff than Nerys. And I wasn't so besotted that I was willing to put up endlessly with Ffion's constant swings of mood.'

'She became obsessed with Carson, I presume. Determined to take revenge on the man she blamed for ruining her life.'

'Impossible not to sympathise,' Virginia said quietly. 'I was extremely fond of Nerys. What that man did was vile.'

'Ffion hatched a plan to kill him,' Rachel said. 'When she discovered that he'd moved to Hemlock Bay, she dreamed of pushing him off the cliffs. Am I right?'

Virginia said, 'Much as I like you, my dear girl, I'm not about to swoon at your feet. You wouldn't expect me to make an incriminating statement, would you?'

Rachel looked this way and that. There was no sign of anyone else hunting Clarion Charlie, or wandering up to take a closer look at the lighthouse or Mermaid's Grave.

'Nobody is listening to us. Not a speaking tube in sight.'

'Once bitten, twice shy.' Virginia shook her head. 'You're a talented storyteller and your voice is melodious, a pleasure to listen to. If you wish to keep spinning your yarn, that is a matter for you. I am willing to hear out your narrative, but don't expect me to offer any embellishments.'

Rachel smiled. She'd never doubted that Virginia Penrhos was a formidable woman.

'Your sketch of Ffion, *The Vow*, suggests to me that you indulged her fantasy. I suppose the vow in question involved murdering the man who caused so much harm.'

She looked at Virginia, who shrugged but said nothing.

'The two of you visited this place and when you found out that a tenancy of the lighthouse was available, you snapped it up. Handy for the cliffs, and also for Carson's home. From an artist's point of view, too, this place was perfect.'

She gestured towards the sea. 'You exorcised your loathing of Carson by painting *Hemlock Bay*. I suppose you found it therapeutic, hence the quality of the finished work. That is his body stretched out on the rocks, isn't it?'

Virginia shrugged. 'You're a student of surrealism. You

understand what we strive for. To reinterpret human experience. To supply a vision of the rational world while
asserting the power of dreams and the uncanny. To challenge
the standards imposed by ordinary society. To champion the
freedom of the individual.'

'Quite a manifesto,' Rachel said. 'I'm not surprised the
two of you were tempted to have a little innocent fun by
having your fortunes told. The psychic world seems so much
more attractive than the drabness of the conventional moral
universe.'

'You understand, don't you?'

'I think I do. But I'm jumping the gun. My guess is that
once you'd finished the painting, you lost the urge to turn the
fantasy of murder into reality. So many dangerous traps lurk
for the unwary, even when one contemplates something as
straightforward as pushing a man off a cliff. What if someone
sees you? What if he survives?'

'Quite. And I need hardly remind you, the swine is still
walking the streets of Hemlock Bay. He has never paid the
price for his crimes.'

'My theory is that you wanted Ffion to give up on the idea
of killing Carson. You regretted indulging her lust for revenge.
But things had gone too far, too fast. She is a stubborn young
woman and you found it impossible to reason with her.'

'Go on.'

'I wonder if one of your reasons for consulting the fortune
teller was the hope that you'd be told something encouraging
about your shared futures that would discourage Ffion from
taking a risk. You were clutching at straws, casting around for
anything that might make Ffion think twice about persisting
with her half-baked ideas about committing murder.'

'You're perceptive, my dear, I'll give you that.'

'The difficulty is that she proved implacable. The murder fantasy had given her a goal. Something to live for. I presume you were arguing in the antechamber, speaking loudly enough for Bellamy to hear. Like you, he came from a Welsh language stronghold. I suppose he could hardly believe his luck. Ffion's interest in Celtic culture caused her to propose committing the crime on the summer solstice, and he latched on to that. It's possible that neither of you even mentioned your intended victim by name. Even if you did, he had no interest in warning Carson that his life was in danger. On the contrary. His priority was to burnish his reputation. What could be better than reporting a carefully garbled version of what he'd heard to a disbelieving world? When, in several crucial respects, his prediction came true, he'd be in clover. The man who foresaw a killing and couldn't persuade anyone to take him seriously. Sensational stuff for the popular press. Jacob Flint's competitors would take great pleasure in recording his failure to save Carson's life.'

Virginia shrugged. 'This is all speculation.'

'Founded on some hard evidence. And it explains one or two things that are otherwise inexplicable. Bellamy needed proof that he'd behaved like a responsible citizen. So he told the police, who were predictably unimpressed. That wasn't enough, so he took the precaution of writing to Jacob – no doubt taking care to keep a copy of his carefully worded letter, so that he could produce it later to substantiate his story about the premonition. Next, he called on his chosen newspaperman in Fleet Street. His plan went swimmingly, and he got hold of Jacob's business card as further evidence of their encounter, but Jacob was prepared to take the story to his editor, and Bellamy didn't want that. It would risk alerting Carson – or the two of you. He was also strangely evasive when Jacob asked him about the accents of the people he'd overheard. That makes sense. He didn't want anyone to realise he'd heard someone talking in his own native tongue.'

'Interesting,' Virginia said slowly. 'Your story, for all its strangeness, has explained one or two things that had puzzled me.'

'About Bellamy's behaviour? There's something else. Martha went to have her fortune told, but she let slip that she knew that The Great Hallemby was really Gareth Bellamy. Something that not even you or Ffion were aware of, I presume?'

Virginia inclined her head.

'I suspect that Bellamy panicked,' Rachel said. 'His original scheme was based on the hope that Ffion would actually kill a man – or attempt to kill him – by pushing him over the cliffs on or around the summer solstice. That was what he'd heard you discussing, and he was confident that the plan was serious, since otherwise why would you talk in Welsh and quarrel about it while waiting to have your fortune told? Perhaps he began to worry that you'd succeed in talking Ffion out of it. So he took a leaf out of Louis Carson's book.'

'What do you mean?'

'You and Ffion gave him enough ammunition to try his hand at blackmail. I think he contacted you, probably by telephone, and made clear that he knew what you were up to. Cross his palm with silver, and he'd keep his mouth shut. He told Winnie Lescott that he expected to come into money, though she didn't believe him.'

Virginia said, 'This is an entertaining yarn. Nothing more.'

'Let me tell you how the story ends. Ffion has a violent streak. She wasn't prepared to submit to Louis Carson's blackmail, let alone Bellamy's. No doubt she realises that once you give in to a blackmailer, he'll never let you out of his clutches. Besides, if Bellamy knew that she wanted to shove Carson off Hemlock Heights, it was impossible for her to commit that crime while Bellamy was alive. She was left in a state of extreme desperation. In her eyes, there was only one possible solution.'

There was a short silence. The inquisitive seagull had flown away. The heat from the sun was less intense and a breath of breeze was coming in from the water.

'I'm listening,' Virginia said.

'I've no idea what the two of you discussed,' Rachel said frankly. 'Or how much collusion there was between you. Ffion may have murdered Bellamy on the spur of the moment, but my bet is that there was some advance planning, even if only on her part and done in great haste. Both Martha and Jacob noticed the gap in the hedge on Hemlock Head, giving access to the Sun and Air Garden. I presume Ffion made use of it in committing her crime.'

'I don't understand.'

'I think you do. She needed an escape route and an alibi. I've never battered anyone over the head with a crystal ball, but it must be almost impossible to avoid having your clothes spattered with blood. Probably a lot of it.'

Virginia shrugged.

'The way I've imagined it is this,' Rachel said. 'You and Ffion go to the Sun and Air Garden together. Once you've made friends with the watchman's Alsatian, she hurries off to Bellamy's hut. She puts on some clothes, perhaps just a macintosh, and crawls through the gap in the hedge, carrying a bag with a change of clothes in some kind of wrapping. I suppose she told Bellamy she was bringing the money he'd asked for. If she was shrewd, she'd have booked an appointment with him, so that he wouldn't be occupied with other customers when she came along.'

'Oh yes?'

'Catching him unawares, she picks up the crystal ball and hits him with it. Then she hurries out through the back of the hut and makes her escape through the hedge. She strips off her bloodstained clothing and shoves it in the bag. Then she rejoins you on the terrace of the Sun and Air Garden. Ten minutes is all it would take.'

'Ffion never left my side that afternoon,' Virginia said steadily.

'Please don't lie to me, Ginny. It's an exercise in futility. I'm not like Bellamy. I haven't threatened you, have I?'

'What exactly do you have in mind?'

Rachel considered. 'A difficult question and I don't have an easy answer. You see, I'm concerned about Ffion's state of mind.'

'Thank you. So am I.'

'She's a troubled soul, Ginny. Angry about her failure to make something of her life, angry that her plan to kill Carson has been thwarted. I imagine she's afraid, too. Afraid that sooner or later, the police investigating Bellamy's death will come knocking at the lighthouse door. My guess is, she feels now she has nothing left to lose. That makes her dangerous, Ginny. To herself and also to you.'

'To me?'

'Yes, you know the truth. She murdered Bellamy in cold blood. Which makes you a threat to her.'

'She cares for me. Despite everything.'

'There's something else.' Rachel was inexorable. 'You've made her bitterly jealous.'

'Jealous?'

'Yes, Ginny, you provoked her deliberately by flirting with me, but that's a risky game with a woman whose temperament is so volatile. Someone with no money of her own, someone who is dependent on you and fears she can't rely on you any more. You changed your mind about helping her to kill Carson and now you've tired of her moodiness and clingy nature.'

'I'm only human,' Virginia said in a small voice.

'And so you've erred.' Rachel shook her head. 'As it happens, Ffion has been on the balcony outside the lantern room for the past five minutes. Watching the pair of us, engrossed in conversation. As if this modelling session is a romantic prelude to our becoming the most intimate friends.'

Virginia looked over her shoulder. Ffion Morris was staring down from the balcony, her slender frame immobile.

Stifling a gasp of dismay, Virginia managed to steady herself enough to give a friendly wave.

'Why don't you come and join us?' she called.

Rachel held her breath as she waited for a reply.

Ffion said nothing.

Instead, she hauled herself up by the balcony railing.

'No!' Virginia screamed. 'Please God! No!'

But Ffion jumped anyway.

29

Rachel and Virginia ran to the edge of the cliff. The drop was vertiginous. Stretched out on the rocks of Mermaid's Grave lay the broken body of Ffion Morris. Even as they watched, a foamy wave broke over the outcrop, as if to wash the blood from the corpse.

Virginia let out a strangled cry.

'You won't believe me,' Rachel said softly, 'but it is for the best.'

'No! You're wrong!' Virginia turned to face her. 'What kind of a woman are you?'

Rachel shrugged. 'That isn't for me to say.'

'You're cold. Heartless.'

'Am I?'

'Doesn't life matter to you? Ffion was young and a beauty. The world was at her feet. She had everything ahead of her.'

'She was deeply disturbed and savage enough to beat Bellamy's brains out. As for Louis Carson, she'd never have got the better of him. Do you truly believe she could ever have come to terms with what she had done?'

Virginia stared into Rachel's eyes.

'So lovely. Yet so cruel.'

'I don't wish to cause you further pain. The simple truth is, you're free.'

A bitter laugh. 'Free? Don't be stupid.'

'I'm trying to be rational. There's no evidence to connect you with Bellamy's murder. In terms of pinning blame on you, the alibi you gave Ffion is neither here nor there. In the unlikely event that any question arises, you can admit that you may have dozed while sunbathing in the nude. Easily done on a pleasant June afternoon. While you were asleep, Ffion may have stolen away and killed the man. Totally unbeknownst to you.'

'We're talking about life and death, and you make it sound like a chess tournament.'

Rachel looked at her. Her gaze was so intense that even Virginia blinked.

'For what it's worth, I don't intend to say anything to the police that would make you liable to arrest.'

'And your pet newspaperman?'

'You've nothing to fear from him. He has more than enough to write about. If you can't bear to stay in England, why not go abroad? Opportunities abound for artists with talent.'

Virginia shook her head. 'It's impossible.'

'Nothing is impossible. You can make a new life, if you wish.'

'Without Ffion?'

'Your affair was doomed before I set foot in Hemlock Bay.'

'My fault. I should have been stronger with Ffion. Made her see sense.'

'Some people never see sense.' Rachel turned on her heel. 'Come on. We must alert the authorities. Ffion's body needs to be retrieved. What story shall we tell them?'

'I suppose you have a few ideas up your sleeve?'

Rachel smiled. 'One or two.'

'I might have known.'

'Courage!' Rachel hesitated. 'Trust me. This is the very worst part.'

'I wish I could believe you.' Virginia closed her eyes. 'All this is just a game to you, isn't it?'

'I play by my own rules.'

'I can't pretend any more. There's nothing left for me.'

'You have artistic gifts.' Rachel spoke in a low voice. 'They count for something.'

'Not enough. People with my amount of talent are two a penny. The best thing I ever did was paint *Hemlock Bay* and now' – she looked down towards Mermaid's Grave – 'it's... forever tainted.'

Rachel breathed out. 'Don't make a rash decision when you're consumed by grief and a sense of guilt.'

'Thank you for your wisdom.' Virginia sighed. 'Will you call the police? I don't have the strength for it.'

Rachel studied her for a few moments. 'Very well. I've said all that I can.'

'Yes.'

'May I take the painting?'

'I didn't get very far.'

'Even so.'

'Then please feel free.' Virginia shook her head. 'And... thank you.'

Rachel walked towards the easel. It wasn't in her nature to look back, but she couldn't help a glance over her shoulder.

Virginia was still standing on the brink, making up her mind.

★

Five minutes later, Rachel was with the Truemans in the garden of Bay View.

'You saw what happened?'

Hetty nodded. 'We didn't want to call the police until we knew what you had in mind.'

'I've spent the last few minutes encouraging Virginia not to throw herself after Ffion.'

'Did you persuade her?'

Rachel sighed. 'I don't know.'

Martha patted her on the back. 'You can't live someone else's life for them.'

'No.'

'I'll call the police.'

'Thank you.' Rachel picked up the accounting ledger containing Basil Palmer's record of his failed plan to murder Louis Carson. 'I'll tell you everything later. Right now, I need to finish reading this.'

Martha got to her feet. The canvas that Rachel had brought back with her was lying on the table. She took a peek.

'How perfect!'

The rough outlines of the picture were there, nothing more. A blurred symbol, with eyes and a mouth below its top.

Virginia had painted Rachel as an elaborate question mark.

At eight o'clock, Rachel met Jacob by appointment in the Hemlock Hotel. The American Bar was filling up, and the orchestra was playing 'What Is This Thing Called Love?', but he'd managed to secure a table in an alcove where they were unlikely to be overheard or interrupted.

'You've spoken to Philip Oakes?' she asked.

'Five minutes ago. He tells me you want to convene people in the smoking room at nine.'

'That's right. Has he been able to organise it?'

'By the sound of things, he's had to twist a few arms, but yes. Everyone you've asked to be present will be there.'

'Excellent.'

'So you reckon you can make sense of everything that's been going on here?'

'I think so.'

'I'm disappointed,' Jacob said. 'Where is your sense of theatre? Surely the Sun and Air Garden would be the perfect venue for all to be revealed?'

Rachel rewarded him with a polite smile which he mistook as encouragement.

'Especially if you exposed a murderer.'

'Very droll. To think that Virginia Penrhos accused me of treating murder as a game. If only she'd met you.'

'You speak in the past tense?'

'When I left her, she was wondering whether or not to jump off Hemlock Heights. I did my best to persuade her not to give up on life, but...'

'Oakes just told me that Inspector Young has interviewed her about the death of Ffion Morris. She said her friend has been suffering badly with her nerves, but Young's mind is working overtime. He's come up with the theory that Ffion was offended by Bellamy's fortune telling, and killed him in a moment of madness. Then she escaped into the Sun and Air Garden. Apparently Virginia was asleep for part of the time on the fateful afternoon, so her alibi for Ffion had gaping holes.'

Rachel nodded. 'I'm glad that is cleared up. And the good inspector deserves a little credit.'

'He's even found Ffion's bloodstained clothes in a laundry basket in the lighthouse.'

'Quick work. Perhaps he's due for promotion.'

'You never know. Even Major Busby may be impressed.'

Jacob grinned. 'There's more to that business than meets the eye, isn't there?'

'Like a surrealist work of art.'

He contemplated her for a moment, before concluding that she had no intention of offering further enlightenment.

'So you think Basil Palmer came here in order to kill Louis Carson?'

Rachel tapped the accounting ledger she'd brought with her. 'It's all here, in black and white.'

'How did you find it?'

'Something Mrs Stones told Hetty was suggestive. She mentioned that Palmer refused to let her dust his "precious books". That made me wonder what was so precious about his books. Rare first editions, perhaps? He didn't strike me as a bibliophile, or even as a particularly keen reader. He was crafty enough to fake up a diary so that nobody would look for anything else. Most of the titles on the shelves were predictable, but there was a row of accounting ledgers.'

'He didn't want her to realise he was an accountant?'

'No, his main concern was that nobody should find his diary. In the circumstances, the ledgers were quite a clever hiding place.'

'Shades of "The Purloined Letter"?'

'Exactly. When I saw them, one question sprang to mind. Why would he bring a load of old accountancy books with him when he was supposed to be on holiday? The only plausible answer was that he wanted to hide something in them.'

Jacob nodded sagely. 'Simple enough.'

Rachel gave him a chilly look. 'I hoped the diary would explain what Palmer was up to. It did that, but much more. Without reading it, I wouldn't have understood the reason why he was murdered.'

'You're sure he was murdered?'

'Absolutely. His death was a clever piece of improvisation. An opportunistic crime, executed very effectively.'

'Until you solved the puzzle.' Jacob looked over her shoulder. 'Well, look who has come along to join the party.'

Bob Harley was coming towards them, a broad smile on his face.

'Well, well, Jacob, didn't realise you had company. Let alone such a charming friend. You've worked fast in a few days. Mind if I join you? Or is this a private tête-à-tête?'

Rachel smiled. 'You are Clarion Charlie, and I claim the prize.'

Bob Harley grinned in delight. 'As the carnival folk say: close, but no cigar. I'm afraid you have to get the precise wording right in order to prise the money out of my editor's wallet.'

'Perhaps you can compensate me in some other way.'

Harley smirked. 'Love to, my dear, absolutely love to. What exactly are you after, dare I ask?'

'You were walking out on Hemlock Heights and Beggarman's Lane yesterday afternoon,' Rachel said.

Harley's brow furrowed. 'That's right. Trying to get my bearings before the hoi polloi descended on me.'

'Tell me what you saw.'

30

'Thank you for coming here this evening, ladies and gentlemen,' Inspector Oakes said. 'I appreciate your co-operation.'

Jacob, sitting to one side in the smoking room, nodded his approval. Oakes was a past master at soft-soaping reluctant witnesses. They had filed in as the clock struck nine and their expressions suggested bewilderment about why they'd been asked to attend.

Sir Harold Jackson, sitting at the front of the room, was chatting amiably to the chief constable. Lady Jackson was pale and drawn, while Louis Carson seemed bored. He'd already made it clear that he had a lot to do, and that it was an imposition to take time out of his busy evening. Pearl Carson, calm and even-tempered, nudged him more than once to encourage him to conceal his discontent. She'd brought her knitting, as if to make sure that the evening wouldn't be entirely wasted.

Inspector Young sat behind the Jacksons while the burly young constable, summoned from Shepherd's Cottage, stood at the back of the room. Bob Harley – much to his displeasure – had not been invited. He sensed that something was up, but Inspector Oakes told him the discussion taking place behind closed doors was confidential. Jacob was there to represent the *Clarion*, but he'd undertaken to follow police guidance about what he could and could not treat as being on the record.

'I suppose,' Sir Harold said to the Scotland Yard man, 'you don't mind explaining what this is all about?'

Oakes cleared his throat. 'We all know there has been a great deal of trouble in Hemlock Bay these past few days. Now we're on the verge of clearing things up, it seemed only right that the people in charge of the Hemlock Bay Development Company should receive a progress report.'

'As I understand it,' Carson said, 'the case is closed. Done and dusted. At least, all bar the shouting. The local grapevine has been busier than ever. I hear that Bellamy was killed by the woman who jumped off the cliff this afternoon. Astonishing. Presumably the inquest will say the balance of her mind was disturbed. So it must have been. Why else would a visitor to the resort batter a harmless fortune teller to death?'

'Why indeed?' Oakes said. 'Inspector Young has been busy. Despite the confusion following yesterday's public meeting, the case has indeed been wrapped up in short order. I can confirm that we are not looking for anyone else in connection with the murder of Gareth Bellamy.'

'There you are, then. Why do we need to go through this rigmarole?'

'Because at present, there are one or two matters that haven't yet been satisfactorily resolved. As we speak, Joseph McAtee is lying in a hospital bed in Lancaster. He's gravely ill.'

Carson reddened. 'The hotel can't accept responsibility for the ailments of its guests. What do the doctors have to say?'

'Their initial diagnosis was tentative. An acute case of Guillain-Barré Syndrome, but they find some features of his condition baffling.' Oakes paused. 'Then there is the death of Basil Palmer, who came here masquerading as a retired doctor from South Africa.'

Sir Harold frowned. 'Didn't the poor devil gas himself? That was my understanding.'

Pearl Carson looked up from her knitting. 'I'm confused. I heard he left a note admitting that he'd killed the fortune teller. Yet now you're saying that the young woman from the lighthouse was responsible.'

'Miss Ffion Morris, yes. She isn't the only visitor to Hemlock Bay who has taken her own life this year. A young man called Edward Hillman threw himself off the cliffs in the spring.'

Sir Harold nodded. 'Sad business, I remember it well. We'd never had such a tragedy before. And now…'

His voice trailed away. To Jacob's ears he sounded weary and defeated, and no wonder. He'd devoted so much energy to creating this resort, only to see the place torn apart by tragedy.

'A short time ago,' Oakes said, 'I had a conversation with Miss Rachel Savernake, whom several of you have already met.'

Rachel was standing at the back of the room and when people craned their necks to look at her she responded with a modest smile.

'I'm acquainted with Miss Savernake,' Oakes said carefully. 'She has given assistance to Scotland Yard more than once. Perhaps I might describe her as an amateur criminologist.'

Sir Harold and his wife raised their eyebrows. Carson frowned, while his wife simply carried on knitting.

'Miss Savernake has formed a theory about the reason for the recent tragedies,' Oakes continued. 'I've therefore invited her to present it to you tonight.'

'I don't see...' Carson began, before Oakes raised his hand.

'If you don't mind, sir, it would be best if I ask Miss Savernake to explain her views and then you can put any questions to her.'

Rachel strolled to the front of the room as the detective sat down next to Young. 'Thank you, Inspector, and thank you everyone for taking the time to come here this evening. I know you're all busy, so I'll be as brief as possible.'

'Please,' Carson muttered.

She smiled at him. 'My interest in Hemlock Bay stirred when I read about the sad death of Edward Hillman. A young man, hard-working and popular, who was about to get married. What could possibly drive him to take his own life? He'd stayed in this very hotel shortly before his death, and he came back here to die, which suggests the place held considerable significance for him.'

'Very distressing,' Lady Jackson said in a soft drawl, 'but he must have been deeply troubled. Surely it's obvious that he came here because Hemlock Bay held happy memories for him?'

Rachel nodded. 'I wonder if he met the love of his life here.'

'His fiancée? Yes, that would make sense.'

'No, he was engaged to the daughter of a man he worked for in Liverpool. But let me turn to Ffion Morris. Unlikely as it might seem, she and Basil Palmer – who called himself Dr Doyle – had something in common.'

The chief constable was beginning to show signs of impatience. 'Such as?'

'They'd both suffered at the hands of a blackmailer,' Rachel said calmly. 'I've read Palmer's journal, which makes the situation clear.'

'Palmer kept a journal?' Sir Harold asked.

'At times of stress, it is therapeutic to jot down one's darkest thoughts.' Rachel gave a wry smile, as if enjoying a private joke. 'Dangerous, though, to give oneself away. The entries make it clear that he came to Hemlock Bay with the intention of committing murder.'

'Good God!'

'Yes. His wife had an affair with another man which was discovered by a blackmailer. They couldn't meet his demands, and the man's wife was told about her husband's adultery. The lovers entered into a suicide pact which resulted in the death of Palmer's wife. When Palmer found out, he became obsessed with avenging her loss. He traced the blackmailer to Hemlock Bay with the help of a private inquiry agent.'

'A private detective?' Sir Harold demanded. 'Extraordinary!'

'Palmer rented Shepherd's Cottage but died before he could put his own plan into action. Meanwhile, Ffion Morris and Virginia Penrhos had come here for similar reasons. Ffion Morris had been blackmailed because of an illicit relationship with another woman. Like the other star-crossed lovers, they refused to pay up, and suffered the consequences. Ffion was also bent on revenge.'

'So Bellamy was the blackmailer,' Carson said. 'That's why she killed him.'

Rachel smiled. 'Bear with me. I wondered if Hillman had also fallen prey to a blackmailer. And I asked myself how a blackmail scheme in a holiday resort might work.'

'Do enlighten us,' Major Busby said gruffly.

'The seaside is a happy hunting ground for someone who trades in dirty secrets. People come to a resort to get away from their ordinary lives. To taste excitement. Hotels are anonymous, guests come and go. You can pretend you are someone else, follow a wholly different way of life. You might bring a lover or pick up a new one. What goes on behind closed doors is no one else's business. Unless a criminal discovers what you're up to.'

Lady Jackson looked bewildered. 'What exactly are you suggesting?'

'Mrs Palmer and Ffion Morris both fell victim to blackmail in Brighton, a raffish place where crime is rife. Hemlock Bay, on the other hand, is famously refined, a Mecca for the respectable bourgeoisie. People with reputations to protect. Individuals with a great deal to lose, if their behaviour is not as impeccable as conventional morality demands.'

'Are you suggesting,' Sir Harold demanded, 'that this town has become home to a blackmailer?'

'Yes,' Rachel said calmly. 'The likeliest explanation for Edward Hillman's act of despair is that he misbehaved so badly here that his engagement was about to be broken and he'd lose his job.'

'What had he done?'

'One possibility is that he consorted with a prostitute.'

'We keep a sharp eye out for trouble in Hemlock Bay,' Sir Harold said. 'Above all in this hotel. Any woman of the streets would be shown the door.'

'The probability is that he succumbed to the charms of another young man.'

'Good God!' Major Busby said. 'In Hemlock Bay?'

'In Hemlock Bay, yes. To cut to the chase, I discovered that a young barman who works in the Mermaid has a penchant for befriending other men who are tempted to… shall we say, feast with panthers? He is in cahoots with the beach photographer. I suspect their modus operandi is straightforward.'

'What do you mean?'

'The barman concentrates his charm on visitors staying at this hotel, on the basis they must have plenty of money. He gets himself invited to the victim's room, and then the photographer bursts in to take compromising pictures. I imagine something of the sort happened to Edward Hillman. Of course, these were exceptional cases where the victims could not or would not buy the blackmailer's silence. No doubt most of the luckless victims paid through the nose in return for the photographs.'

'Appalling,' Sir Harold said. 'Disgraceful.'

'You talk of evidence, Miss Savernake,' Carson said briskly, 'but what evidence do you have to support these distasteful speculations?'

'Not enough to convince a court,' Rachel admitted. 'Palmer's journal is damning, but a document can't be cross-examined. We need more to guarantee a conviction, which is why Inspector Young's sergeant is questioning the barman at this very moment. The beach photographer will be next.'

Carson glanced over his shoulder at the inspector, who responded with a curt nod.

'Blackmail is a lucrative business,' Rachel said smoothly, 'but like most serious crimes, it's fraught with risk. What if, for instance, the blackmailer's scheme is uncovered by someone equally ruthless and amoral?'

'I don't understand,' Lady Jackson said. 'What are you suggesting?'

Rachel folded her arms. 'The private investigator engaged

by Basil Palmer was Joseph McAtee. A capable detective, but corrupt. He was so impressed by the blackmail scheme that he fancied taking a slice of it for himself. Hence his arrival in Hemlock Bay.'

Lady Jackson put her head in her hands. 'This is a nightmare, I can't believe it!'

Rachel looked straight at the Jacksons. 'I understand this must be deeply upsetting for you, but Hemlock Bay is your creation. You need to hear the truth about what has been happening here.'

Louis Carson had grown restive. 'That's all very well, Miss Savernake, but I'm not clear what you're driving at. Are you saying that this blackmail malarkey was masterminded by a young barman? What does McAtee have to do with it all?'

Rachel shook her head. 'You know the truth perfectly well, Mr Carson. Basil Palmer's wife told him in her suicide note that you were the blackmailer. Palmer asked McAtee to trace you and when he ran you down to earth, he decided to get in on your act.'

Carson's face was a deep shade of red. He quivered with temper. 'This is an outrage! I hope you have deep pockets, Miss Savernake.'

'Quite deep, yes.'

'This is slander, plain and simple! Rest assured, I shall instruct my solicitors first thing tomorrow to sue you for every penny you've got.'

Rachel smiled. 'I'm sure you'll be allowed one telephone call from your prison cell.'

'What?' He threw a glance at Oakes. 'I hope nobody else hear believes a word of this fairy tale? To suggest that I'm involved with blackmail...'

'And murder,' Rachel interrupted.

'What? Are you mad? I didn't know Palmer and I certainly didn't kill him.'

'I'm not referring to the death of Basil Palmer,' she said. 'What I'm talking about is the poisoning of Joseph McAtee.'

'You're off your head!' he shouted. 'The man isn't even dead!'

'Not yet, but I fear he soon will be. The last I heard, the doctors were fighting tooth and nail to save his life, but he wasn't responding to treatment. We can only hope that he does recover. Then the charge will be attempted murder.'

'This is a disgrace!' Carson bellowed. Turning to the Jacksons, he said, 'Sir Harold, you're not prepared to stand for this, are you? We're business partners, after all. You said...'

'Whatever I said in the past,' Sir Harold Jackson said icily, 'counts for nothing if there is a scintilla of truth in what Miss Savernake is telling us.'

Lady Jackson gestured to Rachel. 'You say McAtee was poisoned. What proof do you have?'

'Whether he lives or he dies,' Rachel said, 'he'll have to undergo an exceptionally thorough examination. Unless I'm much mistaken, that will yield the required evidence.'

'Evidence of what?' Sir Harold asked.

'Of thallium poisoning,' Rachel said. 'I'm sorry, Lady Jackson, but you were unwittingly responsible for the chosen method of murder.'

'No!' The older woman put her hand to her mouth. 'What on earth do you mean?'

'You mentioned Koremlu Cream to me, and that got me thinking. In your homeland it's attracted a lot of attention as a very effective depilatory. The crucial ingredient is thallium acetate. Unfortunately, that is even more effective when used as rat poison. For a human being, one single dose can prove fatal.'

'My God!'

'I'm sorry to break it to you, but thallium has considerable appeal for a prospective murderer. It is soluble in water and virtually tasteless. The symptoms of thallium poisoning are easily mistaken for various common ailments. And its effects are delayed, although they vary from individual to individual, as well as depending upon the amount of poison administered. I don't claim to be a toxicologist, but given the speed with which his condition has deteriorated, my bet is that McAtee is naturally susceptible. I presume the dose he received was large enough to guarantee death after a period of apparently inexplicable agony.'

Lady Jackson stared at her, ashen-faced. She seemed incapable of finding words to express her horror.

Carson leapt to his feet. 'This is intolerable! Not content with suggesting I'm guilty of blackmail, you're now accusing me of poisoning one of our own guests.'

Rachel smiled, quite unmoved. 'Guests at this hotel receive chocolates on their pillow as a little treat. Is that how McAtee was poisoned? Rather more inventive than simply putting the stuff into his coffee or tea, I agree.'

'I've had more than enough of your nonsense, Miss Savernake. You have no official standing whatsoever. Frankly, it's deplorable that senior policemen are allowing you to parrot your odious theories while they stand idly by.'

Inspector Oakes got to his feet. 'We're not quite as idle as you think, Mr Carson. I've had a quick look at Palmer's journal myself and the accusations about you are damning.'

'The word of a dead man, deranged by grief!' Jerking a thumb at his wife, Carson took a step towards the door. 'Come on, Pearl. We're leaving. If you wish to communicate with me further, Inspector, you can do so through my solicitor.'

Inspector Young interposed his bulky frame between Carson and the door. As Carson hesitated, Pearl Carson rose, clutching her knitting.

'What you're saying, Miss Savernake, is utterly fantastic. The man you're describing isn't the man I married.'

Rachel returned her gaze. 'I notice you don't say *the man I love*. How did you think he made his money?'

'Through damned hard work!'

'Ah, if only.'

Pearl shook her head, in sorrow it seemed, rather than in anger.

'You're making a huge mistake. My husband hiring young men to help him blackmail innocent people? Using a cream of mine to poison a guest in this hotel? It's wild, outlandish. You'll never convince a jury that he's a master criminal.'

Rachel shook her head. 'Don't worry, I won't try.'

Pearl screwed her face up, as if trying to make sense of a cryptic crossword. 'I thought you were saying that Louis…'

'No, no, Mrs Carson. Basil Palmer's wife believed Louis was the blackmailer, and that's why her husband wanted him dead. But Louis was simply the messenger, wasn't he? With the potential to become a convenient scapegoat.'

Pearl held her knitting in front of her like a shield. 'I don't know what you're talking about.'

'Then let me be blunt. You planned the blackmail scheme and put your husband up to moving here and taking over Sir Harold's empire, step by step. And you poisoned Joe McAtee.'

Carson took a stride towards Rachel.

'You're mad! Accuse me of whatever you want, but leave my wife out of it. Pearl is the sweetest, gentlest woman. She wouldn't hurt a fly.'

Rachel stood her ground. 'You think so, Mr Carson?'

'I know so!'

'Touching loyalty. It may be your only redeeming feature. But I wonder how your marital devotion will fare when it's put to the test.'

'You're talking rubbish, absolute rubbish!'

'Am I?' Rachel looked from Louis Carson to his wife and back again. 'I'm sure you've always agreed that, if the worst came to the worst, you'd swear that Pearl is innocent. But how do you feel about her using you as a guinea pig?'

'What do you mean?'

Rachel pointed to his bald patch. 'She tested the thallium on you, I'm afraid. Evidently you only received a small dose, but it left a telltale mark.'

He gaped at her, unable to utter a word. His wife simply stared into space. Her self-control, Jacob thought, was remarkable. He'd thought of her as placid but now he was beginning to believe she was made of ice.

'If she'd got away with killing McAtee,' Rachel said, 'you'd have been the next to go.'

Pearl exhaled, but said nothing. Carson's face was a picture of incredulity.

'Your death would have left Pearl free to pursue her impossible dream. Of becoming the next Lady Jackson.'

'Oh God!' Sir Harold said. 'Never!'

An involuntary exclamation, but coupled with the expression of horror on his face, it was enough to destroy Pearl Carson's unnatural calm.

She picked up her knitting needles and threw herself forward, aiming the needle points at Rachel's throat.

Rachel spun on her heel and dodged out of the way. As Oakes and Jacob rushed forward, she seized Pearl Carson's wrist and twisted hard.

There was a snapping noise that made Jacob cringe.

Pearl Carson stared at Rachel in astonishment and pain and howled like a banshee.

31

'Incredible,' Sir Harold Jackson said as the waiter left the smoking room ten minutes later. 'I don't know what to say.'

Inspector Young had arrested the Carsons. They seemed to be too dazed to offer any further resistance. The looming presence of the burly young constable deterred any thought of a physical fight.

Once the policemen, led by Major Busby, had taken their charges away, Sir Harold summoned drinks from the bar. If ever there was a time for a stiff whisky, he said, this was it. Jacob agreed with more than usual fervour.

'You had no idea of her devotion to you?' Rachel asked.

'Absolutely none. The very idea is absurd.' He glanced at his wife, who looked haggard. 'Everyone who knows anything about me is under no illusion about my love for Sadie.'

'Forgive me for saying so, but Pearl Carson was looking to the future. She knew of Lady Jackson's ill health and she thought that if her husband were out of the way and you were bereft...'

Sir Harold swore. 'Unthinkable! The woman must be mad.'

'In many respects, she is as rational as any of us. She came from a poor background and wanted to be rich, but there's nothing unusual in that.' Rachel smiled faintly, and Jacob wondered if this was some kind of private joke. 'Only when her path crossed with that of Carson, a plausible but unscrupulous rogue, were the conditions met for her to embark upon a life of crime. Psychiatrists call it *folie à deux*. The two of them fed on each other's cold-blooded determination to better themselves. Pearl's agreeable nature enabled her to befriend people in the hope of luring them into an indiscretion. In the Sun and Air Garden, for instance. That's why she was keen for Martha and me to sample its pleasures.'

'They corrupted everything they touched,' Lady Jackson said. 'I suppose that ever since they got married...?'

Her voice faltered. Tears formed in her eyes.

Rachel said, 'At first they must have been nervy about getting caught. Perhaps they began with petty acts of dishonesty, defrauding employers and so on. Their caution paid off, because Inspector Oakes assures me neither of them has a criminal record. As their confidence grew, so did their willingness to take risks. Their talents were perfectly suited to blackmail.'

'And Brighton offered rich pickings,' Sir Harold said grimly.

Rachel nodded. 'Pearl Carson found work as a chambermaid in one expensive hotel after another. If she discovered compromising evidence in someone's room – letters, or photographs, or heaven knows what – Carson would blackmail the luckless guest. I expect most victims paid up without a murmur. If someone refused to comply with his demands – like Alicia Palmer and her lover, or Ffion Morris and hers – Carson had no compunction about betraying their secrets. The consequences were catastrophic. But he grew careless. Alicia and – somehow – Ffion both discovered his real name. And Alicia's widower and Ffion longed to get their revenge.'

'Why did they come here?'

'Pearl realised that Louis was taking too many risks. Moving three hundred miles north made a deal of sense. The chance to run this hotel was too good to miss. The guests – the prospective victims – weren't short of money. Pearl was no longer a chambermaid, but I'm sure she made good use of her supervisory role. Louis hired the barman and beach photographer to manufacture fresh opportunities for blackmail. The profits they'd already made were ploughed into the partnership with you, Sir Harold. They intended to earn enough to buy you out when the time was right.'

Sir Harold nodded. 'These are desperate times for investors. Carson drove a hard bargain, but at least he had the cash available. Please believe that I never had an inkling where their money really came from.'

'I'm sure you didn't,' Rachel said.

'He claimed he'd come into an inheritance. I must say, I didn't care for the man. His obsequious manner grated, but we had to work together and... and his wife was kind to Sadie. Nothing was ever too much trouble for her.'

His wife nodded. 'Pearl gave the impression of being completely under Carson's thumb. Dear God, I actually felt sorry for her.'

'A common technique of swindlers. I suppose you recommended her to try Koremlu Cream as an act of kindness?'

'Certainly, but is there any truth in what you said? Can it really cause harm?'

'Very serious harm. Pearl had worked in a pharmacy and also as a nurse. She knew that thallium is a deadly poison.'

Sadie Jackson shuddered. 'And she actually experimented on her own husband?'

'I'm sure of it. I suspect that not long after arriving here, Sir Harold, she became besotted with you.'

'Again,' he said in a hollow voice, 'I didn't have the faintest notion. And I can assure you, I never gave her the least encouragement.'

'Don't reproach yourself. Pearl Carson saw you as belonging to a different world. Once she had money, she realised it wasn't enough to gain her what she really craved. Respect and respectability. She was skilled at concealing her innermost thoughts from you and from everyone else. Even so, one or two women were sharp-eyed enough to spot the signs of hero worship. Word got around.'

He flinched. 'Dear God. As if I'd ever...'

'Edward Hillman came back here to die, in my opinion, because this was where, fleetingly, he thought he'd found true love. I suspect it was the barman who betrayed his trust. I don't think the young man knew the Carsons had orchestrated his misfortune. With Ffion, the position was different, but Pearl Carson didn't realise who Ffion Morris was, because at the time of her involvement with Nerys, she was using a stage name, Fifi Garcia.'

Jacob couldn't keep quiet a moment longer. 'Did Pearl Carson know that "Dr Doyle" was actually the husband of Alicia Palmer?'

'I doubt it, but already she saw Louis as an encumbrance. She'd given him a small dose of thallium – enough to cause him to lose some hair, but not enough to kill.'

'Why?' Sir Harold asked. 'Some form of rehearsal?'

'Possibly. I suppose she was unsure about the precise effects of whatever dose she administered. Perhaps she did work out Ffion's identity and hoped she'd do her dirty work for her by killing Louis. In which case, there would be no need to spend a penny on buying you out.'

Sir Harold made a noise of disgust. 'Carson made no bones about his hope that, if I decided to step away from business life, I'd sell my remaining stake to him. And I can't deny that following our son's accident and Sadie's illness, I began to contemplate retirement.'

'Forgive an intrusive question,' Rachel said to his wife, 'but am I right in thinking the disease has returned?'

Lady Jackson stared at her. 'For a young woman, you are extraordinarily perceptive. How did you know?'

'You're naturally slender,' Rachel said, 'but now you are so very thin that I feared the worst. You may not have confided in Pearl Carson, but she probably guessed. Your misfortune fuelled her belief that, in the fullness of time, she could become a trusted comforter and, eventually, the new Lady Jackson.'

Sir Harold shook his head. 'There has only ever been one woman for me.'

'I believe that's true,' Rachel said softly. 'If you'll pardon me for saying so, such a love match is rare. Nobody could doubt your devotion to each other.'

Jacob savoured the taste of his whisky. Knowing Rachel of old, he had an intuition that there was more for her to say. Was she waiting for a lead from the Jacksons? Giving them a chance to speak first?

'You mentioned Basil Palmer's journal,' Lady Jackson said. 'I wondered...'

'Whether he said anything about your husband?' Rachel said gently. 'Yes, he did. He recognised you, Sir Harold, and talked about your fleeting encounter outside this hotel. Hooker Jackson, that was the name he knew you by in student days.'

Sir Harold shifted uncomfortably. 'Basil Palmer, good Lord! I thought the name rang a bell. You're right, I did know a chap called Basil Palmer. I've not given him a thought for years but yes, we were at Cambridge together.'

'And he was the best man at your wedding, wasn't he?'

'Spot on! Old Basil, goodness me. Mind you, we were never close, but it was wartime and he happened to be available.'

'The journal suggests he hero-worshipped you.'

Sir Harold drank some whisky. 'I suppose you might say that. Meek little fellow, never said boo to a goose. He hung around, I suppose because he didn't have close friends. So it was his wife who was tormented by Carson, eh? Poor soul!'

'You didn't recognise him when your paths crossed on the esplanade?'

'How could I, if he was in disguise?'

Rachel smiled. 'Disguise?'

Sir Harold stared at her. 'He came here in disguise, didn't he? Took a fake name as well. All in order to deceive Louis Carson. Who would imagine little Basil contemplating murder? Talk about the worm turning. It really is damned extraordinary. But then, this whole business is incredible.'

He spoke rapidly, not pausing for breath. When he'd finished, he took another drink of whisky. His wife rested a hand on his arm. She looked flushed and in considerable distress. Because of the cancer, Jacob wondered, or something else?

Rachel turned to his wife. 'Did you recognise him when he took off his glasses?'

Lady Jackson closed her eyes. 'Our wedding was a long

time ago. The early days of the War. I remember... Basil vaguely, but I only had eyes for Harold.'

'He says in the journal that he found you attractive.'

She blushed. 'Really? That was nice of him, but...'

'He didn't appeal to you?'

'The question simply didn't arise.'

'You didn't want to spend time with him, did you? After the ceremony was over, he asked you out for a drink, but you gave him short shrift.'

'I don't understand,' she said in a low voice. 'Surely he didn't write that down? How could it make any sense? Making eyes at a newly married woman?'

Rachel shook her head. 'That's the point. You hadn't just got married. In those days you were Josie, the impoverished distant cousin. Not the woman with whom Sir Harold tied the knot. His real wife was poor Sadie, heiress to a fortune.'

32

The silence in the smoking room made it seem as dead as a tomb. Jacob's fingers itched. He was desperate to scribble notes but he knew Rachel would never forgive him. Was this a story she didn't want to be told? Otherwise, why wait until Oakes had left before exploding her grenade?

Nobody moved until Lady Jackson, unable to bear it any longer, gave a low moan and buried her head in her hands. Her husband looped a brawny arm around her, murmuring words of comfort.

Rachel tasted her whisky and waited for a reply.

Sir Harold said heavily, 'How did you find out?'

'I'm afraid your wife made a simple mistake. Easily done, even more easily overlooked, but I happened to notice.'

'You don't miss much, do you?'

'What mistake?' Lady Jackson said dully.

'Don't you recall?' Rachel asked. 'You mentioned your mother dying from cancer on your sixteenth birthday. Yet according to *The Illustrated Guide to Hemlock Bay* you were orphaned in infancy by a fatal car crash in San Diego.'

A stifled cry. 'Oh God!'

Rachel continued inexorably. 'A strange mistake to make. Inexplicable. Nobody gets so mixed up about a date that is so important to them. If Sadie lost her parents very young and was raised by her guardian, that meant you weren't Sadie.'

The Jacksons exchanged glances. Jacob held his breath, but neither of them spoke.

'Once I read Basil Palmer's journal,' Rachel said, 'it was easy enough to fit the pieces together. Sadie was due to come into a fortune when she was twenty-five. But her health was poor and the chances of her reaching that age weren't good. She was a shrinking violet, according to Basil. Not like Hooker Jackson, the adventurer who was prepared to cut any corner to get what he wanted.'

Sir Harold finished his drink. 'You seem to know everything, Miss Savernake.'

'I only wish I did. Am I right in guessing that you fell for Josie first? And did she introduce you to Sadie?'

He nodded. 'Two bull's eyes. Sadie's guardian was old and ailing. Josie brought her to Europe to see the world, but they got no further than England before war broke out. I met Josie at a party and from that moment my fate was sealed.'

He looked fondly at his wife, but she seemed incapable of speech.

'When you found out about Sadie's frailty and her financial expectations,' Rachel said, 'you cooked up a plan with Josie. Her cousin had little experience of men. You'd sweep her off her feet and marry her. If she inherited the money, all well and good. Not to put too fine a point on it, she wasn't going to live forever, and the two of you could continue your affair in the meantime.'

'When you put it so baldly, it seems heartless. Cruel. Take it from me, Miss Savernake, the reality was different.'

'You were doing Sadie a good turn?'

'Mock if you wish, but it's not so far from the truth. She'd known little happiness. In the short time we were together, I like to think she experienced some joy.'

Rachel shrugged. 'If Sadie died before reaching the magic age, Josie would step into her shoes and become Mrs Jackson. The strong physical resemblance between the two cousins was a crucial advantage. You'd be living in England, far away from anyone in America who might be able to tell the difference between them. A dangerous game, but I suppose the prospect excited you. You're a born risk-taker.'

'Josie and I have that in common,' Sir Harold muttered. 'Both of us have a reckless streak.'

Rachel allowed herself a glimmer of a smile. 'Like your enthusiasm for taking your clothes off in public?'

'We've never cared about the conventions. Who gives a damn for respectability when you may be blown out of the sky at any moment? None of us knew what was going to happen. I flew out on so many sorties, the odds were stacked against me. It's a miracle I made it through the whole war in one piece.'

'Despite the fact you got married at a time of such uncertainty, you wanted to minimise the chance of being detected in future. So it was a small, hastily arranged ceremony and you chose Basil Palmer as your best man. You'd dropped him long ago and had no intention of seeing him again. He was boring. Far too much of a doormat. But even doormats have their uses.'

'Cynical, but true.'

'As you expected, he was ready, willing, and able to do the honours. What you didn't predict was that he'd be presumptuous enough to take a shine to Josie.'

'She didn't have any difficulty in brushing him off.'

'I felt sorry for him,' his wife muttered. 'Such an unprepossessing creature.'

Rachel asked, 'What happened to Sadie?'

'She was dying of consumption,' Harold said. 'Her inheritance was due to go to distant relatives of her guardian. Sadie didn't even know them. We'd bought a cottage in Epping Forest and Josie rented a room in the vicinity. When I next came home on leave, Sadie was very sick. I berated the nurse we'd engaged and sent her packing. Josie took over from her. I don't mind telling you that I agonised, but… there was the money to think about, you see.'

'Yes, I see that very well.'

'Call me a liar if you wish, but one day Sadie begged me to push the pillow over her face. What could I do? Let nature take its course and see the woman suffer needlessly?'

'So…?'

'So I smothered my wife and buried her in the forest. Her body lies there to this day. Unfortunate, but—'

'Extremely unfortunate,' Rachel interrupted.

'What choice did I have?'

'You could have let her die a natural death and given her a Christian burial.'

'And condemn her to prolonged pain and anguish? Miss Savernake, let us talk plainly. Was it so very wicked to put her out of her misery?'

'We Americans have a term for it,' his wife said quietly. 'We call it a mercy killing.'

Rachel savoured her whisky. 'A slippery phrase. At all

events, you began your masquerade. One pretty American woman looks much like another, was that the idea?'

The other woman took a breath. 'Looking back on it, the confusions of wartime made switching identities as easy as pie. We flitted from place to place, that's how we stumbled across Hemlock Bay. The money came to me without any complications and by the time of the Armistice, we were ready to turn our dreams into reality. This resort is the result.'

'Since the war, everything has gone perfectly here?'

'Pretty much, until the Carsons came into our lives. At first they seemed like the answer to a prayer. After my operation, the outlook was uncertain and Harold and I were ready to wind down. The only question was, how best to do it.'

Her husband nodded. 'To divest yourself of such a big business isn't as easy as people imagine. You need to find a willing buyer with cash in the bank. I had my reservations about Carson, but nobody else was prepared to put up the money. Giving him the hotel to run was akin to putting him on probation. If he made a good job of it, I'd have sold him the rest of my stake in the company at the end of the summer.'

'And then Basil Palmer turned up,' Rachel said. 'His involvement in your big day meant a lot to him. He never forgot it. Even if he didn't see through your deception when he spotted the two of you here.' Rachel looked at Lady Jackson. 'Did both of you recognise him?'

She gave a weary nod. 'He'd taken off his glasses and those small, protuberant eyes rang a bell in my mind. Harold's too, as I soon discovered. For a few moments I couldn't place him, but I knew I associated him with Harold's past and with an unwelcome advance. When the truth dawned on me, I was horrified. A man who had seen me *and* Sadie on a memorable occasion.'

'What terrified us,' her husband said, 'was that we found out that he'd come to Hemlock Bay masquerading as someone else. I established that he wasn't staying at the hotel and when I asked my land agent, his description of the new tenant at Shepherd's Cottage confirmed our worst fears. Basil was here, in our own back yard. Using a false name, trying – not very successfully, but that was typical of Basil – to change his appearance. But he'd slipped up by giving the name of his own accounting practice as one of his referees.'

Rachel winced. 'So much for the best-laid plans. His naïveté is clear from everything he writes in the journal.'

'His refusal to come to dinner seemed deeply suspicious. Had he somehow worked out that we were living a lie? Was he trying to avoid us until such time as it suited him to confront us? We couldn't think of an innocent explanation.'

'You'll never believe it, in view of what the Carsons were up to,' his wife said, 'but we thought he'd fallen on hard times and was planning to blackmail us.'

'Whatever his motives,' Sir Harold said, 'he represented a serious threat. Suppose he was here for some other reason – as now turns out to be the case. He'd taken a tenancy for the summer and had run across us within his first few days in the town. We could hardly go into hiding. If he bumped into us again, there was every chance he'd realise that Josie was pretending to be my wife. And then the balloon would go up. We'd be ruined.'

'Everything we'd created here was in jeopardy,' his wife said. 'The resort. The house. Harold's knighthood. Our children's happiness. We didn't have a clue about what the Carsons were up to. As far as we were concerned, Basil Palmer was the serpent in our Eden. Even if he swore to keep the secret, how could we trust him to keep his word?'

'So you decided to kill him,' Rachel said pleasantly.

'No! For heaven's sake, you make it sound like a cold-blooded plan.'

'I don't believe his murder was entirely unpremeditated.'

The other woman bit her lip. 'The truth is, we didn't know what to do. We were beside ourselves with worry, but we had to maintain a façade. Business as usual, you know?'

Rachel nodded. 'The murder of Gareth Bellamy gave you an idea, didn't it? That crime seemed like the work of a maniac. Who else would batter a harmless fortune teller to death? If a madman was on the loose, perhaps he might choose Basil Palmer as his next victim.'

Sir Harold groaned. 'Inspector Young thought Winnie Lescott was responsible. I doubted he was right. But if she was guilty, Bellamy's murder made it no easier to... remove Basil Palmer.'

He turned to Jacob. 'The moment you revealed that Winnie was innocent, I saw my chance. I didn't have time to think it out in detail, but I've always believed in acting on my instincts.'

'Your preparation was more extensive than you admit,' Rachel said. 'Basil Palmer's supposed suicide note, for instance.'

Sir Harold sighed and shook his head, like a defeated chess player acknowledging the superior skills of a grand master.

'Palmer mentions in his journal that you once forged a cheque,' she said. 'Old habits die hard, and the odd phrasing of the note intrigued me. Am I right in guessing that you copied certain words from his correspondence with your land agent, when taking the tenancy of Shepherd's Cottage?'

'You're exceptionally shrewd, Miss Savernake. As formidable a young woman as I've ever met.' He coughed. 'Except for my beloved... I'll call her by the name she was born with, given that you seem to have penetrated all our secrets… my beloved Josephine.'

'You are familiar with the smugglers' tunnels,' Rachel said. 'Let me explain what I think you did. After dropping off Virginia and myself, you parked your car at the Fisherman's Arms, then hurried back to End Terrace. You were always careful to keep on good terms with the local people who were living here when you and your wife arrived. Mrs Stones thinks the sun shines out of you, and she's not alone. You'd learned that what looks like a well in her garden actually leads to the tunnels. It goes by way of Shepherd's Cottage to the caves by the sea.'

'I did a lot of exploring in my early days here. The tunnel from Palmer's house to the cliffs is blocked, but the section leading back inland is in a surprisingly good state. I'm not quite as fit as I was, but it didn't take me long to get to Shepherd's Cottage.'

'Unfortunately, you were seen.'

His expression was derisive. 'No need to try to trick me, Miss Savernake.'

'There is a witness, I can assure you. Not Virginia Penrhos, because you'd done the deed before she went up to the lantern room, but a colleague of Jacob's called Harley who is masquerading as Clarion Charlie. He caught sight of you hauling yourself down into the well. But he didn't raise the alarm. Clarion Charlie is meant to be elusive and he didn't want to draw attention to himself.'

Jacob felt a prickle of irritation. If Bob Harley had spotted something untoward, it wouldn't have hurt him to alert his colleague, the chief crime correspondent. But Bob only cared about his own position. Besides, he blamed Jacob for the fact he'd been hauled up north in the first place.

'You have an answer for everything,' Sadie – as Jacob still thought of her – murmured.

'You must have given Basil Palmer a shock,' Rachel said. 'Suddenly appearing in his house like that. How did you get the window seat open?'

'There's a tiny slit in the wood beneath the seat. With a pocket knife, it's easy to flick open the catch and lift the lid.'

'Your idea was to concoct a fake suicide and suggest that Palmer killed Bellamy and then took his own life in a fit of remorse. The note was worded ambiguously, in case the real murderer was caught and Palmer's innocence was proven. A wholly explicit confession would have caused the police to become suspicious of the note.'

Sir Harold nodded. 'Right again. I almost managed to kill Basil by giving him a heart attack. Once he'd recovered from his fright, he was thrilled to see me, the poor old soul. I soon realised that he hadn't come to Hemlock Bay to cause trouble for me. But the die was cast.'

'It's clear from his journal that he didn't know you'd changed wives.'

'No, I gathered that. But I simply couldn't risk allowing him to live. We had a drink in the parlour and I managed to slip some of Sadie's Veronal in his whisky when he wasn't looking. He'd just mentioned Carson's name when he dozed off. And so...'

'You killed him?'

'You make it sound very brutal, but I don't believe he experienced any pain. It was surprisingly easy to drag him to the gas oven and turn on the taps. I dropped the note on the floor and locked the kitchen door on the inside before going back the way I came. Never did I imagine... that committing murder can be so straightforward.'

'Yes,' Rachel said softly, 'it can.'

'And I very nearly got away with it.' He gave a rueful smile. 'So, Miss Savernake. You hold the cards. How do you intend to play them?'

Jacob held his breath for what felt like an eternity as Rachel swirled the remains of her whisky around in the tumbler.

'People prate about justice,' she said, 'but it's an unruly beast. Like morality. Each of us sees these things from our personal point of view. Hemlock Bay was built on murder and deceit, but the woman you smothered was dying anyway, and the relatives tricked out of their inheritance had done nothing to earn it.'

Lady Jackson said eagerly, 'You're right!'

'Bellamy was a rogue and so was McAtee. I'll shed no tears if the Carsons go to the gallows. Ffion Morris was doomed to eternal unhappiness long before she committed murder.'

'Exactly!'

Rachel shook her head. 'However. Basil Palmer was different.'

'He was a weakling,' Sir Harold said. 'He'd never have got up the nerve to kill Carson.'

'I agree,' Rachel said. 'His journal makes his failings all too plain. He made mistake after mistake. Trusting his wife. Trusting McAtee. Trusting you.'

'I only did what I had to do.'

'Actually, if you'd trusted him to keep his mouth shut, he'd have kept your secret until his dying day. You were his hero.'

Sir Harold shrugged. 'Easy for you to say that now.'

'Whatever his faults, Palmer didn't deserve to die,' Rachel said. 'That is what matters.'

'Don't forget, he was contemplating murder.'

'Who can blame him?'

He stared at her. 'So what do you propose?'

Rachel looked at her watch. 'I'm not in a tearing hurry. At ten o'clock in the morning, the day after tomorrow, I'll call Inspector Oakes and explain what I believe happened at Shepherd's Cottage.'

His gaze was intense. 'Unless?'

'Unless no purpose will be served by my doing so. You have young children and a dying wife. I have no wish to cause them any unnecessary distress. They have endured enough. But you must disclose where Sadie's body is buried, even if you inform the police anonymously.'

'A little over twenty-four hours?' He shook his head. 'Not much time to set my affairs in order.'

Rachel gave him a wintry smile. 'You're an astute businessman, but let me make one thing clear. I'm answering your question about how I'll play my cards. Not entering into a negotiation.'

33

ANOTHER TRAGEDY
AT HEMLOCK BAY

Jacob flourished the *Clarion*'s headline for the benefit of Rachel and the Truemans. They were back in the drawing room of Gaunt House, and Trueman had just served cocktails. His latest triumph had a rich orange flavour and was called Damn-the-Weather. No question of basking under the sun in the roof garden today. The clouds had burst and the rain was bucketing down.

Hetty peered at the story. 'So Jackson ran his car off Hemlock Heights?'

'Remember the sharp bend on Beggarman's Lane, between the lighthouse and the Fisherman's Arms? Instead of dropping his speed, he pressed the accelerator and went straight over and on to the rocks.'

'A horrible way to go,' Martha said with a shudder.

'At least it was quick and he made his own choice,' Rachel said. 'Inspector Oakes tells me he sent a note describing where his dead wife's body is buried. But the police will handle matters without blighting two children's lives by making their father's crime public. I know you won't breathe a word, Jacob.'

'I gave you my promise,' Jacob said. 'You know I'd never break it.'

'Thank you. The car accident itself can be blamed on the traumatic effect of recent events.'

Jacob nodded. 'Gomersall has ended the Clarion Charlie campaign as a mark of respect. His editorial says the sympathies of all right-thinking people will be with Lady Jackson and her family.'

'Good to see a popular newspaper showing compassion,' Rachel said wryly. 'I suppose you'd describe it a victory for civilised values?'

'You took the words out of my mouth. Anyway, Gomersall has got all the publicity out of the seaside that he could hope for. And Harley was threatening to resign if he wasn't allowed back to report on the cricket.'

'I've had a note from him, inviting me to join him at the Lord's Test match. He's offered to teach me the finer points of the game.'

'Hoping to bowl a maiden over,' Martha said with an impudent grin.

'Will you go?' Jacob asked.

'Let's just say that he was stumped by my reply,' Rachel said. 'What's the latest news? I can see you're dying to tell me.'

'Carson has cheated justice. Hung himself by a shoelace in the prison cell.'

Rachel shrugged. 'Once he knew that Pearl wanted him dead, he had nothing left to live for.'

'Joseph McAtee is paralysed. It's still touch and go whether he'll survive. If so, Pearl Carson will be on a capital charge. Assuming she's fit to plead, that is. Apparently she's raving like a maniac. Her mind has gone.'

'I doubt she'll hang. More likely she'll end her days in a straitjacket.'

'And Virginia Penrhos?'

Rachel handed him a postcard bearing a picture of *S.S. Île de France* and a scrawled message on the back:

On my way to Le Havre and then to New York and on to Santa Fe. Then perhaps Mexico. I miss Ffion but I shall miss you more.

Ginny

xxx

Jacob passed the postcard back to her. 'She shielded a murderer.'

'She cared for a sick lover. For a while she was swept away by Ffion's homicidal fantasy, but working on *Hemlock Bay* offered her catharsis.'

Jacob glanced at the painting. He was beginning to understand what Rachel saw in it. There was something hypnotic about the blend of curve and colour.

'When she came to her senses,' Rachel said, 'she did her utmost to talk Ffion out of her plan to commit the murder.'

He shrugged. 'To no avail.'

'Some people are beyond persuasion.'

Jacob savoured the earthy tang of his cocktail.

'How much does Oakes know?'

'Enough. He may have guessed more, but he'll let well

alone. Meanwhile Inspector Young is lapping up the credit for the arrest of the Carsons.'

'So all's well that ends well?'

Rachel looked him in the eye. 'Not for everyone.'

He shifted in his chair. 'What about the four of you?'

'Our trip to the seaside wasn't entirely restful. But holidays are like the English summer. Like life itself. You can never be sure what will happen next.'

'I still don't know what the future holds in store,' Martha said wistfully.

Jacob was surprised by the bleakness of Rachel's response. 'Isn't it better not to know?'

Cluefinder

The Rachel Savernake books are the first crime novels for about half a century to include a Cluefinder, a long-forgotten trope of Golden Age detective fiction. Readers' enthusiasm for this type of mystery game-playing has delighted me; so has the fact that other crime writers are now joining in the fun. *Hemlock Bay* offers perhaps the most extensive Cluefinder there has been, highlighting forty-six of the hints and tips to the various puzzles within the story.

The impersonation of Sadie

Page 27: *He'd become her guardian while she was still a babe in arms, after her parents were killed in a car crash in San Diego.*

Page 83: *Like Sadie, she was slender, dark, and pretty.*

Page 83: *Sadie was always a sickly one.*

Page 182: *The same disease killed my mother. In those days it was rare and seldom diagnosed until it was too late.*

Page 182: *Birthdays are bad news in my family. Mom died on my sixteenth.*

The Jacksons' relationship
Page 99: *Harold Jackson oozes charm, but I'd say his wife is the power behind the throne.*

Hooker Jackson's risk-taking nature and opportunism
Page 77: *Let alone the scar above his left eyebrow, caused by a fencing accident at school when, with typical bravado, he dispensed with his mask.*
Page 81: *He was reckless, I was irredeemably respectable.*
Page 83: *When Hooker's mind was made up, he was quite unstoppable.*
Page 84: *Hooker was spontaneous and bold, a man who lived for the moment.*
Page 84: *He was always mischievous as well as opportunistic.*

Hooker's ability to identify Basil after so many years
Page 85: *Hooker always had a keen eye*

Hooker's experience of forgery
Page 84: *On one occasion he even forged a cheque from a rich uncle for a dare.*

The secret entrance to Shepherd's Cottage
Page 25: *The fishermen and farmers of Hemlock Bay supplemented their income by smuggling contraband through a maze of underground passages.*
Page 72: *Tunnels beneath Hemlock Heights were used to smuggle ill-gotten gains to their homes.*

Winnie's connection with the libidinous Johnny Gratrix

Page 45: *I don't want my girlfriend hanging round the Rose Garden, either.*

Page 114: *A brawny gardener in a purple string vest paused in the act of deadheading faded blooms to give her a salacious wink, followed by a tuneless whistle.*

Page 175: *I keep my distance from that one. Not like some I could mention.*

The Welsh connection between Bellamy, Virginia, and Ffion

Page 37: *His accent was as Welsh as bara brith.*

Page 43: *'Accents?'*

Bellamy shifted in his seat. 'Hard to say, Mr Flint. I only caught a few snatches of conversation.'

'Did they sound as if they were local to the area?'

An evasive look flitted into the small eyes.

Page 140: *Ffion is Welsh for foxglove*

Page 234: *Ffion and I are Welsh. So was Bellamy. Apparently, he came from Bangor, not far from Llangefni, where I grew up.*

Page 246: *She comes from Machynlleth in mid-Wales*

Ffion's determination to murder Carson

Page 97: *A head-and-shoulders portrait of Ffion Morris, wearing an expression of uncompromising resolve.*

'A wonderful likeness!' Rachel exclaimed. 'You have such lovely features!'

Ffion gave a curt nod of acknowledgment. 'Ginny calls it The Vow.'

Pearl's interest in Sir Harold

Page 104: '*He's a remarkable man.*' *A faraway look came into Pearl's eyes, but quickly she pulled herself back together.*

Page 106: '*He's very good-natured, not at all like some rich folk who wouldn't give the likes of you and me the time of day.*'

Page 112: '*If you ask me, she's besotted with the man.*'

Page 236: *Was it her imagination, Rachel wondered, or did the man's very presence cause Pearl Carson to brighten?*

Pearl's pharmaceutical knowledge and access to thallium

Page 16: '*His wife's name is Pearl. She's worked in shops and as a nurse, but mostly she's been in service.*'

Page 104: *When I met Louis, he was selling wine for a merchant with premises next door to the pharmacy where I worked.*

Page 195: *I've introduced her to Max Factor make-up and Koremlu Cream for removing superfluous hair.*

Pearl's willingness to contemplate crime

Page 107: *We all know what it's like to be tempted to behave in a way that is... out of the ordinary.*

Carson's health and symptoms

Page 76: *With a sallow complexion and irregular bald patch on the crown of his head, he hardly looked like a vicious criminal.*

Page 108: '*I must see how Louis is feeling. He's been under the weather lately, so he needs to take it easy.*'

'*Sorry to hear that,*' *Martha said.* '*What seems to be the trouble?*'

'*Gastric influenza, the doctor says.*'

Page 128: *A sallow-faced man who had lost quite a lot of hair*

How McAtee was poisoned
Page 147: *At least they left some chocolates on my pillow. A special treat, I thought, but apparently they give them to all the guests.*

Pearl's access to McAtee's bedroom to plant the poisoned chocolates
Page 106: *Sometimes I give the maids a hand. I'm not too proud to tidy up bedrooms or make beds.*

McAtee's illness
Page 132: *He was pasty-faced and his breathing was strangely laboured*
Page 133: *There was a faint bleariness in his eyes and he winced as he gave his stomach a quick rub.*
Page 134: *The other man rubbed his stomach again.*

McAtee muscling in on Carson's territory
Page 153: *He put his inquiry agency on the market. His nice little semi-detached in Wimbledon, too. Seems he's thinking of making a move up north.*
'To Hemlock Bay?'
'So it seems.'

How Ffion created her alibi
Page 116: *One patch of lower hedging had died away; a determined intruder could wriggle through*

Page 176: *Surely he wouldn't crawl through that small gap in the hedge into the Sun and Air Garden?*

Page 235: *Making friends with the watchman's Alsatian. We miss not having a dog of our own here.*

Bellamy's plan to make money from blackmail

Page 226: *He was about to come into a good deal of money and would be able to set them up in comfort far from Hemlock Bay.*

Page 246: *Winnie said he was hoping for some sort of windfall.*

Basil's hiding place for his journal

Page 272: *He told her he didn't want her dusting his precious books*

Author's Note

This is a novel, and all the characters and events are imaginary. However, some topographical aspects of Hemlock Bay (notably Hemlock Head) were inspired by a visit to Heysham on a gorgeous summer day in 2023: J.M.W. Turner may never have explored Hemlock Bay, but he did rhapsodise over Heysham. I benefited from studying the informative materials held at the excellent Heritage Centre in the village, and Kath Gregson's evocative account of her memories of the amusements at Heysham Head influenced my general description of Paradise.

The Lobby Lud publicity stunt was indeed inspired by the disappearance of Agatha Christie. Koremlu Cream was a real product which enjoyed a brief vogue in the United States before the disastrous consequences of using thallium became evident. The bold claims made for Koremlu can be found in a booklet available online; today, they make sobering reading. There is an informative discussion about thallium in John Emsley's *The Elements of Murder*.

I'm grateful to Helena Edwards for her work on the maps and also to my agent James Wills and his colleagues at Watson, Little for their help and encouragement. I'd also like to thank my publishers, in particular my editor Bethan Jones at Aries, and Louis Greenberg for his copyediting.

Martin Edwards

www.martinedwardsbooks.com